THE QUALITY OF MERCY

GILBERT MORRIS

Fleming H. Revell
A Division of Baker Book House Co
Grand Rapids, Michigan 49516

Published by Fleming H. Revell
a division of Baker Book House Company
P.O. Box 6287, Grand Rapids, MI 49516-6287

Second printing, October 1994

Printed in the United States of America

Library of Congress Cataloging-in-Publication Data

Morris, Gilbert.
    The quality of mercy / Gilbert Morris.
        p.   cm.
    ISBN 0-8007-5474-3
    1. Ross, Danielle (Fictitious character)—Fiction. 2. Private investi-
gators—United States—Fiction. 3. Women detectives—United States
—Fiction.
PS3563.08742Q35 1993
813'.54—dc20

        93-32432

Scripture quotations in this volume are taken from the King James Version of the Bible.

This is, at times, a very dark and lonely earth
we walk through,
but from time to time we meet those who brighten it.
I have met one who brings splashes of light
into this darkness,
And I dedicate this book to him—

To Bill Petersen, who has made my way easier.

Contents

Contents

1

The Gospel
at the Project

Colonel Daniel Monroe Ross had been a stern comman-
der of his Virginia regiment. Now his portrait, formal in Confederate gray, complete with red sash, glared down from its
place on the wall of Danielle Ross's New Orleans office. The
full lips seemed about to open. And if they had, Colonel Ross
would no doubt have barked at his great-great-grand-
daughter as he had once rebuked his staff officers when he
was displeased:

"Woman—stop that infernal bickering! Do what you're
going to do and stop blathering about it."

But Dani's ancestor could not speak and was reduced to
staring down with fierce disapproval at the two figures below
him. What he saw was a man and a woman in the center of
the room, squared off like boxers in a ring, and biting off their
words as they argued.

Danielle Lynn Ross was tall, and her 135 pounds were trimly clad in a black piqué two-piece dress with large white buttons and a striped jacket with black insets front and back. The jacket, shirred and padded at sleeve caps and tightly fitted at the waist, accented her well-formed figure. She wore no jewelry except a pair of black and white drop earrings joined by a gold ring. It was a simple costume that only a woman completely confident of her appearance could wear— the sort that not only men would turn to look at, but envious women as well.

Her face was squarish and her mouth was too large for classic beauty. It was excellently designed, however, for other things, such as expressing anger, which it did now.

"You can keep your grubby hands to yourself, Ben Savage!" Her voice was deep for a woman, and it rasped when she was angry.

"You've got a one-track mind, Boss," the man snapped back. He was no more than five-ten, and his deep-set hazel eyes flashed with anger as he balanced on his toes, looking more like a champion middle-weight boxer than a private detective. "You think every man who crosses your path goes gaga after one look at you." He had a Slavic face, square with a shelf of bone over his eyes, and his short nose had been broken. His hair and eyebrows were black, very coarse and unruly.

They stood there glaring at each other, and tension filled the office. The quarrel had exploded unexpectedly, like a land mine. Savage had come in to give a rather ordinary report on one of his cases. He did not like working for a woman, a fact he concealed rather poorly, although he had finally accepted the fact that as a boss, Danielle Ross was almost as adequate as a good man.

Dani, for her part, had not wanted to hire him in the first place. When she first assumed charge of Ross Investigations after her father's heart attack, she had planned to use female operatives. She had quickly been forced to rethink that position, however, and reluctantly taken on Savage—whom she disliked on sight. An ex-aerialist with the circus, an ex-Marine (highly decorated), an ex-homicide detective, he had proved to be an asset to the company—and, at least in Dani's opinion, an all around pain-in-the-neck.

But the two of them had fallen into a strange partnership during the first year, a love-hate relationship which neither of them liked, but could not walk away from. Most of their fights centered around Dani's profession. Savage insisted that she was trying to be a man, while Dani insisted he was so threatened by her ability that he used that charge to bolster his own insecurity.

The present skirmish had begun when Dani remarked, "I'm going down to hear Luke speak tonight."

Luke Sixkiller was the head of homicide for the New Orleans Police Department. He had the reputation of being one of the toughest cops in the country, but he had recently been converted to Christianity—mostly under the influence of Miss Danielle Ross. Sixkiller had kept his job but begun speaking all over the city, giving his testimony, and Dani had been so thrilled with his growth that she seldom missed a chance to attend.

Dani's announcement had brought Savage's gaze up in a sudden motion. He had studied her, then said, "You're going to have to decide if you're going to run a detective agency or a Sunday school, Dani."

It was an unexpected reaction, for Savage had generally been supportive of Dani's Christian commitment. He himself was not a believer, and he had come to Ross Investigations with the expectations of seeing his employer fall into inconsistencies. Over time, he had grudgingly admitted that Dani

11

was a Christian on and off the job. Her interest in Luke Sixkiller, however, had for some reason become a sore spot with him.

Then Savage had added fuel to the fire by remarking, "That meeting's over in the middle of the Project, isn't it? Over there, they play with guns in their cradles instead of rattles. It's not safe for you to go."

"I can take care of myself, Ben!" Dani had shot back—and it was at that point in the argument that Savage had stepped forward and put his hand on the small of her back. She knew instantly that he was checking to see if she was wearing the .38 designed to be concealed at that spot, but had been so angry over his attitude that she had shoved him away, accusing him of fondling her.

Now, with her green eyes sparking, she grabbed her purse and stalked out of the room, firing back, "You just do your job, Savage!" She turned to see her father and Angie Park bending over a table, pretending to be deaf. Dani faltered, then added weakly, "Dad, I'll be in late tonight." She shot a bitter look back toward her office, adding, "I'm going to a service with Luke."

"All right, Dani," Dan Ross nodded. He was a tall man with thick white hair and patrician features, but thin and hollow-cheeked since his illness. "I'll leave the light on for you," he added as she left the room. Then he turned to Savage, who had emerged with a scowl on his face. "I take it you've had a little spat with the boss, Ben?"

Savage liked Dan Ross as much as he had ever liked any man, but now he glared at him accusingly. "I'll bet you raised her on the Spock method, didn't you? That old malarkey about not paddling a kid?"

"As a matter of fact, yes."

"I thought so!" Savage scowled, then grunted, "Angie, if

you'll dig up that stuff on Parkinson from the attorney general's office, I'll close the thing tomorrow. Good night!"

He left the room abruptly, his spine still rigid with anger, and Angie leaned back and looked after him. "I'd diagnose Ben's trouble as a terminal case of jealousy," she remarked.

Angie was twenty-nine, but looked at least five years younger. She was an attractive woman with blonde hair and round blue eyes. A disastrous marriage followed by a battlefield divorce had built a wall around her and posted a sign "No Men Need Apply." She was, however, a tender-hearted woman, and was known to violate her own rules. She was totally dedicated to Dani Ross and her father.

Dan gave her a quizzical look that changed to a frown, then shook his head. "When those two first met, I thought it'd be a case of double homicide. Then, when they'd worked on a couple of tough cases, I thought it'd be a marriage. Now—I don't know what it is."

"How serious is Dani about Luke Sixkiller?" Angie wondered aloud. "He's always liked her, but she'd never have much to do with him."

"Don't ask me," Ross said impatiently. "I'm only her father."

"You're closer to her than anyone," Angie persisted. "She's always depended on you, told you stuff."

Ross ran a hand over his hair, a harried look in his fine gray eyes. "I don't know, Angie." He had always hated uncertainty, but since his heart attack, he had been forced to live with it almost daily. He had regretted having to ask Dani to give up her studies at seminary, but Ross Investigations was his life's work. Nobody had been prouder than he when Dani had come at once and had made the agency into a moderate success. Still, he worried about her.

"I don't think she knows what she wants, Angie," Dan said

finally. "She's not really happy—and shooting that man didn't help her any."

"I know. It still bothers her a lot, even though she did it to save those kids. She won't carry that gun, either, and that makes Ben mad."

Ross tried for a smile. "Children never get raised, Angie. The good time is before they learn to walk and talk. You just do what's best for them and then let them bawl. After that, especially after they hit the age of ten, it all goes downhill."

Angie reached out and squeezed his hand. "It'll be all right," she murmured. "She's just not sure about some things yet."

What Dani had not told Savage was that Sixkiller had strictly forbidden her to come to the meeting in the Project.

"This Calliope Project's so bad the police are scared to go in sometimes," he'd said. "I can't come and get you, and I don't want you going in there alone. If you can get Ben to bring you, it's okay."

As Dani drove slowly down the street, she regretted that she had not asked Ben to bring her. That had been her intention, but when he'd acted so—so *sexist*—!

Now, as she drove slowly down South Preiur Street, she was having second thoughts. No shrubs, trees, or gardens. Trash everywhere. Dark shadowy figures moved in the darkness like sharks cruising silently in search of their prey. The neighborhood was a depressing sight.

Dani spotted the squat, flat-topped building, its faded sign lit by a single light bulb: "St. John's Recreation Club." Established by a local church in an abortive attempt to "clean up" Calliope, it had quickly turned out to be a clearinghouse for drugs and prostitution—or so Sixkiller had informed her. "The criminal element is letting us use it for a meeting this one time," Luke had grinned.

Dani drove into the parking lot and killed the engine. She opened the door to a series of whistles from the darkness, a human warning system that usually signaled the police were coming. She only had fifty yards to walk to get to the entrance, but the whistles echoing in the night cut eerie, frightening slices out of the darkness. There were no lights. The parking lot was illuminated only by the moon, and a clammy feeling swept over Dani as she locked the car door.

She knew that Calliope represented the highest crime rate in the city. It was a breeding ground for crime, a headquarters for young hoodlums who *wanted* to be caught breaking the law, considering it a badge, something that would win them acceptance into the only world they knew—and even into Angola State Penitentiary. The police kept trying, but they were overwhelmed. Trying to stop crime in Calliope was like trying to bail out a sinking ocean liner with a tin cup.

She only got halfway to the entrance before a line of young men materialized in front of her. The sight of them was like plunging into an icy pool, and she desperately wanted to turn and race back into the car. Knowing that there was no hope of that, she said evenly, "Hello, I'm looking for Lieutenant Sixkiller."

The leader, a tall rangy man wearing a Kansas City Chief jacket and a snap-brim hat, grinned at her and spoke with courtly malice: "You want the fuzz, pretty lady? You want to report a crime?" A wave of ribald laughter ran down the line, and he added, "I be Jayro. Why don't you and me take a spin in that little ol' bomb you come in?"

"Maybe we all go," another voice said, and a short bulky form came toward her. He was almost as thick as he was tall, with a massive neck and arms that bulged with muscles.

"Naw, Deacon," the one called Jayro said. "This here lady

is accustomed to high-class men friends. When I bring her back, maybe you can go for a little drive with her."

Fear crawled along Dani's nerves, and her eyes swept the lot, but saw nobody except other young men. When Jayro stepped forward and took her by the arm, she protested, "Let me go!"

"Now, don't be like that, pretty lady," Jayro said. He was enjoying himself hugely, winking at the other members of the gang. "You white gals, you don't know what you've been missing. But you won't—"

"Let the lady go."

Dani almost fainted with relief as she recognized Ben Savage's voice. She twisted around and he was there, moving to stand close to the tall man who held her.

Jayro was taken off guard, but only for an instant. He stared at Savage and saw only a rather unimpressive white man— no police. He tightened his grip on Dani's arm. "Whitey, we was doing real good without your help. I expect you better get back downtown—if you can."

A rumble of voices, low and threatening, came from the other men, and the heavy-set one growled, "How much it worth to you to keep your own teeth?" He stepped forward and the others moved with him, but they stopped when a gun appeared like magic in Savage's hand.

"Fun's all over, guys," Savage remarked flatly, looking rather bored. Then, when Jayro didn't release Dani, he slowly lifted the gun and fired.

To Dani it sounded like a cannon. The *kaaawhong!* almost deafened her as the slug delicately plucked the hat from Jayro's head. The echoes of the shot faded, and Jayro stared at Savage with something like awe.

"Man!" he whispered. "You piece of work!"

Then footsteps pounded, and Luke Sixkiller was there. He

looked ominous in the faint light, a gun in his hand and his black eyes glittering. "What's all the shooting about?"

Savage coolly offered, "My gun went off by accident."

Sixkiller studied the scene, taking in Dani's pale face, Savage's casual form, the circle of young hoods—especially Jayro. Then he bent over the hat on the ground, picked it up, and stuck his finger through a hole in the top of the crown.

"This yours, Jayro?"

"I do believe it is," the young man nodded. He took the hat, studied the hole, then smiled. "This gentleman has ruined the crown of my foppish attire, Lieutenant."

Sixkiller smiled tightly. "Make it hard for you to carry out your duties—such as teaching these young folks how to deal dope and steal, won't it?"

"A man is poor indeed, Lieutenant," Jayro said in mock humble tones, "if he don't do all he can to help his people."

"Yeah," Sixkiller mused. He studied Jayro, then put his gun away. "Savage, whoever let you play with guns ought to be booked for contributing to the delinquency of an idiot!" He took Dani's arm, saying, "Come on inside, Miss Ross."

"Can we come, too, Lieutenant Sixkiller?" Jayro asked. "Us members of minority races got to stick together."

Sixkiller was a full-blooded Sioux, and somehow he found Jayro's remark amusing. "Come on in," he said. "You can watch the guns that take up the offering."

Jayro laughed, and turned to say, "You dudes be nice now. I want you to listen to the Reverend Sixkiller's sermon real good! He done hit the glory trail! Give up bustin' heads and shootin' folks to preach the Word."

Dani was escorted into the building which smelled strongly of sweat and a smoke so acrid it had to be from illegal cigarettes. Passing down a short hall, she found herself in a gymnasium. Young blacks were milling around. When Dani, Savage, and Sixkiller entered, someone bellowed, "All right! Sit down!" This was followed by many catcalls, none of them genteel, but the crowd more or less settled down, sitting on the floor.

"Stay here with Ben, Dani," Sixkiller murmured, and walked to stand by one of the goals, directly under the tattered net. He turned to face the crowd, and Dani thought again that he was the most *physical* man she'd ever known. He was under six feet, but his solid chest arched outward, and every move spoke of physical power. He had been a scout in Nam, had been shot three times in the line of duty. The word on the street was, "Don't try to buy Sixkiller—and don't *ever* try to roust him!"

The crowd grew quiet, and Sixkiller began. "Thanks for coming. For some of you, it's the first time you ever went anywhere with me without a summons!"

"You got *that* right, man!" The shout brought laughter from the crowd, and Sixkiller smiled. "I'm going to preach a little at you, but first—just to soften you up—I want you to listen to George Noonan, a friend of mine who thinks he can sing."

He stepped back, motioned to a young black man with a guitar who had been standing beside the wall. He moved forward, nodded, and said, "Glad to see you. I ain't no preacher, but I do like to play and sing about Jesus." That was all of his introduction, and when he made his first riff, Dani and everyone in the room knew he was good.

He played the old hymns, the same ones sung in big churches with stained-glass windows and carpets on the floor—but what a difference! His music was New Orleans jazz, and it was rich and lively, yet somehow mournful, the familiar sound of parades and parties and funerals in the city. The sound was old—but it was new, for Noonan sang the gospel like Ray Charles sang about Georgia. He sang "What a Friend We Have in Jesus," and he sang Andraé Crouch's song, "The Blood Will Never Lose Its Power." When he sang his last song, the rowdy crowd was still:

> Amazing grace! How sweet the sound,
> That saved a wretch like me!
> I once was lost, but now am found,
> Was blind, but now I see.

He sang all the verses, his voice clear as a trumpet, but breaking as it rose and fell, in the style of all good blues singers. Then he sang the last:

> When we've been there ten thousand years,
> Bright shining as the sun,
> We've no less days to sing God's praise
> Than when we first begun.

For a minute he just stood there with his head down, then lifted it. "That song was written by a man who made his living by selling my ancestors. His name was John Newton. He died in 1807. But before he died, he found Jesus—and he lived to set men free." He paused, then said, "I was a slave for most of my life. Oh, I didn't wear no chains you could see. But some of you know, dope can be the worst chain there is. So I wound up with needle prints on my arms, locked up at Dixon Correctional Institution. And it was there I run into Jesus." He told that story briefly, then said, "Ain't nobody can make you do something you don't want to do. But I'm telling you, before I met Jesus, I hated him—just like some of you do right now. But now—he the best friend I got in the world! Nobody else loved me—but Jesus did!"

He stepped away, and Sixkiller moved to take his stand under the net. He said, "I'm a cop. I'm not going to win any popularity contests here tonight, and I don't deserve any. I've given some of you a hard time, and it could be I'll have trouble with some of you later on. But I can't talk politics or racial injustice with you; others can do that, but I can't. What I can do is tell you how my life got changed a few months ago. . . . "

Dani listened as Sixkiller told of how he had come to Jesus. She had been with him, working undercover on the rodeo circuit. Now, as he spoke, his eyes flickered toward her more than once, and she knew he was saying "Thank you."

Standing beside Dani, Ben Savage listened intently. At the same time, he watched the faces of Sixkiller's hearers. Some of them were frozen with sullen hatred, hearing nothing the policeman was saying. They had come out of curiosity and would have no mercy on the man if they met him in a dark alley. On some of the faces, however, Savage saw something different—hope, or something like it. He himself was convinced that Sixkiller was speaking the absolute truth. And strangely enough, Savage, tough and hard-bitten as he was, felt a tinge of envy as the lieutenant related how Christ had brought peace into his life.

When Sixkiller finished, he said, "Most of you know it's pretty common to give an 'invitation' after a thing like this. Well, here's my invitation—if any of you think what I'm saying makes sense, give me a call. We'll talk about it."

A silence followed and Jayro called out, "You mean you ain't gonna take up no collection, Lieutenant? You ain't gonna call us to the mourner's bench to get saved?"

"No collection, Jayro," Sixkiller said. "And I think every man's got to find his own mourner's bench. Most of the time—" he tapped his thick chest, "it's right . . . "

He was interrupted by a young black man who stood up and shouted, "Hey, man, what you have to say to us, anyway? You white! You don't know nothin' about what we feel!"

Sixkiller smiled suddenly. The speaker was Sweet Willie Wine, a famous man in the Project. "Maybe you're right, Sweet Willie. That's why I brought a friend of mine who knows more about how you feel than I do." He turned and called out, "Hoke, you want to tell this dude how he feels?"

A huge black man wearing a suit had been standing near the back. Dani had noticed him, wondering if he might be the director of the club.

But he said, "Sweet Willie, you think I'm black enough to know how you feel? What street you live on?" he demanded.

"Treasure Street," Sweet Willie answered.

"Yeah, well I grew up on Abundance Street, not two blocks from your place. My name's Hoke Waber—which most of you know, because I'm on the homicide squad."

A mutter went over the room, for many of the people there knew Hoke Waber, at least by reputation, as a tough cop. Now he stared at Willie, but he had a compassionate look on his face. "Yeah, I grew up in the Project. I don't know what kind of problems you got, but I had some just as bad. . . . " He related his terrible history, how he had been put out on the street at age twelve, had experimented with every vice offered in New Orleans.

"But I made up my mind I wasn't going to be a junkie. I wasn't going to Angola. I made up my mind I was going to get out of the Project. Well, it wasn't easy. But I made it."

"You ain't nothin' but oreo, Hoke!" someone cried out. "Black outside, but white inside!"

Hoke shook his head. "I can't make you believe what you shut out of your minds. But don't tell me what you told the lieutenant— 'You just don't understand me because you're white.' I'm a black man, and I know what it's like to grow up in the street. I know what it's like to qualify for a job and not get it because I'm black. I know what it's like to have no hope." Then he shook his head, adding, "I'm no preacher, and I run from God a long time. And I never had a minute's peace—until I called on God and he saved me."

Sixkiller said, "Good night. Thanks again for coming—and if any of you want to talk, give me a call."

He stood there talking to some of the men who wandered up to ask questions, and Jayro drifted by where Dani stood with Ben. "Pretty lady, no hard feelings about that little misunderstanding?"

"No, not really."

Jayro looked at Ben and smiled. "Savage? That what the lieutenant called you? Well, now, I figure you owe me one fine hat."

"Get a good one, send me the bill."

"I'll do that, I'll sure enough do that!" He studied Savage carefully, then asked, "You ever think you might have been a little off with that shot? What if you'd missed?"

Savage smiled. "I guess a lot of young ladies would be having hysterics, Jayro."

His answer delighted the young man. "That is true, indeed, Mr. Savage! True, indeed." He examined the pair, and asked Dani, "What I want to know is, are you with this gentleman or with Lieutenant Sixkiller?"

Dani flushed, and the look on her face delighted Jayro. "Well, now, I will be interested to follow your relationship with these two fine gentlemen."

He walked away chuckling, and Dani refused to look at Savage. Finally Sixkiller came and said, "Ready to go?"

"Yes, Luke."

Sixkiller shook his head. "I'm put out with you, Dani. I told you not to come to this place alone. If Ben hadn't followed you, things might have gotten bad."

Dani forced herself to look at Savage. "You were right, Ben. Thanks for your help."

"No charge," Ben shrugged. He turned away and left the gym.

"You two feuding again?" Sixkiller asked.

"Sort of," Dani said shortly. "Let's get out of here." She knew that Sixkiller could read her better than she liked—and she didn't want him to know how much she resented Savage at the moment.

She always resented Ben Savage—when he was right and she was wrong.

2

Flowers for Dan

I wish you'd get a real automobile instead of this micro machine," Sixkiller complained as he wedged himself in the dead man's seat of Dani's maroon Cougar.

"It's a sports car, Luke," Dani remarked. She shifted gears expertly as she exited the parking lot, turned north, and drove through the Project. The service had been exciting, and she asked, "Do you think any of those men will call you?"

"Sure, a few. They'd be afraid to come down for an invitation. Make 'em look bad in front of their peer group. But I get to talk to quite a few on the sly." He laughed and turned to face her. "Getting saved has sure complicated my work. Time was when I got a call, it was from an informant ready to drop a dime on one of his buddies for a few bucks. Those guys are always real careful. Beat around the bush and want all kinds of guarantees that I won't tell on them. Yesterday I got what I thought was one of those—only he was *extra* cautious. Made me swear on my grandfather's false leg I'd never breathe one word of our conversation to anybody. Then, when I finally convinced him, he asked me about how he could get saved."

Dani laughed with him, then mused, "I guess evangelism changes its form from time to time."

"Yeah, I guess. But not its message. That's got to be the same, no matter if you're giving it to a cannibal or a millionaire." Luke readjusted his solid frame in the seat, then added, "I never knew it was such hungry work, preaching. Guess all those stories about preachers and how much fried chicken they can eat have some foundation. Let's go by the Pontchartrain Hotel and get something to eat."

"The Pontchartrain Hotel?" Dani asked with mock horror in her voice. "You want to *eat* there?"

Sixkiller shrugged. "Well, that's where the power is. If you want something done, that's where all the city councilmen and federal judges and big-time contractors hang out. Still I guess the food's not so great. It's legal though."

"Well, we're not eating there; we're going out to my house. Mom and Dad said to bring you home for a late supper."

"All *right!*"

"You want to go by and pick up your car so you won't have to hitchhike back?"

"Naaah! I'll give a call to one of the cruisers. I can tell them I've been investigating you for improper advances to a detective." He moved closer to her, draped an arm around the back of her seat, and said in what he considered his seductive voice, "I'd better start collecting evidence."

"You get back in your own yard," Dani warned. But she didn't object when he leaned over and kissed her cheek.

"I was glad you came tonight," he said. "Means a lot to see a friendly face out in that kind of audience."

He leaned back to his seat and looked out the window as

she steered the small car west on Highway 61, then north on the Pontchartrain Causeway. The vast waters of Lake Pontchartrain lay smooth as velvet under the three-quarter moon. There was no wind, and the late summer heat had not yet left the earth. All day long the concrete, the earth, and the waters of New Orleans soaked up the full force of the blazing sun, and when night fell, it released that stored heat, creating a powerful updraft. Now the worst of it was over, and the air was beginning to cool.

Dani tooled off the Causeway, sped through Mandeville, then hung a right by a small Exxon station. Soon the road narrowed, and banks of huge oaks bearing loads of Spanish moss began to form a corridor, their branches interlocking over the narrow road. She turned onto a gravel drive that made a circle in front of her parents' house.

The house itself was a hundred years old—a small but stately two-story, white with eight columns in front, a restored planter's house. It had been cheap enough back when Daniel Ross had bought it, but he had invested much of his life in restoring the place. Now it gleamed cleanly in the moonlight as Dani and Sixkiller emerged from the car. As Sixkiller stretched, he looked at the large field that lay to the left of the house behind a white wooden fence.

"You ought to get another horse, Dani," Luke said. "I know you loved Biscuit, but you could love another horse."

He saw Dani's lips tighten; had expected it. She had taken her horse, Biscuit, with her to work undercover as a barrel racer on the rodeo circuit. But Biscuit had been killed by a maniac, and she had not stopped feeling the hurt. "Maybe someday," she murmured, and her tone slammed the door on any more discussion.

She was, Sixkiller had long realized, one of the most stubborn people he'd ever known—man or woman. When he'd first met her, he'd been drawn by her beauty but had assumed she would have feminine "weaknesses." But he had quickly discovered that under her svelte good looks lay a will of iron; once she made up her mind, nothing on the face of the earth could change it.

Now as they walked toward the house, Sixkiller wondered about their future. He had long known that Dani Ross would never marry a man who was not a Christian; her commitment was too strong for that. For that reason he had not considered anything more than a casual relationship with her— and he realized that *casual* was exactly the right word, for Dani would never give herself to any man unless he were her husband. He gave her a quick glance, admiring the smooth, rounded form and the classic planes of her face. *She's good-looking enough for any man*, was his thought. *But she's not likely to be a nice, dutiful little wife, staying home to bake brownies and change diapers.*

He shook the thought away as they entered the house and were met by Ellen Ross. She came with a smile to kiss him on the cheek, exclaiming, "Luke, how nice that you could come! I want to hear all about it!"

Ellen Anne Ross was one of those women who age slowly. She was forty-five, but looked ten years younger. One of those striking ash-blonde Texas girls that seem indigenous to that state, she had given up her own career to make a home for Dan Ross and their three children. "I fixed that cheese dip you like so well, Luke," she said, taking his arm and walking him to the dining room. "I've had to fight Dan to keep him out of it. You go down to the den and tell him it's against the law for him to have cheese. Dani and I will finish getting dinner on the table."

Sixkiller made his way down a side hall to the study. He opened the door, and found Dan Ross sitting at a large tiger oak table staring at an array of small metal objects spread out over the surface. The older man looked up and asked in despair, "Can you put this thing back together, Luke?"

Sixkiller moved to take a chair and to stare down at the pieces. "What is it? A clock?"

"No, a fishing reel. I took it apart to see what was wrong with it." Ross gave a disgusted look at the parts, swept them into a wastebasket, and slammed it down on the floor. "There!" he said triumphantly. *"That's* the way to deal with the problems of the modern world! When I was a kid, all a fellow needed to catch fish was a hook, a line, a bobber, and a worm. Now you have to have equipment it'd take a civil engineer to figure out."

Sixkiller grinned. "So we just sweep all the problems we can't solve into a wastebasket? Is that the Ross method of dealing with the world?"

"Well, I don't see that many problems get solved anyway." He sat back in the upholstered chair and considered the policeman. "Look at how much organization and equipment you cops have—and you're not setting any records!"

"I guess not." Sixkiller stared around the room, which was furnished with antiques. None of them was less than a hundred years old, and most were much older. He turned his black eyes on Ross. "Your trouble is, you were born too late."

"Like Miniver Cheevy?" Dan mused. "I guess so, Luke—and so were you. A hundred years ago, you'd have been leading an attack on General Custer and the Seventh Cavalry at Little Big Horn. Now all you do is fool around with two-bit hoods in the Project."

"Some of the cats I run up against are tougher than Custer's boys," Luke answered. "Anyway, you're right about all this equipment. I never knew of a single case being solved or a single crook being convicted as a result of fingerprint evidence. I'd like to go back to the good old days, when you had a cop on the beat, walking around. He knew everybody, and you can't do that sitting in a squad car."

"See?" Ross nodded smugly. "*You're* the one who's living in the past!"

Sixkiller thoroughly enjoyed the verbal sparring. The two men, so different in so many ways, had become fast friends, especially since Sixkiller had become a Christian. They talked for half an hour, then Dani's sister Allison opened the door and stuck her head in. "Time to eat," she said.

Luke got up to give her a hug. "How's my favorite juvenile?" he teased, knowing how much she wanted to grow up.

Allison flushed and tried to pull away, but he held her tight. "Let me go, you troglodyte!"

"Is that sort of like a Presbyterian?" Sixkiller asked, his eyes laughing at her. Then he leaned down and inhaled. "What is that perfume you're wearing?"

"None of your business, Luke Sixkiller."

"It's too dangerous, a good-looking gal like you, going around with potent stuff on. You'll have every male in the neighborhood beating his wings against the screens, trying to get at you. Dan, make her take a bath!"

Allison beat at him with her fist, and he let her go. She was sixteen, in that terrible age between girlhood and womanhood. Not a child—but not *not* a child. Afraid of what was happening, afraid of what lay ahead, yet inexorably drawn to it. She looked like her mother, with the same ash-blonde hair, but her eyes were a much darker blue. In a few years, Sixkiller thought, she would be better looking than Dani—but Allison would never believe it. She insisted she was "too fat."

When Allison turned and ran down the hall, Sixkiller said, "She's a winner, Dan."

"Not at all like Dani," Ross answered. As they walked

down the hall, he added, "Allison's got the world's worst crush on you, Luke. After Ben, that is."

"Doesn't she like anybody but broken-down detectives?"

"Not yet, but I have hopes her tastes will improve."

They entered the dining room, and Sixkiller glanced around appreciatively. Well-rubbed ancient walnut, white linen, fine bone china, and heavy silver tableware all gleamed under a chandelier that had once graced the dining room of Jefferson Davis's home.

"Can't decide whether you're a good cook, Ellen, or if it's just that in a room like this, hot dogs would taste good."

Rob Ross spoke up at once, "You just don't know good food when you taste it, Luke. You think fine dining is a quarter pounder and chocolate shake at McDonald's." Rob was the only son of the family, still tall and lanky at age eighteen. With his mother's blonde hair and his father's finely chiseled features, he looked like a very young Jimmy Stewart. Sixkiller knew that his parents were concerned at his lack of direction.

"That's one of the *better* meals a bachelor gets, Rob," he answered. "I notice you come running back for more of Mama Ellen's cooking every chance you get." Rob was a freshman at Tulane. He was living at home during the summer and working at a refinery to earn tuition money, and spending most of his evenings at the local health club.

"Will you ask the blessing, Luke?" Dan Ross said.

They bowed their heads and Luke gave a short blessing, looking up to say, "Haven't learned any flowery prayers yet."

"Hope you never do," Dan grunted. "Help yourself. It's a poor table Ellen's set, but try to make the best of it."

The "poor table" consisted of a generous array of local favorites. They began with boudin, a spicy mixture of pork, onions, cooked rice, and herbs stuffed in sausage casing. Next came court bouillon, a rich soup made from fish fillets and dirty rice, a dish of leftover cooked rice sauteed with green peppers and onions. The main dish was crawfish étoufée, a succulent, tangy tomato-based stew.

Before the étoufée, Luke and the others worked on the huge platter of boiled crawfish, known locally as "mudbugs." They came whole with head and legs still attached, and the diners worked expertly to shell and devein the little crustaceans. They did this by grasping the heads between the thumb and forefinger of one hand, and the tails between the thumb and forefinger of the other hand, then twisting and pulling until heads and tails were separated. After sucking the contents of the head and discarding it, they squeezed the tails to crack the shells, pulled out the meat, gently pulled the vein free, and popped the meat into their mouths.

As the pile dwindled, Rob said, "You know, one of my classmates is from Arkansas. I took him down to Antoine's and ordered some crawfish, and he took one look at it, and he said, "I'm not eatin' none of that fish bait!""

They all laughed, but Dani said, "Rob, if you went to visit him, he'd probably offer you squirrel stew and let you suck the brains out of the skull." She laughed as Rob made a terrible face and added, "I guess eating habits are hard to break."

"I'd *die* if I had to eat a snail!" Allison said. "Did you ever eat one, Luke?"

"Sure. I ate an iguana once, too. In Belize."

"An iguana?" Ellen frowned. "What did it taste like?"

"Oh—sort of like fox, I guess."

Dan Ross laughed with delight at the stunned expression on his wife's face. He started to speak, but the doorbell interrupted him. Dan exclaimed, "Who in the world can be calling at this hour?"

Ellen started to get up, but Rob said quickly, "I'll get it," and left the room.

"Tell us about the meeting tonight, Luke," Ellen prompted. "Did it go well?"

Luke shrugged and began relating the events of the evening, skipping the bit about Dani's adventure in the parking lot. But he had barely gotten started when Rob came in bearing a long green box. "It's from Majestic Floral," he said, a puzzled look on his face. "And it's for you, Dad."

Dan Ross took the box gingerly, stared at the card, then shrugged. "Must be another Dan Ross in town. Nobody sends me flowers."

They all watched curiously as he untied the red ribbon and lifted the box lid. He looked up at the others and held the box so that they could see the lavish red roses inside. "One of you send this?" he demanded.

When they all shook their heads, Dani asked, "Isn't there a card inside?"

Ross rummaged beneath the roses. "Yes—here's one." He handed the box to Dani and opened the envelope. He stared so long at the small white card inside that the silence grew uncomfortable.

"What is it, Dan?" Ellen asked. She had noted the lines of stress around his mouth and knew something unpleasant had happened.

Ross looked up, his eyes suddenly hard and his mouth tense. "It's from Tommy Cain."

Dani glanced at her mother, whose hand had gone to her breast in an agonized gesture, and whose eyes were large as she stared at her husband. The name meant nothing to Dani. "Who is he?"

"He's a criminal. I helped put him in the pen a few years back."

"What does the card say, Dan?" Sixkiller asked. His eyes had narrowed and his features taken on a professional alertness.

"He says, *Been thinking of you a long time, Dan. Haven't forgotten you. Will look forward to seeing you real soon.*"

Dani was alarmed at the tension in her father's face and knew that Allison and Rob were disturbed. "What does it mean, Dad?"

Ross sat down, lay the card on the table, and said quietly, "When Cain was convicted, he made a lot of threats."

"Against you, Daddy?" Allison asked quickly.

"Against me and others, including the judge and the district attorney."

"Against the foreman of the jury, too," Sixkiller put in.

Dan looked up quickly. "You remember that case?"

"Sure. I was wearing a uniform then, but all of us were glad to see Cain put away. He should have been executed, but it's pretty hard to send a crook that big and rich to the chair."

Dan looked at the faces around him and came up with a smile. "It doesn't mean anything. Happens all the time, doesn't it, Luke?"

Sixkiller spoke quickly, wanting to take the fear out of Allison's face. "I wish one of those birds would threaten *me*! Then I'd be sure of living a long time." He added, "I've heard about five hundred crooks shout about how they were going to get the judge or the D.A. or someone else, and I've never heard of it happening even a single time."

"Luke, is that true?"

Sixkiller looked at Ellen, who had asked the question, and nodded at once. "Yes, Ellen. But I'll have a talk with Tommy when he gets back to town. If he so much as spits on the sidewalk, I can put so much heat on him that he won't be able to breathe!"

"Don't make trouble for yourself over me, Luke," Dan said at once.

Luke shrugged his thick shoulders. "It'll be me making the trouble, not Tommy Cain."

At that moment, Dani thought, Luke looked very much like one of the old war chieftains she had seen in history books. There was a ferocity in his dark eyes that made her feel glad that he was there—glad he was on her side, glad that he would be seeing after her father.

"Well, now, let's see what's for dessert," Dan Ross said.

The dessert turned out to be Dan Ross's favorite—raspberry-tinged white-chocolate mousse—but Dani noticed that her father hardly touched his serving. She noted later on that the roses had been thrown into the trash can. The sight of them gave her such an odd feeling that she turned away and refused to look at them.

3

Fast Company

The only thing Rob Ross hated more than exercise was looking like a bean pole. And that is why he was slumped against the mirrored wall of the health club, watching with envy as a muscled young giant pumped iron on the bench in front of him.

For years now, Rob had seesawed between periods of slothful despair and frantic attempts to build himself up. Not that he was the "skinny" scarecrow he thought himself to be. In fact, his ash-blonde hair, dark blue eyes, and lean good looks caught many a youthful feminine eye. But Rob did not believe anyone could find him attractive. He had gone through high school convinced that his lean frame was the cause of all his unhappiness.

Rob played a good game of golf; he was a fine swimmer and an excellent tennis player—but this all meant nothing to him. His heroes were the Neanderthals who played football, guys whose necks were so thick they could barely turn their heads.

And he was fascinated with bodybuilders. He often picked up bodybuilding magazines, enviously studying the oily, bulging muscles of weight lifters. He never missed a rerun of *The Incredible Hulk* or a movie by Arnold Schwarzenegger. He even bought a book and a set of weights from a discount store and briefly attempted his own (short-lived) self-improvement program. All this, given his slim frame, brought him nothing but despair.

His father, observing Rob's fascination with bulky muscles and noting his frequent references to his "skinny carcass," had divined the heart of the young man's bitterness. He had tried to help Rob by pointing out that he himself had been very thin as a youngster. He had even added, "You know, son, I've known at least three beauty queens—all three of them beautiful enough to become Miss Louisiana. And all three of them were dissatisfied with their looks. I guess when people get to thinking too much about how they look, they're going to become unhappy. I think that's why the Bible says, 'Beauty is deceitful and favor is vain.' Best not to major on those things."

Rob had listened politely to his father but had not profited from his words. Instead, he had finished high school and plunged into his first year of college with high expectations but with the same abysmal picture of his physical self. He had excelled in his classes, achieving a 4.0 on his academic work, yet he remained moody and unhappy over his social life—or lack of it—which he consistently blamed on his physical shortcomings.

Rob admired Luke Sixkiller's heavily muscled frame and would have been happy to have Ben Savage's graceful and proportioned body. And had he asked, either of those men could have helped him. Each in his own way would have told him, "Look, Rob, you've got to build on your strengths. What you need is not bulging biceps or huge pecs, but conditioning. You'll have speed, coordination, and health—and you'll still be going when those body lovers have turned into a tub of fat."

But Rob was too envious and ashamed to talk to either of the men, so he had chosen another route. Determined to gain weight and fill out his frame with impressive muscle before starting his sophomore year, he had been attracted by a health club called "Mack's," one of a chain owned and operated by a former Mr. America, Mack Moran. Moran himself had been at the club when Rob went to inquire about the prices and the program. An amiable giant with curly brown hair, a jaw like the Rock of Gibraltar, and muscles in his fingernails, Moran had worked out at least six hours every day of his life since age fourteen and had kept himself in top shape even after retiring from world-class bodybuilding competition.

"Just what is your goal, Rob?" Moran asked. He listened carefully while the young man expended a great many words to avoid saying what he really meant, which was: "I want to have huge muscles like you so women will look at me when I walk along the beach."

Moran could have guessed this. People came into his place for two reasons, health and pride—usually about 20 percent for the former and 80 percent for the latter. And although Mack Moran was no genius, he had a thorough understanding of one aspect of human psychology: He was totally aware that pride and the desire to be accepted is as much a part of a person as the heart or the lungs. He himself had gone into bodybuilding for these very reasons, and when he had passed the age of active competition, he had parlayed this simple fact of human nature into a multimillion-dollar business.

Now, as he spoke with Rob, Moran surprised himself with a sudden impulse to be honest. He almost said, "Look, kid, you won't *ever* be built like me, because you don't have the genes for it. If you come in here and work out harder than any miner ever worked for about two years, you'll be a little bigger and you'll have some bulges. But you'll have to keep it up for the rest of your life, and nothing on the face of planet earth is more boring than picking up a piece of iron and putting it over your head for four hours a day! You got a good thing going, kid, so enjoy!"

But Moran was a businessman, no more dishonest than most, and he had four young Morans at home who had come into the world owing their government $1840.23 each, and whose college education would cost somewhere close to a million bucks. He rationalized what he was about to do by thinking, *Kid's got the money. Better he spent it here than on booze or betting on the Saints. He won't last long at this stuff anyway—so I might as well take his money as some of the real bad guys.*

"Why, you'll be buying a new wardrobe in three months, Rob," Moran nodded enthusiastically. "Most people who come in here have to shed thirty or forty pounds before I can even *begin* to build them up. You're just the right age, and you've got stamina from swimming and tennis. Why, I wouldn't be too surprised if you didn't muscle up in time for the Mr. Louisiana contest next year!"

That had been at the beginning of summer. Now August was half gone, and Rob was still spending almost every evening at Moran's. By the end of the first month he had grown heartily sick of the routine. He had seen Moran himself only twice, and those visits had been brief. He wasn't sure the owner even remembered him and was not willing to force himself on the man, despite the healthy fees he was paying.

Even worse for Rob than the deadly monotony of the workouts and drain on his finances was the dark suspicion that he was making a fool of himself. Oh, he gained five pounds and could see that his biceps and pectoral muscles were slightly larger. But he had expected more rapid progress. At this rate, it would take him *years* to look the way he wanted.

He spoke of this one night to a young man he had met at the club, the only other "outsider" in this world of the sleek and powerful. Dale Devinny was three years older than Rob, a chunky young man with mild blue eyes, a shock of wheat-colored hair, and a finely developed inferiority complex. His saving grace was a sense of humor. He often made fun of his own inadequacies—usually, it seemed to Rob, before others had a chance.

Rob and Dale had fallen into the practice of "spotting" one another while doing bench presses. Devinny would stand over Rob's head as Rob lay flat on the bench and strained to lift the barbell. In case the barbell got away from Rob, Dale was expected to catch it before it crashed down on Rob's neck. Then they exchanged places; Devinny would do presses while Rob stood sentinel.

They had been engaged in this drill one Tuesday night when Rob spoke of his disillusionment. He had turned purple pressing 175 pounds, then got up from the bench, staggered over to the wall, and slid down against it. Devinny came over and sat down beside him, waiting for Rob to recover and do another set.

As the two crouched against the wall, a heavily muscled young man sauntered over to a nearby bench. He placed a barbell in the holding rack at the edge of the bench and began adding flat disks to the bar. He nodded pleasantly at the two, saying, "How ya doin'?"

"Okay," Devinny answered—Rob feeling too weak to do more than nod. Both of them gaped as the young man kept adding weights. When he was satisfied, he lay back on the bench and put his hands on the bar, which was just inches away from his face. He moved his hands around until he found the grip he liked, then gave a grunt and pressed. The barbell shot up; clearing the rack, the steel bar arching as the heavy weights on each end pulled downward. He allowed the barbell to come down, then pushed it upward again with little sign of strain.

Rob and Dale watched as the young man did twelve of the presses, then settled the bar into the mount and rolled off the bench. He walked around for a minute, resting, then returned to the bench for another set. "See ya," he said, as he finally walked away toward one of the Nautilus machines. A thin sheen of sweat covered his upper body, but he showed no other sign of the effort.

Rob turned with a scowl to stare at Devinny. "That bar had 250 pounds on it, Dale! And he's not even breathing hard."

"Well, he's been at it a long time, I guess. Hey, maybe he's on steroids."

Rob shook his head. "I don't know. I've been working my tail off for weeks. At the rate I'm going, I'll be an old man before I get anywhere *close* to where he is." He rose to his feet, threw a towel around his neck, and stared at the lifter, who was now doing arm work, his biceps muscles bulging powerfully. "You know, Dale, I think it's all a waste of time. I mean, there are two kinds of guys who work out in this place—guys like him who've got muscles in their *hair*, and guys like me who keep on pumping iron but never get anywhere."

"Takes time, Rob."

But Rob Ross was not to be reasoned with. "No, it's not a matter of time. Some guys are muscular and some just aren't. You've seen guys who never even *saw* a barbell who still look like that guy, haven't you? And some of us just don't *have* it."

He shook his head with disgust and headed for the locker room.

"Hey, I'll see you tomorrow night, Rob," Devinny called out.

"Maybe," Rob grunted. With that he left the weight room and turned to go down the wide hall, only to bump abruptly into someone who was hurrying in the other direction. "Hey, watch where—!" he snapped angrily, but he cut his words off abruptly and reached out to catch the young woman he'd collided with. She was not tall, and he caught her easily as she reeled backward. At once he said, "Ah—sorry to be so clumsy."

"Oh, it was my fault. I should have watched where I was going."

Rob was still holding her arms where he had caught her to keep her from falling. She looked up at him and smiled, and he suffered a most peculiar sensation. He had once been struck a hard blow in the stomach and for a brief time had been unable to breathe. The sight of this girl's face had a similar, but less painful, effect.

She had to tilt her head back to look up at Rob. Her eyes were very large, and an amazing violet—the only ones he'd ever seen of that color except for Elizabeth Taylor's. Long, thick lashes swept down over them when she blinked, and she had a long, lovely mouth that somehow made him nervous. He'd read in novels of girls with a peaches-and-cream complexion, but had thought the description was just an imaginative fancy. Now he was seeing the reality of it. Her long, blonde hair was tied back with a ribbon.

She wore a mock thong leotard of heather gray and magenta with a sweetheart neckline and racer back that afforded a provocative view of her full figure. A glance down affected Rob so much that he chose to avert his eyes as he apologized: "I'm pretty clumsy sometimes—"

She was one of those girls who dated professional football players or rising young executives—certainly not the kind who would go for a skinny freshman from Tulane. He wanted to say something clever, but nothing came to him. His face grew red. He mumbled, "Well, sorry about the bump," and would have moved past her, but she asked, "Do you know how to play racquetball?"

"Well—well, sure!"

"I've really been wanting to try it. Is it hard?"

"Easiest thing in the world," Rob said quickly, then dared to suggest, "maybe sometime I could show you how."

She smiled at him, her eyes wide and sparkling, "Oh, would you mind?"

"Just name the time. I'm here every night."

"What about now? Do you have a late date?"

"No!" Rob stumbled over his answer.

"Oh, great! My name's Stormy Carr."

"I'm Rob Ross. Well, let's go get the equipment and we'll hit a few."

Ten minutes later they were in one of the racquetball rooms, laughing at her awkward attempts to hit the small ball.

She finally fell against him, pulling him down with her in a wild attempt to swat the ball, and they fell to the floor laughing. He had cushioned her fall, and she lay across his chest, saying, "You'd better go find another girl, Rob. I'll never learn to hit that silly ball!"

Rob was intensely conscious of her full figure pressing against him, and of her full lips only inches away. He had to clear his throat to say, "Why, Stormy, you're doing fine."

"Am I?" She made no attempt to move, but looked right into his eyes. "Well, I have a good teacher." She seemed to be waiting for something, but after a moment she got to her feet. "I'd like to try this when I'm not worn out from aerobics," she said.

"How about tomorrow night?" Rob asked quickly. "I usually get here about seven."

Stormy smiled at him and nodded. "That's a date." She turned to go, then paused. "I've got to have something to eat. Like to join me?"

"Sure! I'm starved!"

The two left the racquetball room. As they walked down the hall to return the equipment, the same fellow who had impressed Rob with his weight lifting approached them. "Hey, Stormy, how about we go out tonight?"

"Sorry, Juke. Already got a date."

Rob was conscious of a long, hard look from the muscular Juke. But as they walked on, he only asked, "You go out with him, Stormy?"

"Not anymore. He's got nothing but muscles. Can't do anything but grunt. Besides, he's already got a love affair—with himself. See you in the lobby in twenty minutes."

Rob showered and took extra care with his hair. He scowled with disgust at his outfit—charcoal mini-houndstooth slacks with inverted pleats and a Ralph Lauren polo shirt, gray with a three-button placket and rib knit collar and cuffs. "Look like something out of *Tobacco Road!*" he muttered, then hurried out into the lobby, where he waited for twenty minutes. *Probably forgot about me already,* he was thinking gloomily just as Stormy emerged from the hallway.

"Sorry to keep you waiting, Rob," she smiled. "But you know how women are."

Her comment implied—at least Rob took it to mean—that he was quite a ladies' man. He stood straighter, admiring her outfit—a pair of fawn-colored baggy pants with front pleats, a jacket to match—oversized over a pure white camp shirt—

and a pair of dark brown alligator slip-ons. Gold swirl earrings hung from her ears, and a swirl pendant with a strange design hung from a black rayon cord.

Stormy accepted his admiring look, took his arm, and said, "Come on, Rob. We'll take first prize as the best-looking couple at the party!"

"What party?"

She laughed lightly, "You'll see."

She pulled him through the door of the club and down the street to where a jet-black Porsche was parked. "You drive, Rob," she commanded, handing him the keys. "This thing's got too much muscle for a woman. It's really a man's car."

Rob opened her door for her, then went around and climbed down into the deep leather seat. The car was stifling, but it had that wonderful new car smell, and he fumbled with the key, saying, "Never drove one of these, Stormy. New, isn't it?"

"Oh, I've had it a few weeks," she replied carelessly. "Don't hit the gas too hard, or we'll leave the ground."

Rob pulled out cautiously, finding that she had told him the truth about the power of the car. "Where to?" he asked.

"Go to the Quarter. Some friends of mine are having a little get-together. There'll be plenty to eat and drink."

Rob drove to the French Quarter and followed her directions, steering the Porsche by the Jackson Brewery. She directed him to Iberville Street, then said, "That's it , Rob, the Midnight Club." Rob parked the Porsche, scurried around to open Stormy's door, and strolled with her through the front entrance. The first person they met was a big man with forearms like hams. His thick lips split into a broad grin, and he said in a graveled voice, "Hi, Stormy. Go on up. Party's already started."

"Thanks, sweetie," Stormy answered, and pulled Rob

toward a set of black wrought-iron staircases that wound upward. She turned as they got to the first step, looked at Rob, and said, "Come on up. I want you to meet my friends."

When they reached the top of the winding stairway, she led him to a door down a short hallway. It was guarded by a very tall man wearing a shiny gray silk suit and a pink shirt that opened halfway down his chest to reveal three heavy gold chains. He wore four diamond rings, a gold watch on one wrist, a gold bracelet on the other, and dark glasses. A pink silk handkerchief sprouted from his breast pocket.

"Hi, Stormy," he grinned, exposing the over-supply of gold in his teeth. "You're running late."

"Hi, Dude," Stormy replied. "This is my friend, Rob. Be sure you're nice to him."

"Friend of yours is a friend of mine," Dude said. He turned and opened the door, then closed it as Stormy and Rob entered.

It was a crowded room, richly furnished with blue velvet and brass. As they entered, people gathered at once to greet Stormy. She announced, "Hey, this is my new man. Rob Ross—meet the gang."

A tall man with broad shoulders came forward and put his hand out, "Look, Rob, might as well lay it out—I'll steal your girl if I can."

Rob peered at the man through the heavy smoke that hung in the room. "Aren't you Jay Tolbert?"

"Sure am." Tolbert played cornerback for the Saints. He was one of the jet-set crowd, the pet athlete. He looked smaller up close than he did on the field, but Rob was overwhelmed. "That was a rotten call you got last Sunday. That official must be in somebody's pocket."

Tolbert nodded. "That makes two of us who think so, Rob. But he's the man."

For the next ten minutes, Rob was maneuvered around the room, meeting people. Some of them he'd read about in the papers—a TV actress, a high-ranking state official, a New York producer. And Stormy seemed to know all of them well. She stayed close to Rob, whispering choice anecdotes about the guests. She was a "touching" woman, one who seemed to need physical contact, and more than once she leaned on him, pressing her firm body against him. She seemed not to notice—but Rob was acutely aware of her nearness.

She pulled him up to dance, and though he protested, she gave him no choice. He was actually a fine dancer, and Stormy's huge eyes opened even wider as she cried out, "Say, you're not some kind of a chorus boy, are you, Rob?" She laughed at his confusion, pulled him close, and explained, "You know, not many men are good dancers, but lots of them think they are." She pressed herself against him, whispering, "You're really smooth, you know?"

After the dance, they moved toward the table where Cajun waiters were serving a variety of foods. Everyone was drinking, and without asking, Stormy handed Rob a cocktail. Although he didn't normally drink, he held the glass and sipped at it for effect. As the informal meal progressed, he was so engrossed that he gradually drained it without noticing. Later he sat down with Stormy and four or five others. He shook his head when the marijuana cigarettes were passed around. Stormy caught his action and smiled. "Good idea, Rob. I'm cutting back myself."

The party lasted two hours. When Rob finally said, "I've got to go," Stormy responded, "Let me go to the little girls' room, Rob, then I'll drive you home."

She slipped away into the high-ceilinged bath, where she picked up a phone and dialed a number. When a voice said, "Hello?" she said, "Bingo!"

"You got him?"

"Sure. Told you it would be a cinch." She smiled, adding, "He's kind of innocent, you know?"

"Yeah, well, it's your job to see he don't stay that way. Don't move too fast. Let him get a taste of the good life, then sink it to him."

"Sure. I'll take care of it. Gonna be fun taking mama's boy down the garden path."

"Just don't blow it. I'll drop the cash off tomorrow at your place."

There was a click on the line, and Stormy hung up the phone and returned to the large room. "Ready?" she smiled at Rob.

"You don't have to leave, Stormy," Rob protested. "I can get a cab."

"None of that!" she laughed and squeezed his arm. "I don't let my dates take a cab home. Come on, honey, let's go."

A short, muscular man with a dark complexion watched them leave. When they passed through the door, he walked to the phone, dialed a number, and waited. Finally he said, "Okay. She's got the kid in tow." He listened for a moment, then answered, "Not a chance. That kid won't know what hit him! Stormy will have him jumping through her little hoop in a week!"

He replaced the receiver, then leaned back against the wall with a look of satisfaction on his sharp features. He listened to the rock music, shook his head sadly, and murmured, "They sure can't play 'em like they used to!"

4

Dinner at Henri's

W hat's wrong, Dad?"

Dan Ross looked across the chess board, suddenly aware that he had been staring at it for a long time without really studying the game. "I'm trying to find a way to get out of this mess you've put me in," he said defensively.

"No, you're not," Dani answered, her green eyes studying him with concern. "You play chess like Custer fought the Indians. You go roaring in with all you've got, hoping to stampede your opponent. It's just the opposite of the way you work a case—there you're cautious and careful."

"Thank you, Dr. Ross, for a fine psychological profile!"

But Dani refused to be sidetracked. "I know you almost as well as you know me, Dad." She leaned back in her chair, and there was concern written on her face. "Remember that part in *Jane Eyre*, when Mr. Rochester tells Jane she's got to leave him and go to Ireland?"

"My favorite scene."

"He said, 'Jane, sometimes I feel there's a thread attached to your heart, and the other end's tied to mine. But if you go far away, across the sea, that thread might snap.'"

Dan Ross considered his daughter fondly. "Is that your poetic way of saying our communication has gone sour?"

"Yes. You've never been a talkative man, but for the last few weeks you've been a regular clam." She hesitated, then asked, "Is your heart acting up? And I want the truth!"

Ross picked up the ivory bishop, studied it thoughtfully, then carefully replaced it on the board. "No, it's not that," he said slowly. "In a way, I wish it were that simple. Sickness may hurt us, but at least it's something we can fight. There are things we can do, even if they don't always work."

"Tell me."

"All right. I'm worried about Rob, for one thing."

"What's wrong with him?"

"Oh, nothing that I can put my finger on. Maybe I'm just an old fuddy-duddy. A mother hen worried about my only chick." He smiled briefly, his fine eyes almost hidden in the crinkles of his face. "Got my metaphors mixed, I guess. I couldn't be a *mother* hen—and I've got two more chicks." He shook his head slowly, adding, "Rob's gotten secretive. He never was before, not really. Oh, he'd go around carrying some big 'problem' in his head, but if I let him alone, he'd come in sooner or later and tell me about it. But not this time."

"You don't have any idea what it is?" Dani questioned.

"He came in and asked for money early this week," Ross said. "He's seldom done that. Always been proud of being able to make his own way. If he's asking me for money, it means he's spent all his savings for college and is running on the rims."

"Maybe I could find out something."

"I doubt it," Ross shrugged. "He's ashamed of himself. I

gave him the money, of course, but he looked like a sheep-killing dog when he took it." He hesitated, then added, "I'd guess it's a girl, though he hasn't mentioned one."

"He goes out every night, but I thought he was going to that health club."

"He's not going much. I called and found out."

Fine lines had etched themselves in her father's face, and Dani was worried. "It won't kill him to make a fool of himself over a girl, Dad," she coaxed. "Every young fellow does it, sooner or later. Rob's been a pretty straight arrow up until now."

Ross tried to grin. "I guess so. When I was his age, I was studying for the gallows. You may not believe it, but once a young lady's father ran me off with a shotgun!"

Dani reached over and stroked his hand. "I believe it. You're a handsome brute now. I hate to think what havoc you must have wrought with the girls when you were twenty!" Then she asked, "That's not all, is it? All that's been worrying you?"

A shadow touched Dan Ross's eyes and he shook his head. He reached into his pocket and brought out an envelope. "No. I got this in the mail two weeks ago. Since then I've gotten two more like it."

Dani took the envelope, observed that the name and address were typed, then removed the greeting card, noting automatically that it was an expensive Hallmark offering. She read aloud the words on the front of the card: "With Deepest Sympathy for Your Loss." She opened the card, read the insipid verse, then looked up at her father. "It's not signed."

"No."

Dani caught the hard edge of the monosyllabic answer, and then she understood. "You think this is from Tommy Cain?"

"Just the kind of thing he'd do, Dani—threatening to kill

my family." Ross took the card from her, studied it, then shook his head. "Cain liked to torment people. He was charged with some petty stuff before he graduated. He liked to beat up people, especially helpless ones."

Dani was shocked at the fury that shot through her. She didn't speak until she was able to control her voice. "He wouldn't dare touch you, Dad. Luke talked with him when he first got back to New Orleans. Cain knows that if anything happens to you, he'll be the first suspect on the list."

"Sure, I know," Ross said, clearly unconvinced. He replaced the card in his pocket, got to his feet, then said, "Don't mention this to your mother. I don't want her to worry."

"Of course not, Dad," Dani said, getting to her feet. "But I'm going to tell Luke about it."

Ross shrugged. "If you like. But Cain's smart—maybe the smartest crook I ever knew. Luke can't prove he sent the card. He can't scare Cain, either. He's tough, Dani. Tough and smart—and he never forgets a grudge. That's a pretty potent combination." Then he smiled and came around the table to give her a hug. "But remember what David said when Saul was out to get him? He said, 'I will lay me down and sleep.' Now that's faith in God for you!" He released her and left the room, pausing only to add, "Better not tell Ben about this, either. He'd probably go after Cain with a skinning knife!"

Dani picked up the chess pieces, arranged the game in its fine rosewood case, then replaced it in the glass case. She moved to the window and looked out to see Allison bounding up and down on the trampoline. She glanced at her watch, then turned abruptly and hurried to her room, where she threw on tennis whites, tied her hair into a ponytail, and grabbed her racket. When she walked out onto the side yard, where the trampoline was set up, Allison protested, "Oh, Dani, go away! I'm just about to get this back flip right!"

She was poised gracefully in the center of the trampoline, her dark blue eyes enormous as she glared at Dani, then glanced back toward Ben Savage. She had an enormous crush on Ben and resented Dani terribly for taking up so much of his time. When Dani said patiently, "He *works* for me, Allison," the younger girl would pout and proclaim, "That's no argument!"

Now Savage said, "Time to quit, anyway. When you get to a certain point, Allison, it's better to stop. You're doing fine. Practice for two more days—and next time maybe I'll teach you a back flip with a full twist."

"Really?" Allison beamed and sprang to the ground. "Show me, Ben!"

Savage grinned, mounted the trampoline, and began bouncing easily. He was the most graceful man Dani had ever seen, and his years of training in the circus had not left him. He rose high into the air, arched his body sideways, and kicked into a perfect flip that turned into a twist, landing lightly on his feet, then bounding to the ground.

"Show-off!" Dani scoffed, hiding her admiration. "Come on, and I'll beat your ears off on the court." She was proud of her tennis skills and she had finally persuaded Ben to let her teach him the game. He'd never had a racket in his hand until a few weeks ago. But his native athleticism, combined with an overdeveloped competitive streak, had brought him along fast. She still held the advantage that comes with years of practice, but she had quickly moved past the point of holding back to his level.

"Day after tomorrow, Allison," Ben said, reaching out to squeeze the back of her neck. Then he followed Dani to the court and slid his Prince graphite racket out of its case. They began rallying, warming up smoothly and slowly.

"Are you ready?" Dani soon asked, noticing that Ben's strokes were becoming much smoother, with no loss of power.

"Anytime," Ben replied, tossing all three balls to the end of the court. "You serve."

Giving me the service advantage. He must feel a lot more confident with his ground strokes. Dani tossed the ball in front of her right shoulder and hit a three-quarter speed serve into the middle of the service box. Ben bounced on his toes, turning his body to the left, met the ball well in front of him and blasted a topspin forehand down the line. A clean winner.

"You're a great teacher," he grinned, moving over to the ad court to receive.

Dani was speechless. Normally he would have blasted the return against her backstop. She buckled down for a tough match. Her next serve jammed Ben, and he hit a weak backhand reply that barely cleared the net. Dani moved quickly to the net, getting into position for her two-fisted backhand. She noticed Ben sprinting to his right to cover the open court, hit the ball behind him, and watched as he put on the brakes, spinning around to reach her shot. He lost his footing, coming down hard on the green surface.

"You all right?" Dani called out.

Ben got slowly to his feet, brushing the grit out of an abrasion on his knee. "Small scratch on my ego," he replied. "That's all."

Dani won the first game by playing percentage tennis. Shortening her backswing to allow for the pace on Ben's strokes, she used his own power against him in the rallies, where she had the advantage of patience, waiting for a short ball to hit clean winners.

When Ben served, it was a different story. His first three serves were aces, and the last was a winner that she barely got a racket on, the ball dribbling weakly into the net.

Dani tried everything in her repertoire—drop shots, moon balls, topspin lobs. But Ben's quickness and power, combined with his newly found consistency, was too much in the end. The final score, 6-4, 6-4, told the story of the match. One service break in each set was all he needed; she had no hope of overcoming his powerful serve.

"You're getting better, Boss," Savage remarked as they left the court. "If you practice real hard for ten or fifteen years, you may win a game."

Dani clamped her jaws together, and he rambled on. "I think I'll let you win a game every now and then. It'd be the gentlemanly thing to do."

"Don't you dare, Ben Savage!"

Savage shook his head, muttering sadly, "You liberated women sure do miss out on a lot of good stuff."

When they were sitting on the shady patio drinking iced lemonade, she said suddenly, "Ben, Dad's been getting some bad mail—"

Savage listened carefully, his face impassive as she reported the incident, then said idly, "Maybe I better go explain a few things to Mr. Tommy Cain."

Dani shot him a quick glance. "No way, Ben. I know you. You'd 'explain' things by punching him out, and that just won't do. I'll have Luke talk to him again."

"Luke's got to play by the rules, Boss," Savage remarked. "He's got a little book just full of them, and if it's not in the book, Luke can't do a thing." Slouched in the deck chair, he presented an idle shape. He looked mild, even ineffectual, Dani thought, but there was something about his air. And she knew that, like a great cat, he could explode into a driving fury when necessary.

"No, Ben," she repeated. "I don't think Cain will actually

do anything. He'll try to worry Dad, but he'd never dare to touch him."

"That's your idea," Savage said. "It's not mine." He set the glass down on the table and stood. When he arched his back and stretched his arms, muscles leaped into prominence under the thin cotton shirt. "Cain's not your run-of-the-mill hoodlum, Dani. He's smart enough to keep his nose clean, but he's been sitting up at Angola for a few years, doing nothing but thinking of ways to get even."

"You know him, Ben?"

"Never met him, but I've been doing a little listening." He turned to face her, his eyes dark and brooding. "Everybody says the same thing. 'Cain never forgets.' Those cards—they're from Cain, but he's not finished yet."

Dani said slowly, "I'll tell Luke about it. We've got a date later tonight."

Savage had turned to leave, but he pivoted back and stared at her. "Say, what do you two do on a date?" When Dani looked at him blankly, he added, "I mean—since Luke's a Christian now, you two can't go down and park on the levee and do a lot of kissing." He saw the flush that touched Dani's cheeks, but ignored it. "Do you sit around and discuss theology, or what?"

"I don't think you would understand it, Ben!" Dani snapped, rising abruptly.

"Nope, I guess I wouldn't," he called after her as she strode toward the house, her back straight with anger. "I'm just an earthy type, Boss—poor creature made of dust."

He grinned as Dani slammed the door so hard the glass rattled, but then his face grew somber. He looked down at the glass she had left, picked it up slowly and studied it. Finally he set it down firmly, his lips twisted in a bitter smirk.

"Great work, Savage," he said heavily. "Humiliate her on

the court, then make fun of her religion—what a charmer!" He wheeled suddenly and stalked away from the patio toward his car. He slammed the door ferociously, then burned rubber as he sped down the gravel drive.

"Where do you want to eat?" Luke Sixkiller asked. He tooled the Chevrolet Caprice off the Pontchartrain Causeway and onto the interstate, exceeding the plainly posted speed limit by twenty miles an hour.

Dani looked at him with irritation. "Do we *have* to go in a police car, Luke?" She felt strange riding in a car with "New Orleans Police Department" emblazoned on the side.

"My heap's in the shop," he replied lazily, weaving through the traffic with one wrist drooping over the wheel. "Besides, we won't be likely to get a ticket driving this one. Now, how about a nice quarter-pounder at McDonald's? I know the manager personally, and I can probably get us a table by the window where we can watch the kids fighting on the playground stuff."

"They'd never let you in in that outfit," Dani said, glancing sideways at him. Despite his rough power and street-wise manner, Sixkiller dressed like a *GQ* model. She took in the tobacco-colored slacks with the double pleat, the single-breasted olive jacket with touches of red and blue in the mini check, the snowy-white shirt accented by a black silk jacquard tie in a geometric print.

Sixkiller caught her scrutiny and grinned. "My one beset-ting sin—foppish attire," he said. "Now, how about a bite at Henri's?"

"Henri's?" Dani's right eyebrow lifted slightly. "You'd have to give up your pension for a meal in that place."

"It's only money," Sixkiller shrugged. "Doesn't matter in the eternal scheme of things."

He exited to Canal Street, maneuvered through traffic, and finally stopped in front of the Meridien Hotel. Then he let a tall man in a snappy uniform get behind the wheel. Another uniformed doorman, who was opening the door for Dani, gave Sixkiller a slight smile. "Good evening, Lieutenant. Good to see you again."

"Hi, Terry."

Sixkiller and Dani walked through the entrance, and a small man with a brown face and a thin mustache nodded. "Ah, Monsieur Sixkiller," he smiled. "We haven't seen you for some time. Let me take you to a good table."

Dani and Sixkiller followed the maitre d' through the opulent room. He pulled out a chair for Dani. "Always good to see you," he added. "Enjoy your meal."

Dani stared at the man's straight back, then at Sixkiller. "You must eat here a lot, Luke. I didn't know policemen were so well heeled."

"I did a favor for the owners once. They like for me to come in and give the place a little tone."

A trim waiter came to take their order. "I think you might enjoy the filet mignon of venison, sir—and the breast of duck with wild mushrooms is also very good."

Dani ordered the duck, Sixkiller the venison, but they raised the waiter's eyebrows when they both refused the wine. "Probably a first for Henri's—not having wine," Sixkiller remarked. "The waiter looked at us as if we were some sort of barbarians."

"I guess to a French waiter, anyone who doesn't take wine with his meal *is* a savage," Dani smiled. She looked around the room. "Nice little place."

The main dining room of Henri's was paneled with dark wood, but large, gleaming brass chandeliers cast their light over the snowy tablecloths and the pastel-colored chairs with heart-shaped backs. There was a richness in the place, not only in the fixtures and the heavy silver and crystal goblets, but in the clientele. Dani noted the expensive dress of the men and the jewels sparkling on the fingers and throats of the women. "I don't guess they take food stamps here, do they?"

Luke laughed, then shook his head. "They look pretty good, but strip them naked and you couldn't tell them from the bunch eating greasy chicken at the Colonel's. Like the man said, the Colonel's lady and Judy O'Grady are sisters under the skin."

"That's from a poem—" Dani hesitated, then nodded. "Kipling, isn't it?"

Sixkiller's lips grew tight. "Poetry? Never read the stuff!"

Dani leaned back and studied the dark face of Sixkiller. He was by far the most virile man in the room; next to him, the other males looked pale and ineffectual. According to the reports of the other officers on the homicide squad, he was a man who showed no nerves whatsoever. But she could see that his composure was ruffled now. She leaned forward on her elbow, cupped her chin, and said, "Yes, you do, too."

"I do, too—what?"

"Read poetry." Dani studied the effect her words had on him, and added, "I know you do. One time at our house, you and Dad had been playing chess. He went to bed, and when I came in you were reading a book."

"So, I was reading a book," Sixkiller grunted. "I do that once in a while."

"Yes, but you tried to hide it, to keep me from seeing it," Dani probed. Her eyes were bright with interest, and she added, "You got all flustered and shoved it in your coat pocket."

"You're always playing detective. I had a book and put it

in my pocket. Probably a report book on cases. I carry one most of the time."

"I turned the heat up, and when it got warm, you took your coat off. I asked you to get something for me, and when you left, I took the book out and looked at it." She waited for Sixkiller to speak, but he was looking down at his plate. "It was a book of Robert Browning's poetry," she finished. When he still kept his eyes down, she put her hand on his. "Luke, why are you so ashamed of reading poetry?"

He lifted his dark eyes, his mouth a sober line. "I don't know. It just doesn't seem like the kind of thing I'd like people to know about." His lips wrinkled in a wry expression. "I can hear what they'd say in the squad room if they knew about it."

Dani was touched. Here was a man who would walk into an alley full of armed, drug-crazed criminals—yet was afraid to admit he liked literature. "Luke, it's all right for you to like Browning. I like you better for it. Are you angry at me for prying?"

Her words brought a sudden light into his obsidian eyes, and he grasped her hand. "Well, as long as you don't tell Sweet Willie Wine or some of his buddies, I guess I don't mind."

"Good! Now tell me which poets you like."

They sat there enjoying the meal, ordering peaches poached in vanilla with champagne cream sauce, and talking about poetry. Dani was pleased to discover that the policeman, who had never had a course in poetry in his life, not only was well-read but also had fine taste.

They had gone through most of the older poets and were discussing Robert Frost when Sixkiller suddenly broke off his comment to say, "Look, Dani—over by the window."

Dani followed his nod, then jerked her head in surprise. "Why, that's Rob."

"Sure is—and who's his girlfriend?"

Dani stared at the young woman sitting across from her brother, and shook her head. The girl was a flamboyant beauty, and it was obvious that Rob saw no one in the room but her. Dani felt a stab of sisterly protectiveness. "I don't know who she is, Luke. I'd like to know, though."

"Yeah?" Sixkiller inquired. "That shouldn't be too hard. Not too many birds like that in the coop. Want me to find out?"

Dani struggled with her conscience, then nodded. "Dad's worried about Rob—" She repeated the essence of her conversation with her father and added, "I wouldn't want Rob to know I was prying—"

Luke laughed. "What'd you think, Dani—I intend to pull a gun on them and say, 'Up against the wall while I frisk you?' Be back in a minute." He rose and left the room without looking at the pair. While he was gone, Dani picked at her food, feeling troubled.

When Sixkiller returned, he slid into his chair, saying, "Name's Stormy Carr. Lives at the Walford Arms, apartment 334. She's twenty-four years old, is five-feet-six-inches tall, weighs 131 pounds, and has an anchor tattooed on her right thigh." When Dani stared at him, he shrugged, "Okay, so I lied about the tattoo to impress you, but the rest is the straight dope."

"How'd you find all that out so quick?"

"Glove compartment of her car. The registration was there, and I made a call for the rest." He looked across the room, studied the pair, then murmured, "She's pretty hot stuff. Not Rob's type. He doesn't have the coin."

"No. And that's what worries me, Luke. Why would a woman like that be dating Rob?"

"Could be true love. A real romantic story."

"You don't believe that!"

Sixkiller studied the face of Stormy Carr and shook his head slowly, then said, "No. It won't play, Dani."

The light mood had been broken, and Sixkiller said, "Let's stop by and say hello."

Dani hesitated, then nodded. Luke signed the ticket with a flourish, and the two of them made their way across the room. When they approached the pair, Rob looked up suddenly and saw them. His face froze, and Dani recognized guilt. But she put on a look of polite surprise. "Why, Rob! I didn't expect to see you!"

Rob lurched to his feet with a "Hello, Sis." He looked as if he hoped they would pass by, but when they stopped, he said, "This—this is Stormy Carr. Stormy, my sister Dani, and Lieutenant Luke Sixkiller."

"Your sister? You didn't tell me you had a sister, Rob." Stormy smiled and added, "I haven't known Rob long. Why don't you sit down and give me all the dirt on him."

"Well, just for a minute," Dani said. She took the chair Luke pulled out for her, and for the next ten minutes a bright conversation ran around the table, most of it directed by Stormy Carr. She was "fascinated" by policemen, and she "couldn't believe" Dani was a private investigator. Before long, Luke was basking in her charms—so it seemed to Dani. Finally Dani rose. "We've got to run. So nice to meet you, Stormy. Have Rob bring you by the house soon, won't you?"

Stormy smiled and nodded. "I'd love to!"

Outside, in the car, Dani said, "You seemed quite taken with Miss Carr."

"Had her under surveillance," Luke nodded. "Never know when I might have to pick her out in a lineup." He said no more, for he sensed that she was troubled. Soon they were crossing the river bridge, and he let Dani think as the tires hummed. He turned on the radio, found a nostalgia station, and listened as Nat King Cole sang about a ballerina.

Finally Dani said, "Why am I so upset about this, Luke? Rob's grown up."

"No, he's not," Luke shrugged. "Not where that little number is concerned. Nobody's *that* grown up."

"She's very beautiful."

"So is a black panther—but they can eat you alive."

Dani shook her head. "She's too *old* for him, Luke."

Luke dodged to avoid a matronly possum with a tribe of naked-faced babies on her back. He let the music play; this time it was "Green Eyes" with Bob Eberly and Helen O'Connell. Finally he said, "When a cop gets personally involved in a case, Dani, he's not worth a dime."

Dani stared at him. "Why did you say that?"

"Because you're so afraid of Stormy Carr's intentions, you missed something a lot worse."

Dani tried to think back, but could not think of anything. "What did I miss?"

"Rob was high on something."

"Luke—no!"

"He had all the signs, Dani, but you were too uptight to see them. Maybe not hard stuff, but something."

Dani felt as though someone had just struck her in the pit of the stomach. She sat quietly, fear rising like a flood. Finally, when Sinatra began to sing, "Down Mexico Way," the tears started to roll down her face. She was not even aware she was crying. But finally Luke reached into his pocket and handed her a black silk handkerchief that matched his tie.

"We've got a problem," he said quietly, "but God's still with us."

Dani moved closer to him, grateful for his bulk, his assurance, and his reminder that God was in the wings.

5

Fragile Things

I don't know much about this meeting, Luke," Dani said. "Pastor Clay asked me to go. He said the woman who leads the meeting needs some encouragement."

Sixkiller was reading numbers on the houses, or at least trying to find a number, for most of them lacked one. The Gretna neighborhood where they were driving, once inhabited by prosperous upper-middle-class people, had decayed rapidly in the last few decades. "There it is—2133," Sixkiller announced, and Dani pulled the Cougar over to the curb. As they got out, the policeman cast a doubtful look around. "Hope you have your hubcaps when the meeting is over."

"What are 'house meetings,' anyway?" Sixkiller asked as they walked down the sidewalk toward the house. Number 2133 was obviously old, perhaps dating back a hundred years. The red bricks were furred with moss, and the white paint was peeling from the woodwork. "Is it for people who won't go to a church?"

"No, not really," Dani answered. "Pastor Clay says that people don't get close enough to each other in large meetings, so he likes for all the members of the church to be involved in a small group. The idea is that people will share their problems in that sort of situation. There are about thirty house meetings now." They ascended rickety wooden steps that groaned dangerously under Sixkiller's 190 pounds. Dani rang the bell, saying, "I don't know the lady who leads the group, but Pastor Clay told me she's had a hard life. She's got a bad case of rheumatoid arthritis, and it's difficult for her to get to church."

The door opened and a small, elderly woman with a crown of beautiful silver hair smiled at them. "Dani?" she inquired, then put her hand out. "Pastor Clay told me you'd be here. Come in, both of you."

"Mrs. Deveraux, this is Lieutenant Luke Sixkiller. And this is Anna Deveraux, Lieutenant."

Anna Deveraux was in her eighties, and her body was twisted with the crippling disease. Dani took her hand very carefully, knowing the pain that went with arthritis, and shot a quick glance at Luke. She wanted to tell him to be gentle, for he had a grip like a Stilson wrench and sometimes forgot his own strength. But he nodded slightly, and gently took the frail, twisted hand. "Glad to meet you, Mrs. Deveraux."

"Well, then, you're a strong one! But you must both call me Anna. We like to use first names." She turned, saying, "Most of my group are here. Come along and meet them."

The house had the musty smell of age. The high-ceilinged rooms were dark, but the tall windows admitted enough fading sun for Dani to see the old pictures and furniture that filled the rooms. It was a crowded house, jammed with furniture, most of it covered with stacks of newspapers, magazines, books, and a little of everything else. Dani thought of her friend

Caroline's comment after coming back from visiting an elderly aunt: *The only way to help it would be to use blasting powder!*

Anna Deveraux led them down a narrow hall, then through an open door into a sunroom, framed with glass on three sides. The small group of people was sitting around a heavy round oak coffee table, which was covered with Bibles, notebooks, white coffee mugs, and three plates of cookies.

"This is Dani and Luke," Anna said, then began to name the members of the group. There were only six of them, and Dani tried to keep their names in her mind as they were called, fixing their faces at the same time.

Jerry and Sheila Graham—married couple. He, tall, thin, with a long face and a worried look. She, short, very pregnant, also worried.

Helen Baker—about thirty, slightly overweight, very pretty. Blonde hair, blue eyes, no wedding ring.

Maurice Littleton—tall, loose-limbed black man, about twenty-two, tattooed on both arms. Bad scar on cheek, but a gentle look in his eyes.

Pete Carpenter—short, fair, blue eyes. Fairly successful look, like a good salesman.

Rose LaVie—very young, not over eighteen. Dark eyes. Marks of poverty, cheap clothing. Look of dissatisfaction in her eyes. Could be Cajun.

After Anna had gone around the circle, she said, "Now, I hope you two are good singers, because Maurice is the only real musician we have. Even if you can't sing, you can make a joyful noise. Maurice—?"

The young man rose to pick up a battered Gibson guitar, which was leaning against the wall. It looked frail in his enormous hands but made a smooth sound when his fingers ran over the strings. Without preamble he began to play, lifting up his voice to sing, "What a Friend We Have in Jesus." His high tenor was mellow and true; it filled the room, yet was not overwhelming. Dani had grown up with the song, so she joined in, getting a smile from Maurice. The others joined, rather feebly, except for Pete Carpenter, whose voice was powerful though sometimes off-key.

After singing several of the older hymns, Littleton strummed the strings lightly, then said, "You know, we Christians talk a lot about praise and worship, but lately I've been thinking that we don't really *do* much of it." He smiled then, adding quickly, "Oh, I know we have what we call a praise service every time we meet. All churches do that, I reckon. But it seems like the songs we sing ain't really worship songs."

"Why, I think they are," Pete Carpenter said quickly. "Like the one we just sang, Maurice—'What a friend we have in Jesus.' If that's not worship, I don't know what is!"

"Sure, Pete, you're right," Littleton nodded. "And I love the old songs we sing. They been blessin' the people of God for a long time. But I been studying the words a lot here lately, and most of the songs we sing in church—why, they're more about *us* than about the Lord!"

Anna leaned forward, her eyes bright with interest. "Tell us what you mean by that, Maurice."

"Well, I ain't no expert," the young man said, shaking his head. "But you look at that one called 'Love Lifted Me.' Now if they's anybody who ought to love *that* particular song, it's ol' Maurice." He grinned broadly then, saying, "I was sure enough sinking deep in sin, far from the peaceful shore! And sure enough, it was the Lord Jesus lifted me, and I thank him for it every day of my life." He paused, trying to get his thoughts together, then went on softly, "But don't you see? That song is about *me*, about what Jesus done for *me*. And I don't intend to stop singing it—no, sir! That ol' Paul, he didn't miss no chances to tell folks how God knocked him off his donkey and made him a new creature, did he, now?"

"I guess you're saying that we sing mostly about how we got saved." Jerry Graham's brow was wrinkled with thought. "Nothing wrong with that."

"No, Jerry, there sure ain't," Littleton agreed. "But I got to addin' up how many songs we sing like that, and it comes to 'bout ninety percent."

Helen Baker shifted in her chair uneasily. To Dani, she looked slightly out of place, a little overdressed for a meeting like this, and her eyes revealed some sort of despair as she spoke. "It's about all I can do to sing any kind of hymn, and now you're saying we're doing it wrong?"

Maurice looked down at the Gibson, his eyes hidden. There was a silence in the room, somewhat uncomfortable, but no one broke it until Maurice himself looked up and said, "Well, I ain't said it right. Probably I'm all wrong, anyway."

Anna said, "Tell us the rest of it, Maurice. What kind of songs do we *not* sing?"

Littleton gave her a grateful look. "Well, I been studyin' the Bible, tryin' to find out what kind of songs they sung in them olden days. And it seems like in the Psalms, a whole bunch of 'em are just about God—about who he is and what he's done. 'Course, a lot of 'em is about David his self, how he got downhearted at times—but mainly they just bust out with how good God is! Things like 'Great is the Lord, and greatly to be praised,' and 'O Lord, how great are thy works! and thy thoughts are very deep.' Lots of that in the Psalms."

"I've noticed that, Maurice," Sheila Graham spoke up. She was obviously quite close to her time of delivery; her abdomen filled her lap so that she shifted uncomfortably as she continued. "It seems like the same thing over and over, always saying, 'Praise the Lord,' or sometimes, 'Come and praise the Lord with me.'"

Dani said, "I've wondered about that—why the psalmist says over and over, 'Come and let *us* praise the Lord.' Finally, I happened to think—that's just how it is when we love someone or something. We want others to share in that love." She smiled at Sheila Graham. "I'll bet when your baby is born, you'll want everybody you meet to admire him or her."

"I guess I will," Sheila nodded.

"Well, I think the psalmist loved God so much that he just couldn't help saying, 'Look, isn't God wonderful! Come on, let's all just tell him so!'"

Maurice nodded, "Why, you got that right! Man wants others to admire what he takes stock in."

"What else did you find out about praise in the Bible?" Sixkiller asked the singer.

"Found out that the Book of Revelation is 'bout the best song book I know about," Maurice grinned. "Jest one song after another—and all of 'em about the Lord God. Mercy! They's sure good songs!" He shook his head in wonder, adding, "You take that one in chapter four, where John gets that vision of the seven Spirits of God, and the four and twenty elders. Them elders take one good look at God, and they fall down and they sing him a song—" He strummed the guitar, lifted his voice, and sang:

Thou art worthy, O Lord,
To receive glory and honour and power:
For thou hast created all things,
And for thy pleasure they are and were created.

He sang the words several times to a simple melody, then

said, "Now, you all sing it with me." They all began to sing, and Maurice played it over until they knew it.

Finally he said, "You see? That's the kind of song that's *all* praise and worship! Puts our minds and hearts on God, 'stead of on us."

Anna's eyes were damp with tears as she said, "Perhaps it's because we do take our eyes off ourselves that makes it so moving."

"That's it, Miss Anna," Maurice nodded. "And it goes on and on like that. And the next chapter is just *packed* with songs—like this one—"

> Worthy is the Lamb that was slain
> To receive power, and riches, and wisdom,
> And strength, and honour, and glory, and blessing.

Again he played the chorus until everyone could sing along. For the next half hour he played simple melodies, all set to words from the Bible. It was, for Dani, a moving experience, and she saw that Luke felt the power of the moment as well.

Finally, Maurice stopped, and the group became silent. Anna began to pray, and they all bowed their heads. She prayed for each member of the group by name, mentioning specific needs. Then she closed with a brief request for God to bless the new members of their group. "They have their troubles and their heartaches, O Father," she prayed quietly, "but they have the presence of your Holy Comforter, the Holy Spirit. May Jesus Christ continue to be formed in them until they are totally and completely devoted to him. . . ."

Dani felt the power of the frail woman's prayer in her own heart, and when it was over, she looked up with gratitude in her eyes. Anna caught her look, but said only, "We usually have a time of sharing so that we'll know how to pray for one another. Who'll be first?"

For the next thirty minutes, the members of the group shared their problems. This was something new for Luke Sixkiller, who had been brought up to keep his troubles to himself. But as the meeting went on, he saw that what was happening was basically good—with a few exceptions. Sixkiller had spent years as a policeman grilling suspects, interviewing witnesses, and learning how to tell the gold from the base metal, and without meaning to, he applied those same tools to the members of the group.

Within two minutes, for instance, Sixkiller knew that Rose LaVie was acting. She talked the language of the Christians around her, but her eyes gave her away. *Watch the eyes* Sixkiller always instructed a new recruit in his department. *They can lie with their voices, but not one in a thousand can keep the truth out of their eyes.* And Rose LaVie's eyes were hard as arrowheads! She was attractive in a rather sensual way, a Cajun with the fire of her people glimmering in her eyes. She told the group she was having a hard time with her boss, who was "putting the moves" on her. Sixkiller glanced at Dani, who gave one slight shake of her head, indicating she believed not one word the girl was saying. Sixkiller lowered one eye a fraction, as if to say to her, *If anyone's putting the moves on, it's this little doll right here!*

But if he had no confidence in Rose, Sixkiller knew instantly that Helen Baker was real—pitiful, but honest. She asked for prayer in a general way, but as Anna gently drew her out, Sixkiller got the picture. Twice divorced, both times to losers who used her and cast her aside. Starving for affection—and her biological clock was running.

Sixkiller would have written it down as *a good woman with no luck in picking men. Passing thirty and is afraid she's missing it all. Wants nothing but a good man, maybe a child. Security. And she's scared to death she's going to miss it all.* Sixkiller glanced at Dani. He noted she was watching Helen with compassion and knew she felt the same as he did about the woman.

Jerry and Sheila Graham obviously had money problems. Their clothes were shabby, and Sheila's tiny ring gave only a feeble sparkle. But they held hands tenderly and asked prayer for only one thing: a healthy baby. Anna laid her twisted hands on their heads, offering a simple but eloquent blessing on them. As she moved back to take her seat, Sixkiller felt his eyes grow misty. Then he glared at Dani, who was watching him with a covert smile.

Pete Carpenter jumped in at once. "Well, I hate to bring this up again, but I can't help it." He had a stubborn, angry look on his face and his eyes were defiant. "I know what you keep saying about forgiving people, Anna, but you just don't understand what I gotta put up with!" He went on to relate how his brother-in-law had stolen his business, ending by saying, "—so I worked like a dog for that business for eight years. I hired Frank when he was on unemployment—and he undermined me! I trust the crumb—and he steals my business! Now, how can I forget a thing like that, Anna?"

Anna gave Pete a moment's scrutiny. "You probably won't forget it, Pete. I never said you would. But you can forgive. You can stop hating."

"But—it ain't *human*, Anna! When somebody hurts you, it's *natural* to hate them."

"You're exactly right," Anna shot back at him, her head nodding firmly. "It's *human* and it's *natural* to be bitter when someone hurts us. And that's what the people of this world do. But you're a Christian, Pete, and we Christians are marching to the sound of a different drummer." Her wise old eyes grew warm, and she said, "We're asked to follow Jesus, and almost the last act of his earthly life was to forgive those who were crucifying him."

Pete shot back, "Oh, sure, *Jesus* could do that—he was God!"

"He was a man, Pete," Anna rebuked gently. "He laid aside his deity when he came to earth. Everything he did, according to his own words, was done by the Father. He said, 'The words that I speak unto you I speak not of myself: but the Father that dwelleth in me, he doeth the works.' And you remember last week we talked about another thing Jesus said along this line. He said, 'He that believeth on me, the works that I do shall he do also; and greater works than these shall he do.'"

"Well, I don't see that!" Rose piped up. "How can we do greater things than Jesus Christ? It makes no sense!"

Anna gave the girl a compassionate look. "Rose, just read the New Testament. Jesus said over and over again, in many ways, that he would come to live in every believer. And he said that he would send the Holy Spirit, and that through the Holy Spirit all sorts of things that would be impossible for a human being would become possible."

Pete Carpenter said glumly, "Well, I guess I don't have the Holy Spirit, then, because I can't forgive this clown!"

"Yes, you have the Holy Spirit," Anna reproved him quickly. "Every one who is saved is indwelled by the Holy Spirit at that moment. But the Bible says it's possible to grieve the Spirit and to quench the Spirit—and that's what you've done, Pete."

Carpenter gave Anna a wounded look. "Well, if *you'd* been took by someone like I been took by this guy—stole everything I had—!"

Anna Deveraux didn't answer for a moment, and Sixkiller saw that she was pondering something. For one moment she closed her eyes, and then she opened them. "I want to tell you something," she said, her voice quite low, "something I have kept in my own heart for years. I promised God I would not speak of it again, and I have not—but now it seems the Holy Spirit is prompting me to share it with you." She hesitated again, then squared her thin shoulders together. "When I was a young girl, I wanted only one thing—to have a home of my own, with a good husband and children—"

She spoke slowly, and Sixkiller could see she found it painful to open up her past to this group. He listened carefully as she told how she had come from an affluent family, and had not married until she was nearly thirty years old. "I thought I was going to be an old maid," Anna said, a ghost of a smile on her face, "and to me that was worse than death! But then—I met a man. We fell in love, and after a short courtship I married him. He didn't want children right away, so I agreed to wait for five years. At the end of that time, we had a beautiful baby, a boy, and I named him David."

She hesitated, and they all were aware that she was struggling with the pain of the past. Finally she took a deep breath. "When David was five years old, my husband came in one day and told me that he wanted a divorce. He'd fallen in love with a very young woman and wanted to marry her. I said no, that I'd never do it. I tried to make him stay with me for David's sake, but he refused." Again she paused, and this time for so long that Sheila Graham whispered, "What happened, Anna?"

Anna looked at her, saying, "He divorced me. I'd inherited a great deal of money from my parents, and I'd trusted my husband to handle it. I soon found out that he'd put it all in his own name. When the trial took place, I was proven to be an unfit mother. He'd hired detectives, and they'd done things to make it look as if I were unfit. I never understood how they did that."

Sixkiller's eyes sought those of Dani's and they both thought the same thing: *Poor Anna! She didn't have a chance against him!*

Anna held her back as straight as her illness would permit and finished the story quickly. "I was left with nothing but this house and was not allowed to see David—not for a long time. And do you know what I did with my time for all those years, Pete?"

Carpenter shook his head. "No, Anna. What did you do?"

"I hated my husband," she said evenly. "I lay awake thinking of ways to get even with him. It became my whole life."

A silence fell over the group, no one knowing what to say. Anna finally said, "It almost killed me, Pete. I nearly lost my sanity, and some doctors have said that my physical infirmities are partly a result of the terrible bitterness I had for the man who ruined me."

And then she suddenly laughed, so unexpectedly and so freely that both Dani and Sixkiller opened their eyes in shock. "But then I found Jesus, and since then I've been happy. He taught me how to forgive, how to let go of the past." She went into some brief detail of how she had come to Christ through the help of a neighbor. Then Anna said, "Now, Pete, listen to me carefully. Do you know the difference between a scar and a wound?"

"A scar and a wound?" Carpenter echoed. "Why, I guess I don't, Anna."

"A wound," Anna said, "is not healed. You see this scar?" Holding out her arm, she pointed to an old scar on her forearm. "This was a very bad wound," she said. "It was very painful when it happened and for a long time afterward. But now it's not painful at all." She tapped at it with her hand, smiling. "See? It's all healed. I can *remember* how much it hurt—but there's no pain now. And it's like that with my husband. I *remember* what he did to hurt me, but it no longer gives me pain."

"Do you ever see him?" Dani inquired.

"He died ten years ago," Anna said. "I was there, and he asked me to forgive him. I was so glad to be able to tell him I'd done that years ago!"

"And David?" Dani asked.

"He's been a missionary in Peru for twenty-five years," Anna said proudly.

A glimmer of understanding came into Pete Carpenter's blue eyes. "I think I see what you're saying, Anna," he said slowly. His face grew sober. "The doctor told me I'm getting an ulcer. He said it could be from too much agitation." Again he paused, then asked, "You think I can do that, Anna, what you did? So that someday what Frank done to me will be just a memory?"

"Yes!"

Rose said, "I don't see it. How can you forgive somebody you hate?"

Anna took her Bible and began tracing verses that deal with forgiveness. Her crippled fingers moved slowly, but her voice was strong, and Dani marveled at her knowledge of Scripture.

Finally Anna closed her Bible and said, "I want to pray for a miracle for you, Pete. Will you let Jesus do a miraculous thing in you tonight?"

Carpenter looked uncomfortable. "Well—" he hesitated, "I don't think I can do it—forgive the guy, I mean."

"Are you willing to let Jesus come into this area of your life? It's too big for you, but not for him."

A silence fell across the room, and for a moment both Dani

and Luke thought Carpenter was going to get up and run out of the room. There was a haunted expression on his face, and his lips were a mere line. But he finally nodded, "I'll—I'll do it, if you'll show me how," he whispered.

Anna once again got up and went to stand before Carpenter, putting her gnarled hands on his head. She began to pray, and Dani had never felt such an intense pressure. The room seemed to be contracting! Dani began to pray for Pete, and never had she had such a struggle in prayer. Something almost palpable seemed to hover in the room, bringing a sense of darkness and fear. Dani felt it, and then she heard Anna cry out, "You spirits of bitterness and unforgiveness! In the name of Jesus Christ, I command you to leave this man!"

Almost instantly Dani felt a sense of relief, and when she finally looked up, she saw that Pete Carpenter had somehow been changed. Tears were running down his cheeks, but he was smiling tremulously. His lips were moving, and she could tell he was whispering, "Thank you, Jesus!" over and over again.

One more thing happened. Anna came to stand before Dani and, without hesitation, put her hands out. Dani felt them touch her head and blinked with surprise. Then Anna leaned forward and started to speak. She whispered in Dani's ear, "My daughter, you will soon need the grace of God in your life. The hour will come when you will find yourself surrounded by darkness, bound by powers stronger than you dream of now. When that hour comes, if you are to stand the test, you will have to lay yourself open to God in a surrender such as you have never known. God will be there, but he will wait for you to reach out to him. See that you open your lips and your heart to him!"

Anna stepped back, and Dani just sat there, her heart beating rapidly. She realized she was frightened—very frightened, indeed.

She got to her feet, stammering as she spoke to the members of the group, and finally found herself outside. It was a relief, but she found she was still shaky over Anna's final prayer.

"Pretty heavy stuff," Sixkiller said as they pulled away.

"Yes."

He noted her brief reply, then drove her home. When they got to the driveway, he said, "Look, there's Ben."

Dani looked up to see Savage standing on the front porch. "That's odd," she said, and when the car stopped she got out at once and hurried toward the porch. "What are you doing here this time of the night, Ben?"

Savage's voice did not sound quite natural. "A little trouble, Dani. Come inside."

Dani felt faint for a moment. "Is it Dad?"

"No. Go on inside."

Dani ran inside, and Sixkiller came to stand beside Savage. "What's the score, Ben?"

Savage looked at him with eyes that glinted with anger. "It's Allison," he said, biting the words off. "She was picked up by a couple of goons after school."

"Was she hurt?" Sixkiller demanded.

Savage shook his head. "No, not physically, but they frightened her out of her wits. Had to have the doctor come out and give her a shot."

"Who was it?"

Savage rubbed his hands together. "She didn't know them—but it has to be some of Tommy Cain's work."

Sixkiller asked grimly, "Any hard proof?"

"Dan got a card today. A sympathy card again. This one said something about how fragile some things are, and how we ought to treasure them—because we may not have them long."

The two men stood staring at each other. Then Ben said quietly, "Come on in, Luke. They're going to need all the help they can get."

They went into the house, and the door closed gently behind them, shutting them inside with the fear and anguish that had come to invade the home.

6

A Visit from an Old Friend

Once while staying with a friend in the Tennessee mountains, Dani had helped burn off a strip of heavy brush surrounding the house. In case of a forest fire, her friend explained, the cleared strip would serve as a buffer to protect the house.

The two of them were very careful at first, watching like a pair of hawks to see that their fires didn't get out of hand. But later that afternoon they grew overconfident. When the fires they lit kept going out in an area of sparse grass, they took a break and went inside for a drink of water, then lingered a few minutes to answer the phone. When they walked outside, Dani's heart lurched to see flames spreading over a forty-foot area and racing for the trees. The woods were tinder dry, and both young women knew that a runaway fire would destroy thousands of acres of timber, not to mention homes and even lives. Desperately they grabbed up blankets, soaked them in water, then ran to beat out the flames.

They eventually put out the fire, but it was a close call. The smoke gagged Dani; the flames singed her eyelashes and hair and burned her hands. But the worst part was the fear, which threatened her just as violently as yellow-and-red flames that fed hungrily on the dry grass and brambles. She had never known a fear like that, and it nauseated her.

Now, as Dani paced the floor of the den in her parents' house, she felt some of the same symptoms. Anger—raw and potent—roared through her body, as fierce and as difficult to control as those flames in the woods. As she paced the floor, she would gain a momentary victory over her blind anger, only to have it reignite as her father went over some of the details of Allison's ordeal.

She plopped down on her father's cordovan leather recliner and clasped her hands together to control the trembling, forcing herself to listen as clinically as she could as Dan Ross continued, " . . . never saw either one of them before, she said. But she described them in detail, so we should be able to get some kind of make on them." His face was pale, the strain drawing his patrician features tight. "I think we'd better take her down and let the police artist do a sketch from her descriptions—and she can look at the mug shots, too."

"Tomorrow, Dan," Ellen said quickly, her own face tense with worry for both her daughter and her husband. His heart attack had brought them both to a constant awareness of mortality, and Ellen had worked hard to take as much pressure off Dan as possible. "She needs a little time—and you do, too."

"I'm all right!" Dan snapped. Then he went to her and put his arm around her, saying, "Sorry, Sweetheart. I'm a little edgy."

"I'll take her down in the morning, Dad," Dani spoke up.

"I'll go along," Ben said. He had been looking out the window, staring into the darkness, and when he turned, Dani was shocked at the hardness of his eyes. He looked dangerous, though he stood idly beside the brass lamp that cast its gleams over his face. His mouth was a thin line as he added, "Someone will have to watch her until we get these guys."

A silence fell across the room, thin and tense; then Ellen said, "You think they'll try again? I was hoping it was just—"

Dan tightened his grip on her shoulders. "Maybe it was, but we can't count on it."

Ellen looked up at him with fear in her eyes. "You think it was Tommy Cain, don't you?"

"Has to be."

Ben nodded. "I think so, too. And it was just a warning. It could get worse." He reached up and ran his finger along an old scar over his right eyebrow, a habit he had when he was angry. "Maybe," he said softly, "I'd better go by and have a little talk with Tommy Cain."

"No, Ben," Dan said at once. "He'd like that. I know you'd like to go put an arm on him, shake him up. But Cain's smart. That would make it look like we're the ones in the wrong. And you can bet there'll be nothing to tie Cain to the two who abducted Allison!"

Ben stared at Dan, then nodded slowly. "You're right. But I'm still going to do a little looking for those two."

"Better let Luke do it," Dani said, weighing her words as she glanced at Luke. Then she added quickly, "He's got a whole department to work on it, Ben. And we don't need you in jail for aggravated assault. It's like you said, somebody's got to watch Allison."

Her words seemed to mollify Ben, and he shrugged. "Okay, but who's going to watch you—and Ellen and Rob?"

His words brought a blink from Dan Ross, and he nodded.

"That's right. I hadn't even had time to think of that. But Cain will hit at anyone close to me."

"Do you think we ought to pull Allison out of school?" Ellen asked.

"No. We can't live in a cave for the rest of our lives," her husband answered. "But we've got to be careful for a while. Ellen, when you go out, I want someone with you—either Ben or me or someone from the agency. And you've got to be covered, too, Dani."

Dani stood, and her voice was brittle as she said, "I wish that pair *would* come at me, Dad. They wouldn't find me as easy as Allison."

Ben and Dan Ross exchanged a quick glance, and Dan said gently, "Dani, these guys are pretty tough, I'd guess. You can't take on two hoods with a karate chop."

Dani gave her father a level look. "Are they tougher than a .38 slug?" she asked.

"Nobody's that tough, Dani," Ben said when Dan hesitated. "But you're not—" He broke off, remembering their recent argument and unwilling to start another one.

"Don't worry," Dani said in a clipped, unfamiliar tone. "I'll wear it from now on—and I'll use it, too!"

There was an edge to her tone, and her large eyes held a hardness none of the others had seen before. Dan moved toward her, stopping to say, "Dani, we've got to keep cool. I don't think this is going to be a quick thing. Cain wants to get even, and he's found the best way—to get at me through the people I love. But I can't stress enough how clever the man is! My guess is that the two guys who jumped Allison were brought in from out of town and that they're already on their way. Cain knows exactly what we'll be doing, and he'd be stupid to leave anything to tie himself to the pair."

"All the same, we'll take our best shot," Ben said. "It's not that big a world. If we can get anything, I'll run those punks down. That'll shake Cain up, even if we can't tie them to him."

"All right," Dan agreed. "Dani, you take Allison in to see Luke tomorrow. Ellen, you stay home."

"What about Rob?" Dani asked.

"I'll talk to him," Dan nodded. "He'll have to be careful, especially around strangers—" He paused, thinking of his worries about Rob, but said only, "I'll talk to him." He looked at the others, saying softly, "It's going to be a bad time, I'm thinking. But God is with us. It's times like these when we have to live up to the words we've been saying." A slight smile touched his lips, and he nodded, "It's easy to memorize Scripture. But to lean on it when everything seems to be falling down—that's what it really means to have faith!"

"Now, Allison," Luke Sixkiller said gently, "if you'll just describe the two men who did this to you, Charlie here will draw a picture of them."

Allison had dressed up to come to NOPD headquarters with Dani. She wore a cropped cutaway jacket in white and pink check, a white blouse with pink trim at the neck, and a pair of gray pleated trousers. Her dark blue eyes were still apprehensive, despite all attempts to reassure her, and she looked quickly at Dani, who nodded. "You've always had a good memory, Allison. And we need these sketches so that we can be sure these men won't come back to bother you again—or Mother, either, for that matter."

Her words seemed to calm Allison, and she nodded. "Well, one of them was very big—like a wrestler, you know? And his face was all—sort of puffed up, like fighters and wrestlers get. He had a squashed nose, and his ears were all swollen."

"Sounds like an ex-pug," Charlie Devoe, the police artist,

nodded. He was a small man with long, tapering fingers and quick black eyes. "Now, was his face square, round, or oval?"

"It was square," Allison nodded. "He had black hair, cut real short. His eyes were dark, I think. And they were all scarred around the edges, so that he seemed to be squinting. He had a wide mouth with a scar on the right side that drew it up—and there was a tattoo on his right hand, a woman without any clothes on, and the name *Velma* under it."

As Allison spoke, Devoe's pencil flew over the pad in front of him, and the girl was startled at how her words were turned into a sketch as she spoke. Curiosity overcame her fear, and she began correcting the drawing, saying things like, "No, his nose was wider than that—and it was pushed over to one side, the left side—no, it was the right."

Twenty minutes later, Devoe asked, "Anything else, Allison?"

"No, sir," Allison said. "That's what he looked like." The artist saw a trace of fear come to her from just looking at the sketch and exchanged a quick glance with Sixkiller. "Well, let's work on the other fellow," he said quickly. "You've got a sharp eye, young lady. You ought to become an artist yourself! Now, what about the second man?"

Twenty minutes later, Sixkiller was holding the two sketches in his hands. He had a thoughtful expression on his face, and finally he glanced up at Dani and Allison, saying, "I think I know one of these."

Dani was startled. "We thought they'd be from out of town, Luke."

"Yeah, so did I. But this big one is a dead ringer for Moon Mazurki." He stared at the picture, then shook his head. "There *can't* be two punks as ugly as this." He gave Allison a smile and put his hand on her shoulder lightly. "Honey, let's have you look at a picture, okay?"

Allison felt secure with the big policeman's hand warming her shoulder. "Sure, Luke," she agreed at once.

Luke led them out of Devoe's office and down a long hall to an elevator. When they got on, he punched the button, saying, "We'll go to the mug room. Got over a hundred thousand pictures in there, which is pretty discouraging. You could spend weeks plowing through all those shots. But this time we're just going to look at one, so it'll be fast."

When they got off the elevator, he led them to a huge room packed with filing cases. A tall, thin, white-haired man came to meet them. "Hello, Lieutenant," he nodded. "Can I help you?"

"These are the Ross sisters, Leo—Dani and Allison. And this is Leo Hart, ladies," Luke nodded. "He's got a picture of every crook who ever drew breath. Bring us what you have on Moon Mazurki, will you, Leo?"

"Glad to meet you," Hart smiled. "Just have a seat over at one of those booths, and I'll have your order ready."

The three of them sat down. "If this works," Luke said, "I'll probably go into cardiac arrest." He winked at Allison slyly, then added, "If I fall out, Dani, you may have to administer mouth-to-mouth resuscitation." When he got a sour glance from Dani, he shrugged his broad shoulders. "Well, it was worth a try. Anyway, it probably won't be Moon. Nothing's ever that easy in this job." He lolled back in his chair, saying, "I wish being a policeman was as exciting in real life as it is on TV."

"It seems exciting to me," Allison said.

"I get bored to tears," Luke murmured. "On TV, the detective gets a clue, and ten minutes later he's got the suspect in jail. It doesn't work like that. We have to pound the pavement, interview half the population of New Orleans—and most of them don't like cops. Then, when we finally get somebody as a suspect, we have to do the same thing over again just to *find*

85

him. When we do finally nail him, he usually gets out on bail. And finally, about two or three months later, we actually get him in front of a judge—and pretty often the judge turns him loose because we didn't read him his rights or some other technicality."

"But it's more exciting than selling shoes, isn't it?" Dani argued. "If it wasn't, you'd quit."

"Yes, and it is dangerous, isn't it, Luke?" queried Allison.

Sixkiller grinned at them. "Not as dangerous as some other jobs," he said.

"Name one," Dani insisted.

"Cutting logs in the woods." Sixkiller nodded. "Now *there's* a dangerous job! You wouldn't catch me doing a thing like that! Man could get killed or maimed anytime."

"Oh, that's just silly!" Allison exclaimed.

"Fact." Sixkiller straightened up as Hart appeared around the corner of one of the long files and started toward where they sat. "Most dangerous job in the world. Got something for us, Leo?"

"Sure. This the man you're looking for?" Hart passed a picture to Sixkiller, who glanced at it and nodded, then handed it to Allison.

Allison took one glance and nodded vigorously. "That's him!"

"You're positive?" Sixkiller insisted.

"It's him, Luke," she insisted. Looking up, she shivered slightly. "Do you think I'll ever forget him?"

Luke took the picture, saying, "In time you will, honey." He gave the picture back to Hart, saying, "Thanks, Leo."

"Come back any time, Lieutenant—we never close."

"Was she absolutely positive?"

Dani nodded. "No doubt at all. Took one glance at the mug shot and turned pale. No doubt about the identification."

Ben Savage had been sitting in Dan Ross's small office when Dani came in with the news. The two men had grown close in the short time that Savage had been working for Ross Investigations. They were very different in many ways, but each recognized in the other a solid core of rock-hard integrity.

Just before Dani entered, Ross had admitted, "This thing has got me down, Ben. If it was just me that Cain had threatened, that would be one thing. But to threaten my family—!"

Savage looked up at Ross with concern, noting the stretched-out look in the older man's face, and forced himself to speak calmly. "Oh, it won't come to anything, Dan. Cain will keep on sending you those cards and maybe push at Rob a little. But he's been in Angola and he's smart. He won't risk going back."

"I don't know, Ben!"

"Aw, Dan, you know what Angola's like. For guys like Cain, it's death. Luke will put the screws on him, and he'll be a good boy."

At that moment Dani came in with her news. Both men got up, and she shut the door carefully. When she told them about the identification, Ross said, "I'm surprised at that." His thin face took on a perplexed look, and he murmured, "Do you suppose it's just a crazy coincidence? Like maybe those two just saw Allison and hassled her for no good reason—since their kind's never happy except when they're hurting people?"

Dani shook her head. "I wish! But you don't really believe that. We'll just have to assume it's Cain until Luke talks to this Mazurki."

The sound of the buzzer on Dan Ross's desk startled them all. Dan flipped the switch and Angie Park's voice said, "Someone to see you, Mr. Ross."

"Who is it?"

"He told me to tell you it was just an old friend come by for a visit."

"All right, Angie." Ross looked sharply at Dani and Ben. "I want tight security on Allison and Ellen."

"Of course, Dad," Dani nodded. She was touched by the look of helplessness on his face and went to kiss him. "We'll weather this."

"Sure," Ross summoned a smile. "I'm a pretty tough old bird. Wouldn't have made it this far if I wasn't."

He turned to the door, opened it, and stepped back to let the other two leave. When he stepped into the outer office behind them, his view of the man who was waiting in front of Angie's desk was blocked momentarily. But the instant they moved away, he felt a stab of bitter anger run through him.

"What do you want here, Cain?" he snapped, his voice brittle.

Both Ben and Dani halted abruptly and swung their gaze on the man Ross addressed. Even Angie faltered and looked up with alarm.

"Why, I just dropped by to say hello, Dan!"

The speaker was a man just under six feet, well-built, with a healthy-looking tan. His pale blue eyes didn't reflect the smile on his thin lips. He was rather handsome, with even features, but his thin mouth had a cruel curve. His gray suit was obviously expensive and his Italian tie was hand painted.

He looked, Dani thought, like a successful businessman—which, in a macabre way, he was. Except that instead of dealing with stocks and bonds, Tommy Cain merchandised drugs and human bodies. He was one of those who grew rich by trading on human weaknesses—no different, actually, than the young men Dani had met down at the Project.

Cain, of course, hired the rough stuff done. Dani had studied his record after her father confessed his fears and had discovered that few criminals were as successful as Cain. He had grown up in an affluent family, had completed college with an exceptional academic record, and had gone halfway through law school. Then he had left school to become the lieutenant of Dom Lanza, the kingpin of crime in New Orleans. No one had understood why Lanza took Cain in, since the Mafia is for the most part a family affair. Some speculated that Lanza saw Cain as a possible competitor and thought it prudent to use him rather than fight him. But no one really knew.

What everyone did know was that Lanza's scheme had failed. After a few years of learning the trade of organized crime, Tommy Cain had left the Lanza organization and set up shop on his own. Why Lanza didn't eliminate the younger man was also a mystery, but Luke had told Dani, "Cain was too smart to fight, I think. Dom Lanza was never afraid to butt up against muscle, but he knew that Cain was smart enough to hurt him."

Now, looking at Cain, Dani saw what Luke had meant. There was an air of brilliance about the man, observable just by examining him. Brilliance and power. And something sinister as well, even though he was smiling at her father.

"Guess you heard I was out, Dan," Cain said. "So I thought I'd just stop by and say hello."

Dan Ross's lips grew tight and his eyes narrowed. "Cain, I'm glad you dropped by. I was going to have to look you up if you hadn't."

Cain's smile broadened. "Sure! We go back a long time, don't we, Danny? Sure, we've butted heads a few times, but what the hey? I've always admired you, Danny Boy! Always told my boys, 'You keep your eyes on Danny Boy Ross—he's a smart one! Not like some of those other cops!'"

Dani said suddenly, "I'm Dani Ross. And I was planning to look you up, too, Cain."

Cain's eyes touched her, and despite her resolves a breath of fear brushed Dani. But Cain only nodded. "Heard a lot about you, Miss Ross. A chip off the old block." He turned to Dan Ross, adding, "Know you must be proud of this one, Danny Boy! Better take good care of her." There was no threat in the words, but somehow Cain managed to make his statement sound like one. Then he added quickly, "Some guy's going to run off with her pretty soon!"

"Cain, I'll only say this once," Dan Ross said evenly. "Leave me alone—and leave my family alone."

A hurt look came into Cain's face, and he protested, "Why, Danny Boy, that's no way to talk! I told you, I *admire* you!" A subtle change crossed his features then, and he added, "I thought about you a lot up there in Angola. I really did."

Again, the implied threat. Answering it instead of the words Ross said, "Get out of here, Cain, and remember this. If anything happens to my family, there's no hole deep enough for you to hide in! Now, get out!"

Tommy Cain shrugged, saying, "Wish you were a little more friendly, Danny Boy. We're bound to run into each other, you know, and it's better to be on good terms, I always say."

He turned to go, but Ben Savage stepped forward and blocked his way. "My name is Ben Savage, Cain."

He said no more, simply stood there with his eyes fixed on Cain. He made no threat, but Tommy Cain's back straightened suddenly. He had been living in one of the most violent prisons in America—a place where murderers were common as flies at a picnic—and he had survived. Before that, he had been involved with Mafia hit men and every other type of criminal in New Orleans. He was no coward, this Tommy Cain, but he had a well-developed instinct, and something about Savage put him on alert. He studied the detective's squarish face, taking in the wide slash of a mouth, the short nose that had been broken, and most of all the deep-set hazel eyes. Cain's own eyes narrowed, and he said carefully, "I'll remember you, Savage."

"Good idea," Ben nodded. "I'll be seeing you around." He added with a bleak smile, "Mr. Ross may not be friendly, but you and I, we could get real close, Tommy."

The words were softly spoken, but Cain was clearly aware of the message behind them. He nodded briefly, then turned to go. When he reached the door, he snapped his fingers as though remembering something, then turned to say, "I almost forgot! Danny Boy, did you read the paper today? No? Take a look at page three. Something there you might find interesting."

He closed the door, and Ross snapped, "Angie—get me the newspaper!"

"Right here, Mr. Ross!"

Dan Ross took the paper and turned to the inside section; Dani saw his eyes grow bleak. "What is it, Dad?"

"Judge Horstman—he's dead," Ross answered. His eyes ran down the lines, and he looked up finally, saying, "He was the judge who sentenced Cain." He hesitated, then added, "Cain swore he'd kill Horstman."

"How did he die?" Savage asked.

"The paper says he accidentally drowned. He'd retired to Gulf Shores, on the Gulf in Alabama."

Dani studied her father. "You don't think it was an accident, do you, Dad?"

"No. Didn't you see how Cain enjoyed telling us about it?" He said abruptly, "I'm going home," and left the office at once.

Dani bit her lip as she reached over and took the paper. After scanning the story, she shook her head slowly. "I'll run down to Gulf Shores and see what I can find out."

Savage gave her a careful look. "Take that .38 with you," he advised.

Dani nodded. "I'll be wearing it from now on, Ben. You watch out for everything here."

"Sure, Boss." He hesitated, then said, "Look, don't try to be one of those TV lady detectives, all right? If you get a smell of anything that doesn't look right, give me a call."

"Don't worry about me."

Savage's head jerked back, and he said roughly, "I have to. You sign my paychecks!" He left the office, the two women staring after him.

"Tough sort of fellow, Ben," Angie observed.

"He'd better be, Angie," Dani nodded. "That's what it's going to take from here on out!"

7

Death
Out of Season

The sun was already a quarter of the way up the sky when Dani left New Orleans, headed for the Alabama Gulf Coast. She took Interstate 12, passed by Slidell and picked up I-10 just west of the Mississippi state line. Driving steadily at five miles over the limit, she touched on the edge of Gulfport and Biloxi, then passed into Alabama. Turning north, she hit Mobile, then turned south off the interstate and skirted the eastern shore of Mobile Bay, scarcely noticing the small towns that were linked together on State Highway 98. The clock on her dash read 11:57 as she sighted the sign that read "Gulf Shores."

Gulf Shores, she noted, looked more or less like all the other small towns that nestled on the beach from Gulfport, Mississippi, all the way around the Florida peninsula and up to South Carolina. Everything centered around the narrow ribbon of white sugar sand, no more than ten or twenty feet wide at the most, and the span of blue-green waters. High-rise condominiums, the beaches, and the water; bars, fish houses, liquor stores, and souvenir shops—all along a highway that shapes itself around the shoreline, and is pinched in by intercoastal waterways, bays, and rivers. All as flat as a football field.

As Dani drove down Highway 182 looking for a place to stay, she felt the faint impression of sin, just a wisp of brimstone—for people come to the beach in large numbers for iniquity. It is Away from Home, and high-school seniors fill the beach-houses, the motels, the condominiums to capacity at the last of their senior year, all determined to experiment with every form of depravity they have not yet tasted.

The highway was blocked off, thronged with hundreds of people, so Dani took a detour. As she moved along at the pace of a slug, she saw several signs that read "Sea Oats Festival" and noted rows of souvenir booths lining the highway. Most of the people she passed who were headed toward the festival on foot wore swimsuits, and it suddenly occurred to her that there was some sort of inverse ratio to the size of the woman to the skimpiness of the bathing suit.

She tried four motels with no success, then found good fortune at the Alabama State Lodge, which had a cancellation as she was waiting to ask for a room. The rate was a hundred dollars a day, but she was relieved, and when she entered her room she knew she would have paid twice as much! It was a large room with two double beds, a large bath, and a gorgeous view of the Gulf through a large sliding door.

She found a card in her purse, picked up the phone, and dialed a number. A woman's voice answered, "Yes?" and Dani ventured, "Mrs. Horstman?"

"Speaking." The voice was wary, ready to close the conversation, and Dani knew she had to say just the right thing.

"I'm sorry to call at such a time, Mrs. Horstman, but I have an emergency." Dani waited for a response, then getting none said, "My father is Dan Ross. He's a private investigator in New Orleans. He knew your husband—and he's in some trouble that you might be able to help me with."

"I don't know about my husband's dealings."

Dani knew the woman was about to hang up—and she added quickly, "Mrs. Horstman—please let me say one thing. I—I don't want you to be hurt, and I wish I could say this some other way. Some of us think that your husband's death—may not have been an accident."

Dani held her breath, fearing that the next sound would be the crash of the receiver. But after what seemed like a very long silence, Mrs. Horstman said in a hoarse whisper, "You can come to my house. It's on Bon Secour Bay—" She gave careful directions, then added, "Come about nine o'clock—and don't tell anybody, you promise?"

"I promise, Mrs. Horstman," Dani said quickly, her heart beating faster. "I'll come alone at nine. Good-by."

As she put the phone back in its cradle, Dani experienced a strange intuition. *She knows something!*—the thought flashed into her mind. And as certainly as she knew her own birthday, Dani knew that Mrs. Horstman understood more about her husband's death than had been spelled out in the newspaper story.

She wanted to rush out to the house, to begin at once, but the afternoon still stretched out in front of her. So she deliberately put the appointment out of her mind, setting it aside as firmly as she would set a bowl of fruit in a refrigerator and shut the door on it. She had that kind of mind—logical and methodical. It had served her well when she was an accountant, and now it let her approach the afternoon with a determination to spend it peacefully. She had learned that when problems pressed in, the wise thing to do was to deliberately think of something else—anything else! Then, when she picked the problem up again, it was usually with some sort of fresh energy and a fresh insight.

She opened her bag and pulled out a black, one-piece swimsuit. Slipping into it, she stuffed a bag with sunscreen, a book, and a beach towel. Then she left the room, making her way to where the white sand meets the blue-green waters of the Gulf. The beach was no longer crowded, and she put her towel down in the hot sand. She carefully applied sunscreen and, lying down, slipped on her sunglasses. For the next half-hour Dani let the warmth soak into her. She grew sleepy, and when problems tried to edge into her mind, she firmly slammed the door on them, concentrating by an act of will on the world around her—the rhythmic crashing of the surf a few feet away, the harsh voices of the seagulls, the sand beneath her, firm but yielding when she shoved her hips or shoulders into it.

She dropped off quickly, slipping into a restful sleep, and woke with a start some time later. Opening her eyes and sitting up, she looked out over the sea, noting that the sun was lower and the air somewhat cooler.

She rose, took off her glasses, and ran toward the surf, hitting it at full speed. The white, frothy waves grabbed at her ankles; then she stepped into a trench cut by the water and fell sprawling. As she ducked under and the wave rolled over her, she was shaken by the cool water, but it was not really cold, and she came up shaking her head and snorting. Rising, she waded out into the deeper water until finally she reached the point where the waves came in so strongly they rolled her off her feet and flung her back toward the shore. Then, with a fell grip, the undertow put cold green arms around her, drawing her out into the depths. She fought against it, coming to the surface and swimming hard, catching the next wave.

Half an hour later she came wading in, exhausted by the violence of the exercise, and as she emerged from the water, gravity caught at her. In the ocean, she weighed less than 10 percent of her true weight, but when she left the water, mother earth pulled at her. She thought of the old pilgrim in Chaucer's tale, the one who was cursed by losing his right to die. *He wandered around trying to find his place under the earth,* Dani remembered as she struggled to the edge of the surf. *And he was always poking the earth with his staff, crying out "Loving Mother—let me in!" But he never found a way to get in.*

She wrapped the beach towel around her shoulders and sat down to watch the water. *We live—but earth is always pulling at us. We try to put it out of our minds, but we're appointed to die, and none of us knows the day or the hour.* A shiver ran over her in the August heat, and she drew the red-and-green towel closer, staring hard at the line where sea and sky met and putting the grim thoughts out of her head.

Suddenly something broke the smooth surface of the water, out beyond the waves, and she focused on the movement. *Dolphins!* she thought with delight. *Bottle-nosed dolphins!*

Six of them surfaced, all looking like Flipper on the TV show. They were too far away to tell much about their sizes. Father and Mother with young? Perhaps. Perhaps a group of youthful males out for their first adventure away from their folks—a troop of adolescents with flippers!

She watched with delight as the blunt noses broke the water, each followed by a swelling head—a forehead that Sherlock Holmes himself might have envied! Then the curving body, rising sleek as steel—but so flexible!

Dani watched as they passed out of sight, leaving the gray sea unseamed. She was moved by the sight, as always, sensing that she had been granted a glimpse into another world, an empire beneath the surface of the ocean. She felt privileged, and she thought hard about the marvels of the deep.

Finally, she rose and went to her room, ignoring a middle-aged man who hurried up to walk beside her, offering her the pleasure of his company. *"No hablo inglés,"* she said instantly, and left him floundering as she broke into a run. Nothing harder than running in sand, and she felt the muscles of her calves begin to pull as she reached the wooden walk that led to her room.

She spent an hour sluicing the salt from her body, washing her hair, drying it, taking pleasure in the simple acts. Then she slipped into a pair of jeans—baggy, bleached, and belted— and a cool cotton camp shirt with bright periwinkle and white stripes. Donning a pair of navy slip-ons with a tassel, she left the room in search of something to eat. The hostess of the hotel restaurant showed her to a small table beside the outer wall, glassed from top to bottom, and she ordered the catch of the day, which proved to be delicious amberjack. She had not eaten properly that day, and found the white, flaky fish so good that she had to restrain herself from snapping at it like a shark in a frenzy. The hush puppies were only average, but the baked potato was very good. *How can you mess up a potato?* she asked herself wryly before tackling an enormous bowl of peach cobbler. Finally she sat drinking coffee, watching the sun turn the green Gulf waters a fiery crimson. The blazing globe looked so hot that Dani would not have been surprised to see a sudden hiss of steam as it touched the cool waters of the Gulf.

Finally, she rose, paid her bill, and walked slowly along the beach. The air was cooling moment by moment, and she enjoyed the touch of the salty air on her face, which was slightly burned.

She sat down on a round pier and, a few minutes later, had a guest. A solemn blue heron came sailing across the sky, seeming to fly right out of one of Audubon's plates. He made a sweeping turn, then came to her, floating majestically on the air like a clipper ship in full sail, a heavenly argosy.

But if he was the picture of grace in the air, the moment he touched down, he was transmogrified into an awkward clown. As he approached, in slow motion, he reminded Dani of an old vaudeville comedian with an absurd face, dressed in a ragged suit.

Keeping one eye fixed on her, the heron lifted each leg deliberately, three claws pointed forward, one backward. Then he paused and studied Dani with a cold gray eye. She had noticed that raptors, eagles, and hawks have their eyes in front, so that they can focus on their prey. Those that they prey on, however, have their eyes on the sides of their heads, so that they can keep an eye on all directions. The blue heron, Dani noted, had a combination of these two styles. When he turned his head to stare at her straight on, she saw he could see directly ahead.

How thoughtful of God—to make this fellow so that he can see all around to avoid his enemies, yet also right in front so he can see to spear a fish with that long, sharp needle of a beak!

Dani smiled at her own propensity to force everything that came to her attention into her own, rather strict form of Calvinistic doctrine. She studied the ragged feathers and the long neck with its permanent bend. All was for a purpose, she decided—the spearlike beak for taking the fish; the long, spindly legs for wading into the mud and shallow water (confusing the fish, no doubt, into thinking they were some sort of reed!); and the great wings for slipping "the surly bonds of earth." As in all great works of art, all the parts of the blue heron contribute to the overall design—unlike man's creations, which often add frivolous details.

The heron stared at Dani for a long minute. Then, evidently having decided that no welfare was coming, he slowly lifted his wings and sailed away, leaving Dani alone. She watched him disappear into the hazy air.

The darkness had closed in on Bon Secour Bay when Dani pulled up to the beach house perched on top of ten-foot pilings. Her headlights picked up the name *Horstman* on a small sign attached to the siding, and she cut the engine and got out of the Cougar. A mercury light mounted on a high pole cast a greenish glow over the backyard, and as she mounted the steps, Dani could see a white V-bottom and a catamaran docked in the slip.

When she was only halfway to the top, the front door opened, and a voice came to her: "Miss Ross?"

"Yes." Dani reached the top of the stairs, paused and said, "Mrs. Horstman, I'm sorry to trouble you—but it's very important."

"Come inside."

Dani stepped inside, took in the large open space—a combined living room-kitchen-dining room—then turned to face the woman, who said, "Come in. I have coffee made."

"That would be nice."

Dani followed the woman to the small dining table, seated herself, and studied Elsa Horstman as she poured two cups of steaming black liquid into two large white mugs. Mrs. Horstman moved to the table, set the cups down, then took a seat, saying, "There's cream and sugar."

"Just black for me."

Elsa Horstman was a large woman of about seventy, with silver hair and light blue eyes. She was not fat, just big-boned and strong. The white cup looked small in her large hands, and she studied Dani carefully as she sipped the brew. "Tell me," she said abruptly.

Dani put the coffee mug down—it was too hot for her to drink. "My father is a private detective in New Orleans, as I mentioned. Six years ago, he collected evidence for the district attorney's office that resulted in the conviction of a man named Tommy Cain. . . . "

Dani spoke steadily, noting a change in Mrs. Horstman's eyes at the mention of Cain's name. But she listened without comment, and finally Dani concluded, " . . . so when we heard about your husband's death—"

When Dani paused, Mrs. Horstman nodded. "Yes, I see." She took a swallow of the scalding coffee as if it were cool tea, then said, "The police investigated the accident, you know. My husband was a good friend of the police chief's, and he went into it quite thoroughly."

Dani hesitated, then put the question bluntly, "Do you think it was an accident, Mrs. Horstman?"

The words hung in the air—and for one moment Dani saw a break in the features of the woman. Her lips tightened, and then she shook her head, "No, Miss Ross, I do not."

"Did you tell the police what you thought?"

Again a slight hesitation. "No."

Dani leaned forward, her face intent. "Why not, Mrs. Horstman?"

"Because I have no proof. No evidence at all. He had a bruise on his head, and they say the boom swung around and knocked him unconscious." She got up abruptly and, leaving the coffee cup on the table, turned to stare out the window into the darkness. "Felix was such a fine seaman. A thing like that would never happen—though I admit the wind was up. But that's the way they wrote up the report."

Dani wisely kept silent, sensing that no pressure would

make this woman speak. It was one of the things she had learned about interviewing people—that some could be leaned on, and that others would only grow adamant if any pressure was applied.

Mrs. Horstman turned back to face Dani and sat down slowly. There were lines of grief in her face as she said, "My husband and I would have been married fifty years next December. He was so proud of that!"

"He had a right to be," Dani nodded. "Marriages are an endangered species these days."

"Yes, they are. Fifty years—and I loved him more with each year." She seemed to shrink, her face growing more strained. Then she shook her shoulders, forcing herself to say, "But he's gone now."

Although she didn't say so, Dani saw that, for Elsa Horstman, life had become a bleak, unlovely thing. "I'm so sorry," she murmured quietly. "I'll pray for you."

"Ah—you are a Christian, then?"

"Yes."

"So am I—and so was Felix." A softness came into Elsa Horstman's eyes then, and she nodded slightly. "That is what keeps me going, Miss Ross. Do you understand?"

"Yes, I think I do."

Mrs. Horstman picked up her cup of coffee, stared at it, then put it down. "They said that Felix fell out of the catamaran and drowned. That could not be!"

"Why not, Mrs. Horstman?" Dani asked quickly.

"Because he was a distance swimmer! He swam the English Channel when he was a young man. And he would swim all the time to keep in shape. He could not swim the Channel, of course, at his age, but to drown because he fell in the water? No! It cannot be!"

"What exactly happened, Mrs. Horstman?"

"He took the catamaran out for a morning's sail. He liked it, you see. It was what he did when he wanted to think, when he had a problem. He would sail down the Bay, around Fort Morgan, and into the Gulf. And the worse the weather, the better he liked it! He'd stay out all day, sometimes even at night. He—he loved the sea." Her voice grew unsteady, and she cleared her throat. "Last Tuesday, he ate breakfast and told me he was going out for a sail. I didn't think much about it, except it did seem a little odd because he had an appointment to play golf with his brother. They have a fierce rivalry, you see, and I said, 'What about Hoyt?' He said, 'We'll play another day.'"

"And that was unusual?"

"Very! They were like little boys, Hoyt and Felix." She smiled then, and shook her head. "Both so successful—and they played that silly game as if the world depended on it!"

Dani sipped her coffee cautiously, wondering what it would be like to live with another person for fifty years—half a century! The thought of it frightened her for some reason. But at the same time, she had watched her parents all her life, and she knew that a good marriage was one of the richest treasures earth could offer.

Mrs. Horstman said suddenly, "We have one son. He's married to a wonderful girl. They have three children."

"Do they live close?"

"Yes, just over in Mobile."

"That's good. I'm sure you spoil the grandchildren to pieces."

A frown creased the broad brow of Elsa Horstman, and she dropped her eyes. The ticking of the wall clock seemed very loud in the silence. Finally she lifted her head and, in a voice that was almost a whisper, said, "I—I didn't press for a more thorough investigation into Felix's death because of my grandchildren."

Dani stated, "You know about Tommy Cain."

"Yes, I remember the case and how he threatened to kill my husband. But others have done that. It was only when my brother-in-law, Hoyt, told me about Cain getting out of prison that I thought of him again."

"Did your husband talk about Cain?"

"Only to tell me not to worry." Mrs. Horstman turned the coffee mug nervously in a small circle, adding, "But he was worried. I could tell. I always knew when something was bothering him. He never told me things that would worry me—not if there was any way he could handle it himself."

"How wonderful!"

"Yes, he was. But Hoyt told me after the funeral that Felix had heard from Cain."

"In a letter or by phone?"

"Felix didn't tell him, Hoyt said."

"What about his letters? Did you find anything?"

Mrs. Horstman rose and walked over to a rolltop desk, opened the top drawer, and took out an envelope. She came back, handed it to Dani, and said, "I found these."

Dani opened the clasp and removed three cards—all sympathy cards, all unsigned. "My father is getting these," she said slowly. Fear rose in her throat like bile as she noted the postmark on the envelopes. "All mailed from New Orleans," she whispered.

"I—received one more," Mrs. Horstman said, "after Felix died." Her face was haggard as she rose once more to retrieve a single card from the same drawer. Without comment she handed it to Dani. It was a card, Dani saw, much like the others, but with one difference. Printed in pencil was a brief message: "I hope nothing happens to Tim, Leslie, or Angela."

"Your grandchildren?" Dani asked, knowing the answer.

"Yes." Mrs. Horstman looked at Dani with anguish in her blue eyes. "I—I can't help you, Miss Ross."

Dani nodded. "I understand, Mrs. Horstman. May I keep this card? I promise you it will never be used in court." Mrs. Horstman bit her lip, then nodded.

Dani rose, saying, "I'm so sorry to have to bother you. But you understand."

"It's all right." Mrs. Horstman rose, walked to the door with Dani, and opened it. She said only, "I pray that your father will be all right."

"Thank you—and I'll ask God to be very close to you during these days."

Mrs. Horstman summoned a smile, but tears welled in her eyes. "These days—" she said, so softly that Dani barely heard her. "They'll be very long days—"

Then she stepped back and closed the door. Dani descended the steps, got into her car, and drove away. It was not too late to drive back to New Orleans, but she stopped at a pay phone at the gas station and dialed a number she found in her notebook.

"Hello?"

"Chad, this is Dani Ross—" She waited until Chad Boudreaux greeted her, then asked, "Can you take some work? A personal job for me."

A slight pause, then the voice said, "Let's have it, Dani."

Dani spoke rapidly for five minutes, then finished with, "It's a long shot, Chad, but as a personal favor to Dad and me, take your best shot."

"I'll give it all I've got, Dani—and that's all a mule can do."

Dani said good-by, hung up, then got back into the Cougar. She thought of Chad Boudreaux, the best private detective in Mobile, a close personal friend, and said a prayer for his success. It was not a prayer filled with faith, for the odds against success were formidable, but it was all she knew.

She regained Interstate 10 and ground out the miles. And as she drove down the long white strip of concrete, a sense of futility descended on her. She tried to shake it off, but it felt like a thick, choking cloud. She tried to pray, but it seemed that she was talking to herself.

Finally, she shook her head in frustration, saying, "God, where *are* you? Don't you know how bad I feel, how frightened I am?"

As she fought the battle, a large buck with a fine rack of antlers, apparently possessed of a death wish, came bounding out of the woods and ran directly in Dani's path. She stomped on the brakes and threw the Cougar to the left, almost losing control. She missed the buck by inches, fought the car to a stop, then sat there trembling.

Finally, a quietness came over her, and she looked up into the star-studded heavens. "Well, Lord, I guess that if you care for a four-footed deer, I have to believe you care for me!"

She started the engine, pulled back onto the slab, and continued her journey.

The buck waited until the red taillights of the car disappeared, then stepped out of the line of pines. He took several mincing paces toward the highway, then snorted and bolted back into the thickness of the dark woods, his hoofs making a miniature thunder on the hard ground.

8

Ben's New Love

At five thousand feet, Ben Savage decided New Orleans looked much more attractive than it did at ground-level zero. Moving the joystick slightly, he rolled the ancient biplane to the left so that he could enjoy the view better. The darkness flowed around him, tangible as the wind that cut into his lips, and the roar of the engine vibrated through his whole body.

He had bought the wreck of the plane from a pilot who had been lucky to survive the crash and had rebuilt it patiently and lovingly into the smoothly running piece of machinery that now carried him over the city. Gazing down at the myriad of lights that glowed below him, he thought that from the air, at night, a city looked like an old radio with the back off.

He glanced at his watch and noted it was almost six. Reluctantly he turned the ship back toward the airport. Flying the old plane just before dawn had become a ritual in his life—a way to escape from earth for a short time. He remembered a line from one of Robert Frost's poems: "I'd like to get away from earth for awhile," and thought, *The old man knew something. Wonder if he's happy now that he is away from it all?"*

He suddenly shook off the solemn thought, for he flew to get away from things, not to solve deep philosophical problems. He wrenched the joystick back, thrusting it to one side, at the same time stomping on the pedals and shoving the throttle forward. The biplane threw itself into a wrenching turn, the frame protesting. Savage lost all sense of up and down, all sense of earth itself, as the motion threw him against the side of the cockpit. He steered the plane over the sky, spinning like a leaf in a storm, enjoying the violence of the action.

Finally, he leveled off, shook his head, and grinned at his own foolishness. Looking down at the stick in his hand, he said mockingly, "A joystick, that's what you are. No more like you around." He shifted the stick slightly, adding, "Know what they call things like you now? *Control columns.* That's what we've come to in this world—all control and not much joy."

He shook off the thought as he approached the small airport just west of New Orleans, slightly disgusted with himself for dabbling in amateur philosophy—a habit he'd found himself falling into of late. He touched down, wheeled the ship around, taxied into the small hangar, and cut the engine. Climbing out, he slid into in his car and headed to the Ross house on the north side of Lake Pontchartrain.

The sun was up, filtering yellow bars of light through the thick branches of oaks that lined the driveway, bathing the white house with faint tinges of gold. As Savage pulled up to the entrance, Allison came running out to say, "Dani's on the phone, Ben. She wants to talk to you."

"Okay."

Savage entered the house and picked up the receiver, saying, "Yeah, Boss?"

"Ben, I've got to have the report on the Gerhart case. It goes to court today instead of next week."

"It's at my place. You want me to bring it to the office after I drop Allison off at school?"

"No, I'll pick it up at your apartment. We need to go over it. See you there in thirty minutes."

The phone clicked abruptly, and Savage stared at the receiver. "So much for courtly manners," he remarked sourly. He placed the receiver in the hook and walked out to the car where Allison was already inside waiting. "I'm late, Ben," she urged. "Break a few speed laws."

"It's only seven forty-five," he said, sliding into the seat and starting the engine.

"I have to be there early."

"Okay."

Savage drove to the school, listening with half an ear as Allison chattered about people and events in her life. Finally, as they approached the school, she grew quiet, and he noted the anxious expression on her face. "Not worried about seeing those two goons, are you?"

Allison shot him a quick glance, surprised that he had read her so easily. "Well—to tell the truth, I see them behind every bush."

"That's natural, Allison. A thing like that, it takes time to get over it."

"Ben, I'm scared." As Savage pulled up to the side door of the school, Allison seemed to settle down into the seat. "I don't want to go out of the house. I'm having bad dreams about all this—not just what happened to me at school, but about all of it."

Ben understood her words as a plea for reassurance and said easily, "You know what, Allison? Nothing ticks me off more than the guy who, when I tell him I'm worried, says,

'Don't worry.'" He reached over and pulled gently at a strand of her blonde hair. "Don't worry," he said, then grinned. "See how stupid it is?"

A smile curved her smooth lips, and she took his hand. "It's not stupid, Ben. I need to hear you say it."

He shook his head, then quoted, "Man is born to trouble as the sparks fly upward."

"Is that from a poem, Ben?"

"From the Bible. I heard a sermon on it once, a long time ago. Never forgot it." He wanted to reach out and hold her close, to tell her she didn't need to be afraid. But he knew she needed more than a shoulder to lean on. "People talk about these 'bad times' as if there were some other kind of times. But it's always been 'bad times,' I think. Now we've got AIDS killing people; a few years ago, it was diphtheria. People are afraid of getting killed by a gang on the street, but there's always been somebody out to get us—outlaws or bandits or somebody. And it's never going to be any different."

Allison listened to him, her dark blue eyes sober. "Not a very cheerful preview of things to come, is it?"

"Sure it is," he shot back. "You're healthy as a horse, you're a gorgeous woman, you've got a fine family—and a good-looking guy like me to haul you everywhere you go."

Allison smiled then, and leaned over to pull his head down. She kissed his cheek, then whispered, "Ben—don't get too far away, will you? Not for a little while?"

Savage squeezed her shoulder. "I'll stick like a limpet. Now, go let those teachers stamp out your ignorance!"

"Ben—what's a limpet?"

He grinned at her. "See how dumb you are? A limpet is a marine gastropod with a propensity for adherence." He laughed at her expression, adding, "It's a sea critter that clings to things real tight. And that's what I'll be doing as long as it takes."

Allison laughed at him, then got out. She joined two girls her own age and gave him a cheerful wave as they entered the building. Savage eased out of the parking lot, thinking how vulnerable the girl was. He felt a fierce surge of protectiveness, accompanied by the anger of knowing that if Cain wanted to hurt her, there was no way to stop him. A thought began to grow in his mind, and by the time he arrived at his apartment he had made a decision—one which he would not mention either to Dani or to Sixkiller.

He pulled up in front of the Launcelot Arms—thinking sardonically that the fanciest thing about his apartment house was its name—and spotted Dani's Cougar in the parking lot. He shut off the engine and got out of his car as Dani climbed out of hers. She asked, "Allison all right?"

"She's still shook up."

Dani shook her head. "Mother says she's having nightmares. I'm worried about her." She turned to go with him, and they walked along the sidewalk that buckled abruptly, as though a miniature earthquake had occurred. Dani looked up at the ugly front of the old, red-brick structure, but said nothing. They entered, and he turned to the right, leading the way up a set of rather narrow stairs.

"Elevator's broken," he commented. Since his apartment was on the fourth floor, Dani's breath was beginning to shorten as they approached the top. "Good for your heart," he commented. "Aerobic."

Dani shook her head. "Have you complained to the owner?"

"No, he's too sensitive. He wants to be a poet, I think. I don't want to hurt his feelings." As they reached the fourth floor and stepped out into the hall, Savage said, "Don't guess I mentioned it—but I don't live alone anymore."

Dani blinked with surprise, but she nodded. "You got someone to share your place? No, you didn't mention it. What's his name?"

They reached the door with 410 over the lintel, and Savage reached for his keys. "Jane."

Dani froze for an instant. "Jane?" she asked. "What's his first name?"

Savage found his key, but looked up at her. "It's not a 'he,' Boss. A female type."

Dani was aware that Savage was watching her with a peculiar expression in his hazel eyes. His statement seemed to rob her of speech. Though she was aware that Savage dated, it had never occurred to her that he would live with a girl. She had wondered often about him—what he thought about marriage and sex—but the news that he had actually entered into an "arrangement" came as a shock to her.

She was suddenly aware that she did *not* want to meet the woman and said hastily, "I don't want to intrude, Ben. I'll go on down to the office. Bring the papers there."

He took her arm as she turned to go, his grip firm. "You won't bother Jane, Boss," he shrugged. "She's probably asleep, anyway. Come on in."

Dani wanted to pull away, to leave at once. She didn't consider herself a prude, and every day she encountered what had been dubbed the "new" morality a few years earlier. Many of the people she knew personally and in the business world lived together without being married—and no one could live in New Orleans, Louisiana, without being constantly confronted with sins of the flesh in all possible forms. Still, she didn't like to have her nose rubbed in it—especially by someone she worked with this closely.

She hesitated, then said, "Well, all right. But I'll just take the report back to the office."

Savage ignored her, opened the door, and stepped back to allow her to enter. Dani walked in as if she were stepping into a field with live land mines, her eyes sweeping the living area. She was relieved to see that the woman was not there, and she glanced at the door to the bedroom, which was slightly ajar.

"Have a seat," Savage nodded. "I'll make some coffee, and we can go over the report. A few things I need to explain to you."

Before Dani could protest, he walked into the kitchen, and she followed him with alacrity, taking a seat at the table. He went about putting coffee into a small filter cone and setting the teakettle on to boil the water. Then he said, "I'll get the report. It's in the bedroom."

After he left, Dani sat staring out the window at the clouds rolling by like huge cotton balls. She was struggling with the strange sensation that Ben's announcement had aroused. The two of them often argued and fought, but Dani knew that beneath Savage's caustic manner he felt something for her. Two or three times he had kissed her, and she had felt herself drawn to him strongly. Since he was not a believer, she had refused to entertain any thought of a permanent relationship with him, yet she had come to depend on his being there.

Now in one instant, all that had changed, and she felt a sudden emptiness in her stomach. She'd felt the same way when Biscuit was killed—as if she had been walking along a level road but had stepped off into a deep hole. The shock of it numbed her.

Savage was back then and handed her the report. "There it is, Boss. Look it over."

Dani stared at the pages, trying to focus on the first page while he poured the boiling water into the cone. She tried to concentrate on the report as he moved about, buttering some

English muffins and popping them into the toaster oven. By the time he had put some saucers and strawberry jam on the table, she had collected herself enough to ask a few questions.

Savage rattled off a list of comments on the case, interrupting himself long enough to pour the coffee and set out the buttered muffins. "Better try one of these, Boss," he urged.

"No, I've already eaten." Dani stirred her coffee, then asked suddenly, "Where did you meet—Jane?" There was an awkward pause as she tried to put a title in place. *Friend? Lover? Old lady?*

Savage shrugged. "Over on Burgundy Street, in the Quarter," he said. He took another bite of his muffin, chewed it thoughtfully, then added, "She was in pretty bad shape, so I picked her up and brought her home."

Dani sipped the coffee to conceal her disgust. She well knew the type of woman who'd be "in pretty bad shape" on Burgundy Street in the French Quarter. "That was nice of you," she said, trying to keep the sarcasm out of her tone.

Savage shrugged. "I thought I'd keep her a few days, then pass her on to somebody—but she's a pretty thing, and I got used to having her around." He finished off his muffin, then stared at the second one. "Sure you don't want this?" He picked it up, smeared jam on it, and took a huge bite. "You ever eat Smucker's strawberry preserves?"

"No."

"Their sales pitch is, 'With a name like Smuckers, it's got to be good!' I think they've got the right idea. Stick with your own name, even if it's Smuckers."

He appeared to have forgotten his narrative, and Dani finally said, "Well, it'll be a new lifestyle for you. You've been alone a long time, Ben."

"Oh, I don't think so." Savage sipped the scalding coffee, adding, "It's pretty nice not having to come home to an empty apartment—but Jane won't make much difference in my lifestyle. I come and go pretty much as I please. As long as she's got something to eat, she'll make out."

Dani could stand it no longer. "Ben," she demanded suddenly, "do you love her?"

Savage looked at her with absolutely no expression. "She's okay. She can stay as long as she doesn't give me too much trouble."

Dani got up abruptly, anger on her face. She snatched up the report and turned to leave the kitchen.

Savage caught up with her as she reached the door. "What are you so sore about?"

"Let me go!"

As Dani struggled to free herself, Savage turned his head toward the bedroom door. "Hello, Jane," he said, a smile stretching his mouth wide .

Dani's head jerked as she whirled to stare across the room. She saw a beautifully groomed white cat with enormous green eyes walk daintily across the carpet, leap up onto a red recliner, and gaze across at the pair who stood at the door.

Dani faltered. "This is—Jane?" she whispered.

"Sure." Savage turned to look into Dani's face, saying, "Good-looking thing, isn't she?"

Dani swallowed and managed to say, "Very fine-looking cat." She felt like a fool, and she was furious with herself. "You didn't mention—"

Savage waited for her to finish. Then, when she said no more, he remarked blandly, "I've had her for three months now." Then he added, "Want to go over the rest of the report?"

Dani wanted to leave, but forced herself to say, "Maybe we'd better." She was not, she decided, going to be put to flight by a cat!

"Have a seat on the couch, I'll get the report."

Dani sat down gingerly, and for the next few minutes Savage went over the fine points of the report. He was sitting close to her, and suddenly the cat jumped up between them. Surprised, Savage looked at her, then grinned at Dani. "She's jealous of you, Boss."

Dani had to smile, then. "She doesn't have to worry." She put out her hand to stroke the cat's head, and yanked it back when Jane's paw shot out and scratched her wrist. "Why, you—!"

Savage said quickly, "I'll get some antiseptic for that."

"It's just a little scratch."

But Savage had already disappeared into the bedroom and come back with a small tube of ointment. "Let's see," he commanded, took her hand, and smeared some of the ointment on the scratch. "Sorry. I should have warned you. Jane doesn't like to be petted."

"Does she scratch you?"

"Not always," he said, looking down at the injury. Suddenly he looked up with a grin. "Her real name is Jane Eyre. I just call her Jane for short."

"Jane Eyre?"

"Yeah. I was walking home in the rain on Burgundy Street, and I saw her in an alley. Just a ball of wet fur. I thought she might even be dead, but when I stopped and reached out to touch her, she tried to scratch me. I liked that, Boss. She had true grit, just like Rooster Cogburn in that old John Wayne movie."

Dani became aware that Savage was still holding her hand, and pulled it away abruptly. "You *would* like a cat that has a temper!"

"Well, I guess so. I brought her home, fattened her up. Thought I'd give her to somebody when she got well. I could see she was going to be a looker. She's Persian, I guess." He looked fondly at the cat, which seemed to be listening carefully to what he said. "Well, I got hooked in a week. Got so I'd hurry home to see how she was doing. So we just decided to make it permanent."

Dani watched curiously as Savage stepped over and picked up the cat; then she asked, "Why'd you decide to call her Jane Eyre?"

Savage smiled briefly. "Because she was so blasted independent—just like the Jane in Brontë's novel. You know how stubborn that woman was! Always thought she could have bent a *little*—but she never did."

"I always liked Jane."

"Sure you did—because you're just like her. Stubborn as a mule, the two of you, and suspicious of men." He smiled, adding, "You and Jane here are different from the original Jane Eyre in only one way."

Dani stared at him. "How?"

"Both of you are good-looking, instead of being plain like Mr. Rochester's Jane."

His compliment pleased Dani, for he was not given to praising her. "Well, you two make a nice couple. I hope the honeymoon lasts a long time." She turned to go, saying, "I've got to run. Be sure you pick Allison up when she gets out of school."

Ben asked as she opened the door, "What did you find out about Judge Horstman's death? Was it accidental?"

"His wife doesn't think so." Dani ran through Mrs. Horstman's suspicions, but ended by saying, "She won't press the thing. She's afraid of Cain."

"Guess she's got a right to be," Savage nodded. "Maybe I better take a run down there and check it out."

"No need for that, Ben. I hired Chad Boudreaux to do some checking."

"Chad's smart." Savage thought hard, then said, "I've been

thinking about the other two men that Cain threatened—
Mack Carver and Henry Sweet. We know Cain's threatening
your dad, and it's possible he had something to do with Judge
Horstman's death. I think we better have a talk with Carver
and Sweet."

Dani nodded. "I've thought that myself. You take Sweet. I
know Mack Carver slightly. Let me tackle him."

She turned to leave, and he asked, "That .38 loaded, Boss?"

He had noted she was wearing the pistol, and now Dani
nodded quickly. "I told you, Ben. I'm playing for keeps with
this one. If it were just me, I'd be more charitable. But this
man could kill Allison or Rob—or Mother. I've thought about
that. It would be the way to hurt Dad the most, and Cain
might just figure that out. That's why I want to pin it down.
I want to put Cain in the pen for the rest of his life."

"Hard thing to do," Savage murmured. "Look how he got
out of the last rap. Anybody else would have been in Angola
for life. But Cain got out. He's smart; he's got money and no
scruples. A bad combination."

"We've got to nail him, Ben," Dani insisted. "We can't live
under this thing forever. You go see Sweet, and I'll talk to
Mack Carver."

"Got one little job to do first—something on my own," Savage answered. "I'll take care of it today, then try to see Sweet
tomorrow."

"All right." Dani turned to leave, then stopped. Savage saw
that she seemed to be struggling with something, and finally
she turned and said quietly, "Ben, that was mean of you—to
make me think you'd—taken up with a cheap woman."

Savage stared at her, admiring the clean lines of her features, and he nodded. "I always carry things too far. Sorry,
Boss. Can you overlook a dumb acrobat?"

Dani could see he was sincere, and she gave him a warm smile. "Sure. I'm—I'm glad you were just kidding, Ben."

She turned and left him, and he stared at the door for a long moment. Then he crossed the room and sank down on the couch, his eyes thoughtful.

Jane came over and lay down in his lap. When he paid her no mind, she reached up and pawed at his chest, saying "Meow?"

Savage looked down, then slowly stroked her. "You fickle female! When I want some affection, you stick your nose in the air and rake me with your claws. When it's *you* who crave some love, you think all you have to do is cuddle up and ask for it."

He stroked the cat's silken head, then looked thoughtfully across at the front door. "I guess all you females are about alike," he finally said, a thin smile coming to his lips.

9

Savage Sends an Invitation

Savage caught up with Sixkiller after convincing the offi-
cer at the NOPD that he *had* to find the lieutenant. She finally
admitted reluctantly, "He's at the morgue," and that was
where Savage cornered the policeman. They drove on to El
Zarape Mexican Restaurant on Magazine Street, and as soon
as they'd given their order to the waitress, Ben started in.

"You put the squeeze on those two goons who shook Allison up?"

Sixkiller's square face assumed a pained expression, and
he shook his head. "No, Ben, I can't do it."

"Why not? You've done it before."

"I'm on good behavior now." Sixkiller stared moodily
across the room, where sombreros and serapes and bull horns
lined the walls. The tables were actually railroad spools, and

the tablecloths were black-and-red serapes. He commented sourly, "I hate the phony decorating these places do."

Savage looked around the room. "They have to do it. The food's so bad, they have to give you something to take your mind off it." He took one of the chips from a basket, dipped it in the red sauce the waitress had put between them, brought it to his mouth, then spit it out at once. "That's *hot!*"

"This is a macho restaurant," Sixkiller grinned. He extracted a large chip, scooped up an enormous amount of the sauce, and stuck it in his mouth. He crunched the chip between his strong white teeth, showing no evidence of discomfort. Finally he said, "You white eyes are soft. Can't even eat a little hot sauce."

Savage stared at him, but chose to ignore the jibe. "What's the use of being a cop if you can't pull in a suspect and lean on him?"

"You're thinking of the good old days, Ben. Was a time when we could pull off a stunt like that—and sometimes it still works. But you got to remember I was suspended not too long ago for being a bad boy. Now I've got everybody from the ACLU to the DAR making sure I cuddle the little darlings who are shooting up New Orleans at a record rate."

The waitress brought in tacos filled with strips of beef, lettuce, tomatoes, and sour cream. The two men pitched in, and after the tacos came *grillades*, veal cut into squares and cooked in a thick, spicy, brown gravy.

"This isn't Mexican food, is it?" Savage inquired.

"No, it's Cajun. Owner married a New Orleans girl, and she does the cooking. Says she has to throw some Cajun cooking in with the Mexican or she'll go crazy."

"Makes sense, I guess." Savage finished off his meal and, while Sixkiller poured honey into a huge *sopapilla*—a hollow, rounded fried pastry—he said stubbornly, "Luke, we got to do *something* about Tommy Cain. He's not going to be a good boy and forget the whole thing."

"No, he's not. But it won't help matters if I get myself suspended for brutality." The honey was leaking out of the pastry, and he held it up, trying to catch it before it fell. "These things are impossible to eat!" he complained. "If they weren't so good, I'd give up on them."

"Too bad," Savage remarked. "You have a real problem, I can see. Why don't we go to Dani and explain how you can't stop Tommy Cain because your honey won't stay in your Mexican doughnut?"

Anger flared in Sixkiller's dark eyes. "Look, Ben, you've carried a badge, but you've forgotten what it was like, I guess. A homicide detective is part junkyard dog, part psychologist, and part vampire, prowling the night, despising the day shift. He's got to be Sherlock Holmes and Wyatt Earp rolled into one. He's got to be smart, patient, and lucky—and he's got to have some kind of drive that makes a man go for the jugular when he has to. And he has to live with the fact that there are boards and newspapers that can put him back to walking a beat."

"Yeah, Luke, I know." A morose expression came to Savage's face, and he shook his head. "Well, you have to keep the rules—but I don't have a board to answer to."

"You can get your license revoked," Sixkiller reminded him. "Or Cain can revoke *you*. He's done it plenty—even if we haven't put him away for it." He stared thoughtfully at Savage across the table. "I've got a feeling you're going to bust loose. Is that right?"

"If you say you've got a feeling like that, Lieutenant, I guess you have it," Savage said, grinning slightly.

"Yeah, I know you. But it won't do any more good for you to get yourself offed and dumped into the river than it would do for me to get busted. Dani needs you alive, not dead. So don't go turning over any old boards, Ben—something bad might come crawling out and bite you."

The two men stood up, and Sixkiller took Savage to where his car was parked. He pulled a traffic ticket off the windshield and handed it to Savage, saying, "You've got to learn to keep the rules, Ben. Now pay your ticket like a good boy."

Savage crammed the ticket into his pocket, climbed into the car, and drove to the office. Dani was out, and Angie Park handed him a folder, saying, "Dani said for you to take care of this." It took most of the day to accomplish half of what Dani had dumped on him, and it was six o'clock by the time he quit. He drove to his apartment, and was greeted affectionately by Jane Eyre.

"You must want something," he muttered as she rubbed ecstatically against his calf. He offered her some Cat Chow, and she looked at him reproachfully. He opened a can of tuna and dumped half of it in her bowl. She ate it daintily, then moved off to the bedroom, ignoring his existence.

"Good how you lavish all that love on me," he called after her. He fixed a sandwich, ate it, then lay down and slept for two hours. Then he got up, put on a pair of New Balance running shoes, jeans, and a blue sweatshirt—extra large to cover the .38 he wore in a holster on his left side. Leaving the apartment, he got in his car and headed for the Quarter.

As Savage turned down Bourbon Street, he thought suddenly how much he hated the place. It was all a front—neon and jazz on the outside, lots of good food and laughs, but mean underneath.

Rolling the old Charger slowly down the street, Savage saw dozens of people dealing drugs. Half the business in the Quarter was dopers selling to one another. The owners of lots of little mom-and-pop operations kept turning up dead in the trunks of cars—casualties of the fierce competition of the drug war.

He passed by the Jackson Brewery building, watching the tourists mill in and out, then moved on around Jackson Square, past St. Louis Cathedral. St. Peter Street was quiet, the sidewalks almost blocked by parked cars. As he drove, Savage let his mind range, trying to find some way to get a handle on what was happening. He wanted to steamroller somebody—particularly Mr. Thomas Cain—and part of his mind was struggling to cap the hot anger that kept trying to surface. He had the scars on his body to prove that untempered fury could often lead to broken bones and worse. He knew it was better to keep control, but at times the fiery response to some injustice overcame his better judgment. He muttered, "Steady down, Savage—" then finally left the Quarter and headed for the Calliope Project.

He turned down Louisa Street and the beginnings of the Project began to appear. Savage felt his senses snap to alert at the sense of danger. At one time he had thought that *nothing* could be worse than the Quarter. Now he dreaded even driving through this dilapidated area.

"A good idea gone bad," he murmured, his eyes taking in the crude graffiti and the broken-out windows. The idea had been, a long time ago, to build cheap public housing for people who weren't going to make it. Nothing fancy—just nice and clean with a few flowers, maybe, and a place for the kids to play.

But the people who dreamed it all up never lived there. They slapped together the buildings, then rushed off to do good for other people. He thought suddenly of Thoreau's statement, "If I knew for certain that a man was coming to do me a good deed, I'd run for my life." Savage nodded slightly, not taking his eyes off the street.

The Project was a doper's paradise, of course—sort of a discount warehouse. If they didn't stock what you wanted, they could get it for you in twenty minutes. The kids—the little boys and girl—were the runners. The teenage boys would sell and collect. Some of the stuff was put together right in the Project. Drugs were to the Project what the mountains are to Colorado and the beach is to Florida—and it would be about as easy to control the mountains or the sea as the drug traffic in the Project.

Suddenly Ben put on the brakes and rolled down his window. "Jayro," he called out to a tall figure leaning against a lamppost. The young black man was wearing Ray Ban sunglasses. He came to stand beside the car.

"Why, it's the man who shoots the hats off innocent young dudes," he grinned. His white teeth made a slash across his black features.

"Get in," Savage nodded. "I'm buying."

Jayro stared at him, his eyes hidden behind the glasses, but he nodded finally. "Why not?" He moved to the other door, opened it, and slid into the seat. He examined the interior of the car carefully, then asked, "What variety of car is this, Mr. Savage?"

"Dodge Charger, Jayro—born in 1966."

"Before my time," the black man grinned.

"They knew how to make cars in those days," Savage nodded. "I picked it up for three hundred dollars."

Jayro looked at the duct tape patching the brittle vinyl seat covers, the gaping hole in the dash where the radio had been, and remarked, "I think that dude you bought it from saw you coming."

"This heap is like most things in this world, Jayro—what you sees is *not* what you gets."

Jayro was not impressed. "When I get my car, it's gonna

have it all hanging out, Mr. Savage. I don't intend to race at Daytona with it—so I'll just get me a nice red Porsche, or a black BMW, maybe."

The night was falling fast, casting a cloak of darkness over the buildings. The streetlights were on, bathing the concrete below in pale circles of light. Figures began to move out of the buildings, dark and ominous. "Always think of vampires when I see the folks coming out as the sun goes down," Savage remarked.

"Take lots of stakes to stop all the brothers, true enough."

Savage asked curiously, "It's not like you to be idle, Jayro. You on vacation?"

"No, indeed! I'm a victim of the times."

"How's that?"

"Well, you know, in my business, Mr. Savage, I don't require a regular office. But I do need a telephone. So I been using the pay phone that used to be where you picked me up. But they came and took it out last week."

"Why'd they do that?"

"I believe the reasoning was that dealers and gang members use that phone as a rent-free office—which indeed was true." Jayro settled down in the seat, took off his shades, and tucked them in his pocket. He was wearing ostrich-skin cowboy boots, a pure white shirt, and skin-tight black jeans. A gold herringbone chain dangled from his neck, the yellow metal glinting against his ebony skin. "This country going defunct."

"Because they took your pay phone?"

"Naw, it's bigger than that. Look, you go in now and buy some Tylenol, and the thing is sealed so tight it'd take a cat burglar to get at the stuff." He grinned at Savage in the fading light. "It's another of those subtle societal shifts, Mr. Savage. More repression for the brothers."

Savage said, "There was a story in the paper yesterday about a guy named Larry Hogue. He's a crack addict, lives in the Upper West Side of New York. His hobby was chasing pedestrians with machetes and ice picks."

"Sounds like an okay guy."

"Sure. He's been arrested or sent to mental hospitals thirty-seven times since 1985, but he always goes back to his neighborhood when he gets out."

Jayro nodded. "I admire a man who sticks to his roots."

"New York law says a person can't be committed to a mental hospital until at least two doctors agree he's a threat to himself or others—so it's in again, out again."

"What's your solution? Pop the crazy off?"

"Don't have one—but I don't think taking a pay phone off the street is going to shut down your average pusher."

Jayro studied the man beside him for a long moment, then asked, "You pick me up to deliver a lecture on social ills?"

"No. I want to know about a pair of cheap hoods named Moon Mazurki and Whitey Harms."

A silence settled in the car, broken only when Jayro asked, "What you want with them?"

"Just have a little talk, that's all."

Jayro said cautiously, "Better have that little gun on you when you do—and don't try shooting their hats off."

"No trouble. Just talk."

"I ain't sure Mazurki *can* talk. He got his brains scrambled so many times when he was in the ring he don't make much sense. Harms do most of the talking for the both of them."

"Who they hooked up with, Jayro?"

"Anybody who needs strong-arm work."

"Ever hear of them being on Tommy Cain's payroll?"

Jayro reacted strongly, his lips tightening as he shot out, "Cain? Who said anything about Cain?"

"Me. I just said it."

"Wouldn't be using that name loosely, I was you."

"He some kind of tin god? Got fur on his knees?"

Jayro shook his head. "Cain ain't nobody to mess with, Savage."

Savage drove slowly, thinking about the dealer's reaction. Something about it bothered him, but he said only, "Look, can you get word to Mazurki and Harms that I'm asking questions about them?"

"You don't want that!"

"Can you do it?"

"Yeah. But you better get some backup when they come to find out why you're reaching for them."

Savage said, "Just let it leak out that I'm asking around about them. Let it slip that I live in the Launcelot Arms." He pulled some bills from his pocket and handed them to Jayro. "Anywhere I can drop you?"

Jayro stared at the bills, then turned his gaze on Savage. "Right here is all right." When Savage pulled over, he got out, then leaned in to say, "You ain't a brother, Savage, but I'll give you some free advice—you steer clear of those two. Maybe you can take them—but there's lots more where they come from."

"Get the word out, Jayro," Savage said. He smiled and added, "I'll take it up with the mayor about having your phone replaced."

Jayro stepped back as the Charger accelerated and quickly disappeared down the street. He tucked the bills into his pocket, shrugged, then turned and walked down the narrow street.

As soon as Tommy Cain heard the voice on the phone, he frowned. "I told you never to call me," he said coldly.

"Sure, Mr. Cain—but you gotta know. There's a guy asking questions about me and Moon."

"Questions? What kind of questions?"

"I dunno. Just asking about us. Name's Savage."

Cain had been ready to blast Whitey Harms, but now he paused. "Is it Ben Savage?"

"Yeah, I think so," Harms said. "And I found out he works for the—"

"Shut your mouth! I know who he works for."

Harms said no more, and Cain stood there thinking. Finally he spoke, "I want you to discourage him."

Harms asked, "Discourage him? You mean lay him out?"

"I mean I want you to see to it that he stops asking questions."

A long silence, then Harms said, "Okay, Mr. Cain. We'll take care of it."

"Do a good job. I'll send you some cash by Marcel." He hung up the phone and turned to the woman half reclined on the pale blue silk couch. She smiled at him, her rich lips curving seductively. He walked to the liquor cabinet, poured two drinks, then moved to sit beside her. She moved closer, and he reached out and took a strand of her blonde hair lightly in his fingers. "How are you doing with your pupil, Stormy?"

"The kid?" Stormy Carr shrugged carelessly. "Like shooting fish in a barrel, Tommy. Almost a shame to take the money."

"You got him on coke yet?"

A frown crossed the woman's face, and she said in a puzzled tone, "Well, not yet. He's a real square." She took a drink from her glass and looked up at Cain with a sudden grin. "Would you believe he hasn't even tried to hustle me?"

"Boy's been raised right."

"It kind of shocked me at first, Tommy. I spend a lot of my life fighting guys off—and this kid acts like I'm Rebecca of Sunnybrook Farm." She put her forefinger in the glass and stirred the liquor gently, adding almost wistfully, "You know, I think he's got ideas of marrying me, Tommy."

Cain's lips curved slightly, and he gave her hair a sudden pull. "If he's hooked that bad, you ought to be able to get him to do more than take a few puffs on some of that Acapulco Gold I gave you."

"Sure, Tommy," Stormy said quickly. He was holding her hair so tightly that she winced, and knowing her man, said, "I'll get him started on a little coke tonight. In a few days he'll be hooked good."

Cain pulled Stormy's head back and kissed her, then whispered, "See you do it, sweetheart. I'd hate to have to punish you again—like last time."

"No!" Stormy cried out quickly. She draped her arms around Cain's neck and held him tightly. Her eyes were wide with fear as she added, "He's ready, Tommy. I promise you!"

Cain's pale blue eyes studied her, and he nodded. "That's a good girl. I knew you'd take care of it." A thought passed his mind, and his thin lips curled in a smile. "Got to see to it that old Dan's little boy learns what the real world is like. Soon as he gets hooked, I'll give him a job to support his habit." His shoulders shook with a spasm of laughter, and he thought, *Wouldn't it be something if Dan Ross's boy wound up in Angola—the same place old Danny boy put me?*

10

A Message for Tommy

That's the guy—the one wearing the light blue jacket."

Whitey Harms peered across the darkening street, squinting to make out the group standing in front of the old brownstone apartment house.

"You sure, Deacon?"

"Yeah, it him." Deacon Williams was so thickened with muscles that he had no neck. When his head bobbed in affirmation, it was only a bare nod. "He been asking all over the project fo' you two."

Moon Mazurki grinned, a wicked light in his ebony eyes. "Well, he's gonna find us."

"You need some mo' muscle?"

"For one guy?" Mazurki snorted. "Get serious."

Williams shrugged. "He carrying."

"So am I," Harms snapped. His eyes narrowed, and he

moved quickly toward the black Lincoln he and Mazurki had driven there. "He's coming this way. Get in the car, Moon."

The two of them slid into the Lincoln and watched carefully as the man they'd come to intercept left the group he'd been talking to and walked at a casual pace along the crumbling sidewalk. He passed close enough for the two men to see him clearly. When he'd moved on out of hearing distance, Whitey Harms nodded. "Come on, Moon. It's dark enough now. Drive around the block, and we'll take him into that old burned-out house."

"Yeah. Sure."

Mazurki started the engine and drove by the single figure, turning into a driveway where the hollow shell of a brick building loomed. It had long ago been gutted, and now its empty windows stared with dead, hollow eyes. The two men got out quickly, and Mazurki whispered, "You want I should take him, Whitey?"

"No. I'll nail him when he comes along the sidewalk. Then we'll take him inside and work him over." Harms moved to stand behind the brick wall that formed a border for the burned-out building, pulling a Colt Python from beneath his jacket as he spoke. He motioned for Mazurki to get against the wall and then stood poised, his pale eyes gleaming. The faint sounds of the man's approach alerted him. He waited until the form of his quarry passed the wall, then stepped out, saying harshly, "Hold it, dude!" He leveled the Colt on the chest of the man who whirled around, adding, "Don't pull that gun. You'll never make it."

"I may be dumb, but not dumb enough to carry a lot of cash in this neighborhood."

"Your name Savage?" Harms demanded.

"Sure." Savage took in the forms of the two men, then said, "And I would guess you two are Harms and Mazurki."

"Smart guy, ain't he, Moon?" Harms grinned, his thin lips drawing back at the corners to reveal a mouthful of bad teeth. "Now, move along, Savage." He waved the gun toward the gutted building, adding, "Take his gun, Moon."

Mazurki came forward and pulled Savage's jacket open, ripping the gun from the shoulder holster. Holding it in his left hand, he gripped Savage's arm and sent him reeling, grunting, "Hear you wanna talk to us. Well, get in there—and I'll give you some 'talk'!"

There was no door, and Harms' gun prodded Savage through the gaping opening. The streetlight was out, so the room was pitch black. "Hold on to him, Moon, 'till I get a light," Harms instructed. He produced a penlight from his pocket and directed the thin sliver of light into Savage's eyes, causing him to blink. Harms grinned. "Comfortable?" he asked. "Now, you've been doing a lot of looking for us, Savage. Moon and me would like to know why."

Savage turned his head to avoid the light. "Got some business to talk over with you, Harms," he said.

"Always glad to do business," Harms said. "What kind of business?"

"Like to get some information on a friend of yours."

"A friend of ours? Who you talking about?" Harms demanded.

"Why, Tommy Cain, Whitey."

His words dropped into the darkness, fading into silence, but Savage knew that Harms was shaken because the slender light in his hand wavered.

"Tommy Cain? We don't know any Tommy Cain, do we, Moon?"

Moon's voice was coarse, as if he had a throat full of rocks. He cursed roughly and suddenly struck out with one of his massive fists. The blow caught Savage on the cheek, the force of it driving him across the room. He stumbled over an upturned sink and fell to the floor. Moon's hands were like hooks as he grabbed him up, and the big man spat out, "What you talking about Tommy Cain for?"

Savage said, "Sure, you know Cain, Moon. You and your buddy work for him."

Mazurki drew back his fist, but Harms broke in suddenly, "Wait a minute, Moon. Let's hear what this smart guy's got to say. Plenty of time for you to work him over. Just hold on to him." He moved closer, bringing the penlight in close to Savage's face. "Everybody knows about Tommy Cain, Savage. But we don't work for him."

"What about the job you did for him on Dan Ross's daughter?"

"Dan Ross? We don't know nobody named Ross."

"What about Felix Horstman? Know anybody by that name?"

Again, the silence, then Mazurki said, "Lemme shut this guy's mouth, Whitey. He's too nosy!"

Harms nodded slightly. "Maybe that'll be enough, if you do it right."

"I'll bust his teeth to snags!" Mazurki snarled.

Harms said, "Savage, I'm giving you a break. Moon's going to rough you up pretty good. I ought to put a slug in your brain—which is exactly what you'll get if you ever open your kisser again!"

Savage said, "I'm going to give you one chance to spill what you know about Cain, Harms."

Harms stared at the face of Savage, then laughed harshly. *"You're* giving *us* a chance? What you on, Savage? Moon, bust him up!"

"Yeah! Hold his gun, Whitey! "

Mazurki passed Savage's gun to Harms, who jammed it in

his left pocket and stepped back to give his partner room. His lips curved in a shark-like grin; he always enjoyed watching the burly Mazurki in action. Mazurki had been only a prelim fighter, winning his fights by virtue of a thick skull and powerful muscles. But if he was too slow for the ring, he was admirably constructed for street fighting, where there were no referees. His favorite ploy was to pen his victim into a small space where there was no room to maneuver and then pulverize him with smashing blows to the face and body. He was abnormally strong, able to break ribs with a single blow.

Now he grabbed Savage and shoved him back toward the wall. He needed fights as other men need food and drink, and having been without one for several days, he felt a gush of pleasure as the smaller man hit the wall. Drawing back his fist, he aimed a tremendous punch at Savage's stomach—but somehow it never landed. He felt a steely set of fingers close on his wrist. Suddenly he was yanked forward—just in time to receive a stunning blow on his throat.

Mazurki had a nose like a saddle and had become inured to pain from blows on the face, but he crumpled at the sudden spasm of pain that shot through him as the hard edge of Savage's left hand made contact. And even worse than the pain was the fact that he couldn't cry out. The blow had taken away his speech. He tried to call out to Harms, but only a rough gurgling sound came from his thick throat.

Harms saw the huge form of his partner lunge forward at the smaller figure of Savage and expected the usual—a sudden blow and a cry of pain from the victim. What he saw instead was Mazurki stopping short as if he'd run into a brick wall—and then came the weird sound of a gagging scream. At first Harms thought it was Savage and was pleased, but then he saw by the slender beam of light that fell on Mazurki's face that the big man was in trouble. "Hey, what's—!"

But Harms never finished the question, for things happened so quickly that he didn't have time. He heard a solid *thunk* and saw Mazurki crash to the ground. It looked as though Savage had struck the big man with a club—but what Harms couldn't see was that the club was Savage's forearm striking the back of Mazurki's bull-like neck. It would have killed a man who lacked Mazurki's padding of fat and muscle, and it drove the form of Moon Mazurki to the floor. He fell, Harms saw, in that loose-jointed fashion of the totally unconscious.

Harms had the quick reflexes of a cobra, and at once he lifted his gun and drove a shot toward the shadowy figure of Savage, but the light was bad, and he knew at once he'd missed. He was certain Savage had moved to his left, and he swept the narrow beam of light from the penlight in that direction—but he was mistaken, for Savage had faked in that direction like a good basketball player and then dodged into the shadows at Harms' right.

Harms tried to correct his error by swinging to his right, but even as he turned he sensed a shadowy form, and he cried out as a hard object came down on his right wrist. The Colt was driven from his hand, and he heard it skitter along the floor. Before he could go after it, the penlight was plucked from his left hand. A faint *click,* and the beam disappeared, throwing the room into stygian darkness.

Harms had good nerves. He had gone up against blazing guns without a qualm, but the thick darkness, and the sudden silence was something he'd never faced. Sweat popped out on his forehead.

"What about it, Whitey?"

The voice came from his right, and Harms suddenly remembered that he had thrust Savage's gun into his coat pocket. He grinned in the darkness, reaching carefully for the gun and speaking to cover his movement: "Well, now, Savage, you're pretty good! I didn't think any dude living could take Moon out like that!"

"Ready to talk about Cain, Whitey?"

The voice came from a different spot in the room, though Whitey had heard nothing. The man must move like a cat! Harms had the gun free now, and he knew he couldn't take any chances with this man. "What you want to know, Savage?" He held the gun up in a ready position, and waited for the sound of Savage's voice.

"Just what he paid you to rough the Ross girl up—that'll do for openers."

The voice came from in front of Harms, slightly to his right.

I'll empty the whole clip at him, Harms thought. *Some of them slugs'll have to get him!*

Carefully he pulled the muzzle of the automatic to the right, tightened his finger—and all that happened was a futile clicking sound!

"You didn't think I'd hand you a loaded gun, did you, Whitey?" The voice was mocking, and then it grew harder. "Game's over, Harms," Savage said. There was no sound, not that Harms could hear—but suddenly the gun was plucked from his hand. An instant later, a blow to the solar plexus doubled him over. He would have joined his partner on the floor if powerful hands had not caught him.

Gasping for breath, Harms found himself pushed against a ruined wall, and the voice came floating out of the black void almost as if from a disembodied ghost.

"From the first, Whitey. When did Cain set up the hustle? What's next on his schedule?"

Whitey Harms was a tough one—but only in his own element. In the darkness, with no gun in his hand, and facing a man who apparently could see like a cat, he suddenly knew that, no matter how much he hated squealers, he was about to join their ranks!

Tommy Cain leaned forward in the stylist's chair, looked at himself in the mirror, then nodded.

"Good job, Sam." Rising, he reached into the pocket of his pearl-gray slacks, pulled out a packet of money, and slipped a fifty from under the flat gold clip. He handed it to the hairdresser and accepted the man's thanks, saying, "You do my hair just the way I like it. If I could get my people to do their jobs like that, I'd be happy."

"Thanks, Mr. Cain."

Cain left the small shop, which was located on the first floor of the Crescent Condominium. He greeted Nelson, the security man, who nodded and called his name with respect, then he stepped into the empty elevator. As it shot up to the tenth floor, he realized he was tired. It was only three in the afternoon, but his eyes were gritty, and he thought with both regret and satisfaction of yesterday's all-night poker game. He'd lost a bundle, but a certain state senator had been in attendance. By the time the party was over, Cain and the senator had spent half an hour in a conference. They had gone out onto a balcony that overlooked the city. And when they returned to the party, Cain was assured that the next man appointed to the lottery board would be *his* man.

As he entered his apartment, he was already thinking of ways to tighten his grip on the Louisiana lottery. He was a simple man, this Tommy Cain, in many ways—despite the contradictions that sometimes confused his friends and enemies. He'd said once to his most trusted lieutenant, Louie Zapello, "Louie, there's only one rule—know what you want, and don't let anything keep you from getting it."

Zapello, a tall, cadaverous man of forty who was dying of

cancer, had grinned mirthlessly. For the past five years he had worked as a hit man, doing his job with reckless efficiency. Since he was dying, he had no fear of being killed by a bullet. And he was the one man who was not afraid of Tommy Cain, the one who always told Cain the truth. He'd said, "That's okay if you want a woman or cash. But some day you're gonna want something you can't take away from some guy, Tommy. What'll you do then?"

Cain thought of Zapello's question as he stripped out of his jacket, but only for a moment. He rarely bothered himself with philosophic speculation, preferring to deal with matters at hand. He undressed, showered, then threw himself on the bed for a nap. He went to sleep at once, like a cat, and slept for over an hour. When he awoke, he shaved, then put on a pair of gray Venetian dress slacks, a white silk dress shirt, and a paisley tie. He slipped into a silk maroon blazer, put on a pair of black Italian shoes, then padded out of the bedroom on the thick carpet.

Cain was an observant man, and he saw the note at once—a single sheet of paper affixed to the inside of the outside door with a slender, golden letter opener driven into the wood. Instinctively Cain looked around the room, and he moved swiftly to the rosewood desk beside the mauve couch. He slid open the left-hand drawer and took out a .32 automatic before going to the door. Carefully he wrenched out the letter opener and unfolded the note which was written in bold strokes:

Hey, Tommy, remember me—Ben Savage? We met at Dan Ross's office. I came by to talk a little—mostly about what we can do about your problem. You were sleeping so soundly, I hated to wake you up, so I'll drop in again some night. Don't bother to leave the key under the mat—I don't need it.

Oh, by the way, you'd better go down to the garage. I had

a package to give you, but since you were catching up on your shuteye, I left it in the trunk of Whitey's Lincoln. Key's on top of the left front tire. Catch you later, okay?

P.S. Your diamond cufflinks were on the table. I got worried that some cat burglar might come in and help himself, so I put them in the safe.

Your friend, Ben Savage

Cain wrenched his eyes away from the note, stuffed it into his pocket, and hurried to the bedroom. The small safe was behind a painting on the wall, and with quick, jerky movements he twirled the dial. When the door opened, he reached inside, pulled out something, and stood there staring at it. Two one-carat diamond cufflinks. They'd been on his table, right beside his bed, when he'd lain down for a nap.

The hair on the back of Cain's neck rose. He slammed the door of the safe shut and moved to the phone on the bedside table. His motions were choppy as he dialed the number, and he drummed his fingers nervously while he waited.

"Louie? Get here quick as you can."

Without waiting for a reply, he dialed the desk, and said at once, "Is Nelson still here? Get him to my room right now!"

He slammed the receiver down and walked back to the living room. His eyes were half-shut, and he lit a cigarette, then poured himself a stiff drink from a bottle at the bar. He was on his second cigarette when the doorbell rang, and he went at once to open it.

"Mr. Cain, you want to see me?"

"Yeah, come in." Cain stepped back, and the security man, a black-haired man with heavy shoulders, entered. Cain shut the door and turned to face him. "Somebody got into my apartment, Nelson."

The security man's eyes narrowed. He looked around quickly, taking in everything. "Anything missing, Mr. Cain?"

"I don't know—but what kind of security are you providing around here?"

"Nobody came through the front door, Mr. Cain—nobody I don't know."

Cain knew full well that Nelson was a competent man, but his anger was boiling over. "Don't tell me who came in or who didn't!" he grated. "I'm telling you somebody came in while I was asleep."

"How many keys do you have?"

"Two—and I keep both of them."

"We've got the best locks on the market, Mr. Cain. Guy don't have a key, he's going to have trouble opening this door—especially with that deadbolt lock."

Cain forced himself to calm down. He lit another cigarette, thought hard, then asked, "You know anybody named Ben Savage?"

"Savage? Don't know him."

"Medium height, well-built, black hair, hazel eyes."

Nelson shook his head. "Nobody like that's been in through the door on my shift."

"What about—?"

The doorbell rang, and Cain went to open it. "Come in, Louie."

"What's up?" Zapello's face was thin and pale, but his brown eyes were sharp.

"Somebody got in my place this afternoon," Cain repeated. He related what had happened, leaving out some of it. Finally Nelson said, "I'll go check with the cleaning people. Only way I can think of for anybody to get in without going through a checkpoint is through the trade entrance. I'll get back to you, Mr. Cain. Meanwhile, I'll have the lock on your door changed."

"Yeah, you do that, Nelson." Cain waited until the door

closed, then took the note out of his pocket. He handed it to Zapello, who read it carefully.

"Were the cufflinks in the safe?" he asked.

"Right in there, just like he said." Cain went to get another drink, then asked, "You realize what happened, Louie?"

Zapello nodded. "Sure. The guy gets into a full-security building, past every checkpoint. Then he opens a door with a tough lock *and* a deadbolt. He comes into your bedroom, takes your cufflinks, finds the safe, opens it, then writes you a note."

Cain's forehead was glossy with sweat, despite the air-conditioning. "He could have offed me, Louie."

"Sure he could." Zapello studied the note, then asked in a bemused half-whisper, "Wonder why he didn't?"

"Come on," Cain snapped. "Let's go see what's in the Lincoln."

The two men rode down in the elevator, hurried down the corridor, then passed through a door that opened into the garage. "He could have come through here," Zapello nodded.

"TV camera up there," Cain pointed out. "Nelson would have to look him over and open the door from the front." He led the way down a line of cars, then stopped. "That the car Whitey and Moon drive?"

Zapello moved closer to the big Lincoln, then nodded. "That's it." He moved to the front of the car, stooped over, and came up with the key. "Stay back, Tommy," he ordered as he walked to the trunk and inserted the key. "Might be a bomb."

"Maybe we ought to get help?"

A humorous light touched the gunman's austere face. "Want me to call the police?"

Cain stared at Zapello, then waved his hand. "Open it up. If Savage wanted to waste me, he had a good enough chance."

Zapello turned the key and stepped back quickly, a gun

appearing in his hand. He peered inside, then put the gun away.

"What is it?" Cain stepped closer for a look, then cursed. He saw two men bound hand and foot with duct tape. The silver tape covered their mouths, and their eyes blinked in the sudden light.

"Let me cut them out of it, Tommy." Zapello produced a wicked-looking knife with a five-inch blade and leaned forward, slicing the tape. As he snapped the knife shut, Cain reached down and half pulled Whitey Harms out of his cramped position. Harms tried to help, but his limbs were numb, and he sprawled on the ground.

Tommy Cain reached out and ripped the tape from Harms' mouth. "All right—what's the story?"

But the mouth of Harms was too dry for speech. Mazurki was floundering in the trunk, and it was several minutes before Cain could get anything from either of them. Zapello produced a small, silver flask of brandy from his pocket, and the shock of the alcohol finally freed the throat of Whitey Harms.

"Let's have it, Whitey," Zapello rasped. "How'd Savage get to you?"

Harms told the story, trying to make it sound better than it was, but Cain said in disgust, "So you had Savage between you with a gun on him, and he kicked the daylights out of Moon, took your gun away, and made you spill your guts!"

"We didn't say nothing, Mr. Cain!" Whitey protested.

"That's right," Mazurki nodded. "Me and Whitey—we don't sing."

"You'd sell your own mother!" Cain snarled. "He got something out of you—now let's have it! If you lie to me, I'll let Louie take you for a walk down to the river."

The threat was effective, and the two at once began to

protest, but in the end Cain was convinced that the pair had not given away anything vital.

"All right, you two get out of town."

"But—where to?"

Cain took his money roll out, peeled off a few bills, and handed them to Harms. "Go to Baton Rouge and stay with Jimmy Buchannon—and don't leave any forwarding address!"

"Aw, we wouldn't do that, Boss!" Mazurki protested. "Besides, that guy caught me off guard. I can take him!"

"You couldn't take my grandmother!" Cain snapped. "Now get out!"

Louie Zapello tossed the car key to Harms, who dropped it nervously. As Harms picked it up, Zapello said, "Better hide good. This Savage seems to be handy at things."

Cain led the way back to his apartment, and Zapello went to pour himself a drink.

"You're not supposed to drink, Louie," Cain observed mildly.

"Going to report me to AA?"

"You really ought to take care of yourself."

"What for?" Zapello downed the liquor as if it were spring water, poured more, then said, "Savage, huh?" He sipped at the drink, then suddenly turned to face Cain. "Want some advice, Tommy?"

"From you? Always, Louie."

"Buy him off."

Cain stared at Zapello's cadaverous face. He valued the opinion of few men, but Louie was special. He was the only friend left. The rest were dead or in jail.

"He's pretty slick, isn't he, Louie?" Cain finally said slowly. He paced the floor, thinking hard, then stopped and gave Zapello an odd look. "No. Won't work."

"Why not, Tommy?"

"I know faces pretty good, Louie," Cain said. "I saw this guy only once, in Ross's office, but I knew as soon as I saw him he was bad medicine. He didn't say much—but I can tell. He's one of the stubborn ones." Cain laid his hand on Zapello's thin shoulder, adding, "He's like you, Louie. You can't be bought—and this guy is the same."

Zapello stared at Cain for a long moment. "Well, if he can't be bought, that kind of cuts the options down, don't it, Tommy?"

"He's a tough one, Louie. Get him out hard and quick. Don't waste your time on anything else. He didn't get much out of Whitey and Moon, but he'll keep on turning over boards until he gets what he wants."

Zapello stood there, his thin face turned toward his friend. He was a dead man and knew it. Every day was a coin out of a quickly dwindling pile. He had only one loyalty—and that was to Tommy Cain.

"I'll take him out, Tommy," he promised quietly. He left the room without another word. Cain stared at the door when it closed, disturbed by the hole where Savage had driven the letter opener into it.

"Do it, Louie!" he whispered. "Do it quick!"

11

Sixkiller
Makes an Offer

Life had become an arid desert for Dani, with the oasis mostly out of sight. The pressure from the Tommy Cain affair came trooping into her mind the moment she awoke and lurked around in dark corners of her subconscious all day as she went through the routine of working and living. When she closed her eyes at night for sleep, it shouted so loudly that she sometimes had to get out of bed to exorcise the thing.

Sunday night was particularly bad. She fought with Cain all night, his face drifting in and out of her mind for most of the night, and when she crawled out of bed at the ring of her alarm on Monday morning, she felt like a used dishrag. Only sheer willpower got her out of bed at all, for nothing seemed so inviting as to lie back and fall into unconsciousness.

Dani stripped off her nightgown, marched to the shower, and turned the cold water on full force. Gritting her teeth, she stepped into the stinging spray, endured it until the mental cobwebs were driven away, then dried off and plucked a new Leslie Fay dress from her closet. It was a black and white Glen plaid with long sleeves and black buttons bearing a gold crest. She slipped into it and noticed it did not fit as snugly as it had the last time she'd worn it. As she put on her makeup, she saw that her cheeks were slightly hollow and that fine lines were etched around the edges of her eyes and the corners of her lips.

Dani was not a woman who lived for her looks. As a young girl, she had experienced that typical adolescent stage of despair, when all seems hopeless. She had been taller than most girls her age and had developed a stoop from trying to look shorter. She had wept on her mother's shoulder, calling herself a "giant" and moaning that no boy would ever ask her out. To make matters worse, she had developed a mild case of acne when she was fourteen. Even now she recalled vividly the anguish this condition had caused her. Her father had finally said, after countless trips to the dermatologist, "Dani, it's just part of growing up. It'll pass, but I know that's no help right now."

The acne *had* passed, and she had gradually come to regard her height as an asset. She had passed out of the coltish stage into young womanhood, and despite a few forays into high fashion, she had finally learned to accept herself more or less as she was. Now, as she applied a plum-colored Clinique lipstick, she thought suddenly of the Basic Youth Conflict Institute that had changed her life.

In her mind she could hear Bill Gothard, the speaker, ask, "How many of you, when you look in the mirror, see anything you'd like to change?" Dani smiled as she traced the corners of her lips, thinking of how she'd cried out in her spirit, *Anything? I'd change everything!*

But then Gothard had shaken her ideas of beauty to the foundation. He'd said, "If you want to change something, you're saying, 'God, you've done a poor job on me! I want to take over your job and make myself into something *I* want.'"

It had taken a while, but Dani had grown to see the wisdom of that teaching. Now, looking into her mirror, she remarked, "Well, Dani Ross, you'll never decorate the cover of *Vogue*." The face she contemplated was too square and too strong for that world. The eyes were too far apart, the mouth too wide, the figure a bit too full for current tastes.

With a wry smile, she mused, "Well, so much for a career in the movies. Let us then be up and doing—just a hard-working PI."

Fully dressed, she moved over to the cordovan Lane recliner, sank down, and picked up her Bible from the table. For half an hour she sat there, sometimes reading, sometimes just letting the words soak in. The Bible was open to Proverbs, and as the age-old wisdom came off the page and into her mind, she prayed for the essence of the Book to take root in her spirit.

When Dani had first become a Christian, she had tackled Bible study the way she approached any other task—all set to master it by sheer determination. She had become a CPA by sheer intelligence and will, and it seemed logical to her that she could become a good Christian the same way.

It took her a while to realize that the Bible just could not be mastered that way. What happened was that she memorized huge chunks of Scripture, absorbed an enormous amount of background about the Bible, and could rattle off verses appropriate for any situation. She was the joy of her Sunday school teachers, for she always went beyond mastering the lesson; she also searched through commentaries for comments on the text by Bible scholars. The trouble was—all was in her head, not in her heart.

She had discovered this largely through the influence of a young woman she met while working in the attorney general's office in Tennessee. Her name was Ginny Tallifero, and Dani had met her in a sharing group that gathered in the home of one of the elders of her church. It took some time for Dani to get to know Ginny, for she was a shy young woman who rarely spoke. But the leader had asked for volunteers to minister at the jail. He had placed Dani in charge, saying, "You're the most mature of the group, Dani. You know more about the Bible, and you've got confidence. I want you to take Ginny with you. She's so shy, and I think this might help bring her out."

It hadn't worked that way, not at all. Dani, so calm and capable and assured, had gone blank when confronted with the hard faces of the inmates. She had stuttered, stammered, and made a hash out of the whole visit. It had been Ginny who'd been able to smile and begin to reach out to the hardeyed women. Her knowledge of Scripture had been limited, but what little she knew was real in her. Soon it had been Dani who was the pupil, learning from Ginny how to approach the prisoners.

Finally she had asked, "Ginny, you do so well with the inmates. How do you know so quickly which way to go with them? How do you make them like you?"

Ginny had answered, "Oh, Dani, I don't know! I just love them, I guess. And when they have a need, I ask God, and he tells me what to say."

"He actually talks to you?"

"Oh, no! Not like that, Dani." Ginny had thought hard, then finally ventured, "I'm not much of a student. You know a thousand times more than I do about the Bible. What I do is read the Scripture, and when part of it seems to be interesting, I think about it all the time. I guess you'd say I meditate on it. At work or wherever I am, I just think on it. And then, when I need something to help somebody, one of those things will come to my mind, and I just share it."

It had been a life-changing lesson for Dani, and she had gone on to learn from experience that meditation on the Scripture was the most effective way to let God speak to her. She'd tried to explain it to Luke once: "You know a cow has several stomachs? What she does is just chomp the grass and it goes into one of her stomachs. It's not chewed, but it's inside her. Then later you see the cow lying down, chewing and chewing. She brings up the unchewed grass from one of her stomachs and chews it until it's ready to be digested. Well, I sometimes listen to a sermon, and part of it goes into me, but I don't understand it. Then I meditate on the Scripture as I go through the day—and usually God lets me learn something from him."

Dani's habit of meditating on Scripture had served her well for years—but the trouble with Cain had shaken her more deeply than any trouble that had come into her life. She had never been a fearful woman, but in recent days, fear had come to live in her. Now, as she read her Bible and meditated, she asked God to show her how to be rid of the fear. After a time, a thought arose in her mind, so clearly that it startled her: *Your problem is not fear, but anger and hatred.*

Whether the words came from God or from her own mind, Dani could not decide, but the thought troubled her. She finally closed the Bible, prayed for a short time, then got up and left her room.

It was too early for anyone else to be up, so she left the house and got into her car. When she turned the key, all she heard was a faint groan as the engine made one feeble attempt to start, then died.

"Oh, fine! A dead battery! That's just what I need." She thought suddenly of one of the verses she had just read: *In everything give thanks, for this is the will of God concerning you in Christ Jesus.*

A wry smile turned up the corners of her mouth, and she said tartly, "Well, thank you, Lord, for this dead battery." She got out of her car and looked in her father's Blazer, but could not find the jumper cables. Her brother's car, a ten-year-old Ford, was parked beside the house. Dani knew Rob kept jumper cables as standard equipment, and she knew also that he kept a spare key wired underneath his license plate. He was always losing his key, or locking it inside, so he used it pretty often.

Dani had to get on her knees to get the key from beneath the plate and stared with disgust at the mess she'd made of her pantyhose, but there was no help for it. She unlocked the trunk, took the cables out, then unlocked the door and slid into the seat. As she did, she saw something white in the crease between the seat and the back. She picked it up to keep from sitting on it, then blinked violently when she saw what she was holding.

It was a small glassine packet, no more than two inches square, filled with white powder.

Cocaine!

There was little chance of a mistake. Dani had seen the stuff often while working for the attorney general in Tennessee, and on more than one case in New Orleans she had been there when the police had confiscated drugs. Sixkiller had once shown her a black garbage bag filled with such envelopes, saying, "Coke. This bag holds enough to buy a mansion in the Garden District, Dani."

Numbly, Dani stared at the small object, her mind rebelling against all it meant. She was well aware that, Miami aside, there was no city in the country where a hit cost less. This was because dealers found it relatively safe to do business in the Crescent City. The interplay between the legal and the illegal is as old as the Black Hand, the Mafia's granddaddy, founded in New Orleans a hundred years and more ago. People move back and forth across the line the way people move across a border in Western Europe nowadays. She knew some of the street language for drugs—agates, apples, artillery (for injection paraphernalia), bindles, Boy (heroin). But the terms changed constantly, so unless you were on the street or worked in vice, you were always behind.

And she had seen some of the horrors of the drug world. Stiff bodies with staring eyes—dead of an overdose. One man who'd clawed his own eyes out under the influence of LSD. Women turned to living skeletons by living on coke instead of food.

And now it was her baby brother, Rob, who was into the stuff.

The thought sickened her, and she began to tremble. Her first impulse was to storm into his bedroom, screaming at him, her fear laced with anger: *How could he do this to us?* And she knew that this was wrong, though the relatives of most addicts would understand. The addict doesn't go down alone, but drags his family and friends along as he plunges into the horrors of the drug world.

Dani tried to pray, and became aware that she had to talk to somebody. She sorted out the possibilities as she went through the process of jump-starting her Cougar. She thought of her parents, but they had all they could handle. Finally she decided to go to Luke.

She got the car started, carefully locked Rob's Ford, then left the driveway. She knew that Luke would come on duty at 7:45, but she dialed his home number from her car phone.

"Hello?"

"Luke, this is Dani. Can you meet me?"

"What's wrong?"

"I can't talk on the phone. Can I come to your place?"

"Sure. I'll put the coffee on."

Sixkiller's house was located on a cul-de-sac just east of Bayou St. John, a long finger of water that bore off from Lake Pontchartrain to form the eastern boundary of City Park. Some called it the Cultural Corridor, for it contained the New Orleans Museum of Art, Storyland, and the Botanical Garden—and stood near two colleges, Dillard University and Delgado College.

Dani crossed the Causeway, took a left on Zachary Taylor Drive, then exited on St. Bernard Street. Sixkiller had found the house by accident while investigating a murder. It was the only house on Jade Street, a three-bedroom traditional hidden by a stand of oak trees. Dani pulled up, cut the engine, and climbed out as Sixkiller appeared to greet her.

"Coffee's ready," he said, then impulsively put his arm around her and kissed her cheek. "You smell better than the coffee," he smiled. "Come on in."

He sat her down at a solid oak table in the country kitchen, poured coffee into two mugs, then sat down himself. He said nothing, his quick black eyes studying her.

Dani pulled the glassine envelope from her purse and put it down on the table. "I found this in Rob's car."

Sixkiller picked up the envelope, studied it carefully, then opened it and, wetting the tip of his finger, collected some of the white dust. He tasted it, then looked at her.

"Cocaine—high grade," he murmured.

"I thought so."

Sixkiller sipped his coffee, noting the lines of strain on Dani's face. *All this is getting her down,* he thought. *She can't handle much more than this.* "Any idea where's he's getting the stuff?" he asked, keeping his voice casual.

"That girl!" Dani's nostrils flared, and the words came out hard and flat. "It has to be her—the one we met in the restaurant."

"Stormy Carr?"

"Yes. Rob was fine until he met her." Dani rose suddenly and went to the window where she stared out at a squirrel marching across a power line with his jaws stuffed. She stood there watching him as he came to earth, industriously dug a hole, put whatever he had into it, then covered it up. "He'll never remember where he put those nuts next winter," she murmured.

Luke came to stand behind her and on impulse pulled her around. She tried to turn her head away, to pull away from him, but he held her, studying her face. Pulling a fine linen handkerchief from his pocket, he removed the tears that wet her cheeks, then put his arms around her and held her tightly.

At first Dani resisted, as she always did when someone violated her sense of independence. She had been that way even as a child, and many times she had suffered needlessly rather than run to her father or mother with her problems. As she blossomed into young womanhood, she had kept the wall around herself, learning how to cover up her fears and insecurities. Now that she was a mature woman, it seemed that she still had not learned to receive help.

As Luke held her, she suddenly began to sob, and she thought of something her father had said to her once—something about learning to receive help.

"It's more blessed to give than it is to receive, Dani," he had remarked when she had been through a hard time and was handling it, as usual, by herself. She'd stared at him, and he'd explained, "Strong people like to give help. It makes them feel stronger—and they hate to ask for help because that's a weakness." He'd come to put his arm around her, adding, "You need to learn, daughter, to receive. It's hard, because you've got a mule-stubborn spirit. Got it from me, I guess. But no matter how strong you are, you're not strong enough to bear all that life's going to pile on you."

Dani remembered how she'd listened to her father then, but she remembered also that she'd resisted his advice.

The arms of Luke Sixkiller were strong, and relief washed over her as she leaned against him, aware not only of his physical strength, but of the forcefulness of his spirit. She realized that this was the real reason she had come to him, and it was like coming out of a raging, storm-tossed sea into a quiet, placid harbor.

Then Luke said, "I'm glad you came to me, Dani." He drew back and looked into her eyes. "I'd like to be the one you always come to when you get hurt."

Dani blinked her eyes, knowing that Luke was offering more than a casual willingness to be of help. She had been engaged once, and it had ended badly, so she had shut an invisible door on that part of her life. Maybe somewhere down the way she would think again of such things—but not now. At least, that was the way she'd handled it in the past. More than one man had come knocking at her door with a serious offer in his eyes, if not on his lips, but she had become adept at fending off such overtures.

Ben Savage had said once, "You're going to be the best-looking old maid in New Orleans, Boss. Too bad you're going to waste all that woman on nothing."

Dani had resented Ben's statement, but had ignored it rather than debate him. Now, however, she felt a strange weakness come over her. Brought on by the strain, no doubt, but there was also something about the feel of Luke's arms around her. . . .

Sixkiller sensed the struggle his words had set off in her and said gently, "Don't try to solve everything with your mind, Dani. Some things just can't be handled that way—and that includes the way of a man and a woman, I think."

When she didn't answer, he leaned forward and deliberately put his lips on hers. She could have turned her head, or moved away from him. But something in her desired the kiss, and when their lips met she felt a sudden release—a swelling fullness that had been locked in some dark place in her heart. Now she found herself pulling his head closer. He was, somehow, rough and gentle at the same time, his arms tightening, the force of his lips crushing hers, and yet there was a care in his manner, as if he were holding a rare and delicate object that might easily be broken.

Time seemed to stop, and Dani clung to him almost desperately, seeking to draw from his touch relief from the fears that had been haunting her. As long as his powerful arms were holding her tightly and his lips were on hers, the specters seemed faint and dim.

Finally, she drew back, shaken so that her voice was reedy and thin. "Luke, I—I don't know—"

She faltered, and Sixkiller reached out and brushed her cheek tenderly with his hard hand. "I know, Dani." He smiled then, his tough face made gentle by the curve of his lips. "You're the only one for me, Dani. I'd like to take care of you for the rest of your life."

Dani dropped her head, her mind fluttering. Finally she raised her eyes and whispered, "Luke—I'm so confused. It would be so easy to say yes." She stood there, struggling to put into words the things that were flying through her mind. She was a woman of logic, and she hated it when logic failed—as it did now. The touch of his hands made it even harder for her to think, so she moved away from him, returning to stare out the window. She stood there struggling to contain the emotions that had broken out of their long-buried stronghold. Then she finally turned to say, "Luke, thank you. Any woman would be privileged to have a man like you."

Sixkiller grew serious, his lips drawing tightly down. "Thanks—but no thanks. Is that it, Dani?"

"Oh, don't put it that way!" Dani cried. "You don't know how easy it would be for me to just let you take over my problems, Luke! But I'd never know if it was right—if maybe this was my test, and I was too afraid to stand up to it." She mustered a smile, then came to put her hands on his shoulders. "Luke, don't force me to make a decision. I can't! Not now!"

Sixkiller took her hands, held them tightly, then nodded. "Sure." Then he came up with a grin, adding, "Don't think you've heard the last of this. I'm an awful pest when I want something."

Dani nodded, relieved by the release he was offering her. "Better be careful," she warned. "I might take you up on it. Then you'd have to spend the rest of your life trying to make a good, docile wife out of me."

They both laughed then, somewhat shakily, for both had been stirred by the kiss. "I've got to go to work," she said. "Why don't we—"

The phone rang, and Sixkiller said, "Just a minute—" He went to the phone and picked up the receiver. "Sixkiller."

Dani was watching idly as he listened to the caller, but something came to his face—shock or anger, perhaps both. "What do the medics say?" He listened carefully, his face fixed, then said, "I'll be there." He turned to Dani and said, "Bad news."

Dani stared at him, her heart seeming to miss several beats.

She could not bring herself to ask. Images of her father and mother, then of Allison and Rob swept through her mind. "Who is it, Luke?"

Sixkiller said, "It's Ben. He's been shot."

Dani had not even thought of Savage, so certain she was that it was one of her family. "Is it bad?"

"Don't know," Sixkiller said. "He's in Sacre Coeur. Come on, we'll go find out." He disappeared into his bedroom and returned at once, strapping on his shoulder harness, then slipping a gray jacket over it. He took her arm, starting her toward the door.

Dani moved uncertainly, and Luke said when they were outside, "We'll take your car. I'll drive."

They got in, and when they were halfway to the hospital, Dani said, "If he dies—"

Sixkiller cast a covert glance at her, noting the set tension in her cheek. "He's alive. Probably be all right."

Dani gave him one of the hardest stares he'd ever seen from her—and when she spoke again, there was a hard, adamant edge to her voice: "If he dies, Luke, I'll put Tommy Cain in the electric chair—no matter what I have to do to get him there!"

12

Ben Goes Home

Yellow sunlight splashed cheerfully from a pastel blue sky as Sixkiller pulled up to Sacre Coeur Hospital. As Dani left the car, a mockingbird perched on a branch of an azalea bush puffed his chest out and anthemed the day. For one moment Dani's thoughts were wrenched away from Ben Savage, and the thought came to her that no matter how bad things were, mockingbirds still sang their songs—the world still went on.

As they entered the building and Sixkiller spoke to the receptionist, Dani thought of how often she was like the mockingbird, making happy noises in the presence of those who were hurting. *No other way to live, is there? You can't go around wearing black and pulling a long face, can you? You never know what's going on inside the person you pass—maybe they've just lost their child to a dreadful disease . . . or been laid off from the only job they know . . . or found out a friend has been shot . . .*

Sixkiller came back, nodding toward the elevator. "Second

floor, room 232." As they waited for the elevator, he looked around the lobby. "Oldest hospital in New Orleans," he remarked. "Someone told me the nuns put up tents for the wounded when Bienville was storming around the swamps, trying to find out what it was he'd claimed for France."

"Is it a good hospital?"

"Yeah. Looks funny, with all the old crucifixes and holy pictures on the wall, but the equipment is first class, state of the art." The door slid open, and he added as they turned left and walked down the wide corridor, "The help is good, too. Most of the interns come in from the LSU and Tulane medical schools—all tough and hard-nosed, the way fresh interns get. All ready for gunshots and stabs and dope and car crashes and the rest of the crud we've built for ourselves since we whipped yellow fever and malaria."

"They look so young!" Dani exclaimed, taking in the faces of the interns who were moving down the hall dressed in white and stethoscopes. "Maybe I'm getting old."

"Know what you mean," Sixkiller nodded. "A guy gets sick, he has to put his life in the hands of a snub-nosed kid he wouldn't trust to change the points in his car from the looks of him." He stopped at the nurses' station and showed his badge to the almost comically small nun who stared at it calmly. "How's Savage doing?" he asked.

"The doctor's just left," she replied. "Let me see if I can get her. You can use the waiting room." She led them to a very small room just to the left of the station, then marched off down the hall.

Dani could not sit down. There was no window in the room, so she moved to one wall and stared at the picture of Jesus with his hands outstretched. It was a very old picture. She stared at it silently, and Sixkiller came to stand beside her. "Doesn't look like the way you think of him," he remarked.

"None of the pictures do."

"Mistake to try it, I think." Sixkiller glared at the picture, then shook his head. "Look how pale he is. Half a day under that sun in Judea would cook him."

Dani's mind was on Ben, but she welcomed the diversion. "Yes, and did you ever see a carpenter as *frail* as that man? All the carpenters I've ever seen were rough men, most of them missing a finger or two. Jesus was an outdoor man; the one there looks like a shoe clerk or a poet."

"Be better if they didn't even try to paint Jesus, I think."

Dani had a sudden memory. "I read about a big church in Chicago that hired a world-famous artist to paint a picture of the Lord. He agreed, but insisted that he'd have to be free to paint Jesus without any restrictions. And he did."

"What was it like—the painting?"

"It was a portrait of Jesus in a three-piece business suit. The face was about like most paintings of Jesus, but the suit threw the leaders into a tizzy."

"I'll bet!" Sixkiller grinned broadly. "Know what? If I was a painter, I'd paint him close as I could to what he'd be like if he came today instead of two thousand years ago." He narrowed his eyes in thought, then added, "I'd have him wearing Wranglers—maybe cutoffs—an old T-shirt and a pair of Nikes."

Dani laughed, amused despite her fears. "You crazy cop!"

"No, it'd be a lot closer to truth than this one," Sixkiller insisted. "I haven't been a Christian for very long, but I've seen some people who worship some kind of an—an *image*, not the real Jesus. They've got him stuck back in one spot of time, and it's like there's something *spiritual* about the sandals and togas."

"Hard to think of Jesus riding a Honda, isn't it?" Dani smiled. "It's an anachronism."

"And besides that, it's like something in the wrong time," Sixkiller deadpanned, then shook his head, a thoughtful expression in his dark eyes. "But if God had sent Jesus to die in our time, I guess he'd have ridden a Honda—or maybe a secondhand bicycle."

"He was for all time," Dani mused, then turned at the sound of a door opening.

"Lieutenant Sixkiller?" The doctor was a slim woman of thirty, with large, brown eyes and short, curly hair. "I'm Dr. Lane."

"Glad to meet you, Doc," Sixkiller nodded. "This is Danielle Ross."

"Are you a relative, Miss Ross?"

"Why, no," Dani answered. "Mr. Savage is one of my operatives—Ross Investigations."

Dr. Lane gave her an interested glance. "You're a detective?" She smiled, two dimples appearing in her cheeks. "I didn't know they came in such an attractive package."

Dani ignored the compliment, asking, "Doctor, how is he?"

Dr. Lane, noting the strain on Dani's face, said quickly, "He's going to be all right." Seeing relief wash over Dani's face, she added, "It was one of those injuries that looked very bad at first, but it's not nearly as serious as I thought when he was brought in."

"Where'd he get it, Doc?" Sixkiller demanded.

"In the back." Dr. Lane took a small brown envelope out of the pocket of her white jacket and handed it to the policeman. "This is the bullet."

Sixkiller shook the slug out, looked at it carefully, then replaced it in the envelope and pocketed it. "Handgun—a .38 would be my guess."

"When I saw the location of the wound," Dr. Lane said, "I thought it was fatal. It was on his left side, and if he'd been standing squarely, the bullet would have gone right to the heart." She shook her head, curls bouncing, and added, "He must have turned his body just as the bullet was fired, and it's my guess he ducked at the same time. The bullet followed a path up and to the left. It tore up some muscle and cracked a bone in his left shoulder."

"He going to have any permanent damage?" Sixkiller asked.

"No, I don't think so. But he'll be very sore for a while, and I'll probably want him to keep his left arm in a restraint for a time after he's released."

"Thank God!"

The words issued from Dani's lips, and she discovered that her knees were weak. She saw that both Luke and Dr. Lane were watching her. "Can we see him?" she asked quickly to cover her slip.

"Yes. I just left his room. Come along." She led the way down the hall and entered room 232 without knocking. "Visitors, Mr. Savage," she said, as they all trooped into the room.

Savage lay flat on his back, staring at a television mounted high on the wall. The voices of Kermit the Frog and Miss Piggy filled the room. When the wounded man turned his head, he smiled faintly and said, "Good stuff here. Want to watch?"

The sight of Ben lying on the bed, his face pale and his lips taut with pain, brought a sudden stab of pain to Dani. To cover it, she moved to the bed, crossed her arms in front of her, then shook her head. "Some people will do anything to get out of working!"

A faint gleam of humor flickered in Savage's hazel eyes. "Thought I'd see how long it'd take the agency to fall apart without me."

Sixkiller came to stand beside Dani. "Hear they got all the leaks plugged. You feeling okay?"

"Peachy."

"Yeah, I bet! Nothing like a hot .38 slug plowing through your back to perk a fellow up. How'd it happen?"

Dr. Lane said, "I gave him a shot for the pain. He'll be getting fuzzy pretty soon."

"I don't think we'll be able to tell the difference," Sixkiller jibed. "How long you going to keep him here?"

"About a week."

Savage shook his head. "It won't take that long."

Dr. Lane lifted an exquisitely formed eyebrow. "No? We'll see about that."

She turned and walked from the room. Savage glared after her. "I'll have her eating out of my hand in two days." He nodded at the chairs. "Sit down."

"We wouldn't want you to miss *The Muppet Show*," Sixkiller joked. But the two of them sat down, and he took a pad and pen from his pocket. "Just a few questions, Mr. Savage. We just want to get the facts." He nodded sagely. "Saw the cop on *Dragnet* do that. Now, when did you first suspect you had a problem?"

"When the slug knocked me down," Savage said gloomily. "I knew right off I was in trouble."

"Who did it, Ben?" Dani leaned forward, her lips drawn tightly together.

Savage shook his head. "I didn't get a look at him—but I've got a pretty good idea he gets his employment benefits from Tommy Cain."

"Cain!"

"Yeah, I think so." A slight look of embarrassment crossed Savage's face, and he glanced at Sixkiller in a peculiar way. "I guess I kind of ran around you a little bit, Luke."

"Not the first time. What'd you do? Rattle Tommy's chain?"

"Yeah. I looked up his two leg-breakers and had a talk with them."

"Moon and Whitey?" Sixkiller shot a quick glance at Savage. "Tell me about it." He listened as Ben gave the essence of his encounter with the two hoods and his visit to Cain's apartment, then leaned back with a hard glint in his ebony eyes. "So you roughed up Cain's pet gorillas and sent word to him that you were on his trail. Great!"

"Ben, you shouldn't have done that," Dani protested.

"Things weren't moving," Savage shrugged, and the movement brought a gasp of pain from him. The medication was taking effect, and he had to frame his words carefully. "Cain only understands one thing. I want him to feel the weight of mortality."

"How'd you get shot?" Sixkiller asked.

"Stupidity," Savage responded. "I figured Cain would send somebody—but he moved faster than I expected. Something to keep in mind. I was going into my apartment, and he came out from someplace. Let me have it as I was turning the key in the door. I heard him breathing and started to turn, but I didn't make it." His lips tightened, and he added, "He's pretty cocky. Didn't take a second shot."

"Cain's pretty swift," Sixkiller agreed.

"You really did that, Ben? Broke into his apartment while he was asleep?"

"Stood right over him while he was all tucked in."

"You think about offing him?" Sixkiller inquired.

Savage's eyelids were getting heavy. "Sure I did."

"Glad you didn't," Sixkiller said. "It's against the law."

Savage opened his eyes, glanced at Dani, then said in a blurred voice, "Don't worry, Boss. Soon as I get out of here, I'll—take care—"

He dropped off abruptly, and Sixkiller said, "Guess we'd better go."

When they reached the nurses' station, Sixkiller stopped long enough to say to the small nun, "Sister, I'm going to put a man here to watch Mr. Savage. Can you fit him out with one of these intern outfits?"

"Yes." She had a birdlike expression, alert and watchful. "Do you think there'll be trouble, Lieutenant?"

"Just a precaution."

When they had found her car and were driving away from the hospital, Dani asked, "What will you do, Luke?"

"About Ben or about Rob?"

"Both of them. It's all one thing, isn't it?"

"Probably. Well—first I'll pick up Harms and Mazurki. I'll talk to the captain of vice and see if he can put a man on Rob—no, wait, that won't do!"

"Why not?"

"Because Rob's into the thing, and he might be the one to get busted."

"Probably what Cain's got on his mind," Dani nodded, a bitter twist to her lips. "Let me take care of that. I'll put an operative on Rob."

"That'd be better. If you get anything, come to me." He drove without speaking until they reached his house. He didn't shut the engine off, but turned to her. "You all right?"

Dani gave him a smile, then put her hand on his cheek. "Thanks, Luke. I—I needed you."

"Sixkiller's Care for Distraught Women—we never close," he said. Then he got out, saying, "Call me."

Dani drove away, and as Luke watched the Cougar make a turn that took it out of view, he shook his head. "Would have solved a lot of problems if Ben had stopped Cain's clock." But the thought displeased him, and he shook it off as he got into his car.

The small nun was named Sister Veronica, and Savage came to know that she was the best the hospital had to offer. No bigger than a cricket, she handled him as if he were filled with Styrofoam instead of solid flesh and bone. The younger nurses and aides tried to be careful when they changed his bandage or bathed him, but somehow Sister Veronica's firm movements were less painful than their attempts to be gentle.

She came in on the third day of his stay, her eyes bright as usual, and asked, "Are we ready for our bath now?"

Boredom and lack of activity made Savage irritable, and he stared at her. "Are we bathing together?"

His remark failed to shock the diminutive nun, who had heard far worse in the emergency room. She smiled sweetly, then proceeded to scrub his face and upper body. "What is that, lye soap?" he demanded.

Ignoring his question, Sister Veronica gave him a critical look. "You need a haircut, a shampoo, and a shave."

Savage stared at her in alarm. "The haircut can wait. And I can shave myself."

"Don't be stubborn, Mr. Savage. You need to learn how to receive." She moved to the small table, pulled out a kit, then returned to the bed. Taking out a small can of Colgate shaving cream, she uncapped it and filled her palm. As she layered his face, she asked, "Have you always been a detective?"

"No one is born a cop," he answered, eyeing her cautiously as she picked up the small disposable safety razor. "Have you ever shaved a man before?"

"Dead and alive," she answered calmly.

"Dead? You've shaved a dead man?"

"Many times—in Calcutta. I worked with Mother Teresa for

three years. The men we took in off the street were not able to help themselves, so I shaved them. Sometimes after they died."

Savage stared at her with a new respect as she raked the whiskers off his cheek with firm competence. "Pretty rough work, wasn't it? Got pretty dirty sometimes?" She made no answer, moving the razor slowly around his jawline. "I wouldn't do that for a million dollars."

Sister Veronica removed the razor, swished it in the basin of water, then looked him in the eye. "Neither would I, Mr. Savage."

Savage was rebuked by her reply and sat there silently until she finished. As she was wiping his face off with a damp cloth, the door opened. Dr. Lane came in, accompanied by Dan Ross.

"Good morning, Mr. Savage," the doctor said cheerfully. "You're lucky to get Sister Veronica. She's the best barber here." A smile pulled the corners of her lips upward, and she added, "When some of the less experienced nurses and aides try it, I have to come in and do stitches."

"Better than most barbers," Savage nodded. "Thanks, Sister. You ever want anybody beat up, call on me." A glint of humor came to his eyes, and he announced as Sister Veronica prepared to leave the room, "I've decided to let you—" He paused dramatically until she turned and waited curiously. "I've decided to let you—pray for me!" he ended triumphantly.

Sister Veronica said quietly, "I haven't waited for your permission."

As the small nun left the room, Savage glared after her, then turned his glance toward Dr. Lane. "That woman drives me crazy! I've tried every way I know to get her goat—and she hasn't even *got* a goat."

"Higher class folks than you run with, Ben," Dan Ross grinned. "How are you feeling?"

"Good enough to go home."

Dr. Lane gave him a cryptic stare, then said, "Let's take a look at that wound." She removed the old bandage, probed at Savage for a time, then changed the dressing. "You can put your gown on now," she said.

Savage shoved his arms into the gown and grunted, "Well, what about it?"

"Mr. Ross wants to take you home with him," Dr. Lane said. "It's a little too early, but he says he's got three women to wait on you—so I've agreed."

Savage grew alert, his eyes brightening at once. "Get my pants," he commanded.

"Not just yet," Dr. Lane admonished, putting a hand on his chest. "I've got a few little things I want understood before I sign you out—"

Ben listened impatiently as she ran over the do's and the don'ts, then nodded, "Sure, Doc—scout's honor."

"Were you a scout?" Dr. Lane asked.

"No."

"I was," Dan Ross nodded emphatically. "Eagle scout. I'll see he behaves himself, Dr. Lane."

"Very well, I'll get your release. But no walking to the car. I'll send someone with a wheelchair."

Savage started to protest, but one look at the expression on the doctor's face changed his mind. "Why, sure, Doc. And thanks for all you've done. I'm going to recommend you to all the people I shoot from now on."

His breezy manner amused Dr. Lane, but she frowned, saying, "I take it someone is trying to kill you. You'll be more vulnerable in a private home than here."

"Well, they can't kill me but once, can they, Doc?" Savage put his hand out and took hers firmly. "No kidding—thanks a lot."

"Just don't come back with another bullet."

Two hours later Savage was in the guest room of the Ross home. There'd been no wheelchair, but Ellen and Allison had practically carried him in, one on each side. They'd tried to put him to bed, but he'd held out for a time in the rocker. Now, since the women had gone to fix something to eat, he talked with Dan Ross.

"I ought to be paying rent here, Dan," he said, looking around the room. "Every time I get hurt, I come running here like a whipped puppy." It was true that Savage had been injured the past year, badly beaten by an assailant at a rodeo in Texas. Dani had come to his rescue and hauled him to her home, where Ellen had taken care of him.

Dan Ross was standing at the window, watching the sun go down. He turned and came to sit in the recliner against the wall. His face, Savage noted, was thinner than the last time he'd seen him, and he seemed very tired. "Ben," he said, ignoring Savage's remarks, "I'm going to go after Cain."

Startled, Savage said quickly, "Sure—but wait until I'm on my feet, Dan."

"No, there's no time." Ross shook his head, his eyes hooded. He said no more, for in his chest was the now familiar sensation that had been coming to him more frequently— a wind-blown vacancy. It would come on him suddenly—this feeling that his body was enormously fragile. With it came a gray emptiness like nothing he'd ever known before. He felt as if he were made of finely spun glass, and that one blow would shatter him totally.

After his heart attack, Ross had decided he had the willpower to come back, to be the man he was before. But the heart muscle is not subject to the will; it cannot be forced, and the futility of living with his weakness had drained his spirit.

Sometimes he seemed to hear a voice whispering: *Going—you're going soon now, very soon!*

But he ignored the weakness and lifted his head to say, "I've got to do something, Ben. Can't wait and let Cain whittle us down. He's gotten to Allison and you."

"He got me because I was stupid!"

"No, it was because he's got resources. He can send his soldiers anytime, anyplace. We've got to nail him, Ben."

Savage clenched his fists. "I should have killed him when I had the chance!"

"And go to jail for murder? No, we've got to do it legally."

"Any ideas?"

Ross said, "I'm going to put all the pressure I can on him, Ben. Tomorrow I'm going to talk to Mack Carver and Henry Sweet. Did you know Dani got a call from Chad Boudreaux?"

"No. He turn up anything?"

"Maybe. He's got a witness who rented a boat to two men the afternoon Judge Horstman died. Lots of people rent boats, but these two attracted attention. Both of them were carrying guns, and they were in a hurry when they turned the boat in."

"Descriptions?"

Ross smiled slightly. "One of them was 'big as a boxcar,' and the other one was an albino."

"Mazurki and Harms!"

"So I assume. I'll go down and talk to the witness."

"Let me do it—or somebody else from the agency."

Dan Ross got up and walked back to the window. He had felt a familiar thump in his chest, as if someone had struck him with a hammer on the inside, and then a new kind of flutter that alarmed him. He waited until it passed, then turned. "No, Ben, I've got to get into it."

Savage sat there silently, thinking of arguments. But he knew well the steel resolution that lay in this man, so he finally shrugged. "You won't do Ellen and the kids any good dead, Dan."

Dan Ross said evenly, "That may be. But a man has to lay himself down for his family. I'd rather die trying to help my wife and kids than live to see them hurt by Tommy Cain."

He moved to the door, but paused and turned. A smile was on his lips, and he nodded. "If it did happen—if Cain got me—I'd be sorry to leave my family. But I'd be leaving them in good hands." He hesitated, then asked quietly, "I can count on you to take care of them, Ben?"

Savage felt a thickness in his throat. He nodded, saying, "I'll be there, Dan."

Ross came back and put his hand out, his fine eyes warm as they rested on Savage. "God has blessed me with fine friends, Ben. Thank you." He wheeled and left the room, and to Ben Savage it seemed as though he heard the tolling of a bell in those last words of Ross.

13

Dan
Makes a Case

Dani tasted the crabmeat salad she'd been laboring over, then frowned. "Darn it!" she muttered darkly. "Why can't I *ever* make this stuff so that it tastes like Mom's?"

She studied the salad, wondering what it lacked, then shrugged and glanced at the clock. "Time to add the andouille to the gumbo." It was the one thing she could cook that came close to Ellen's standard—chicken andouille gumbo. She'd come home early and gotten the gumbo started, which meant cutting the chicken, browning it, and adding it to the roux. The roux itself contained onion, celery, bell pepper, and garlic. The spicy aroma had filled the kitchen as she'd added the chicken to the gumbo and left it to simmer on the stove.

Now, as she carefully added the andouille sausage and began stirring the gumbo, she thought of how strained the past week had been. Ben was little trouble—none at all to Ellen or Dani, for Allison had waited on him hand and foot! But her father's actions were a matter of deep concern to both Dani and Ellen. He would disappear for long periods and then refuse to say where he'd been—something he'd never done before. And though he obviously did not feel well, he'd turned away the attempts of the two women to slow him down, saying brusquely, "I'm all right. Don't worry about me."

Once Dani had asked Ben if he knew what her father was doing, and he'd been noncommittal, saying only, "Guess he's minding the store while I'm laid up."

An impulse took Dani, and she snatched off her apron, turned the fire down under the gumbo, and left the kitchen. She found Ben in the study, playing Monopoly with Allison. "Allison, will you go set the table, please?"

Allison looked at her sharply. "If you want to talk to Ben without me around, just say so!"

Dani was tired, her nerves ragged, and she spoke with irritation, "All right, I want to talk to Ben privately."

"All *right!*" Allison got up, her face stormy. "You never want us to have any time together!"

Dani was sorry at once, and she caught the girl as she moved toward the door, blonde head high in the air. "Allison—" she said, pulling the angry girl around. "I'm sorry. I've been an awful grouch lately. Forgive me?"

At once Allison's frown disappeared. "Sure, Sis," she nodded. "I guess I'm kind of a grump myself." She gave Dani a hug, saying as she left, "Ben's about to land on Boardwalk. If he does, make him pay up! He always begs when he goes broke!"

"I'll gouge him, don't worry," Dani assured her. When Allison left the room, she sat down across the table from Ben, who was watching her closely. "Made a fool of myself, didn't I?"

Savage shrugged. "I've seen you do worse."

Dani frowned, then a smile broke across her lips. "You do have a magic way with words, Ben Savage!"

"Charm the birds out of the trees." He held up the dice, then stared at the board. "If I roll a six, I'll hit Boardwalk and have to pay the kid two thousand dollars and lose the game." He rolled the dice, eyed the double four, then said evenly, "Six." He moved his piece to Boardwalk, glanced up at Dani, and said, "How about a loan—just until I get on my feet."

"Not a chance, Bud!" Dani said. Holding out her hand, she said, "Two thousand—cold cash."

Ben looked at her hand, then reached out and took it. She felt the hard edge of Ben's hand and watched him carefully. He held her hand, studying it as though he were a palm reader, then let it go.

"You worried about your dad?"

Dani was always startled when he seemed to read her thoughts. "Don't *do that!*" She pulled her hand away, irritated with herself for being so obvious. "You think you know women pretty well, don't you?"

"Well, I have a lifetime subscription to *Cosmopolitan*," he shrugged. "And I watch *General Hospital* every chance I get." He leaned back, his face serious. "Not too hard to figure out you're worried. We all are."

"Ben, what's Dad up to?" Dani asked quickly. "Do you know?"

"Why would I know? You're his daughter and his partner. I'm just hired help."

"That's not exactly true," Dani protested. "Dad's always felt close to you."

"He's closer to you than anyone, except Ellen."

"Then why won't he *tell* me what he's doing?"

Savage shook his head. "Doesn't want to worry you." He picked up one of the yellow five-hundred-dollar bills from the game, studied it, then put it down. "I think you've got a pretty good idea what he's doing."

Dani bit her lip, then said slowly, "He's working to get Tommy Cain off our backs, isn't he? Oh, don't play dumb, Ben! You know more about this than you're telling."

Savage leaned back carefully, testing the pain. The worst was over, but there was still some soreness when he twisted his torso. Now he stood up and turned carefully, first to the left, then to the right.

"Not too bad," he announced. "I'm getting out of this room tomorrow." He came to stand over her, which brought her head up to look at him. "I guess you're right, though Dan hasn't told me much. I tried to get him to wait until I got all mended, but you know Dan when he takes a notion. Stubborn as a mule—like all the rest of the Ross clan."

Dani rose and turned to face him. "Ben, don't try to be the U. S. Cavalry riding to the rescue."

A smile softened Savage's lips. "Already tried that. Wound up about the same as Custer at Little Big Horn, didn't I? But Cain's pets won't catch me off guard again."

"I don't want you hurt, Ben," she said quietly. "I—we all depend on you around here."

Savage saw the fear in her eyes, and even as he watched, he was surprised to see her eyes begin to fill with tears. "I feel so—so *helpless!*" she moaned, and without warning she began to tremble. Her voice held a trace of panic as she shut her eyes, saying, "If anything happened to Dad—!"

She seemed to sway, and without purposing it, Savage reached out and put his arms around her. It was, to him, a sign of how distraught Dani was when she moved against him, holding him tightly. Her body began to shake with suppressed sobs, and Savage said nothing. The pressure of her body reminded him of what a lovely woman she was, but there was nothing but compassion in him at the moment. He was aware of the soft bubbling of the small aquarium, of the fragrance of her hair. He held her until finally she moved back and gave an embarrassed half-laugh, saying, "Sorry, Ben."

"That's all right." He wanted to say more, but he always had trouble saying certain things to Dani. He struggled with his words, then said lamely, "I'll be more help now, Boss."

At that moment, Allison burst in, asking at once, "Did he hit Boardwalk?"

Ben grinned and nodded. "I tried to negotiate with your big sister, but she turned me down. I'll have better luck with you, sweetie. You wouldn't be hard on a poor old invalid, would you?"

Dani left them arguing, and as she made her way back to the kitchen she felt a surge of gratitude for Savage. She'd fought with him since the day they met and would no doubt fight again. How he felt about her was a mystery—and still more perplexing was the way she felt about *him*. He was one of the most attractive—and irritating!—men she'd ever known. Now, as she picked up the wooden spoon and stirred the gumbo, she thought abruptly, *The woman that marries Benjamin Davis Savage might go crazy putting up with him—but she'd never be bored!*

The house was dark when Dan Ross pulled up in front. Pale moonlight silvered the white pillars that held up the portico.

Ross shut off the engine, listened as the silence flowed back, then got out of the car and shut the door. He moved slowly, carefully, and as he climbed the steps he was aware that each tread called for a distinct effort. He remembered the days when he had taken them three at a time, and the thought depressed him.

As he reached the front door and stood there fumbling for his key, it suddenly swung open and the circle of light from the brass lamp on the hunt table in the foyer outlined the figure of his wife.

"Ellen, you shouldn't have stayed up."

She moved to put her arms around him, held him tightly, then said, "I couldn't sleep." She was soft and fragrant, and the light cast a dim halo around her ash-blonde hair as she slipped her arm into his, adding, "Come and have something to eat."

"I'm not hungry," he protested, but he allowed her to lead him to the kitchen. He took a seat on one of the tall oak stools at the bar and watched as she went to the stove. "Smells good," he remarked.

"Dani made her famous chicken andouille gumbo," Ellen said, spooning some into a white bowl. Bringing it to where he sat, she added, "When she gets married, her husband will get sick of this. It's about all she ever cooks."

Ross spooned up some of the spicy broth, tasted it, and said, "She did a good job." He was not hungry, but he forced himself to eat for Ellen's sake.

They sat quietly together as they had so many times before, Ellen telling him about the little things that had happened that day. As she spoke, he sipped at the skim milk she had poured into his glass, thinking of their years together. When he'd finished, she said briskly, "Now, up to bed with you, Daniel Ross!"

They went upstairs and he showered, enjoying the feel of the warm water. When he had dried off and put on his pajamas, he moved into the large bedroom, stopping to say as he stared at his wife, "Well, I see you've been to Victoria's Secret again."

Ellen was wearing a soft, shimmering pink chemise with spaghetti straps and floral embroidery on the bodice. Over it she wore a wrap-style robe of the same material. Although she was in her mid-forties, Ellen still had the same rich figure she'd had when she'd been runner-up for the Miss Texas beauty contest. She smiled at him, saying, "I've been reading one of those books on how to hold on to your husband."

Ross lay down on the bed, looked up at her, and though the weariness pulled at him, teased, "You are a brazen hussy, I do believe."

Ellen laughed softly, turned out the light, and slipped into the bed beside him. She moved very close, threw her arm around him, and whispered, "Dan—I love you so much!"

Ross turned to face her, and they lay there quietly, holding on to each other. He stroked her hair and said quietly, "I may not have done much in this life, but when I got you, Ellen—that made my life."

"Dan—!" She was too full of emotion to speak for a moment, but finally whispered, "We have such a wonderful marriage. I feel so sorry for women who have bad husbands."

"I'm not such a prize, Ellen."

"Yes, you are!" she insisted. "You've always treated me like a queen."

"Well, I always wanted to be a king," he said, smiling in the moonlight as it fell through the high windows. "And the only chance I had to make it was to be married to a queen."

She hesitated, then said, "Dan—let's move away from here."

"Move? Move where?" He waited for an answer, then guessed, "Away from Tommy Cain, you mean?"

"Yes!"

Ross felt the tension in Ellen's body and stroked her silken shoulder. "There's no place to run, Ellen. It would make Cain's day if we tried it. He'd hunt us down, and the torment would begin all over again."

"We could go to England. You always wanted to live there."

He wanted to tell her he didn't have the strength to pull up stakes, that he was too sick for that. But he only said, "We'll have to stay here, honey. This is our place, and if you let the Tommy Cains move you from your place, you're lost forever."

Ellen listened as he spoke, knowing that he would never run. She had really known it all along. Now she simply said, "All right, Dan."

"I know it's foolish to say 'Don't worry.' But I think it's going to be all right. I've found out a few things, and I believe we can put a damper on Mr. Thomas Cain."

"How, Dan?"

He pulled her close, saying, "Not now. Maybe I'll tell you tomorrow."

She moved against him, holding him tightly, and as his lips came down on hers, there was a hunger in her own. "Dan—" she whispered. "Oh, Dan—!"

Dan came down late for breakfast. "Haven't slept this late for years!" he announced to Ellen as he entered the kitchen. He moved to stand beside her at the sink, put his arms around her, and kissed her neck. "Your fault, I think!"

Ellen giggled like a schoolgirl, turned and kissed him. "Me and Tammy, we stand by our man!" Then she pushed him toward the table. "Here, sit down and tell me about Cain while I—" She broke off as Savage came into the room. He was wearing a pair of charcoal slacks, a blue knit shirt, and a pair of scuffed loafers. "Where do you think *you're* going?" she demanded.

"Back to work," Savage grinned, sitting down carefully.

"It's too soon," Ellen protested.

"Got to get out of here, Ellen." A glint appeared in Savage's eyes. "Read a verse in the Bible that says so."

Ellen stared at him. "Nonsense! No verse says that!"

"Sure it does." Savage nodded. "It says 'Withdraw thy foot from thy neighbour's house; lest he be weary of thee and so hate thee.'"

"Where does it say that?" she demanded. "I don't think that's in the Bible!"

"Proverbs, the twenty-fifth chapter, verse seventeen," Savage announced.

Ellen stared at him. "Oh, it doesn't mean you have to leave."

Savage shrugged his shoulders. "Better if I move back to my place. I can go into the office and help Angie with the paperwork."

Dan was smiling at Savage. "How'd you happen to come across that verse, Ben?"

The question seemed to embarrass Savage. "Oh, I ran out of something to read and was thumbing through that Bible your wife left on my table." He picked up the cup of coffee that Ellen brought to set before him and sipped it. "That Book of Proverbs; it's got some good stuff in it. Pithy."

Dan nodded. "It was written by the wisest man who ever lived—Solomon." He began to speak of some of the verses, and by the time Ellen had cooked the bacon and eggs and sat down, the two of them were in a deep conversation about the Bible. "Well, let's thank God for the food," Ross said. He bowed his head and put out his hand.

Savage hesitated. He had eaten many a meal in the Ross household and been included in the grace, but somehow this felt different. But he took Ross's hand, and then Ellen put out her own hand, so he gripped that as well. An odd feeling came to him, for there was an intimacy about the thing that broke the wall that he usually kept up. Not just that holding hands with two other people was of itself intimate, though the Ross's warm hands gripping his made him feel peculiar.

But Dan's prayer somehow seemed to bring the presence of God into the kitchen. It was not a formal or a long prayer, but Ross thanked God for the food, then asked the Lord to bless his family. And then he added, " . . . and bless our friend who shares this meal with us. Bless him by bringing him into your own presence, Lord. Give him a hunger for Jesus Christ—and then satisfy that hunger. Amen!"

Ben fumbled for his napkin, and as the other two began to eat, he tried to collect his thoughts. He listened to the talk of the couple, admiring as always the handsomeness of the pair and wondering what it must be like to share life with someone for twenty-five years. Then he became aware that Ellen was speaking to him. " . . . you've got to keep a close eye on this one, Ben. He's got some scheme to take care of Tommy Cain."

"Not a scheme," Ross protested. He spread some red raspberry jam on a final morsel of toast, put the toast into his mouth, and chewed on it thoughtfully. "I've been doing a little digging around, and I think we can get something together that'll put Cain away."

Savage studied Ross's face. "You been throwing rocks at the barn to see what rats will come out, Dan?"

"Sure have—and I think we can put a little pressure on Cain. For one thing, I've been to see Mack Carver, and he's with us."

"Has Cain tried to get to him?" Savage asked.

"Yes—and Mack is mad. You know what they call him in Baton Rouge?"

"Mack the Knife," Savage nodded. "He is one hard-nosed D.A., I hear. What'd Cain do to him?"

"Some cards, like the ones that came here. Mack drove to New Orleans, found Cain, and faced him with it. Cain denied it, of course. But three days later Mack's dog was killed—poisoned."

"How awful!" Ellen exclaimed.

"Yes, and the next day another card came offering sympathy for the 'loss of a loved one.'" Dan Ross's face grew bleak, and he shook his head angrily. "Mack is running around looking for someone to bite—and he knows Cain is behind it all."

"He got any idea?" Savage asked.

"Just one," Ross nodded. "Mack says we're never going to pin much on Cain using what we've got now—just a few anonymous cards. He thinks we'll have to nail him on something else."

"He's probably right," Savage agreed. "But maybe not. I shook him up by roughing up his boys and breaking into his apartment. Do that some more, rattle his cage, and he'll make a mistake."

"Maybe so. And I've started some cage rattling myself." Ross smiled in a satisfied way, saying, "I visited Henry Sweet. He works for the Aquarium of the Americas."

"He the foreman of the jury that convicted Cain?" Savage questioned.

"Yes. Well, he's a pretty simple guy really. But Cain made the mistake of hitting at him through his kids. Sweet's got two small children, aged five and nine."

"What did Cain do to them?" Ellen asked.

"Sweet got the same kind of sympathy cards, and they scared him to death. He's a pretty timid man. But when one of the kids told him that a strange man had been trying to lure them into a car with him, he kind of lost it." A perplexed look came to Ross, and he said with a trace of wonder, "He took time off from his job and bought two things—a gun and a camera. Every day he took the kids to school, then he stayed around and watched—always out of sight."

Savage leaned forward, his eyes bright. "He didn't get a picture?"

"He did!" Ross nodded. "And he took a shot at the guy who was trying to get at the kids. Missed by a mile—but that didn't satisfy Sweet. He went downtown and confronted Cain in broad daylight. Told him he had the pictures of the man who's tried to hurt his kids and said if anyone ever came *near* them, he'd blow Cain away!"

"What did Cain do?" Ellen demanded.

"Nothing, because Sweet had his brother with him." Ross smiled and added, "And his brother happens to be a Louisiana State Trooper."

"So Cain had to stand still for it," Savage smiled. "Wish I could have seen that!"

"One more thing. I went over to talk to Chad Boudreaux. He's been working hard, and he's got something. It *was* Mazurki and Harms who rented the boat—and they're the ones who killed Judge Horstman."

"Any proof?" Ben asked.

Ross gave Savage an odd look. "Know anything about gliders?"

Ellen and Savage exchanged puzzled glances. "Gliders?" Ellen inquired. "You mean, the outdoor furniture that swings?"

"No, I mean *flying* gliders," Ross said. Shaking his head, he gave them both a reluctant smile. "I've spent half my life trying to find witnesses, and usually you can't find one. But believe it or not, a guy was flying a glider over the Gulf, and he *saw* two guys pull up to a boat. He *thinks* he saw them get into a fight with the man on that boat."

"He *thinks*?" Ben demanded sharply. "Wasn't he sure?"

"I think he was, but he wants money to say so." Ross shrugged and went on, "He came to Mrs. Horstman, told her about it, and said he'd be willing to testify if she paid him. But she was afraid for her family and told him no."

"How'd Chad dig this guy up?" Savage asked.

"Well, it was funny. Chad went to Mrs. Horstman, and somehow she got to talking. You know Chad—the world's best listener! Anyway, she finally told him, and he's got the guy pinpointed."

Savage thought quickly, "If we can pin Judge Horstman's murder on Moon and Whitey, they'll sing."

"Won't they be afraid of Cain?" Ellen asked.

"Not afraid enough to take a life sentence," Ross declared. "Anyway, I'm going to hit Cain with all this. It's really not enough to nail him, but when he sees I'm going to push it, I think he'll back off. He's cruel, but he's not stupid!"

Savage sat there, his mind working rapidly. "Don't go to him in person, Dan. Let me do it—or even better, let Luke do it."

Ross shook his head. "No, I'm going to have to do this myself, Ben."

"Let me go with you, Dan."

"No, you're in no condition to move around. I'll drop you off at your place, and you can go to the office tomorrow if you feel up to it." He smiled at the worried looks on their faces. "Hey, it's not dangerous. Cain wouldn't dare try anything. I'll see him, warn him, and that'll be it. Maybe it won't work, but I've got to try it." He rose and kissed Ellen. "I'll call you after I've seen him."

"No, don't call," she said quickly. "Come home."

"All right, I will."

As the two men left, Ellen forced herself to keep a smile on her face. But as the car left the driveway, she slowly sat down. Her hands were trembling, and she clenched them tightly. Closing her eyes, she sat there a long time, praying hard. Finally she took a deep breath, got to her feet, and began to clean up the breakfast dishes.

14

A Favor
for Stormy

Marcel Delgard resembled Paul Prudhomme. Round-faced and bearded, and weighing over three hundred pounds, he shared the same Cajun heritage with the famous chef—as well as the same enormous appetite. His profession, however, was crime, not cuisine.

As he sat at a table at Broussard's on Conti Street, Delgard was doing what he liked best—discussing food with the chef, a tall man named Louis DeSpain. The two men were great friends, and Delgard sighed, "Ah, Louis—if I'd had your good luck, I'd be cooking. I could have been an artist, like you, my friend, if I'd had the luck."

DeSpain shrugged in the Gallic fashion. "You haven't done badly, Marcel. Lots of men envy you."

Delgard glanced down at the huge diamond ring that glittered on his pudgy finger and came up with a smile. "It is nothing, what I do, Louis. You are an artist—and I curse the day I turned from my true calling to become a bookkeeper."

The tall chef shot a cynical smile at his friend, for he had heard all this before. Marcel Delgard was not "a bookkeeper" except in the loosest sort of definition of that term. Though he had never seen the inside of a college, he was a genius at any sort of accounting. And he had put his skills to a bad use, using them to juggle the books of highly placed criminals. He knew how to launder money so expertly that the IRS could never get a handle on it. He was an artist at juggling funds, hiding expenses, uncovering tax loopholes, and was known as the slickest man around with a calculator.

His chief client at the present was Tommy Cain. And though Delgard never showed it, he disliked Cain and felt somewhat contaminated by the association. He liked to describe himself as a businessman, and he looked down on his employer as a barbarian who ate like a field hand, with no appreciation for the finer points of artistic cuisine.

Even as the two men plunged into a discussion of the best way of producing Cajun smothered roast duck, they were interrupted by Louie Zapello, who appeared suddenly at Delgard's elbow. "C'mon, Delgard. Tommy needs you."

"But I haven't had my lunch!"

"You want me to go tell Tommy that?"

"No!" Delgard might dislike Cain, but he had the sense to fear him as well. He got to his feet with that extraordinary lightness some very fat people possess and said, "Louis, I will come back tonight—and we will, perhaps, attempt my new recipe for salmon Lafayette."

The two men left, and thirty minutes later they entered Cain's office. "Here he is, Mr. Cain," Zapello said. "He was stuffing himself, as usual."

"Not so!" Delgard protested. "I was just about to have my

lunch—a filet de boeuf Wellington." His large eyes saddened at the thought of the missed meal, and he asked, "What is the crisis, Mr. Cain, that takes me away from such a meal?"

Cain was standing at his window, staring down at the traffic below. He didn't answer Delgard for what seemed like a long time. This interested Louie Zapello, for Cain was a man who did most things very quickly. And then, as Cain turned, Zapello noted that his employer was in a cold rage. He knew the signs well—the thinned lips, the steely eyes, the slight twitching of the cheeks. He had seen it before, and it always meant trouble for someone.

Cain advanced to his chair, sat down, and stared at the two men. "I just had a caller, Louie," he said evenly. "Dan Ross was here while you were gone."

"Ross? He want you to lay off?" Zapello asked.

"Sure, he did."

"Not a bad idea." Zapello shrugged. "No money in chasing around after him, Tommy." He'd argued this with Cain many times, but now he saw that argument was useless. He asked, "How'd he get you so stirred up?"

"He's been busy, Danny Boy has. Got some stuff he thinks will hurt us." Cain related the essence of Ross's visit, summing it all up by saying, "He's got nothing—but he could become a nuisance."

"Drop it," Zapello urged. "We don't need any hassle. Like I say, there's no profit in it."

To the tall henchman's surprise, Cain nodded. "I agree, Louie. We'll drop it—but we'll drop Ross, too."

"Put him down?" Zapello's eyes narrowed. "Not smart. Sixkiller will be right on your tail. You forget what he said?"

Cain smiled with a hawklike cruelty coming to his lips. "That dumb cop won't be able to do a thing. He's hit the glory trail, Louie, haven't you heard?" The idea amused Cain, and he added, "He's too busy preaching and taking up collections to know what's happening."

At this point, Marcel Delgard grew alarmed. He understood they were talking about murder, which was *not* his area. He spoke nervously, "Mr. Cain, would you like for me to do something with the books?"

Cain had forgotten the fat man. He gave him a sudden glance and snapped, "Get out, Marcel!" Cain watched as Delgard scurried out of the office, then said, "Fat slug! If he couldn't do things with the books, I'd feed him to the fish!"

Zapello stood there, tall and pale, but secure in the imminence of his own death. He spoke with the bluntness of a condemned man. "Tommy, you're making a fool out of yourself." Ignoring the flash of anger in Cain's eyes, he spoke with a lack of fervor, but with absolute certainty. "You've always been smart. This is *dumb*! So we waste Ross, what's it get you? A hassle from the cops. You know how they are when a detective gets it, Tommy—they *never* let it go!"

Cain nodded. "Sure, Louie, I know that. But I want to make sure that everybody knows it's bad news to cross Tommy Cain. Everybody knows who put me in Angola. Well, when I'm through, the state won't be able to dig up a prosecuting attorney with the nerve to go after me." Cain's eyes took on a hard glitter as he added, "We're going to get Ross—and that guy Sweet and that D.A. in Baton Rouge!"

"It's not smart," Zapello shrugged. "But I can see you're going to do it no matter what. You want me to take care of it?"

Cain smiled, "I'm going to handle this personally, Louie."

"That's even dumber, Tommy. All they need is you with a gun standing over Ross—they'll nail you for sure."

"Not going to use a gun, Louie," Cain said. "As a matter of fact—Danny Boy, why, he's not to be a homicide! He's going to die a very *natural* death." Cain's face was lit with an unholy joy as he leaned forward, speaking rapidly for the next ten minutes. Finally he asked, "What do you think about it now, Louie?"

Zapello shrugged, his gray face expressionless. "Guess it'll work. Ross will be dead—and someday I'll be dead—and someday you'll be dead, Tommy."

The words sent a chill through Cain, but he only blinked rapidly a few times, attributing the sudden stab of fear to Zapello's condition. It was strange to be talking with a man who'd be in the ground in a few months. Everybody died; it was the *knowledge* of it that was weird. He shook off his thoughts and said, "Get Stormy, Louie. Go by and tell her to get Ross's kid to take her out tonight."

"Maybe he won't go for it," Zapello suggested.

"Tell Stormy I said for her to get him—any way she can. And tell her I'll be real unhappy with her if she don't deliver the kid. She's got him following her like a lost puppy; now's the time to sink the hook!"

Dan Ross looked around the table—as he had a thousand times before. But somehow, this time, the sight of all his family together brought him a special sense of joy. They were all eating Ellen's banana pudding, washing it down with strong, black coffee. Without meaning to, Ross blurted out, "Nice to be together—the whole family."

Ellen looked at him quickly, knowing what was in his heart. "Yes, I've missed these suppers together. Maybe we can play one of those dumb games that I always lose."

Rob dropped his head in shame. He had been gone night after night and was leaving to meet Stormy in thirty minutes. He was aware that none of his family were looking at him, but he knew they were all thinking the same thing. Hastily he said, "Gosh, I'd like to—but I've got a date. How about tomorrow night?"

"Oh, Rob!" Allison pouted. "Break your old date!"

Seeing the look on Rob's face, Dani said quickly, "Tomorrow? Sure, Rob. We'll all set that time aside." She cast a warning look at Allison, then said brightly, "How about you and I do the dishes and let Mom and Dad have a date?" She winked at her father adding, "Take her out to the river and park."

"I might just do that," Ross grinned. "Will you give Allison her bath and put her jammies on?"

"Daddy!" Allison squealed, getting up with a red face. "I'm not a *child!*"

"Don't tease her, Dan," Ellen smiled. She reached across and patted Allison's hand. "You know," she said warmly, "I think a lot about the days when you were just a baby—when all of you were little." Her eyes grew thoughtful, and she added, "Those are the best days, I think."

Dan Ross nodded in agreement. "Sure. When you want a child to do something, you just pick him up and set him in place. Can't do that with the grown-up variety."

Rob felt a sharp jab of conscience, but could not say a word. He toyed with his coffee, thinking about what a turn his life had taken since he'd met Stormy Carr. He was dead broke, had borrowed from every friend he had, and was desperately trying to blot out of his mind the question of how he would pay his tuition for the fall term at Tulane, which was about to start.

More than once he'd tried to cut himself free from the crowd Stormy ran with—had even told her he was finished. But somehow she'd smoothed his protests away, her warm lips blotting out his good intentions. Now he wanted to stay at the table, to be with his family. *Not worth it! I'm going to get myself back on track!*

"Let me make a call," he said abruptly. "I'll break my date." He leaped up and left the room so quickly that the rest of them stared after him speechless.

"Well—that's a switch!" Allison said with surprise. Then she shook her head. "He won't do it, though."

When Rob got through to Stormy, he spoke quickly, "Stormy, I can't make it tonight."

"But, Robbie—you've just got to!"

"No, I'm broke," he said. He wanted to tell her that he was sick of the whole thing—the drinking, the drugs, the immorality that characterized the whole bunch he'd been with. But he said only, "Maybe we can get together sometime when I get my act together."

Once Stormy was convinced he meant what he said, she spoke gently, "Robbie, if you want to break it off, that's okay. You're a sweet boy, and I love being with you—but you know best about our seeing each other." Then she went on in a voice that seemed to be filled with fear, "But—I *need* you tonight, Robbie! Really, I do."

"What's the problem?"

"I—I can't talk about it on the phone, but I'm in a jam. I need one little favor, Robbie. Just one, I promise. Will you help me?"

Rob tried to imagine what sort of problem Stormy could have that he might help with. "I don't have any money."

"It's not money," she said quickly. "Look, it won't take but a little while. Meet me at my apartment in an hour. Will you come?"

"Well—" Rob hesitated, then said, "okay, but this is it, Stormy. I'll be there as soon as I can."

He hung up the phone, walked back to the dining room, and stood in the doorway. "I couldn't exactly break the date—but I'll be around more from now on."

Dan Ross took a deep breath, stood up, and walked toward his son. "Fine, Rob!" He turned to the others and said, "You know, we haven't prayed together for a long time. I'd like to get back to it. How about it?"

The three at the table got up at once, and they all joined hands. Rob felt sheepish, but his father's hand was warm and comforting—as he remembered it from his childhood days.

"Oh, Lord," Ross prayed, his voice clear and firm, "we are helpless, but you are the helper of the helpless. We have no power, but you have all power. Nothing is impossible with you, and we ask you tonight to bring us through the troubles that surround us. . . . "

As his father prayed, Rob felt tears sting his eyes. Remorse swept over him, and he cried out in his own spirit, *Lord, forgive me for failing you—and for failing my family!*

When Ross said, " . . . in the name of Jesus Christ we pray," they all looked up, and Ellen said, "This was so nice, Dan!"

Dani said little, but made it a point to give Rob a hard hug. "You big lug, I love you!" she whispered in his ear.

Allison always found it hard to show how she felt. But her face was radiant, and she felt warm and safe as her father put his arms around her. "Don't grow *all* the way up so quick, sweetheart," he said. "You're still my baby girl!"

Rob turned and left, and Ellen and Dani began clearing the table. "I haven't seen Dan so relaxed in weeks," Ellen whispered to Dani.

"I know he's been very worried about Rob."

"Yes, and so have I." Ellen looked at her daughter, her face filled with hope. "Do you think Rob means it? That he's leaving that crowd?"

Dani put her arm around her mother's waist. "We've been praying for it, haven't we? So let's just believe God together!"

*   *   *

"All right, Stormy, what's the big problem?"

Stormy had met Rob at the door, but he avoided her embrace. He was afraid of himself, afraid that she would weaken his resolve as she had at other times. He walked past her, turned, and said, "I'll help you if I can, Stormy, but you're just too rich for my blood."

Stormy hesitated, for it was not often that she met resistance. Rob had been different from the beginning. At first she'd laughed at his innocence, certain it would not last long. But she'd been wrong, and she had lied to Cain about her progress. She'd never been able to get Rob Ross to try hard drugs. A few drinks, a puff or two of marijuana—that was it. She knew it was hopeless to try to get him drunk or high on drugs tonight, as Cain had ordered. Quickly she said, "It's—not easy for me to talk about, Robbie. Can't we have a drink?"

"Just Pepsi for me," Rob said quickly.

"Sure. Sit down, and I'll fix it and make myself a Bloody Mary." She went behind the bar, worked busily on the drinks, then came back and sat down. "Here's your Pepsi," she said. "Lots of ice the way you like it."

Rob was thirsty and drank half the Pepsi before he lowered it and asked, "What's this trouble you're in?"

Stormy said, "It goes back a long way, Robbie. I'll have to tell you all of it so you'll know why I'm asking you for a favor."

Rob shrugged. "Go ahead." He sat there listening, taking another sip from his Pepsi as Stormy began to tell him about a man she met a year earlier. It was a complicated story, and he had trouble following it.

The room began to grow warm, and he interrupted her to say, "Can you turn the air-conditioning up? I'm getting pretty warm."

That was what he intended to say. The words that actually came out were: "Cus zoo tin duh air customer? Gissing hod innear!"

He stopped abruptly, shocked at his own babbling. When he glanced over at Stormy, he seemed to be looking at her through the wrong end of a telescope. Even as he stared at her, she seemed to shimmer, as though illuminated with some sort of inner light.

Lurching to his feet, Rob took one step—then the room tilted and he fell headlong. In his ears he heard the rushing of mighty waters, and in his veins the blood had turned to molten lava. He tried to cry out, but no sound came. Then the room began to spin like a gigantic kaleidoscope, and he was caught by it, pulled into the whirling colors as he uttered a voiceless scream.

15
Fatal Call

The women of his house had gone shopping at the mall, leaving Dan Ross to read. When the phone rang, he put down the book he was reading—*Mere Christianity* by C. S. Lewis— and picked up the receiver, saying, "Dan Ross."

The voice that answered stiffened him, for he recognized it instantly.

"Hello, Danny Boy. How's it going?"

Ross said, "What do you want, Cain? I said my piece in your office."

"Sure you did, Danny Boy. But now it's my turn."

"No deals, Cain. Leave me and my family alone—or I'll have you put back in Angola."

His threat seemed to amuse Cain. "You got moxie, Danny Boy, I'll give you that." Then Cain's voice grew hard. "Maybe we can deal—but we've gotta hammer it out."

"The only deal I'll make is the one I laid out. If you bother me or my family one more time, I'll nail you if it takes all I have."

"Know where Rob is right now?"

Ross's hand tightened on the phone until his knuckles turned white. He'd been fearful for weeks that Cain would somehow get at Rob, for his son was the one member of his family he could not keep close. Keeping his voice steady with an effort, he said, "What about Rob?"

"Why, the kid's in a little trouble, Danny Boy—could be real *big* trouble if you don't get right on it. Why don't you and me get together and see what we can do?"

Ross decided instantly. "Where are you?"

"You know Port Sulphur—how to get there?"

Port Sulphur was a small town on Highway 23, which led down the peninsula that extended south from New Orleans and into the Gulf. "I know where it is."

"Great! Now listen—you better write this down. About five miles before you get to Port Sulphur, there's a dirt road that bears to the right. It's right beside an Exxon station and a little hamburger joint called the Blue Goose. You start down that road, Danny Boy. I'll be waiting for you about five miles down the way. It's a deserted spot, so we can talk real private. But come alone, got it? I'll have you watched, and if anybody's following you, that kid of yours won't be in such good shape."

Ross drew a rough map on the pad beside his chair. "I'll be there, Cain. But if you harm my son—"

"Hey! We'll work it out, okay? I've had enough hassling, Danny Boy, so let's talk things out. Only—come alone."

A click sounded in Ross's ear, and he replaced the receiver. Getting to his feet, he walked to a desk and took out a shoulder holster holding a .38. He put the rig on, pulled a jacket off a rack beside the door, then hesitated. Going back to the desk, he pulled off the map he'd drawn and scrawled on the pad, "Got a call from Cain about Rob. Have to go meet him." He hesitated, then added, "All my love." He signed the paper and laid it on the desktop.

In a matter of minutes he was crossing the Causeway. He made his way to Gretna, where he turned off onto Highway 23. As he sped down the highway, he tried to think. *Maybe I ought to get Ben or Luke in on this.* But Ben was still crippled, and just the sight of a policeman might set Cain off. *No, I'll have to take care of this myself.*

He passed through the small towns that had grown up beside the highway—Dalcour, Carlisle, Myrtle Grove. The Mississippi River rolled through the low ground on his left, and he thought about how far it came, starting all the way back in Minnesota as a small stream, growing as it swept south until it spread to a mile-wide river, moving thousands of tons of rich dirt from the midland to the Delta he now drove through. He had heard once that when a drop of water fell on the eastern slope of the Rocky Mountains, it would eventually find its way into the Gulf right at this spot.

He passed through Socola and grew careful, watching the side of the road. Soon he saw the lights of a gas station, and as he slowed down he spotted a small, unimpressive cafe next to it. The Blue Goose.

A hundred feet north of the cafe, he saw the dirt road and turned down the rutted surface. The land was low and he knew it was one of those roads that no one could use in rainy weather. It led, he guessed, to a private hunting club on Barataria Bay, and was used by fishermen and hunters.

Scrub timber and thick underbrush closed in on the road, so that there was room for only one vehicle. Ross had to hold the wheel carefully, for the ruts wrenched the tires around so violently that he had difficulty keeping the car steady. "Should've taken the Blazer," he muttered. "Not thinking straight." The headlights made twin cones of light, stabbing the darkness, and to the side he saw the luminous eyes of a deer, which bolted at once, disappearing into the thicket.

His heart seemed to be functioning well; at least it was not trying to burst out of his chest. He prayed steadily—not for himself, but for Rob. As for trusting Cain, he knew better than that. The man was a wild beast who would kill at the slightest provocation, but he felt he had no choice. And as the car thumped along, dragging bottom almost constantly, Ross was surprised to realize he felt no fear. He wondered if it was because he'd lived with death at his elbow for so long that the specter had no power over him.

He thought of his family, what would happen to them if he died. But he'd been through all of that, and God had given him peace about that matter. He knew Ellen would be lost for a time without him—as he would be lost without her. But she was a strong woman, and she had Dani to help her. Allison had been more of a burden, for he knew how fragile her spirit was. He struggled once again with his concern about his youngest daughter. Then a verse came into his mind: " . . . casting all your care upon him; for he careth for you."

I've just about worn that verse out, Lord, but I've got no one else to turn to. I'm asking you to keep me alive. But if that doesn't happen, make Rob into a strong man of God. Keep Allison close and don't let her fail. He prayed for Ellen and Dani, but his prayer was more of a thanksgiving than a plea, for he knew how strong they both were.

Suddenly a light flashed on in front of him, and he braked quickly. As the car slowed, the parking lights of the other car came on. As the car came to a full stop, he automatically touched the gun he wore, then reached into the glove compartment for a flashlight. He got out of the car and walked forward, but he'd gone only twenty feet when Cain's voice came to him: "Danny Boy? You made good time."

Ross continued to walk toward the car, and Cain's form materialized out of the darkness. He wore an expensive suit, Ross noted, and there was no sign of a gun in his hand. "Get in my car," Cain said, slapping at his neck. "Mosquitoes are eating me alive!"

As Cain moved around and got into the dark-colored BMW, Ross hesitated. He knew that Cain could have stationed his thugs in the car or the shelter of the trees, but he saw nothing, so he opened the door and slid into the car. As he entered, he sensed the presence of someone in the back, and the gun seemed to leap into his hand as he commanded, "Hold it!"

A woman's voice broke the silence, a half-scream, and Cain cried out, "Don't shoot, Ross! "

Ross threw the light on the woman in the back and noted the fear in her face, but saw no sign of a gun. He turned the light back on Cain's face, and his voice was gritty as he asked, "What's all this, Cain?"

The light etched the features of Cain, giving him a hungry appearance and making his cheeks and eye sockets appear cavernous. "Take it easy," he said quickly. "I don't even have a gun—you can check."

"I will," Ross said, and ran his hands over Cain. He found no weapon, so he slipped the .38 into the holster and demanded, "Spill it, Tommy. Who's the woman?"

"You never met? Why, she's Stormy Carr, Rob's main squeeze! Ain't that right, sweetie?"

Stormy's voice was thick with fear as she answered quickly, "That's right, Mr. Ross. Rob and I've been dating."

"He couldn't afford the price of one of your diamond earrings," Ross stated flatly. Stormy was a flashy beauty and probably could have plenty of men. Ross knew that Rob had little to offer her.

"Well, he's a sweet boy," Stormy said quickly. "I just like him, that's all."

"Stormy tells me the kid's really a straight arrow," Cain put in, his voice amused. "You must be proud of him."

"I am," Ross said. "Where is he?"

"Well, that's kind of complicated," Cain answered. "Stormy here got into a little trouble, and she asked the kid to help her out."

"What kind of trouble?"

"It was a hassle with one of the Colombian dealers." Cain shook his head, stating, "Stormy don't know those guys! If she'd come to me, I could've told her they're poison!"

Stormy broke in, speaking rapidly. "I knew this fellow, and it was really his problem. But he dragged me into it. What he made me do was agree to meet some of his—friends. To—to give them something."

"He forced you to make a drop?"

"Well, yes. So I asked Rob to come along. I was afraid to go alone."

At her words, Ross grew sick at heart. Once a man got involved with that kind of business, there was little hope of turning back. He asked harshly, "What happened?"

Cain took up the story, his voice sharp and clear. "You know how these greaseballs are, Danny Boy, ready to do anybody in—and even each other. A rival gang leader got wind of the drop and set a trap. They got to the spot first. Stormy saw them coming and hid in the bushes, but they got your kid. Tell Mr. Ross about it, Stormy."

"I could hear them talking. I was afraid they were going to shoot Rob, but they didn't. One of them said, 'We'll nail this thing down. This is Domingue's car, and the stuff is in it. We'll drop a dime on him, and when he comes to, he'll find the cops here.' And then one of them asked about Rob. The leader said,

'We'll leave him here, but we'll shoot him up enough to keep him still until the cops get here.'"

"Pretty smart—for a spick," Cain said, his voice tinged with admiration. "Now when the cops get there, they'll get Domingue—wipe out the competition for these guys."

"Where's the car?" Ross demanded.

"Down that road," Stormy said. "We went in my friend's Bronco. We needed the four-wheel drive; nothing else would make it, he said. After they left, I called Tommy on the car phone. I tried to get Rob to wake up, but he was out. So I made it down the road to where Tommy found me."

"Cops'll probably be tipped off pretty soon—" Cain looked at his watch and nodded. "Nearly eleven. Stormy said the drop was set for midnight. They'll make the call in maybe half an hour."

Ross thought rapidly. "I'm going after him."

"Thought you might do that," Cain responded. "And here's the deal, Danny Boy. I'm handing you a chance to get your kid out of this jam. You stop poking around in my business. From here on, you leave me alone, I lay off you. Is it a deal?"

Ross instinctively distrusted any sort of proposition offered by Cain, but the clock was running. If Rob got picked up in a car with a kilo of heroin, he'd do time. "All right," he agreed.

"Sure, I knew you'd be smart," Cain nodded. "Now, I'm getting out of here. If I get picked up anywhere within ten miles of a drop, the feds'd lock me up and throw away the key!"

Stormy said, "They took the key to the Bronco, but I had the spare in my purse." She handed it over, saying nervously, "Rob won't be able to drive. I tried to wake him up, but they gave him something pretty strong." She shivered and added with a trace of hysteria, "Tommy, let's get out of here!"

"Yeah, that's a good idea." He put his hand out to Ross, grinning. "No hard feelings?"

"Just leave me alone," Ross said. He got out of the car and walked down the rutted road.

As Ross disappeared into the darkness, Stormy whispered, "I don't get it, Tommy. There's no cops coming."

"But Danny Boy thinks there are," Cain laughed softly. "And he'll never make it down that road—not with a bum ticker. It gets worse, and he'll kill himself trying to get there before the cops." He shook his head, adding, "I'm giving Danny Boy an easy way out. I'd like to pull him apart, piece by piece. But this way is safe. Nobody can blame me if the old guy has a heart attack, can they, babe?"

As he drove away, he had another thought. "Only thing I hate is—I can't watch Ross kick off. But he'll catch on pretty soon. When that ticker of his starts busting through his chest, he'll know it's ol' Tommy Cain who set him up!" He laughed loudly, then said, "How about we get us a steak, honey? You hungry?"

Stormy was so scared she was nauseated, but she smiled and said, "Sure, Tommy, that'd be fine." As the car rocked over the ridges of hardened mud, she was wishing fervently that she'd never heard of Tommy Cain!

When Dani heard her mother's cry, she whirled and ran to the den. Ellen Ross was standing at her husband's desk, her face pale as chalk. "He's gone!" she gasped, and held out a notepad to Dani.

Dani scanned it, and the fear rose in her, strong and bitter. But she forced herself to think. "We've got to find them," she whispered.

"But—we don't know where he went!"

Dani had a flash of insight. "The phone! Dad records all his calls!" She ran to the machine that monitored the phone system and, with the speed built of long practice, started the machine. A wave of relief washed over her as she heard Cain speaking. "It's him, Mother!" she cried, then strained to listen to the conversation. As soon as it was finished, she said, "Get Allison. We can't leave her here alone!"

As her mother left the room calling for Allison, Dani pulled the .38 from the holster, checked the loads, then stood there uncertainly. She made a decision, picked up the phone, and dialed. When Savage's voice said, "Hello?" she felt some relief.

"Ben, Dad's gone to meet Cain. He went alone without telling us. Can you go with me?"

"Pick me up," Savage said instantly. "Better not call the cops yet."

Dani said, "I won't," then hung up. She ran toward the door, meeting Allison and her mother. "Why didn't Dad take the Blazer?" she wondered. "That's rough country out there."

They piled into the Blazer and, as Dani spun the wheels out of the driveway, she called out, "Hang on, I'm going to break some traffic laws!"

The limbs seemed to reach out at Dan Ross, clawing at his face like demented goblins. One of them slashed him across the eye, and he stumbled along, his eyes watering with pain.

But the worst pain was in his chest. He had done very well for the first mile or so, but then the old familiar feeling began—like a spear being prodded from the inside of his chest. Ordinarily he would have stopped at once and waited for it to pass, but he could not do so now; he was racing against time.

Ragged clouds moved across the sky, pulling veils across the face of the moon and then whipping them away again. The woods were quiet, broken only by the sound of his own hoarse breathing.

He stepped into a hole and threw his hands out wildly, but fell sprawling headlong to the dirt. For a second he lay there, every nerve in him crying for rest. But then he took a deep breath, got to his feet, and staggered on. The flashlight beam jerked up and down—now on the road, now up in the treetops. Cold sweat dotted his forehead; the stabbing in his chest grew more insistent.

He had not gone a hundred feet farther before the pain doubled him over, and his trembling legs collapsed. He sat down and stretched back, his breath coming in great, jagged gasps. The moon overhead was only a worn yellow disk, like an old shell washed by the sea.

Ross lay there, knowing he would never make it. Desperately, he cried out in his heart: "God—help me—got to get to Rob—no matter about me—but help me get to him!"

He lay there for ten minutes, and the racing of his heart seemed to slow. The pain lessened, and he got to his feet carefully. "Got to take it slower," he muttered thickly. He moved along the road at a slower pace, each step a deliberate effort, and waited for the pain to sweep back. When he had gone two hundred yards, the road grew rougher—little more than a rutted track—but he said, "Thank you, Lord—for giving me strength."

The air was still, and the small creatures of the night watched the figure of the interloper creep down the road. A curious raccoon peered down from a large branch, then scrambled to a higher limb for safety.

Ross grew weaker, for his careful program of exercise since his heart attack had done little to prepare him for a task like this. It was a chore that would have been difficult for a healthy man, and it proved to be too much for Ross. He collapsed again and lay there almost sobbing for breath, but again forced himself to get up.

He lost his clear logic as he staggered along the rutted road. He could do no more than put one foot in front of the other. Blindly he moved along, lost to all but the need of pressing on.

He came upon the Bronco so suddenly that he could not take it in at first. Then he saw Rob lying on the ground and lurched toward him, falling on his knees. "Son! Rob!" he cried out. He thought for one terrible moment that Rob was dead, that it had all been for nothing. Then Rob's eyes opened slowly.

"Rob—are you all right?"

Rob tried to answer, but could only move his lips, making inarticulate sounds.

"We've got to get out of here, son!" Ross got to his feet, reached down, and began to pull at Rob. But Rob was still drugged; he could not help. Desperately, Ross leaned over, picked the boy up, and shoved him over the lip of the door opening. The effort tore at him, and the pain came roaring back. Falling forward, he leaned against the Bronco, nauseated and faint.

The old familiar sensation of a vast emptiness in his chest came to him, and he felt the world receding. He had no strength, but he had to get his son out of there.

Clinging to the vehicle, he crept around until he got to the driver's side, then gripped the wheel and took a deep breath. Gathering all his strength, he gave his best effort and pulled himself up into the seat.

Searing pain struck him then, and he fell forward, grasping at his chest. He knew he was dying, but something inside kept him from giving up. Reaching into his pocket, he found the key the woman had given him, and inserted it into the slot. Ignoring the pain that seemed to pull him into knots, he started the engine. Looking over toward Rob, who was sprawled half on the seat, half on the floor, he gasped, "We'll make it, son—!"

The engine roared to life, and Ross slipped the vehicle into gear. The lights reached out into the darkness, and Ross released the clutch. The Bronco pitched as the wheels bounced off the hardened ruts, and each jolt seemed to be a knife in Ross's chest.

As they moved along the old road, he prayed steadily. He turned on the dome light, and more than once he looked down at Rob, whose head bounced against the seat. But the bouncing had somehow stirred his mind, and he began to grope around. Rob raised his head, opened his eyes, and looked around wildly. "What—" he muttered thickly. Then he twisted his head and stared at the driver. "Dad—?" he gasped. "What is—!"

A violent jolt as the front wheels hit a large hole broke off his speech, and Dan Ross managed to say, "Be still—Rob—we'll be all right—!"

But he had not driven a quarter of a mile when it hit—the pain that struck like nothing he'd ever felt. It took his breath, and the road grew faint as his vision faded. He tried to stop, but the effort of lifting his foot was too great.

He didn't even know when the Bronco left the road and rammed into an oak tree a foot in diameter. He heard the crash, and then everything was silent.

"Look—there's something over there—a wrecked car!"

Dani saw the dark shape of the vehicle as soon as Ellen cried out. She brought the Blazer to a stop and almost fell out of it. Clutching the flashlight, she ran toward the car, ignoring Savage, who was calling, "Dani—hold on—!"

When she got to the car, she threw the light inside. "It's them—Dad and Rob!" she cried out. She yanked the driver's door open, and her father fell out into her arms. She held him until she felt Savage at her side, taking part of the weight. "Let's get him out," Ben said. "Ellen, see about Rob!"

They eased Dan Ross to the ground, and Dani at once put her head to his chest and listened. She was aware of Allison and her mother speaking to Rob, who seemed to be mumbling in return.

"Hear anything?" Savage asked urgently.

"I—I think so," Dani whispered.

"Let me see." Savage held a finger against Ross's neck, waited, then shook his head. "Bad! We've got to get him to a hospital. We'll take him in the Blazer. Pull up as close as you can."

Dani ran to the Blazer, started it, then edged it as close as she could. When she got out, she saw that her mother was seated on the ground with her husband's head cradled on her lap. Looking up with tears in her eyes, Ellen whispered, "He's trying to speak, Dani—!"

Dani fell to her knees. Allison was on the other side of their mother, and Rob came staggering to fall beside the form of his father. Savage stood slightly to the left, holding the flashlight on the group.

"Dan—can you hear me?" Ellen cried. She pushed the hair from Ross's eyes and saw them open. "Oh, Dan!" she whispered.

They all saw Dan's lips move, and instinctively leaned closer.

" . . . made it!" he whispered. "Thank God!"

"Don't try to talk, Dad," Dani said quickly. "We'll get you to the hospital."

But Ross shook his head, whispering, "No—want to say—something. Help me—sit up, Ellen—"

Ellen helped him to a sitting position, but held his head against her breast, holding him like a hurt child.

Ross turned to Allison, whose small body was racked with sobs. "Allison—?" She came to him, and he put his arms around her, smoothing her hair. "You are my beautiful little girl—don't grieve too long. We'll see each other again."

Allison stepped back blindly as he released her, falling against Dani, who took her, pressing the younger girl against her chest.

"Son—Robbie—" Ross said, and reached out for Rob, whose eyes were staring, tears running down his cheeks. He gripped his father's hand, and then put his arms around him.

"Dad—it's all my fault!"

Ross shook his head, and his voice grew a little stronger. "No! Son, promise me something?"

"Anything!"

"Don't ever feel guilty about me! It—will ruin your life. You've been—such a fine son! The best a man ever had! Made a mistake—but you'll be all right—just don't blame this on yourself—promise—"

"I—I promise, Dad!"

Rob couldn't seem to move. He knelt there, holding his father's hand, but Ross whispered, "Dani—give me—"

Seeing his arm outstretched, Dani released Allison and came to put her arms around her father. She held him, tears burning in her eyes, her body aching from unreleased sobs.

"Dani—we've been close—haven't we? Always—best of friends?"

"The—the best, Dad!"

"Take care of your mother—and take care of yourself—learn to be happy. You are—my pride!"

Dani stepped away, blind with tears. She felt Ben catch her, and she grabbed at him for support.

"Ben—see to them—you promised—"

Savage nodded, his face a mask. "You can count on it, Dan."

Ross looked up at Ellen, lifted his hand, and traced the smooth line of her cheek. A faint smile soothed the corners of his lips, and he whispered, "Ellen—sweetheart—you have been my life!"

He took a deep breath and whispered so faintly that only Ellen caught his final words: "Lord Jesus—I'm—ready—"

They heard his breath as he released it slowly. Then his eyes closed, and he smiled. Ellen felt his body relax, as if he were a tired child who dropped off into sleep.

"Good-by—!" Ellen whispered, pressing his head against her in one final gesture. "Oh, good-by, my darling—!"

16

Celebration

"I never did like funerals," Savage muttered, his lips pulled to a tight line.

Luke Sixkiller turned to regard Savage. "Well, I guess nobody does—but we ought to."

"Ought to like funerals? That's *sick*!"

"Is it?"

"Why, sure it is!"

The two of them were standing outside the white wooden church, waiting for the body of Dan Ross to arrive. Even at this early hour, the sidewalk was already beginning to heat up like a stove. The two had stood there watching the flow of people as they entered the church, and Savage felt uncomfortable, wishing he had not agreed to be one of Ross's pallbearers. Sixkiller's remark irritated him, and he shook his head stubbornly. "What's to like about a funeral, Luke?"

"Nothing—in the natural sense, I guess. We all hate death. It tears things away from us that we want to hold on to. And it reminds us that one day we'll be the ones in the casket—something most people don't like to think about." Taking out a snowy white handkerchief, he wiped his brow, then putting it back, remarked, "There's a verse in the Bible that I found the morning after Dan died, and I've been thinking about it a lot. It's in the Old Testament—the Book of Ecclesiastes. It says, 'It is better to go to the house of mourning, than to go to the house of feasting: for that is the end of all men; and the living will lay it to his heart.'"

Savage grew thoughtful, mulling over the words. "I don't get it," he admitted. "Sounds like it's saying that it's better to go to a funeral than it is to go to a party."

"That's exactly what it says," Sixkiller nodded. "And it makes no sense at all—from the world's point of view." He paused, looked down the street, then announced, "There it comes." Both men watched as the two long black shapes rounded the corner—the hearse bearing the body and the limousine with the family inside.

"Well, I don't care what that verse says!" Savage shook his head, his eyes rebellious. "Give me a party anytime!"

Sixkiller said gently, "You've been to quite a few parties, Ben. How much good did they ever do you?" When the smaller man only shook his head, he added, "The verse just means that we don't really learn anything or get any better from good times. It's the hard times that make us what we are."

Savage stared at the funeral home employees as they got out of the car. They were all impeccably groomed, in neat dark suits. As one of them moved to open the door of the limousine, Savage muttered thoughtfully, "Yeah, I can see that. You can't make a soldier by taking him out to parties. Have to work him until he's ready to drop—" He cut his words off as Dani got out of the car, followed by her mother, Rob, and Allison. He gave the husky policeman a bitter glance, saying, "It's a rough way to go, Luke."

"Like they say—they never promised us a rose garden."

The two of them watched as the family was met by the pastor, who walked with Ellen into the church. As they moved past the pallbearers, Dani looked up suddenly, catching the eyes of Savage—and Ben was shocked at the bleak despair on her face. Her eyes were unreadable, and she turned without a word and went inside.

"If you gentlemen will step over here—" The speaker was a short, middle-aged man with a shock of reddish hair and tangled red eyebrows overlooking cool gray eyes. Savage remembered his name—Olan Miller. "Just make two lines here, if you will."

Savage got into one of the lines—four men to a side—and watched Miller swing the doors of the hearse open. He lifted something from the rear, which proved to be a sturdy cart with large wheels. "Just guide the coffin as it slides out," Miller said quietly.

The coffin—bronze, with a swinging handle on each side— was propelled slowly out of the vehicle. As Savage reached out and touched it, a chill shook him. It was impossible to think that his friend was inside that gleaming metal box. *Not Dan. He was always so alive!* he thought as they took hold of the handles and began guiding the cart and coffin down the sidewalk. *He was the most contented man I ever knew. Now he ends up like this!*

Shaking his shoulders, he forced himself to concentrate on the task ahead. Miller guided them down a short hall, through an extra-wide door, then into the cool darkness of the church. The sanctuary was packed—with every seat filled and people standing against the walls. Savage stepped back with the others as Miller and his assistant positioned the coffin, then he sat down with the other pallbearers to the right of the center aisle.

He saw many people he knew—including what seemed to be a large delegation from the New Orleans Police Department. Many of Sixkiller's staff were there, and over in one corner sat the mayor of the city and his wife. It was a heterogeneous group—some wearing expensive jewelry and fine clothing, but others dressed very poorly.

"Dan had a host of friends," Luke murmured as Miller finished his work, which included placing a blanket of red roses on the coffin. He moved away, and the strains of music filled the auditorium. At the same moment, the pastor left the family pew, where he had been whispering with the family. Loren Clay was a tall man with short brown hair and a wide expressive mouth. He seated himself in one of the dark oak chairs at the front of the church and dropped his head as the words of the hymn began.

Savage had been expecting a slow, mournful dirge, the sort he'd heard at the few funerals he'd not been able to avoid. Thus he was caught off guard by the sudden burst of sound—joyful and exuberant—that issued from where a small choir stood to his left. He blinked, slid his eyes around toward Sixkiller—and was shocked to see a tear run down the face of the toughest cop in New Orleans! The words of the song were clear, and he listened carefully:

> What can wash away my sin?
>   Nothing but the blood of Jesus;
> What can make me whole again?
>   Nothing but the blood of Jesus.
> Oh! precious is the flow
>   that makes me white as snow;
> No other fount I know,
>   nothing but the blood of Jesus.

A shock ran through Ben as the verses were sung. He was a self-contained man, not given to much emotion, but there was *something* in the large auditorium that refused to fit the catalog of his experience. He thought, *It's just emotional—that's all it is!*

But he knew it was more than that. The phrase, "Nothing but the blood of Jesus," hammered at him, bringing an unaccountable weakness. He bowed his head and set his jaw; his feet pressed against the carpet so hard that they cramped.

When the song was over, Pastor Clay rose and came to stand casually in front of the pulpit. His voice was a rich baritone, and though he seemed to speak in a conversational manner, it carried easily to the furthermost reaches of the room.

"We are here this morning to celebrate," he observed. Looking out over the crowd, he added, "I have been to many funerals, and some of them were not in keeping with the gospel of the Lord Jesus Christ. The songs were mournful! Most of them seemed to imply that once a person becomes a Christian, all he can do is endure the misery of this world until he's lucky enough to die so he can go to heaven. But the funeral songs I remember were not very happy." He shrugged his shoulders expressively, a small twitch of disapproval on his wide mouth. "We acted like—well, like the very *worst* thing in the world had happened!"

A slight murmur ran across the room, and Pastor Clay nodded. "I see some of you remember those funerals!" He lifted his fine head, his voice rose, and a smile came to him. "Well, our friend Dan Ross has left us. But I want to tell you that's not the worst thing in the world! No, for a man or a woman to lose their faith—that's worse! For a person to live to be old and miss out on knowing God in his heart—that's a *lot* worse! For men and women and boys and girls to go through suffering, that's worse, I think, than what we have here this morning—!"

Dani sat beside her mother, listening as the young pastor spoke. She tried to let his words comfort her, but all she could do was stare at the bronze coffin. The minister's words seemed to fade into a drone, so that they lost all meaning for her. And inside her head other words were forming:

You'll never see him again! He's gone—and you'll never be able to go to him—as you have a thousand times—and let him help you! And all because a man more vicious than any animal—!

Ellen sensed that Dani was not listening. She turned and put her hand on her daughter's arm. Dani did not look at her. Ellen saw that her jaw was set, that she was pale as a ghost. She wanted to throw her arms about Dani, to hold her tight. But she understood that this grief was something they would all have to endure alone. Others could say words and try to comfort—and that sometimes helped. But her own heart was a desert, and she knew that only faith would get her through the years to come. She turned her attention back to the minister, offering up a swift prayer for Dani: *Lord, they were so close—so very close—! Take the burden from Dani—don't let her grief destroy her!*

Pastor Clay didn't speak long. He quoted many promises, weaving them naturally into his remarks. He spoke of Dan Ross's life, of the many fine things he had done, of his long record of charity and willingness to help the weak. He spoke of Ross's outstanding role as a father and husband, his rock-like presence as an elder of the church.

Finally, he said, "We cannot but miss him, our brother, Dan Ross. Ellen will miss him; Dani and Rob and Allison will feel the loss. His many friends will constantly make the mistake of looking for him—only to realize that he's gone from them."

He hesitated, turned to gaze at Ellen and the family for a

long moment. Then he said, "We're celebrating the promotion of Dan Ross. But a promotion to be with Jesus—while it means glory for him—means loss for us. But I try to think of moments like this—of losses of friends and loved ones—in terms of someone going on a long ocean voyage."

Ellen leaned forward slightly, her eyes fixed on the pastor, her hands clenched tightly as he continued. "When that happens, we go down to the dock where the liner is waiting. And we say our good-bys and give the last kiss or handshake. Then we leave the boat, and we stand on the dock as the big ship begins to move slowly away from the dock. It turns and heads out to the open sea. We stand there watching, and as it gets smaller and smaller, sadness comes to us. We think of the loneliness that will greet us, of the warm hands and warm eyes of the one who's being taken away by the ship—"

Clay described the scene vividly, and then he said, "Finally the ship becomes a mere dot on the horizon, and then—it disappears. Someone cries out— 'She's gone!'"

Clay raised his head, and his fine eyes were filled with pain, yet his voice was strong as he added, "But somewhere—far away, on the other side, the other shore—somebody's waiting! And at the same moment that we're crying, 'She's gone!'—they're shouting with voices filled with victory: 'She's come! She's come!'"

A cry of pure joy rose from the throat of someone in the congregation—"Thank God for the victory!"

Ellen could not stop the sudden flow of tears, but she knew afresh what the peace of God and the joy of God were! The pastor held up his hands in a gesture of surrender and praise, saying, "We grieve and know our loss. But on the other side, there's rejoicing as Dan Ross comes home!"

The choir suddenly lifted their voices in a tremendous hymn of praise, their voices ringing as many of the congregation joined them in a spontaneous demonstration of the power of the Spirit:

> All hail the power of Jesus' name! Let angels prostrate fall;
> Bring forth the royal diadem, and crown him Lord of all. . . .
>
> Oh that with yonder sacred throng we at his feet may fall!
> We'll join the everlasting song, and crown him Lord of all!

The entire congregation rose to their feet, their voices rising, filling the auditorium with praise. Dani came to herself and stood up with her mother. Then the four of them drew together, holding desperately to one another.

Pastor Clay closed with a prayer, then said, "There will be a graveside service for those of you who would like to come." He stepped back, and the funeral director moved forward. He removed the flowers from the casket, opened it, and arranged the white silk inner covering. Then he stepped back, and as Pastor Clay came to stand at the head of the casket, motioned to the row on his left. At once the people moved forward and passed in front of the casket for their last view of Dan Ross.

It took some time, but finally all the mourners were gone, and the pastor went to stand beside Ellen. She tried to smile at him; then they walked together, followed by the children.

Ellen looked down at the still face of her husband. For the last time on this earth, she let her eyes rest on his strong features, thinking of the good years she'd had with this man. He looked younger than he had for some time—more handsome. She reached out, touched his face lightly. "Good-by, my darling!" she whispered, then turned blindly away.

Dani stood with Rob, the two of them holding tightly to Allison, who shook with sobs. Dani forced herself to look at her father—but could not stand it. She wheeled and left the church, head down and stumbling so that one of the director's assistants caught her arm and led her outside. Rob and Allison followed her out, their arms wrapped tightly around one another.

When the family was gone, Olan Miller efficiently rearranged the coffin, closed it, then said, "Now, gentlemen—"

Ben Savage followed the coffin to the hearse. The handles seemed cold to his touch as he gripped them to help move the coffin into the hearse. He stepped back, his mind empty, and it was only when Sixkiller touched his arm, saying, "Come on, Ben—" that he looked up and found his place in the car.

The drive to the cemetery was a blank for him. Sixkiller spoke with one of the other pallbearers, but Savage didn't hear the conversation. He was locked inside himself—his mind in stasis. He tried to pull himself together as they finally got out of the car and carried the casket to the small canopy where the hole gaped blindly—covered by green astroturf to blunt the sight of raw dirt. He helped place the coffin on the wide canvas straps that spanned the grave, then turned away at once, taking a spot near the far edge of the canopy.

The service was brief, consisting mostly of readings from the Scriptures—the same age-old promises that have been read over untold millions of graves. Finally the pastor prayed a brief prayer, then went around to say a word to each member of the family.

Ben felt very much alone as he stood there, his face in the canopy's shade, his back in the relentless heat. He knew some of the policemen and a few of the politicians, but except for a few nods and muted greetings, he spoke with no one.

Finally, he saw the family leave the canopy. Pastor Clay spotted him and came at once to say, "Mr. Savage? I think it would be better if you took the family home. I'll be by this evening to see them—but right now they need an old friend."

He turned to say a word to Ellen, leaving Ben little choice. Ellen looked at him, saying only, "Ben—?"

He took her arm and the two of them walked toward the long black car. On the way back, Ben tried to say something, but couldn't find words. He said finally, "I never—"

Ellen turned to him and saw his difficulty. "You never saw a funeral like that? Neither did I, Ben! It was good for me!"

The others said little, and when they got to the funeral home where the family had parked their cars, Dani said, "Rob, the Cougar is too crowded with five of us. I'll ride with Ben."

"All right, Sis." He hesitated, then asked, "Can we change clothes and go someplace, Mom?"

"Of course." Ellen smiled tiredly, knowing what lay behind the request—that Rob didn't want to go to the house so soon.

Dani got into Savage's old Charger, dodging a spring that threatened to puncture her. She said little as Savage started the powerful engine, and it was not until they were on the Causeway that Ben said, "Dani, I'm sorry. It's—worse for you, I know, than for me. But I've got a great big hole in my life."

Dani remained silent, watching the endless water of the huge lake. Finally she spoke. "A big hole—that's just what it's like, Ben."

Savage struggled, knowing that nothing he could say would change what was tearing at Dani. Nevertheless he tried. "I guess it'll get easier as time goes on."

Dani turned her head so suddenly that he was startled. She said evenly, "It'll get easier when Tommy Cain is dead!"

A shock ran through Savage. He turned to look at Dani, and saw that her lips were a thin line. Rage burned in her eyes like hot coals. He'd never seen her like this, and he didn't know what to say.

Dani looked away, nodded slightly, then murmured, "Yes, it'll be all right—when that monster gets what he deserves."

Then she added in a voice hard as agate, "And I'm going to see that he gets it, Ben!"

The tires of the Charger sang on the highway, and as it flashed along the strip of concrete, a brown pelican folded its wings and dropped in a steep dive not fifty feet out. It hit the water, making a small irregular geyser, then rose and floundered awkwardly upward—the scales of a long fish glinting like silver as it struggled frantically to free itself. Even as Savage watched, the pelican gulped convulsively, and the fish disappeared into its gullet.

17
A Visit with Dom Lanza

Late summer heat humid enough to suck the breath held New Orleans in its grip. Tourists from the colder north got off the plane, felt themselves struck in the face by the torrid breath, and scurried from one air-conditioned haven to another. The rich turned their thermostats down five or ten degrees, and the poor in the projects moved doggedly through the days, then lay out on balconies and in postage-stamp backyards after the sun went down.

Luke Sixkiller, emerging from a ratty apartment in the Calliope Project, felt the pressure of the blazing sun. His coppery complexion protected him from sunburn, but coming out of the dark interior into the incandescent brilliance caused him to squint his eyes. Turning to his companion, Sergeant Jerry Pierce, he grinned, saying, "This heat is pretty bad on you palefaces, isn't it, Jerry?"

Pierce was a small man, no more than five-eight with a florid complexion. He shot an irritated glance at his boss. "Like to get you up in North Dakota in a blizzard, Lieutenant." He fished a limp handkerchief from his pocket as they walked down the sidewalk and wiped his dripping brow futilely, then jammed it back into his pocket, and grunted, "Looks like it'd be too hot for the punks to shoot each other up, doesn't it?"

"Makes it worse, I think," Sixkiller shrugged. He was thinking of the room they'd just left, of the fifteen-year-old boy who had been shot full in the face by a nine-millimeter pistol. *Drug related*, he'd mark on his report. A scowl turned his heavy lips downward. *What's not "drug related" in this job?*

"You want me to pick up Ducote?"

"Yeah, I guess so. Watch your rear, though, Jerry. He's a shooter."

"Sure." Pierce didn't look it, with his thinning brown hair and gentle eyes, but he was one of the toughest cops in the NOPD. He'd killed three men and had taken two bullets himself in his eleven years with the department. He yawned hugely and blinked, still watching the streets carefully out of long habit. "Open-and-shut case. Looks like if Ducote wanted to blow the kid away, he'd try to do it when nobody was looking—not in front of three witnesses."

"They don't care much, I guess." Sixkiller thought for a minute and finally commented, "Seems like another world, the one I grew up in. If a murder took place, it made the front page. Everybody was talking about it, and the trial was covered from start to finish." A streak of fatalism brought a heavy expression to his brown face, and his black eyes were dull with weariness. "This one *might* show up on page ten."

Pierce's eyes were fixed on a small group of youths who stood congregated in an alley. He was a hunter, this nondescript policeman, who moved in danger as a fish moves through water. "I'll have to flush Ducote—but he won't run."

"No, he won't. He's only been out of Angola three months, and now he'll be going back for a stiff jolt." The thought depressed Sixkiller, and he drove it from his mind. "Take Hoke with you."

"Won't help," Pierce shrugged. "I can remember when it did make a difference—taking a black cop to pick up a black suspect. No more, Luke. They shoot anything that moves."

Sixkiller nodded, then asked, "You pick up anything on Tommy Cain yet?"

"Nah, nothing. He's a responsible citizen now, haven't you heard? Next thing you know, he'll be going to church." Pierce fixed his steady brown eyes on the big lieutenant. "You make him for the Ross killing?"

"He's the man."

"No charges in that one. Ross died of a heart attack."

"That's what it said on the death certificate." Sixkiller turned a fierce stare toward Pierce. "He's going down for it, Jerry."

"You know how hard it is to put a man in the chair," Pierce remarked. "And Cain is about the cutest bad guy we've had in this part of the world." He sat there beside his chief, thinking, *Luke knows more than he's telling about this. It's got to be tied up with the Ross girl. He's been walking around in a purple haze over her. Can't blame him much—that's one good-looking chick.* He admired Sixkiller greatly, and now thought he saw peril ahead for the big detective. He spoke offhandedly: "Be careful about Cain, Lieutenant. He's poison."

Sixkiller gave him a bleak smile. "Sure, Jerry. Just keep pumping your informants. You know, and I know, that he's the man behind most of the real bad stuff on the streets. I want him taken out."

Sixkiller pulled into the parking lot behind the New Orleans Police Complex. The two went inside, and for the rest of the day, Sixkiller worked steadily on his caseload. He and his squad were chronically overworked, for New Orleans held the dubious record of having more homicides per capita than any city in the nation. He sat in his office, going over cases with the men of the squad, making assignments for new cases, planning strategy for putting men and women behind bars. He spoke with lawyers, with prosecuting attorneys anxious to cut deals for their clients, with distraught family members frightened over the fact that their sons or daughters or husbands or wives were facing prison or the electric chair. He reviewed old cases, deciding which ones to archive and which to pursue a little more.

Finally, he got a call from his boss, Captain Lou Tournillon, chief of the New Orleans Police Department. "Get up here, Luke," Tournillon's soft voice said over the phone. "Right there, Captain," Luke responded. Hanging up the receiver, he left his office and went at once to Tournillon's office, an austere room furnished with an antique oak desk and only three chairs.

"Luke, what's with you and Tommy Cain?"

Tournillon didn't bother with a greeting, but turned from the file he was going through to hit Sixkiller abruptly with his question. "You don't have enough cases without trying to make a new one?"

Sixkiller eased his bulk into one of the black leather chairs and studied his boss. Tournillon was a Cajun, no more than five-ten and slender as a distance runner. He had the swarthy complexion, brown eyes, and black hair that were standard equipment for his people—and although he was in his middle sixties, there was little in his appearance to reveal his age. He had come up through the ranks, climbing to the pinnacle of the department through a rare combination of intelligence, guts, and tact. (The intelligence and guts were not rare in his ethnic group, but Cajuns are not noted for their gentle tempers or tact.) Tournillon had an impossible job—catching criminals and at the same time satisfying the crowd. Usually, when a man was arrested for murder, he had someone to fight for him—the NAACP, the ACLU, or some other advocacy group.

Captain Tournillon had survived because he knew when to be hard-nosed and when to bend. No man could survive in the jungle of Louisiana politics without getting along with the stream of movers and shakers such as Huey P. Long, Earl K. Long, and Edwin Edwards. The captain had managed to keep his place, despite efforts from powerful men to oust him. And the strain showed, Sixkiller noted, in his manner, if not in his appearance. "He's the man," said Sixkiller, "now that Dom Lanza's out of it."

"I hear you're trying to pin Daniel Ross's death on him."

"He set it up, Captain."

"Sure, you told me—three or four times." Tournillon slammed the file drawer shut, rolled to the window, and stared out. Then he wheeled back behind his desk. He gave Sixkiller a hard stare, then shook his head. "Luke, I'm going to be stepping down in a year or two."

Sixkiller's eyes opened in surprise. "Why would you do that, Captain?"

"Because I'm sixty-three years old. Because I've got a wife who's never had much of my time. And because I've got six grandchildren and not long to be with them."

"Won't be the same with you gone, Captain."

Tournillon said suddenly, "You ought to step into my job, Luke."

Sixkiller was not a man who was easily surprised, but his black eyes flew open and he could not answer for a moment.

Finally, he said, "You know better than that. I've made too many waves. It'll be some political appointment. The boys want somebody they can handle."

"I don't give a rat's rear what they want. I've given my life to this job, and I want a man sitting here who'll keep the department clean. You can do it, Luke. You're not as smart as I am, but you're clever, and you've got guts. But—"

"Let's have the rest of it, Captain," Sixkiller said.

Tournillon seemed to have difficulty finding what he wanted to say. His lean face was still, but the angular planes of his cheeks showed strain. "It's this religious kick you're on that bothers me," he admitted finally. "I'm a Christian myself—but with you it's different." When Sixkiller made no reply, the chief shook his shoulders restlessly. "No good to talk to you about it, I guess?"

"No."

"Thought not. Well, what about the Ross thing? It bothers me, Luke. I'd like to see Cain put where the dogs won't bite him, but I think it's personal with you. Ross was a good friend of yours, wasn't he?"

"Yes. And don't waste your time telling me about how it's not professional, Captain. When we lost Nap Poirrier, you swore to get the punk that did it. Wasn't too *professional* the way you nailed him, but I always admired you for it." Sixkiller shook his heavy head, his eyes half hooded as he stared at Tournillon. "I don't care what charge we nail Cain on, Captain. He killed one of the finest men I ever knew, and I'm going to pull him down!"

Tournillon could not restrain the slight smile that came to him. "Ross's daughter have anything to do with it, Luke?" He noted that his words had hit a sore spot with Sixkiller and waved his hand. "Never mind. Just don't let yourself get to thinking that all's fair in nailing Cain. Get him according to the books, Luke."

"Sure, Captain." Sixkiller saw that the interview was over and stood to his feet. "I'll watch it."

He left the building, found his car, and drove at once to Bourbon Street. Ross Investigations was located on the second floor of a white stucco building flanked by a small cafe and a souvenir shop. Sixkiller mounted the stairs, pushed through the door, and found Ben Savage perched on the desk of Angie Park.

"Hello, Lieutenant," Angie's usual bright smile was subdued, but she greeted him with as much good cheer as she could muster. "Catch any desperate, crazed killers today?"

"No, but I gave an old lady a ticket for double parking," Sixkiller parried. He took in Ben's outfit—worn Wrangler jeans, black Nikes, and a faded navy T-shirt with "I've Been to Gulf Shores" across the chest. "Like that outfit, Ben. Catch a yard sale?"

Savage shook his head sadly. "We can't all afford the best. You look nice, Lieutenant."

"You got nothing to do but put the moves on Angie?" Sixkiller shot back, embarrassed by the reference to his taste for high fashion.

Angie smiled again as the two of them carried on their war of words. Finally she asked, "Do you want to see Dani, Lieutenant?"

"Yeah, I do." Sixkiller hesitated, then asked, "How's she seem to you two?"

Savage and Angie exchanged a quick glance, and it was Angie who said, "Not good, I'm afraid."

"She talk much about her dad?"

"No, not at all—and she cuts me off if I say anything about him." Angie shook her head sadly, her long, blonde hair swinging with the motion. "It's like she's walled herself in, isn't it, Ben?"

Savage nodded shortly. "Be better if she'd talk about him." He hesitated, then added tentatively, "It's like she really hasn't said good-by."

"That's bad," Sixkiller murmured. He chewed thoughtfully on his lower lip, then said, "Tell her I'm here, will you, Angie?"

Angie pressed a button and, when Dani's voice answered, informed her, "Lieutenant Sixkiller is here, Miss Ross."

Luke nodded at Angie and Savage as Dani said, "Send him in." He passed through the heavy oak door into the darkened room. Only the late afternoon sun illuminated the office, falling in pale bars through the blinds. Dani made no move to get up from her desk. "Hello, Luke," she said quietly. "Want something to drink?"

"No, thanks." Sixkiller took a seat and looked around the office, studying as always the fine portrait of Dani's great-great-grandfather in his Confederate colonel's uniform. Something about the fierce-eyed man always reminded Sixkiller of Dani—either the iron determination in the mouth or the concentration in the eyes. "We on for tonight?" he asked, bringing his eyes back to Dani.

"Oh—I don't think so, Luke." Dani moved impatiently in her chair, bringing her hand to her mouth. She chewed on her thumb nervously, then, feeling the weight of Sixkiller's attention, jerked it away. "I need to stay around the house."

"Your mom's taking it bad?"

Dani rose, walked over to a small cabinet, and poured black coffee into a blue mug. "Better than I am," she shrugged.

Sixkiller sat still, studying her. She had lost weight over the past month, and her white, double-breasted jacket hung loose over her straight black skirt. Her square jaw was set; her wide mouth, which usually curved self-confidently, had tightened into a stubborn line. The hardness in her eyes disturbed him, partly because he had seen the same look before in his own mirror.

Sixkiller was a man wholly confident of his chores in the surface world, but greatly troubled at times by the problems of those close to him. He rose from the chair and went to her, and as he put his hand on her arm, she felt the warmth that he usually kept under lock and key.

"Don't mind me," she murmured. Suddenly she leaned against him, and he took her weight, his arms going around her. She rested against him, but there was no ease in her. He could feel the tension in her muscles, reflecting the stress that he knew lay inside. "Let it go, Dani," he murmured.

Dani drew back at once. "Tommy Cain? You want me to give him up?"

"Something will catch up with him," Sixkiller said slowly.

Dani's eyes shone with an adamant light that Luke had never seen in her. When she spoke, her words were clipped. "Something will catch up with him," she said. "And it'll be me, Luke!"

"Let me do it, Dani," Sixkiller urged. "He's bound to slip—and I'll be on him the minute he does."

Dani shook her head. "No. I'm going to see that he pays for what he did to my father." She drew away from him, and he knew she had put up some sort of wall between them. "Have you got anything on Cain?"

"Not yet. He's pretty slick, Dani."

"I don't think he'll let himself get caught again," Dani said. She moved back to the cabinet and picked up the coffee. Sipping it, she mused, "Got to get him off guard."

Something in the way she spoke caused an alarm bell to go off in Sixkiller's skull. "Dani—don't try anything fancy. Tell me before you make a move against him."

Dani found a smile. "Luke—thanks for everything. I'll be all right. You just do all you can to find a weakness in Tommy Cain."

Sixkiller was not satisfied, but knew it was pointless to say more. "I'll call you tomorrow."

"Be sure to," she said, and as soon as the policeman left the room, she went to her desk and found a number in a small book. Dialing it, she waited, then spoke. "This is Dani Ross. I'd like to come and talk with Mr. Lanza." She listened, then said, "I understand. And I'll be very careful not to tire him. Would it be all right if I came right out? . . . Fine, thank you very much."

Replacing the phone, she rose and went to the long credenza that lay just beneath the portrait of her great-great-grandfather. Opening the drawer, she took out the .38, donned the harness, then slipped the jacket over it. The weight of the gun pulled at her, and she looked up suddenly into the eyes of her soldier ancestor.

She stood there for a long moment, then whispered, "It's not as easy now as it was for you, Colonel. All you had to do was find the blue uniforms and blaze away—" A thought came to her, a flicker of uncertainty, but she only looked up, saying, "I guess you must have had some second thoughts, too, didn't you, Colonel?"

Picking up her purse, she strode out of the office. "I'm leaving for the day, Angie."

Angie watched Dani until the door shut behind her. Slowly she leaned back in her chair, shook her head sadly—then began to type steadily at her computer keyboard.

"I'm glad to see you, Miss Ross. Mr. Lanza has spoken of you often lately."

Thomas Rossi opened the door for Dani, his eyes warming at the sight of her. He took the hand she'd offered, saying,

"The family are all gone right now. They'll be sorry to miss you." Rossi was a tall, thin man with a pair of steady gray eyes. He'd been at the right hand of Dom Lanza for many years. Now he said, "I'll take you to him."

"How is he, Thomas?" Dani asked as she followed Rossi down the carpeted hallway.

Rossi shrugged, and there was pain in his eyes. "Not well. He—can't make it much longer." He said no more, but Dani saw the grief that lay below the stolid surface of the man.

She remembered when she'd come to Dom Lanza's house—she and Ben Savage—to guard the old man's grandchildren. The Lanzas had been engaged in a gang-style war with one of the powerful New Orleans drug lords. Somehow she had been able to win the old man's confidence enough to share her faith with him—and had often prayed that she might see Dom Lanza find God. Now, however, her faith seemed far away, her prayers futile. And she had other things on her mind.

"Miss Ross is here, Mr. Lanza."

Dani nodded at Thomas Rossi, who left the room at once. Dani moved to the bed—and was shocked at the sight of the sick man. Lanza, who had been one of the most feared men in the country in his heyday, now looked like a very sick child. He had always been a small man, but since Dani had last seen him, he had dwindled and shrunk. His dark skin was gray, and his white hair looked thin as it clung to his skull.

The eyes, she thought, retained much of the same strength she remembered. Dark eyes that could be fierce and proud. Eyes that men had dreaded and feared. Now they were still bright, though with pain rather than pride.

"Dom, I'm glad to see you." She sat down in the chair beside the bed, reached over, and took the hand he held out.

The bones felt fragile under the loose skin. "I'm sorry I've been so long getting back to see you."

Lanza held onto her hand for a moment, and then he smiled slightly. "I'm glad to see you." He fixed his eyes on her, then added, "Your father—I was sorry to hear about his death."

Dani dropped her eyes, for she had not mastered the art of keeping the sharp grief from showing when her father was mentioned. Just when she thought she had her emotions under control, someone would say something, and the tears would well up, though she willed herself not to allow it. Finally, she was able to nod.

"It was very hard for me," she said finally. Then—"How is your family doing?"

He seemed to understand that she didn't want to speak of her father—couldn't speak of him. "Very well—all of them." He was still holding her hand, and the pressure of his grip increased. "Your doing, Dani."

"Oh, Dom—!"

"Yes. If you hadn't come, my family would have been lost." The fierce old eyes sobered as he thought back to that time. His eldest son had just been gunned down by a rival organization, and his second-born son, Frank, had been forced to step in. But Frank and his wife, Rosemary, had been on the verge of separation, and their three children had become unmanageable. The stabilizing influence of Dani Ross had been the salvation of the family.

Now Dom said, "And I have good news for you, Dani." He waited until her eyes came up to meet his, and his thin lips curved upward in a genuine smile. Dani knew that Dom had just a short time to live, and her eyes opened wide as a thought came to her. She rejected it instantly, but Dom had seen her expression. "Yes—you have guessed it, I think. I have found the Lord."

"Oh, Dom!" Dani's eyes filled with tears, and before she thought what she was doing, she came up off the chair and threw her arms around the sick man.

Dom Lanza, a man who had been hard to take off guard, was not expecting such a strong reaction. He felt her soft form shaking with sobs, and he put up a trembling hand to stroke her glossy hair. Then she drew back saying, "That's all you need, Dom—a hysterical woman messing you about."

Dom drew the back of his hand across his eyes, then cleared his throat. "I—don't mind," he said quietly. Then he asked, "Can I tell you about it?" He lay there for the next ten minutes, telling how he'd never been able to get away from Dani's words when she was in the house. "I tried to laugh at them," he said, "but they kept coming back. And finally, Rosemary began to tell me about how God had put such joy in her." It had been his daughter-in-law, he said, who'd led him to call on God.

As he came to the end of his story, his eyes glistened, and he said, "I just asked God to save me, in the name of Jesus Christ. It seemed too *easy*, somehow, Dani. But I knew it had to be easy—a dying man can't do much." Wonder came to his eyes, and he whispered, "It was so quick, the way it happened! I've lived with doubt for so long. But as I called on God, peace just—just came to me, I don't know how!"

"Thank God!" Dani cried. "I'm so happy for you, Dom!"

The old gang leader looked at her, tears running unchecked down his worn cheeks. "Not any too soon, Dani," he whispered. "But now I'm ready." He looked at her, then said, "I only wish I could do something for you."

Dani hesitated, her smile fading. Slowly she said, "There is something you can do for me."

"Name it!"

Dani said slowly, "I want to put Tommy Cain away."

"Cain? Why?"

Dani explained what had happened and ended by saying, "He'll never be tried for killing my father, Dom, but he murdered him! I want you to help me bring him down!"

Lanza studied her face. "You want to put out a contract on him, Dani?"

He had known this would shock her, and it did. "Oh, no, Dom! Not that! I just want him stripped—in jail for the rest of his life."

Dani felt the weight of the old man's eyes on her. She looked up defiantly. "It's important. This man is vicious. He'll hurt others if he's not put in jail."

Lanza said, "Dani, your greatest charm for me was always the way you told the truth—no matter how much it hurt. Don't start lying to yourself about this. You don't really care about the people Cain might hurt. You just want to get revenge for what he did to your father."

Dani flushed, but shook her head stubbornly. "Call it anything you want, Dom. Will you help me?"

Lanza dropped his eyes. Pain ran along his nerves, but he had learned to endure that. What he could not stand was the hardness that had come to this young woman who had brought so much joy into his own life.

"Dani, you know what my life's been like. An eye for an eye—*especially* when it was a member of my family who was hurt. Now I'm an old man, and I can't go back. But if I could, the thing I'd change would be—the kind of thing you're letting control you."

"I'm going to get Cain, Dom, with or without your help. I just thought you might make it safer for me." As she said these words, Dani realized with a shock that something had changed inside her. She was *using* Dom Lanza—in a way that disgusted her. It was worse because he was in that first glow of finding God—and she was asking him to turn his thoughts back to the old ways that had almost destroyed him.

But she discovered that she could not turn back. The thing in her—the huge, black thing that pushed at her whenever she thought of Tommy Cain—was getting stronger. She mentally shrugged off her misgivings, waiting for Dom to speak.

The big clock on the wall ticked loudly in the large room, marking off time, slicing it into small segments—each tick measuring a fragment of a person's life. Dom Lanza knew he had very few fragments left, and it grieved him to use any of them in such a way as Dani Ross had suggested. He knew, better than she, how little satisfaction came from revenge. Yet he also knew how perilous her quest would prove—for he had been contending with carnivores such as Tommy Cain for half a century. This girl, who had become so precious to him at the last of his journey, was facing a terrible danger— and he had the knowledge to make her venture a little safer.

Reaching out, he took Dani's hand and held it quietly. Finally, he nodded. "I will help you, Dani. It is not wise—but I must do all I can to keep you from harm."

"Tell me, Dom!" Dani whispered intently. She leaned forward, her eyes fixed on his. "Tell me about Tommy Cain!"

18

Undercover

For a week after Dani's visit with Dom Lanza, she worked long hours at the office. When Angie asked her why she was working so hard, she said, "I've got to get away from things, Angie. I think I'll take a few days off."

"Be good for you, Dani. We can manage without you for a little while. Take a good rest."

The next day, Dani called Savage into her office and said, "Ben, I'm going to take some time off. Are you well enough to hold things down here?"

Savage gave her an odd look, then nodded. "Sure. No problem."

Dani waited for him to ask her where she was going, but he merely said, "Don't worry about the agency. If things pile up, I'll get Phil Carlisle to help."

Dani went over all the current cases with Savage, then drove home, tired to the bone. When she got home, she found the family waiting for her. "Crab salad, Dani," Ellen smiled. "A treat for you."

"Oh, Mother, you shouldn't have gone to all that trouble," Dani protested. She had little appetite, but she forced herself to sit down and eat some of the meal.

"We've been living on sandwiches and sweets." Ellen shook her head. "That's no way to eat." She looked over and saw that Rob was merely picking at his food but said only, "Did you see the registrar today, Rob?"

"No, I didn't," Rob said. He put his fork down and took a deep breath. "I've decided not to go back to school—not for a while, anyway."

"Rob!" Ellen exclaimed. "You can't drop out of college!"

Rob shrugged his shoulders. His face was haggard and there was no life in his voice. "It costs too much, Mom. I've been thinking of getting a job on one of the offshore rigs. It pays good."

"No need for that, Rob," Ellen protested quickly. "The insurance check will be coming soon. Dan saw to it that we wouldn't have to scrimp."

Dani, watching Rob closely, saw his lips tremble slightly when Ellen mentioned his father's name. But he tightened them quickly and said, "I'm glad of that, Mom—but I need a little time. Somehow learning how to diagram a complex sentence in English class doesn't seem too terribly important right now."

He got to his feet quickly, went over and gave Ellen a kiss. "I'm going out for a while. Be back in an hour or so."

When he was out of the room, Allison asked, "Mother, do you know Rob cries sometimes?" Her smooth, youthful cheeks were slightly concave, for she had lost weight since her father's death.

"I know, Allie," Ellen said quietly. "It's all right to cry sometimes. I do it myself."

"Don't we all?" Dani said. She rose, went over and gave

Allison a quick squeeze. "We'll make it, though, won't we?" She straightened up and gave her mother a glance. "Mom, I know it's a rotten thing to ask, but could you do without me for a few days, maybe a week?"

"Why, of course, Dani," Ellen said. She started to ask Dani where she was going, but changed her mind. "It'll be good for you to have some time to yourself. We'll hold the fort, won't we, Allie?"

Dani went over and gave her a hug. "When I get back, why don't we all go to Asheville? We need to see some mountains! I get tired of this flat old swamp!"

"All right, we will."

Later, when Allison and her mother were doing the dishes, Allison asked, "Mom, where do you think Dani's going?"

"I don't know, dear. But you know how close she was to her father. I think she just needs to get away for a few days."

Allison thought about it, then said in a subdued voice, "I wish I could run away! That all of us could!" She turned to her mother with tragedy etched on her lips. "Everything about this place reminds me of Daddy, Mom." She dropped her head and her voice quivered as she added, "I was looking for a pen today, and I found the card Daddy sent me on my last birthday. It said—it said, 'We'll have lots of birthdays together—'"

Ellen took Allison in her arms, soothing her with her hands and tender tones. She wanted to give way to the sudden and unbearable pangs of grief that rose in her, but she pushed them back, saying only, "It will pass, Allison. We haven't lost him forever."

"But—I want him *now!*" Allison wailed.

And inside Ellen a voiceless cry almost broke free: *So do I! So do I want him now! Oh, God—how I want him!*

But she only waited until Allison's spasm of grief passed, then said, "Let's go to the mall and pick out a new gymnastics outfit for you. Ben will be coming tomorrow for supper, and you're bound to end up on the trampoline. I'm ashamed of that old outfit!" She smiled as Allison blinked, then began hurrying to finish the dishes. *I wish a new outfit would take my mind off Dan*, she thought as she listened to Allison describe just the outfit she wanted.

Dani left at dawn the next morning, leaving a note for her mother: *Woke up early, so decided to get a good start. I'll call you tonight. Sorry to be such a wimp. It'll be better soon. I love you.*

She fastened it to the refrigerator door with a blue magnet shaped like an elephant, then left the house. She took the Causeway, turned left as it touched the southern shore, and soon was on Interstate 10. By the time she reached Baton Rouge an hour later, the first skim-milk color was beginning to dilute the coffee-black shadows of the sky. It was too early for offices to be open, so she wended her way through the city until she passed Cortana Mall. A few blocks west of the mall, set back off Airline Highway, she pulled off into a packed parking lot. A sign in front proclaimed, "Frank's—World's Greatest Biscuits."

She found a place at the rear of the lot, then walked back to the restaurant. It was crowded to the wall, and the hum of many voices almost drowned out the voice of the waitress who said, "Got one place left."

Dani followed her to the table, took a seat, and nodded when the waitress asked, "Coffee?" When she got the cup of steaming black coffee, she glanced down at the menu. "I'll have the buttermilk biscuits and white gravy."

"Anything else?"

A whim took Dani and she said, "I'll have some alligator sausage."

"Got it."

Dani sipped the coffee, wondering what alligator sausage tasted like. She'd eaten breakfast at Frank's a few times when she was working on a case, but she had never had the nerve to try such a delicacy. *You only get one time around*, she mused, *so eat all the alligator sausage you can.*

A short, muscular man of about thirty, with cowboy boots and a huge belt buckle, was watching her from the next table. Dani knew he would have something to say to her, but she almost smiled at his direct approach.

"You got an ol' man?" he asked. He had a round, red face and a reddish mustache that covered most of his mouth.

"Just a boyfriend," she said.

"You tight with him?"

"Pretty much."

"Ah, me, I don't ever have no luck, me!" He shrugged, then turned back to his meal.

When Dani's meal came, she discovered she was hungry. The biscuits lived up to their advertising; she ate both of them. And the alligator sausage was surprisingly good—so spicy that she could not really tell much difference from regular sausage. Still, she had a mental image of an armored back and eyes like walnut shells as she swallowed the meat. *No worse than eating a pig*, she told herself.

For an hour she lingered in the cafe, thinking of what lay ahead of her. She was cursed with a fertile imagination, and several distinctly unpleasant scenarios came trooping through her mind as she sipped the strong, black coffee. She could shrug those off, but the image of Dom Lanza's face came to her more than once, and she could not forget the pain in his eyes as she'd insisted on going through with her plan for getting Tommy Cain.

The thought of Lanza made her so uncomfortable that she

rose and started for the cashier. Her admirer called out, "Hey, pass a good time!"

She gave him a brief nod, paid her check, and left. It was warming up, early as it was, and she thought of the cool Smoky Mountains around Asheville, wishing she were there. She left the parking lot and began the irritating chore of driving through Baton Rouge to get to Louisiana State University. It was possible to go from east to west on Highway 10, but there was no easy way to move from north to south in the city. The town seemed to have been planned by people who were determined to route all traffic by the most inconvenient streets. As she wound around, she noted that as usual most of the streets were under construction. *They tear up a street, get all the traffic blocked—then go find a new one to tear up. Never finished a job that I know of! Whoever sells those plastic orange barrels they use to mark off street repairs must be a millionaire!*

She followed Acadian, crossed Highway 10, and finally arrived on the LSU campus. Summer classes were meeting, but only a few students could be seen. She parked the Cougar and made her way to the building where drama was taught; the first person she saw was Tanya Meno.

"Dani!" Tanya flew toward her and gave her a bear hug that robbed Dani of breath. "Why didn't you tell me you were coming—come on and let's go eat breakfast—"

Tanya was a tiny woman of thirty, no more than five-six, with the perky manners of a cheerleader. She had the blackest possible hair, chopped short, and dancing black eyes. Dani had once saved her father from a bad situation and Tanya had sworn to pay her back. But she had little money, and when she did save a little, she went to New York and tried to get into show biz.

Dani let the small woman bully her into the cafeteria, where she drank more coffee and listened while Tanya told her about her latest trip to the big city. "I didn't get any parts," Tanya said, "but I met an agent. He's going to take me on."

"That's wonderful, Tanya," Dani smiled. She knew in her heart that Tanya would never make it on the stage. Tanya loved the theater but had little acting talent. She reminded Dani of a young man she'd known in high school—Jimmy Singleton. Jimmy had burned to play professional football, and he *had* possessed the talent; he'd been a terrific halfback. Unfortunately, he was only five-feet-six and weighed 130 pounds. He had eventually shelved his dream and had become a first-rate auto mechanic.

But Tanya Meno was still clinging to her version of Camelot, and she was itching to tell Dani all the details. Dani drank cup after cup of coffee until finally Tanya paused for breath. "Tanya, I need help," she said.

Tanya at once grew intense. "Anything! Just ask, and if I got it, it's yours, Dani!"

They were seated at a back table, but Dani lowered her voice as she began speaking. "Tanya, I've got a job to do, and to do it I need to change the way I look."

"Oh, that's *easy!*" Tanya cried. "We can dye—"

"No, Tanya, I mean I have to look so different that even my own family wouldn't recognize me," Dani said. "It's a dangerous job, and if I get found out—well, it won't be nice."

Tanya, for all her cheerleader behavior, was a shrewd woman. "And you came to me because I'm in makeup and costumes, right?"

"Right! If you'd just do that instead of beating your head against the wall trying to be another Meryl Streep, you'd have a great career."

Tanya gave Dani a searching glance. "Been thinking about that some, Dani," she murmured. "I've had some good offers on the coast. May take one of them." Then she said, "Let's get out of here. We've got work to do."

"This has to be between you and me, Tanya. I'd rather none of your associates know about it."

"Not to worry! They're all gone except me. All off getting a fat Ph.D. Come on."

Dani followed Tanya back to the red-brick building, where the two of them wound up on the second floor. "Got everything we need right here, Dani," Tanya said, waving her tiny hand around. "Complete style shop, for one thing. Thought once I'd be the world's greatest hair stylist. Got my license and all—but I hated listening to those old hens jabbering all day!" She laughed and pulled Dani around the room, waving at the costumes that lined the walls. "If we don't have it here, I can make it," she boasted, motioning at the sewing machines over on tables beside the wall.

Finally, when Tanya had showed Dani everything, she said, "Come over here and sit under this light. I need to study you."

Dani took a seat under a powerful floodlight. Tanya grew silent, her face intent as she moved around Dani, studying her from every angle. "All right," she said finally. "Now, what sort of person do you need to be?"

Dani took a deep breath, then said, "I need to look as much like a cheap, conniving, low-life woman of the streets as you can arrange, Tanya. Good-looking, but hard."

Tanya Meno nodded. "You want it, you got it! Now, what we'll do first is—"

As soon as Jap Gatlin opened the door and saw the woman, he knew she was trouble. Gatlin knew trouble pretty well, having been drowning in it most of his life—some of the worst of it stemming from women like the one who stared at him now. As manager of the Camelot Hotel, he'd learned to spot the tough ones, and the woman who stood there definitely qualified.

"I need a place," she said in a husky voice. "Let's see what you've got."

"Only got one suite—and it's pretty steep," Jap said. "Fifty bucks a day."

"I hope it's cleaner than that shirt you're wearing, Clyde," the woman said, her lip curled. "Let's see it."

"Up on the second floor." Yes, she was trouble—but a real looker. Her hair was too blonde to be for real, but nothing unusual about that. Real big eyes, with phony lashes, mouth all swollen like the women wanted—and a figure that made Jap swallow. He took it in as she preceded him up the stairs and grew so jittery he fumbled with the key in the lock.

"What's the matter, Clyde?" the woman asked, laughing at him with her sexy eyes. "You nervous around girls?"

Jap looked away from her, stepped back, and muttered, "Go take a look."

He went in with her, trying not to stare as she walked around the room. She was tall, and the dress she wore clung to her full figure. *Pretty hard number,* Jap thought sullenly. *Be bringing men in here—but that's not my problem.*

The woman looked around casually, then nodded. "I'll try it for a week."

"Got to have cash rent up front," Jap protested. "Not my rule, lady."

"My name's Margo St. Clair," the woman said. She dug into her gold purse, fished out a roll of bills, peeled off several, and tossed them at the manager. "But don't let it get out, Clyde," she added. "I don't like surprises. No visitors unless you clear it with me first."

"Okay, Miss St. Clair."

She handed him her car keys. "Have the boy bring my suitcase in. It's in the trunk of the white Town Car in the parking lot. And have him bring a fifth of Wild Turkey when he comes."

Jap nodded, left the room, and descended the stairs back to his office. A lanky man of about fifty was leaning against the wall, watching a football game on television. "Legs, get the suitcase out of the white Lincoln in front and take it to 204. Take a fifth of Wild Turkey, too."

"Okay." The bellhop straightened slowly—in sections, it seemed—then asked as he took the keys, "Anything I need to know?"

Jap scowled. "Keep an eye on the babe. She'll draw men like flies."

"Just what we need, ain't it?" The black man ambled off, and Jap sat down to watch the game. When Legs came back, he sat down loosely. "Be action in 204. Don't send me if they get to shootin'."

"Let 'em knock each other off," Jap grunted. "It'd be the kind of thing that broad would enjoy!"

Upstairs, in room 204, Dani was sitting on the bed, a smile on her heavily painted lips. She was physically exhausted, but her nerves were drawn tight as a piano wire. The Camelot was in the heart of New Orleans, not many blocks from her own office. She had rented a car in Baton Rouge and driven back as Margo St. Clair. Now, for the next few days, she would have to play a role more difficult than any she'd played on stage in her younger days. She had no illusions about the character of the men and women of the streets; they would kill her out of hand if they suspected for one moment that she was not what she seemed.

She got to her feet, stretched, and started for the bathroom, thinking longingly of a long hot shower. But even as she crossed the room there was a tiny clicking sound, and the door suddenly opened.

Dani took one frantic look at the man standing there and whirled. She lunged for the .38 she'd removed and placed on the chest beside the bed—but she never made it.

Strong hands seized her, and she was whirled around to face the man who'd broken in. He had black hair, slicked back like a fifties rocker, and he wore a pair of dark sunglasses. His lips were puffy, and when he spoke his voice sounded as though he had rocks in his throat. "Come on, baby!" he whispered. "Don't be a stranger with ol' Newt!"

Dani opened her mouth to scream, but at once he shifted his grip, holding her tightly with his left hand, and clamping his right over her mouth.

Terror ran through her—a raw, hot fear that seemed to drain her strength. She fought to free herself, but she was a child in his steely grip.

He turned her head to face him, and he smiled suddenly, saying in a voice she knew very well: "Aw, come on, Boss—don't act up so!"

The hand left her mouth, and she stood there, legs rubbery and mind reeling. Then Savage pulled the dark glasses off and grinned at her. "How do you like my undercover disguise, Boss? About as good as yours, wouldn't you say?"

Dani glared at him, but discovered that her knees were giving way. She staggered back toward the bed, sat down abruptly, and then, with anger flashing from her eyes, spat out, "I *hate* you, Benjamin Davis Savage! You're fired!"

Then she crumpled and to her absolute disgust began to cry. The hot tears rose to her eyes, and she turned away from Savage and choked as she said, "Get out of here—!"

Suddenly she discovered that sniffles wouldn't do it—so she stretched out on the bed and loosed great ropy sobs that shook her body.

19

Doing Business in the Quarter

Savage stood over the form of the sobbing woman, his eyes fixed on her, indecision on his face. His first impulse was to reach out, to try and soothe her, but he held back. Long before, he had learned that something in Dani resisted such comforting, so he walked over and sat down on the maroon recliner beside the window.

Dani was aware that he was still there, but it took some time for her to get a firm grip on herself. Finally, she took a deep breath, got up off the bed, and walked into the bathroom, slamming the door. Turning on the cold water, she soaked a towel and pressed it to her face. The rough surface felt good on her heated cheeks, and as she stood there, most of the anger left her. The heavy makeup, she saw as she looked into the mirror, had run, and there was no way to clean up because her cosmetic case was in the outer room.

She had no choice, for she knew Savage would not leave until she came out. *Why does he always have to see me at my absolute worst?* she thought grimly, then opened the door and went out.

"All right, Ben, what's the big idea?" she snapped. Stalking across the room, she picked up her cosmetic case and slammed it down on the dresser, adding, "You have to prove what a marvy detective you are?"

"I was worried about you."

Dani, ready for a wisecrack, paused abruptly at his words. She cast a searching glance at Savage, but saw no trace of the cynicism he sometimes used with her. Turning back to the mirror, she covered her confusion by applying a layer of Clinique makeup remover to her face. When she finished, she asked in a less strident tone, "How'd you find me, Ben?"

"I didn't buy your story about getting away for a little vacation." Savage watched with interest as Dani began to wipe the goo off with Kleenex. "I followed you to Baton Rouge." A smile came to his face as he added, "When you came out of that building at LSU I nearly lost you. If you hadn't got in your Cougar, I'd still be there."

Dani finished cleaning her face. The simple task had given her time to cool down, so she came over and sat down on the bed across from Savage. "I suppose you've figured out what I'm going to do."

Savage shrugged. "Not too hard, even for an ex-acrobat. You're going on the street to try to get the goods on Tommy Cain."

"That's right. There's no way to get him for murdering my father, but I'll come up with something to put him away." Dani was acutely aware that Savage's gaze was doubtful. "I know—you think it's crazy, that I can't do it."

"I think you can get killed, that's what I think," Savage said instantly. "Dani, there's guys out there who'd slit your throat for ten bucks. Cain hires them for peanuts."

"I'm going to do it, Ben." Dani's voice was flat, and her jaw was tightly set. "I talked with Dom Lanza, and he gave me some direction."

"Dom Lanza?" Savage's face was swept by surprise. "I thought he was too sick to get into stuff like this." He gave Dani a closer look then, and understanding came to him. "Oh, I see."

Dani felt distinctly uncomfortable. "All I did was ask him to tell me how I could nail Tommy Cain." Her words seemed to hang in the air, and as the silence ran on, she finally spoke with asperity. "There was nothing wrong with asking Dom for help."

Savage was staring at Dani, his dark eyes accusing. "I guess if I was dying, there are things I'd like to do besides being a button man."

A button man, Dani knew, was a small-time criminal who went around setting up jobs for others. His words cut her, and she stuck her chin out aggressively. "I thought you were Dad's friend. If you really were, you'd want to do something to the man who killed him."

"I don't think using a dying man to get your revenge is the best thing you've ever done. Besides, I thought Christians were supposed to forgive their enemies."

"Why, you—!" Dani was filled with a sudden flare of anger. "What do you know about Christianity?"

"Not much."

Dani knew she was making a fool of herself, but she could not seem to control the scene. Finally she said wearily, "Well, Ben, think whatever you please. I'm going to do everything I can to get Cain. You just run along and mind the store."

Savage shook his head firmly. "No, I'm sticking with you. Tell me what Dom said."

Dani should have felt a thrill of victory at seeing Ben come over to her side of the argument, but she did not. There was a look of—disappointment on his face, and she knew she had fallen in his judgment. She almost gave it up, but the thought of letting Cain go free came back bitter and strong in her, so she pushed on stubbornly.

"Dom said the police would have a hard time getting Cain on anything. If he takes a fall, it'll be because somebody blindsides him."

"Dom's probably right," Ben nodded. "Cain's got his mind made up that he's never going back to Angola—and to him that means he doesn't do anything that would give the police a handle on him."

"Yes, so Dom said somebody would have to get close to Cain."

"And then what?"

"It'll have to be a drug bust, Dom said. Everything else in the rackets is tied to that these days."

"You'll never get Cain within ten miles of the actual stuff. He'll always use someone else to make the buy. And whoever he sends will be so scared of Cain he'll never talk—or if he does, it'll be just his word against Cain's." A double furrow appeared between Savage's eyebrows as he struggled to make the thing clear to Dani. "Contract killers hardly ever get caught, Dani. The best contract killer has no ties to the victim and no motive other than the money he receives from a third party. He's practically a phantom. That's why mob-related hits have only resulted in a handful of convictions. And if Cain gets one glimmer of an idea that you're a threat to him, you'll have a caller—one who can open doors as easy as I just did."

Dani shook her head. "You know about all these things, Ben, but all we need is one break. Dom says that since he retired, someone has taken over almost all the dope traffic in New Orleans—and it's bigger than ever, he says."

"Does he think it's Cain?"

"Well, he didn't know. But he said even *that's* a tipoff, because he still knows everybody in that world. He says Cain's the one smart enough and tough enough to handle it."

"What's his idea about trapping him?"

"The big dealers all have the same problem—getting enough dope. They have to get it from outside the States, and that's why the Gulf Coast is the hot spot; that's the easiest place to bring it in. Florida was the center for awhile, but now it's Louisiana. And Dom says there *has* to be some place in the city or close to it where the stuff is really stockpiled."

"Sure, it'd almost have to be," Savage nodded in agreement. "He have any idea where it is?"

"No, but he said he'd have someone ask around." Dani leaned forward, her face almost pale without the heavy makeup, her eyes intense. "Dom says if someone could make Cain believe he had a huge shipment of dope—really gigantic!—Cain might risk taking part in the actual sale."

Savage leaned back, his eyes thoughtful. "Yeah, I see that. It'd have to be really big to bring him out, though." He rubbed the scar on his forehead, thinking hard. Looking up, he shot a question at her: "So you're going to go to Cain with this story that you've got a mountain of dope, but he's got to come in person to make the payoff?"

Dani smiled a little nervously. "It sounds silly when you say it like that, Ben, but it could work, couldn't it?"

"Not the way you're set up."

"Why not?"

Savage shook his head. "A lone woman making a deal like that? No chance! Cain would send his thugs for you. They'd take you to some little cabin out in the swamp, and they'd have you telling them everything. Why should Cain pay for the dope when he can wring it out of you, then feed you to the alligators?"

The jarring harshness of his speech brought a slight shudder to Dani's shoulders, but she kept her eyes on his. "Well, what can I do, Ben?"

Savage grinned suddenly, his teeth white against his tanned skin. "Do? Why, Boss, you get a real tough honcho who can handle the goons that Cain hires."

Dani saw that, unlike her, Savage seemed to have no fears. The idea of dealing with merciless criminals was, to him, a game. She leaned over and put her hand on his forearm. "Know where I can get such a man?"

Savage looked down at her hand, then nodded, his hazel eyes gleaming. "You got the best there is, Boss!"

He got up and stretched. "Ready to go?"

"Go?" Dani stood up, but looked mystified. "Go where?"

"I thought you wanted to smoke Tommy Cain out of his lair. You can't go up to his front door and offer to sell him coke like a Girl Scout peddling cookies, can you? Cain's got to hear about us—the good-looking broad who's got something to sell and her pet gunny."

Dani stared at Savage, asking, "Where'd you get that outfit, Ben? You look like a bouncer in a Mexican bordello."

Savage cocked his head, a glint of humor touching his eyes. "How'd you know what one of those look like? Never mind, Boss," he said when she looked nonplused. "It was in my trunk. I used it over at Lafayette on the Belgrade case. Just remember—I'm Flash Manti. Grass never grows where I spit!"

"All right, Flash." Dani rose from the bed. "Just let me put my face on again." She got up and saw him looking at the skin-tight dress with its thigh-high slit. A slight smile came to her lips, and she quipped, "Flash, you have no idea how expensive it is to dress this cheap!"

The French Quarter is only about a square mile in area, but for Dani and Savage it proved to be a colossal haystack with no needle to be found.

For four nights they cruised the backwaters of the Quarter, spending time in bars like Mom's Society Page and Dungeon. The former was a hangout for female impersonators, the latter a rough dive where individuals could easily get hurt. They sauntered down a narrow four-block section of Decatur Street, near several big convention hotels and dodged tourists passing through on their way to Bourbon Street. Dani noted that most of the tourists were approached by panhandlers and prostitutes. Ben noted her look of distaste and remarked, "It's New Orleans Times Square—but not as well-lit."

Dani, despite an earlier nap in her hotel room, was exhausted by three A.M. "Ben, we're not getting anywhere," she complained.

They were in a dark, smoke-filled bar, tucked into a booth against the back wall. The barmaid had brought them drinks, but both of them carefully emptied them into the water glasses. Savage said, "Don't call me that—I'm *Flash!* Yeah, we're making headway, Margo. See that pair over by the door, the big ones?"

Dani saw two men standing at the bar. Both of them wore sport coats despite the heat, a sure sign that they were carrying. She saw that they were watching her and Savage, though trying to appear casual. "That's Nellie Box and Enos Riker, two of Cain's favorite leg-breakers. They've been following us for two hours. Didn't you see them?"

Dani gave him a startled look. "No, I didn't. You think Cain sent them?"

"I doubt it. Box is just muscle, but Riker is a different story. He's tight with Cain, I hear, though nobody ever sees them together. Luke thinks Riker is the point man for Cain." He straightened his tie, pulled his hat down in front, then said, "Let's go give Tweedledee and Tweedledum a chance to talk to us."

"Here?"

"Nah, they like privacy to beat their victims up. Let's go find a dark alley and give them a shot at it."

Dani's heart began racing, but she set her jaw and rose from her chair. Ben dropped a twenty on the table and stepped back, allowing her to go first. Most of the men, he noted, watched her as she moved across the floor. He didn't look at the pair at the bar, and as soon as they were outside, he said, "Let's head this way. Lots of dark alleys."

The streets were not so crowded now, and as they moved away from the line of bars and clubs, the sounds of music grew fainter. The streetlights were much dimmer than the neon lighting, and as they walked into the thicker darkness, the muted sounds of the bars seemed ghostly to Dani. They had not gone more than two blocks before they came to a small parking lot filled with cars. A single light faintly illuminated a sign that read, "Parking by the Month."

"Steady now—" Savage spoke in a whisper, but Dani had already heard the sound of footsteps behind them—footsteps that grew more rapid as she listened.

"Hold it right there!"

Savage wheeled at once, pulling Dani around with him. Two men surfaced out of the darkness. "Don't be a pair of fools!" Savage snarled. "We're not carrying any big money."

"Just hold it right there, Flash," the shorter of the two men said. He was no more than five-eight, but very thick and strong. "Just a little conversation—that's all we want."

"I don't talk to strangers," Savage shot back. "My mama taught me better."

"Yeah, I can see you had good raising," Box said. He was overweight and had a nose like a saddle. His voice was raspy from too many blows in the throat during his days as a heavyweight boxer. He reached out and slapped the side of Savage. "I'll just take that iron, Flash," he grinned. He cocked his head to one side, studying Savage, then suddenly reached out and cuffed the smaller man on the side of the head. The blow drove Savage backward, and his hat fell off.

"Never mind that; check the woman's bag," Riker said sharply. He waited until Box took Dani's purse, peered into it and said, "No gun."

Riker relaxed, letting the snub-nosed pistol droop. "Now, you been doing some talking—some pretty big talking. I think you're both a pair of phonies, and we don't need any more of them around here."

Savage touched his jaw, glaring at Box, then he turned to face Riker. "You two got names?"

"I'm Riker—this is Box. What's that get you, Flash?"

Dani spoke up, hiding the fear that rose in her throat. "You want to make a buy?"

Riker grinned at her. "Buy what? Do we look like holiday shoppers, Margo?"

"You obviously know our names, Riker," Dani said, making her voice as hard as possible. "If you didn't think we had something, you wouldn't fool with us. But I don't do business with little boys. Tell the main man if he's in the market for the biggest buy he ever heard of to give me a call."

Box chortled in a raspy voice, "Feisty broad, ain't she, Enos? I bet if me and her had some *private* time, she'd tell me all about it."

Riker stared at Dani, considering the idea. "Maybe so." He

teetered on the brink of a decision, then made up his mind. "Tell me all about this big deal. What is it, blues and bennies? Or you got a kilo brown stuff—some of that Mexican H?"

Dani laughed at him, her voice shrill in the quietness of the alley. "Riker, you're out of your league. I'll tell you this—just to get your attention." She lowered her voice and leaned forward. "Four hundred keys of pure white stuff!"

Translated that meant four hundred bags of heroin, each bag weighing 2.2 pounds—and her words brought the eyebrows of Riker up abruptly. He giggled, saying, "You wouldn't be trolling if you had that much China white. Lemme see your arm—" He took the arm Dani held out at once, studied it carefully, then muttered thoughtfully, "No tracks."

That, Dani saw, meant something to him, and she laughed, "I sell the stuff, Riker. Only a fool uses it."

Riker hesitated, then said, "I guess we'll have to go to some quiet place and talk about this. Just move along in front—and remember, a .44 makes a pretty big hole in the head." He waved the pistol, and Dani thought with a single flash of terror of what Savage had told her.

But there was no place to run. Riker would shoot—of that she was sure. And then Savage said, "I'm not going, and neither is Margo." Then he spat out, "And nobody clips me, Box—!"

Dani saw Savage reach out and drive his fist into the face of the heavy-set man, but the blow didn't move Box. He let out a roaring curse, saying, "Don't burn him, Enos—let me take him!"

Dani saw the huge man throw a punch at Savage. When Ben fell, she knew all was lost, for he was no match for the huge boxer. She saw Riker grinning. He said, "He's going, all right, but we'll have to carry him."

Box leaned down and jerked Savage to his feet, pulling his hamlike fist back for a blow on Savage's unprotected face— but then something happened. Dani could see only a blur of Savage's arm, but she heard a solid *thunk*—like someone hitting a melon with a wooden mallet.

Box seemed to—to *melt!* Dani watched with fascination as his legs folded and he hit the concrete bonelessly, his face slamming into it with a meaty sound.

Riker was a man of chain-lightning reactions. Even as his partner was collapsing on the ground, he was wheeling to put the muzzle of his revolver on Savage—but he was too slow.

This time Dani saw it—the blur of motion and the short stick that Savage held in his right hand. It moved faster than a striking snake and caught Riker's wrist with a sharp *splat*. Riker cried out and grabbed his wrist; the gun fell with a clatter to the sidewalk.

Savage scooped up the .44 and handed it to Dani saying, "Bust him if he moves, Margo—!" He leaned over, reached inside Box's coat, and came up with a pistol, then retrieved his own gun from the gutter where Box had dropped it when he went down.

"I—think you broke my arm!" Riker moaned. His face was suddenly pale and dripping with sweat.

"No, it's not broken," Savage said. "You can hear the bone snap when that happens. Sounds like a dry stick breaking," he added with clinical distraction. Then he turned to Dani, asking, "Well, what's the game plan, Margo? Want me to dust these two?"

The explosion of violence had brought a dryness to Dani's throat. She swallowed quickly, then said, "No. They're good guys—just overmatched." She studied Riker, then noted that Box's legs were beginning to twitch. "I think we'll have a word with your man," she nodded.

"We're freelancing, Margo," Riker said. He was holding his injured arm carefully, his eyes fixed on her.

"Now, Riker," Dani smiled. "Don't tell me we're going to have to take *you* to a nice quiet place where Flash can persuade you to do some talking?"

Savage suddenly reached out and tapped the top of Riker's hand—the one at the end of the injured wrist—and the pain of the light blow brought a gasp from the gunman. "This stick will outlast your wrist, I gar-on-tee," Savage said, slapping it into his hand thoughtfully.

"Okay! Okay!" Riker gasped. "But I do the calling."

"Fair enough," Dani nodded. "I think you will find I'm a reasonable woman."

By the time Box recovered enough to walk, pain was raging in Riker's wrist. "You *did* break it!" he accused Savage.

"Put some ice on it," Savage suggested. "Or is it heat? I always forget. Anyway, it's one or the other."

Fifteen minutes later they were standing at a phone booth on a deserted street. Dani got a quarter from her purse and put it into the slot. Riker growled through tense lips, "You get back there with your man. I don't want you to hear me dial."

"Pretty smart," Dani agreed, and she nodded at Savage. They drew off about thirty feet, Savage remarking, "Don't either of you clowns get the idea you can outrun a slug." They stood there watching carefully as Riker dialed, then began talking. They heard nothing, but it was obvious that what Riker was hearing was not pleasant. Finally Riker looked at them venomously and raised his voice—"He wants to talk to you."

Dani and Ben moved forward, and Dani took the receiver. "Hello," she purred. "I hope you don't blame your boys too much. They were just out of their league."

A small silence, then a voice: "You must play in a pretty

fast league, Margo. Box isn't much, but I don't remember anyone ever taking Enos."

It was a smooth voice—the voice of Tommy Cain. He spoke easily, as if he were chatting with an old friend about pleasant matters. That in itself was enough put Dani on her guard. His best men had just been had—and he showed absolutely no concern.

Got to remember all the time that he's as unpredictable and poisonous as a king cobra!

"I understand we might do a little business," Cain said cheerfully. "Tell you what, Margo. Just as a sign of good faith, why don't you let my two boys go, give me your phone number, and we'll see about this thing."

Dani laughed. "I'll let your men go, but I don't give my number out to strangers. You name a place, and I'll be there. Anywhere you like—in the middle of Jackson Square or in the darkest section of the Atchafalaya Basin."

"I don't do much business personally, Margo."

"Then I'd better see what your competition will offer. Maybe they've got an up-front man who's not afraid of his shadow."

The taunt cut Cain, as she'd hoped. "Hey, it's okay. I'll just see what kind of a hand you've got. Me and my rabbit will take a look at your stuff. Tell you what, I keep a low profile, so I'll pick a good spot where we won't be bothered with too many people."

A rabbit, Dani knew, was a specialist used by the buyer to test drugs. "Where and when?"

He laughed with pleasure. "You're a real businesswoman, Margo. I like that!" The line went quiet, then he said, "There's a phone booth in front of the Aquarium of the Americas. Be there at ten o'clock tomorrow morning, and it will ring. I'll tell you where to bring the stuff—and come alone."

"Where I go, Flash goes," Dani countered. "You bring the rabbit, I bring Flash."

"Fair enough. See you tomorrow, Margo." He laughed and added, "Riker says you're a real looker. Maybe we can make this deal for fun and profit?"

Dani said, "I don't think you can handle a real woman." She hung up firmly, then turned to say, "You two can go."

"Our guns?" Riker demanded.

"I'll give them to your boss tomorrow. Come on, Flash."

When they got to the Lincoln and Savage pulled away, Dani collapsed into the soft cushions. "Oh, Ben—we did it!" Then she straightened up and turned to face him. "*You* did it, I mean. Where'd you get that stick?"

"Hid it in my sock. Had to let Box put me down to get at it."

"Is it some kind of mysterious Eastern form of martial arts?"

Savage turned to grin at her, his eyes laughing.

"No. It's something I learned as a very young man."

"How does it work, Ben?"

"When anyone threatens you, you pick up a stick and hit them in the head with it."

Dani thought that was the funniest thing she'd ever heard, and she was still giggling as he opened the door to her room.

On impulse she kissed him on the cheek, saying, "Good night, Ben. You're—quite a guy!"

Savage stared at the door as it closed. The smile left his eyes, and he murmured, "Yes, I am, aren't I?" He slammed his fist into his palm, then wheeled and stalked down the hall, his back stiff and unyielding.

20

Rendezvous at Alligator Annie's

Dani tossed in bed for hours, seeking sleep, but it avoided her. She would shut her eyes, willing herself to drop away into unconsciousness, only to realize that her hands were in fists and her teeth were clenched. Finally, she dropped off, but nightmares haunted her sleep. Most of them were vague and filled her with a nameless fear, but one was so vivid it seemed to be etched on the lining of her eyelids.

She was running down a long dark street, so dark and shadowy that she could see only the outline of a form ahead of her. The only sound she could hear was the pounding of her feet on the earth—that and the hoarse breathing of the man she was pursuing. It seemed to go on for hours, the chase, and as she ran, anger was building in her breast. She carried a gun in her right hand, and she longed to use it on the fugitive who fled before her.

Then, without warning, the man's mad flight ended, for he had encountered some sort of a barrier. As Dani drew closer, she saw he had run into what seemed to be a barbed-wire fence. He was struggling, trying to free himself, and Dani felt a wicked streak of glee run through her.

She raised the gun slowly, savoring the moment. Then, when the sight was on the trapped man's chest, she pulled the trigger. The explosion from the cartridges bracketed the whole world, and she saw her victim's body shudder as the bullets struck, one after another.

Finally, she lowered the gun, and a heavy silence rolled over Dani. As she stood there, her eyes fixed on the body that now hung limply, like a dead insect trapped in a spider's concentric web, she seemed to hear her heart thudding. Then she walked toward the man, and as she walked the darkness seemed to give way to an arboreal light.

In the dream, as Dani approached the still figure, she felt a savage satisfaction and a longing to look on the dead face.

She walked toward the corpse and, seeing the head drooping down, reached out and grasped the hair, pulled the head upright, and stared at the face—

And she came out of the dream screaming soundlessly—for the face was her own!

"No! Nooooo!" she moaned, and fought the covers, escaping from the bed to stand trembling, every nerve alive with fear. Her breath came in great gasps, and she was weeping helplessly.

Finally, she stumbled to the bathroom and turned the cold water of the shower on full force. Stripping off her gown, she stepped into the stinging spray, gasping when the cold water took her. For a long time she stood there, letting the water play on her face, then finally got out and dried with trembling hands.

Fumbling to pull on a short robe, she went to look out the window. The ragged edge of dawn had begun to break up the blackness of the sky, and when she glanced at the clock, she saw that it was only ten after six.

Four hours to wait. To sit around the hotel room was unthinkable, so she put on her makeup and slipped into the clothing she'd decided to wear for her meeting with Cain—a pair of Levi's stretch-denim jeans, and a turquoise hooded top. She slipped on a pair of white Reeboks, then paused. Slowly she opened the top drawer of the chest and stared down at the .38 that rested in the holster. The smooth sheen of the metal glinted, reflecting the light overhead. Gingerly Dani picked up the weapon, handling it almost as if it were some sort of deadly viper, fastened it around her waist, then pulled the top down to cover it. As she picked up her purse and left the room, the pressure of the gun against the small of her back seemed to increase. The weapon seemed to have turned to ice, the cold of the metal chilling her spine.

She fled the hotel, getting into the Town Car and almost blasting out of the parking lot. She left the city, and for hours she drove the state and rural roads that spread outward into the many small towns that sprouted like mushrooms across the countryside. Once she stopped for coffee at a tawdry road-side restaurant. The occupants—most of them men wearing jeans, faded shirts, and big belts—stared at her openly. She drank the thick, bitter Cajun coffee, then left and drove until the clock on the dash informed her that it was nine o'clock.

She caught the heavy morning work traffic, and by the time she had parked and walked to the Aquarium of the Americas, only a few minutes remained until ten. She found Savage already there and nodded at him. "He call yet?"

"No calls so far." Savage was wearing a pair of charcoal slacks and a loose-fitting white pullover. At that moment, two harried-looking middle-aged women were herding a gaggle of small children toward the entrance, and one of the flock looked up at Dani. She was no more than six, with red hair and round blue eyes. "We're going to see the sharks," she announced.

"That's fine, honey," Dani answered, and even as she spoke, the phone rang. Taking a deep breath, she picked up the receiver. "Hello, Tommy," she said, making her voice as neutral as she could manage.

"Hey, Margo," Cain's voice came to her, strong and confident. "You ready for our date?"

"Where do we meet?"

"You know about Alligator Annie?"

Dani had to think for a moment. "You mean the tour of the swamp out by Houma?"

"Right. Meet me there in one hour."

"Kind of public, isn't it?" Dani had been expecting Cain to suggest some obscure spot, far from any activity.

"Way to hide is in a crowd, honey. See you in an hour."

Savage watched Dani carefully as she hung up the phone. "What's the plan?"

"He wants to meet at Alligator Annie's."

A glint of humor came to Savage's eyes. "If he acts up, we can throw him to the gators," he remarked.

They walked to Dani's car, and when she said, "You drive, Ben," he slid in behind the wheel. They drove down Canal and turned left on Magazine Street under the approach to the Greater New Orleans Bridge. Savage cast a covert glance at Dani as he looped back to the Mississippi River Bridge, noting that she was pale under her makeup and that lines of strain were etched around her mouth. As he cleared the bridge and drove down the Westbank Expressway, he said, "This might be a little more exciting than a high tea, Boss."

Dani answered sharply, aware that he was watching her. "I'm all right, Ben. He won't try anything."

"That's your opinion—not mine," Savage returned. He laid the needle on sixty, and the large car glided along until they came to Bridge City, where the highway turned into U. S. 90. He followed a series of signs that led south of Houma, the roads winding through bayous and swampland.

"There it is," he murmured, nodding at a large white sign that announced, "Annie Miller's Swamp Tour." A small frame building perched on the brink of the open water of the bayou. He parked the Lincoln between a bright red Ranger truck and a battered Impala that had passed up no opportunities to be involved in any collisions. Savage shut the engine off, then turned to face Dani. "We stay with the crowd, Boss."

"All right." Dani nodded, and as she got out of the car, she spotted the two men at once. "There they are, Ben," she murmured. "You go buy the tickets while I meet with the man."

"Okay, Boss."

Two flat-bottomed aluminum barges were anchored next to the shore, and a few people had already found places on one of them. Dani walked toward the two men, and Cain at once strode up to meet her. He was wearing a pair of white pants and a dark blue T-shirt. A white billed cap was pulled down over his eyes, which were hidden by reflective silver lens. He was, Dani thought, a good-looking man. "Margo?" he smiled. "Just in time." He put out his hand, and Dani took it, letting nothing show in her eyes.

"How about we do it like this," Cain said easily. "Your guy and my guy stay here. My rabbit checks out the stuff. You and me go for the tour, sit in the back, and get acquainted. What do you say?"

"All right. Flash has the samples."

That was the way it went. Dani told Savage, "Flash, wait

here with this dude." She waved a hand toward the small, thin man who seemed slightly nervous.

Cain said at once, "Check it close, Charlie." Then he stepped back, leading Dani toward the barge. One barge was almost full, but only half a dozen people were in the second. Dani stepped into the craft, which rocked slightly. A low rail ran around the boat, and a sign warned, "Do Not Touch the Alligators!"

As soon as they were on board, a short woman emerged from the small building. She had a round, tanned face and the placid expression of one who has found satisfaction in life. She wore a baseball cap held on by a veil, shapeless men's work pants, and a plaid shirt with the sleeves rolled up over strong arms. "Let's go feed my babies," she nodded and, stepping into the crowded barge, sat down and started the twin Evinrudes.

A short swarthy man with a heavy mustache had stepped into Dani and Cain's boat and said, "Keep your hands out of the water, folks. These things ain't pets."

Cain asked, "Anybody ever get bit?"

"Woman two years ago." The man eased the craft out of the shallows and turned it around with a practiced hand to follow the leading barge. He fished in his shirt pocket and came out with an amber square of Red Man. He carefully picked some lint from the tobacco, bit off a healthy chunk with a set of bright teeth, then added, "She reached out and that gator stripped her whole han' off. Nothin' but bones that woman draw back."

Dani felt Cain's arm pressing against her and resisted the impulse to draw back. "I guess that proves something, doesn't it, Margo."

"Yes. Don't put your hands where they don't belong—or

you might draw back a nub," Dani said evenly and moved away from his touch.

Her reaction amused Cain. He grinned and made no attempt to come closer. Turning his attention to the banks, he said, "I'll remember that. But a good-looking woman like you has got to expect that a man will take a try, right?"

Dani made no answer. She was watching the banks slide by as the two barges moved smoothly along. The bayou narrowed into a channel no more than forty feet wide, and the tall cypress trees that lined the shores reached out and shut off some of the bright sunlight. The limbs were loaded with moss, dangling down in bundles like knitting yarn. Dani remembered that the old-timers during the Great Depression—and even before—had collected the moss and used it to stuff mattresses.

The water ahead of the leading barge was brown and smooth, with an oily cast, and the banks were lined with some sort of tall, weedy plant with a blue blossom that drew many bees. As they proceeded deeper into the swamp, water lilies and hibiscus made a green carpet on much of the surface, and large frogs took alarmed dives into the water, sending out spreading concentric circles. The heavy odor of the swamp was a miasma of rotting vegetation, rich dirt, woody cypress, all wrapped in an envelope of moist air.

Annie cut the Evinrudes back, as did the pilot of the second boat, and the two crafts slowed until the churning behind the boats was just a smooth roiling of the brown water.

"There's one!"

Dani looked up as someone from the lead boat cried out, and she saw what appeared to be a log on the bank. There were other logs, but this one was different, for it rose up on four scaly legs, turned, and slid with a plop into the brown water. She watched as the gator moved across the water toward the boat, leaving only a slight ripple. There was no sign of effort on the part of the reptile, just a smooth, easy glide with the eyes just above the surface.

As the beast reached the first boat, Annie extended a pole with a large hook on the end and a chunk of raw meat attached. "Now, Baby," she crooned, "here's your breakfast!"

She held the meat about two feet over the water, and the gator's tail disappeared. He rose straight out of the water, his grinning jaws spread wide. The inside of his jaws and his throat were white, and the teeth curved like small scimitars. He rose effortlessly, closed his jaws on the meat, then swallowed it with one convulsive movement. Dani saw the bulge in his throat as the meat passed down, and she felt slightly ill. The big gator slid back into the water, turned, and in the same smooth fashion made his way back to the shore.

"Some 'baby' she's got there," Cain remarked. He shook his head, saying, "I hear some of these Cajuns get in the water with those things and fight them with just a knife—the big ones, too." The thought seemed to disturb him, and he shook his head. "They got to be nuts to do a thing like that, don't they?"

"I guess it's some kind of initiation with them," Dani murmured. "Like the Masai in Africa. The young men aren't counted as men until they've taken a lion with nothing but a spear."

Cain considered that, then said, "Well, I guess it's the same everywhere, Margo. Man has to fight something to get to the top. And some of the guys I've had to go up against—well, I'd just as soon tackle that gator as them."

"I've heard you're tough, Tommy," Dani ventured, turning to look at him. His eyes were hidden behind the reflective lenses. She could see twin reflections of herself—which gave her something of a shock, so different did she look in her disguise. "You've had to put a few dudes down."

Cain instantly grew reserved. "I stay away from stuff like that, Margo. It can get you a jolt in the chair in this state."

"I know. You hire it done."

Cain said nothing, but turned to watch the show. Annie was calling the beasts by name—"Cherry," "Boudreau," "Tina Belle." As the barges moved down the waterway, the crusty backs would appear, take the meat, and disappear.

"Let's sit down," Cain said. "You see one gator, you've seen 'em all." He sat down on the back seat and Dani sat beside him. The other four passengers were in the front of the craft, watching the show and talking to the pilot. Cain held his hand out before him—strong, tanned hands with long fingers and well-manicured nails. He made fists, stared at them, then clasped his hands and said, "All right, what's the story?"

"I've got enough H to fuel your operation for a long time, Cain."

"You tell me that? But where'd you get it, Margo?" His voice was easy, but there was no real ease in the man. He was like a cat, able to go from a relaxed mood into full alert with no warning. He would not have survived, she realized, if he had not had this quality.

"I got it in from a seaplane that landed in the Gulf—ten miles offshore. We loaded it into a cabin cruiser and brought it right into New Orleans. That's where it is now, but it's where nobody would ever guess."

Cain shook his head. "Nothing's that easy, Margo. Who's going to hand over eight hundred keys of heroin without getting the cash?"

Dani said evenly, "The pilot was my brother, but Nicky never knew that."

"Nicky?" Cain snapped. He thought rapidly, then shot a question at her. "You don't mean Nick Defronttio!"

"Sure I do," Dani said. She and Savage had worked on the story carefully, knowing that Cain would demand some explanation. "My brother brought the stuff in from Colombia, using Nicky's money. He was supposed to make the drop on Friday. But he came a day earlier—and a hundred miles away from where Nicky was waiting. I was there with the boat to take the load."

Nicky Defronttio was Cain's chief competitor in the world of drugs. The two of them had never met, but their underlings were waging a fierce battle for control of territory. If Tommy Cain had one overriding obsession, it was to bury Defronttio. Now he said sharply, "Nicky's not a safe man to cross. He'll skin you alive, Margo."

"Not when I get the payoff," Dani smiled. "I'm leaving this country, Tommy, and I'm going with enough money to pay for plenty of bodyguards."

Cain was unconvinced. "I don't buy it. Nick Defronttio's no kid. He'd never let himself get took by a couple of mules."

Mules was the title given to those men and women who moved drugs from place to place. Dani suddenly reached out and put her hand on Cain's cheek. She smiled and whispered, "He's a man, Tommy. And any man can lose his smart when the right woman comes along."

Cain suddenly pulled his sunglasses off and looked into Dani's eyes, now turned bright blue with colored contacts. "You're something else, Margo," he murmured. "I never saw a woman with more nerve." He ran his eyes along her body, adding, "And in such a nice package."

Dani said, "I don't think it would be as easy to fool you as it was Nicky."

Cain was a vain man, and the compliment pleased him.

"No, I'm a different sort of fellow." He reached over, pulled her toward him, and as he kissed her, Dani felt her nerves crawling, but forced herself to put her hand behind his neck. When he drew back, Cain was pleased with himself. "Be a new thing for me."

"What will, Tommy?"

"Having a woman for a partner."

"Just for this one deal," Dani said. "What's your offer?"

As the boat nudged its way through the oily smooth waters, with Annie calling out, "Come on, Baby—come to Mama!" the two of them sat in the stern, making a deal.

They came to the halfway mark, and Dani and Cain watched as the gators came swarming from the banks. A ramp built of cypress rose out of the water, and Annie led the gators up by holding the meat in front of them. They marched out on their scaly legs, snapped the meat, then rolled back into the waters.

Finally, the pilots turned the barges around, and they cruised back down the narrow neck of water, the Evinrudes barely turning. The banks were fertile with vegetation and animal life. White egrets rose from time to time, floating lazily over the water, rising like white ghosts to sit in the tops of the tall cypress trees.

A red-tailed hawk returned from the hunt, and Dani's boat passed underneath. She saw a limp form dangling from his talons, and the deep piercing eyes of the fierce raptor seemed to focus on her. He was a machine made for killing—deep-set eyes with binocular power for spotting prey, wide, powerful wings for propelling the bird at tremendous speed for short distances, and needle-sharp talons to pierce to the heart of a hapless animal when powered by the huge muscles of the bird's legs.

A killer, Dani thought, *but only to meet his need. He kills for food, in order to stay alive—not for gain.* She thought suddenly of her dream, and despite the heat of the swamp, a cold chill seemed to roll over her. *He doesn't kill for revenge, either,* was her thought. She drove it away, focusing on a big nutria that looked up from the bank, staring at the boats as they passed. Twenty yards further, she saw a cottonmouth as thick as her thigh draped over a limb. When he opened his mouth, she saw the whiteness that gave him his name, and one drop of pristine liquid formed at the tip of one needle-sharp fang.

As they approached the bank, Cain said, "We both know that the stuff Flash brought proves nothing. Anybody can pick up a deck of China white."

"Sure, I know that." Dani saw Ben Savage leaning against the frame building, watching them come in. "And you know that I'm not about to let anybody get within a mile of the place where I've got the load stashed until I know I'll get the cash."

Tommy Cain shrugged. "Always that way, Margo. No trust left in this world."

"Get real, Tommy!" Dani snapped. "I'd as soon trust one of those gators with a big T-bone as I would you with eight keys of H!"

"Okay. What you got on your mind?"

"One thing—money. You come up with my price, we do business."

"Raising that kind of dough's not easy. Have to laundry a batch."

"Give me a number where a message can get to you. I'll call you tomorrow."

"That's not enough time!"

Dani smiled. "Nicky's mad at me, but if he could get his junk back, he might be willing to forgive—or forget. I'll be calling him, Tommy. I always believed in free enterprise. If you can't handle it, Nicky can."

"All right, all right," Cain protested. "All I need is a little time—two days maybe, three at the most. Give me a call day after tomorrow."

Dani said, "One thing, Tommy. I don't deal with anybody but you. I know you don't like to get involved directly—who does? But with a deal this big, I'm not taking any chances. I'm flexible on the time and place—but I want you on the spot with the cash. Bring all the rabbits you want, but you be there!"

Cain hesitated, and for one moment Dani thought she'd gone too far. But his greed was too great, and Cain nodded. He took a card from his pocket, wrote a number on it, and handed it to her. "All right, but it's gotta be fail-safe, Margo. I'm not going to Angola again, and that's flat!"

"No need for that," Dani nodded. The boat touched the shore, and she murmured as they moved to step out of the boat, "You be careful—I'll be careful. We make a mint, and nobody goes down, right?"

"Right!"

They moved to where the two men waited, and the nervous young man reported, "First class, Mr. Cain."

"All right," Cain said. He slipped his shades back on, adding, "Call in two days, right?"

Dani nodded and turned to go to the car with Savage. They drove off quickly, and when they were out of sight of the bayou, Savage asked, "He go for it?"

"I think so. He wants a couple of days to get the money."

Savage studied the road ahead. "You're gonna have to come up with some way to close the door on him. And it won't be easy."

"Will you help me, Ben?"

Savage blinked, then turned to give her an odd look. "You're asking for help? What about the independent liberated woman who needs no man?"

Dani was thinking about the alligators with their great teeth and fixed smiles. They reminded her of Cain, and she looked down at her hands, noting that they were not steady.

"He's a monster, Ben. He's got to be put away."

Savage tried once more. "Look, Dani, let Luke do it—or me." He struggled for words, and finally said, "I—don't like what's happening to you."

Dani turned her eyes on him in a startled fashion. "Happening to me?"

"You're getting hard," Savage stated flatly. "I've seen it before, Dani. Always happens when a man—or a woman— sets out to get somebody. I saw it in the Corps and on the force in Denver. It even happened to me. I set out to get a guy, and in the end I got him. But it got me, too," he ended, his face tense. "Let it go. Cain will die of a bullet or of cancer or of old age. What's the difference?"

Dani, for one moment, was tempted to agree. But even as she considered it, she saw her father's gray, dying face—and then the cold eyes of Tommy Cain.

"Just this one thing," she said quietly, an iron stubbornness in her voice. "I'll do this one thing—and then it'll be over."

Savage dodged an armadillo that scurried out from the bushes. When he had straightened the car, he murmured, "A thing like that—it's never over, Dani!"

The armadillo, almost flattened by the wheels of the Lincoln, dashed madly for half a dozen steps—then, as the sound of the car faded, forgot all about its brush with death and began nibbling contentedly on a juicy stalk.

21

"Don't Let Yourself Hate—!"

After the meeting with Cain on Tuesday, Dani decided she could not face being cooped up in her hotel room until the next contact. She felt cheap and tawdry in the role of Margo St. Clair. So she dressed in a simple, light burgundy dress and put her hair up. It was an effort to become herself again, but it did little good; she still felt grubby and unwashed. "I've got to get out of here or I'll explode," she told Savage when he stopped by at eleven the next morning to fill her in on what was going on at the agency.

Savage was out of his Flash Manti disguise, wearing instead a pair of light tan slacks, a white shirt, and one of the four neckties he owned. When Dani stared at it, he said lightly, "I like to dress up on holidays."

"Holiday? What holiday?"

"Carrie Nation's birthday," he said. He grinned at her, then sobered. "It's time to bring the fuzz in on this thing, Boss."

Dani shook her head. "No, we'll wait until we've got it pinned down. Otherwise they might get in our way."

Savage shook his head shortly. "Look, it's got to be a federal bust, somebody from narcotics."

"We can wait."

"Wait for what?" he demanded. "Have you got some kind of idea that you're going to pull this off alone?" His angular face bore a streak of irritation as he jibed, "You been watching too many of those dumb women television cops. They always get their man—and in exactly one hour. But Cain's no actor, and if we nail him, it's going to take the best we got at the ranch!"

"Ben, I—"

"Dani, this thing's got you hooked! You've got a personal vendetta, and you've got this fixation about nailing Cain and watching him squirm. But you can't do it without help—and more help than I can give you."

Dani was angry with him, and for half an hour the two of them argued. Dani knew her case was weak, that Savage was right—and this made her all the more stubborn.

Finally, she threw back her head, crying, "Oh, all *right*, Ben! We'll do it your way. Now go on and get that awful look of superiority in your eyes like you always do when I give in to you."

Savage glared at her, but there was no satisfaction on his face. "Just give Luke a call. And if you think I'm getting any fun out of this, you're nuts!"

Dani knew she had gone too far—that she ought to ask his pardon—but she couldn't do it. With jerky motions she dialed a number, and after going through a sergeant, heard Sixkiller say, "Sixkiller here."

"Luke, can you get loose for a little while? I—I need some help."

A short silence, then—"You want to come down here?"

"No, not there."

"Okay. It's about time to eat. You know Della's Delight?"

"I don't think so."

"It's down in midtown," he said, then gave her the address. "See you in thirty minutes."

Dani hung up the receiver and turned to say to Savage, "We'll meet him at a place call Della's Delight. Do you know it?"

"No. Probably a fancy place with tablecloths. You ready?"

They drove at once to midtown, a neighborhood that used to be high rent and silk stockings. The houses were enormous and had once been beautiful and ornate. Now they were deteriorating hulks, like derelicts parked forever in a ship's graveyard.

Dani grew depressed as they drove along the streets. Some of the houses were three stories tall, with balconies, gingerbread carving, and bow windows. Most of the mansions had been carved up into eight or ten small apartments. But the first floor of one of them had been made into a restaurant. "There it is," she said, indicating a sign with peeling paint that read, "Della's Delight."

Savage stared at the building and nodded as he eased the Lincoln into a slot. "Just as I thought. One of those snooty places the rich tourists flock to."

But there were no rich tourists inside Della's. It was crowded, but mostly with a mixture of poorly dressed whites and blacks who eyed Dani and Savage as they entered. A tall woman with a regal face came to greet them. "Table over here," she said, and led them to a small table with four chairs. She asked as they sat down, "What you want to drink?"

"Lemonade for me," Savage said. Dani ordered the same.

At that moment, Sixkiller came through the front door. He walked over and grinned, saying, "Hello, Della. You're looking mighty fine."

"Hello, Lieutenant. You with these folks?"

"They're oil people from Texas, Della. Got me down here to bribe me to fix a ticket for them." Sixkiller had not seen Dani with her hair bleached, and a slight shock ran over his face as he looked full at her.

"Uh-huh." Della's face was smooth, but a light of amusement flickered in her golden-brown eyes. "Gone on the take, have you, Lieutenant? I'll pass the word around."

She placed three menus encased in clear plastic on the red-and-white checked tablecloth, then stood there patiently talking to Sixkiller while Dani and Savage looked over the selections. It didn't take long, and the two of them exchanged stunned glances. Sixkiller watched their reactions with a deadpan face. He was wearing a light-gray double-breasted suit, a dark-blue shirt, and a maroon tie with flecks of gold. His shoes were alligator, and the Rolex on his thick wrist caught the light from the hanging lamps, making a rich glow.

"I'll have the pig's lips, Della," Sixkiller announced, then glanced over at his companions. "What looks good to you two?"

Savage asked gravely, "Do you recommend the neck bones and gravy?"

"Not bad, " Sixkiller shrugged. "Miss Ross, you'd go for pig's feet, yams, and dirty rice."

"Chit'lins are fine today," Della nodded.

Dani suppressed a shudder, then picked what seemed like the most civilized item on the menu. "I'll have some of the boiled river shrimp," she announced.

Della picked up the menus, and Sixkiller sat there idly, a big man at ease. "You look like a real dame, Dani," he remarked coolly, taking in her bleached hair. "I hope you don't get addicted to that rig." He spoke randomly of his work, asking no questions, and when the food came he looked across at Dani, remarking, "Maybe we better ask the Lord to bless these pig lips." He bowed his head, either not knowing or not caring that the action brought some startled reactions from customers who were watching the fuzz covertly. When he had finished, he started on his food, and Dani, to her surprise, discovered that the shrimp were delicious. She entered into the talk, allowed herself to be talked into tasting samples of pig lips and neck bones from the plates of the others, and all the while she felt apprehensive about Luke's reaction to her plan.

Finally, they finished, and were eating slices of buttermilk pie and sipping the café au lait that Della brought in tiny china cups. Luke gave Dani a straight look, raised one black eyebrow, and said, "Okay, what's up?"

Dani flushed and dropped her eyes, then had to smile ruefully. "I feel like a kid caught with his hand in the cookie jar."

"Wouldn't be Tommy Cain's cookie jar, would it?"

"Well—yes," Dani stammered slightly. She never knew exactly how much the big policeman understood about what was going on in her mind, but it was almost always more than she was comfortable with. She gave Ben a quick glance, then began to relate what she'd done. But the telling of it was difficult. No matter how she put it, she sounded to herself like a fumbling amateur. But she grew more aggressive, ending by saying, "Cain's getting the money for the payoff. In a day or two, he'll be ready to meet me. All you have to do is be there when he makes the buy."

"That's all?" Sixkiller mused. "I'm surprised it's so easy. Here we've been trying for a long time to clean up the drug traffic in New Orleans, and the answer's been right under our noses."

Dani's face burned, for though Sixkiller's tone was mild, there was a slight touch of acid in his words. He sipped his coffee, stared at her for a long moment, then asked, "Ben, have you talked to her about this?"

"No use."

Ben's short answer angered Dani. She glared at the two men, and her temper slipped. "What's wrong with you two? Don't you *want* Cain to be put away?"

Neither of them answered, and Dani at once said, "Oh, I'm sorry, Luke, but can't you see? This will work!"

"I don't see how." Sixkiller shook his head. "Dani, this bird is no patsy. If he does show up for the payoff—and I'm betting he won't—he'll have it fixed so that no cop can get within ten miles of the spot. It'll be some spot where he can take the dope, keep his money—and put you in the river wearing concrete shoes."

Dani shook her head. "I know that's what he'll do if he gets the chance. But I've been thinking about it—and there's a way to get him cold."

Sixkiller said tersely, "I'd like to hear it."

Dani leaned forward and began speaking earnestly. She spoke rapidly, and both men saw she'd gone over her plan many times. She used her hands, making gestures in an eloquent fashion as she spoke, and in her intensity her eyes grew luminous. Both Sixkiller and Savage were aware of her appeal, for in the soft curves of her body and the shape of her face lay a femininity that could not be denied. Still, she had a lot of Dan Ross's drive, and there was a steely side to her that glinted at times like this.

Finally, she put her hand out and gripped Sixkiller's wrist hard. It was an unconscious act, something that one man might do to another, but Sixkiller stared at her long slender fingers with an odd expression.

"It'll work, Luke!" Dani insisted. She started to say more, but broke off, and pulled her hand back quickly. A slight flush tinged her wide cheeks, and her lips were drawn into a line. "Can't we try it?"

Sixkiller stared down at his wrist, his brow knitted. Finally, he shrugged. "It'll probably get me fired—and you and Savage thrown into the river—but I can see you're going ahead with it no matter what I say. So why not?"

"Oh, Luke!" Dani exclaimed. "It'll be all right, you'll see."

Sixkiller picked up the last morsel of buttermilk pie, nibbled at it, then put down his fork. "Well—" he muttered dolefully, "I've got to go talk to the head of narcotics." A scowl pulled at his lips, and he said while rising to his feet, "Ed Hidalgo is his name. He's going to *love* my butting in and doing his job!" He gave Dani a sour look, said, "You pay for the lunch," and left abruptly.

"I don't think he's happy in his work," Savage spoke up. Then he snapped his fingers. "I forgot—urgent call for you. Angie left the number on her desk, but she was gone, so I don't know who it is."

Dani stared at the number. "That's Dom Lanza's private number." She got to her feet and walked to where Della was seated behind a register. "Is there a phone I can use?"

"Local call? Okay."

Dani took the phone the woman handed her, dialed the number, and waited. A man's voice answered, "Hello?" and Dani recognized it. "Frank, this is Dani."

"Dani—it's my father." A thickness came to the voice of the oldest son of Dom Lanza, and he cleared his throat. "It's a bad spell. The doctors say—he can't make it."

Dani gripped the phone tightly. "Oh, Frank—!"

He cut in, "Dani, he's been asking for you. Can you come?"

"Of course. Which hospital?"

"He's here. Wouldn't go to a hospital. Says he can die better at home with family."

"I'll be there as soon as I can, Frank."

She hung up, said, "Thank you," in a wooden tone, then turned to face Savage, who had come up to pay the bill. He dropped a twenty on the glass countertop, then took Dani's arm and guided her outside. "Is it Lanza?"

"Yes. He's dying, Ben!"

Savage said nothing, but when they were in the car, he left the parking spot at a fast clip. "No chance?" he asked.

"Frank says not." She thought about the last time she'd seen the old man, who had become very precious to her. "Drive as fast as you can, Ben!"

By the time Savage pulled up to Twelve Oaks, the fortresslike estate of the Lanza family, he had broken every traffic law in the book, but somehow they had avoided being stopped. As they pulled up to the cast-iron gate, a tall, uniformed guard took one look inside and waved them on. "Go right in, Miss Ross. I'll call Frank to tell him you're here."

The gate swung open, and Savage whipped the car through the curving road that wound through a forest of oak and pine. When he came to a jolting halt in front of the large white plantation house, Dani slid out. "I'll hang around out here," Savage called out as she ran up the steps.

The door opened, and Rosemary Lanza rushed out, grabbing Dani in a fierce embrace. "Oh, Dani—" she cried out, and for a moment Dani could do no more than hold the sobbing woman. Then Rosemary, a tall woman with dark blue eyes and startling good looks, stepped back, wiping her eyes with a handkerchief. "I'm glad you're here," she said thickly. "Frank said for you to come up as soon as you got here."

Dani followed the woman down the long hall, asking, "Is he any better, Rosemary?"

"No—he's dying," Rosemary said, shaking her head. "I think he's been holding on just to see you." She opened the door to Dom Lanza's room and stepped aside, allowing Dani to go first. When Dani stepped inside, she scanned the room, noting that Thomas Rossi was standing back against the wall and that another man—presumably the doctor—stood beside him. Frank Lanza sat beside the bed, holding his father's hand. He looked up at Dani, leaned over, and said, "Pop— Dani's here!" Then he got up and turned to Dani, motioning at the chair. His eyes were sunken, and there was a bitter cast to his lips.

Dani sat down and reached over at once to take the trembling hand that Dom Lanza held out. The old man's face was ashen, and his eyes were closed, but as her hand touched his they fluttered, then opened. Dani leaned forward and brushed the white hair back from his forehead, whispering, "I'm here, Dom—"

He turned his head, his eyes dulled by pain, but a smile came to his lips. "Dani—didn't know—if I could—wait—"

A host of memories rose in Dani's mind—clear images of the many hours she had spent in this room with Dom Lanza. He had been a skeptic of all things religious when she had first arrived as bodyguard for his grandchildren, believing in nothing but power and loving nothing but his family. It had taken all the courage Dani could summon to share her faith in Jesus Christ with the old man, and at first he had scoffed at her. But slowly that had changed, for the aging crime lord had seen a peace in the young woman—along with courage enough to lay her life on the line for him—and he had sat for long hours listening as she had read to him from the Bible and shared what Jesus had done for her.

Now as he smiled at her, tears rose in her eyes, and her lips trembled.

"No—don't cry—" he whispered. His eyes seemed to grow brighter, and he nodded, saying in a stronger voice, "You have been—a great joy to me, my Dani. Without you, I would never have known—what peace in this world is." He groped for her with his free hand, captured her in a frail grasp, then gazed at her, his old eyes growing softer. "It's time for me to go— and I am ready—thanks to you, daughter."

The use of the word *daughter* brought the tears in Dani's eyes down her cheeks—for she knew how the old man felt about his family. He had called her by the most prized name he had ever known.

"Dom—it's so hard—!" she began, but broke off when he shook his head.

"No—staying here—that would be hard," he said. Then he suddenly loosed her hand, reached up with both hands, and cupped her face. "Come closer—" She bent over and he kissed her forehead, then held her there for one moment. Then he dropped his hands, and tried to speak. His voice was so weak that Dani had to lean forward. She knew he wanted desperately to tell her something. She caught the words, " . . . promise me, Dani!"

"Yes, Dom—what is it?"

He caught his breath, and his lips framed the words carefully: "Don't let—yourself—" His voice was merely a sibilant breath, but as she leaned forward, she could read the words his lips were framing. "Don't let yourself hate—my daughter! Never—never do that! Let—the great love—I've seen in you—let that love—come out of you!"

The lids closed, and his lips grew still. Dani got up quickly, and moved away from the bed as the doctor hurried over. Dani heard him say, "Get the rest of the family—" and left the room as Rossi almost ran through the door. She made her way down the hall, slipping out the side door.

Savage saw her and came to walk with her to the car. He said nothing, and when they got to the car, he saw that Dani was blinded by tears, so he opened the door and gently guided her inside. When he got in and sat down beside her, he asked, "Is he gone?"

Dani shook her head, unable to speak.

Savage started the car and pulled away from the house. When they had cleared the gate, he asked, "He say anything?"

Dani swallowed and waited until she could speak.

"He—told me—" She shook her head, unable to continue, then finally whispered, "He told me not to hate anybody."

Savage didn't take his eyes from the road, but finally nodded briefly, and his voice was terse.

"That's not a bad idea—not bad at all." He shook his head, wonder in his tone as he added, "Not a bad thing—to come from a man like Dom Lanza."

22
The Drop

All right, Margo," Cain's voice said confidently. "Time for the balloon to go up."

The suddenness of Cain's proposal took Dani off guard, so much so that for a split second her mind went blank. She had called him early on Thursday morning, fully expecting him to put her off, and his ready acceptance was completely unexpected.

"Why, that's great," she said inanely, wishing desperately that he *had* required more time. She knew she'd sounded uncertain and forced a laugh, saying, "I've got to admit, I'm a little bit surprised, Tommy. I thought it'd take a little longer for you to raise that much cash."

"Yeah? Well, I'm ready—how about you? You ready to make the drop?"

Everything in Dani warned her to wait, to play for time, but there was always the possibility that Cain would be scared off. She calculated rapidly, thinking of the long session she'd had with Sixkiller and Ed Hidalgo, head of the narcotics squad. The two of them had hammered at her for hours, and only after going over every detail had they agreed to lay the trap for Cain.

"Sure, I'm ready. You name the time and place." She had known that he'd insist on this and on controlling every other detail, so she had made her plan flexible enough to accommodate whatever he came up with. "You got someplace in mind?" she asked.

"Well, sure, but I'm not telling you over the phone. What I want is, you load the stuff in that cabin cruiser. I get me a boat, and we meet at a good place where we got no problem with crowds. Just the four of us."

"Sounds okay to me," Dani said quickly. "How'll I know where to make the drop?"

"You get the stuff loaded, then you call me. I'll tell you where to go." A thin note of warning came into his voice then. "Like I said—we don't trust each other in this thing, so no radio in that boat! If it's got one, tear it out. First thing we'll do when we meet, I'll check your boat for any kind of radio. I find anything—it's likely to be messy. You clear on that?"

Hidalgo had warned her it would be like that. "I see that, Tommy. No problem."

"Right! Now, the time. We go this afternoon."

Dani was surprised, but thought rapidly. "That's pretty quick," she said. "What time do I call?"

"Call at one. You can use this number, but I won't be here. You'll get told what to do. Are we straight?"

"Just have the dough, Tommy—and no fancy stuff."

"Right!" Cain laughed, saying, "You're a piece of work, Margo! I'll be waiting for your call."

The phone clicked loudly in Dani's ear, and she was suddenly aware that she was gripping the phone so tightly that her fingers were cramped. She slammed the receiver down, and looked over at the three men who'd been monitoring the call. They were in Captain Ed Hidalgo's office, which was mostly filled by a huge desk buried in papers.

"Well—curtain going up," she said, trying to inject a light tone into her voice, but neither of the two officers nor Savage was fooled by it.

Ed Hidalgo, a stump of a man with red hair and frosty blue eyes, said at once, "I don't like it." He chewed viciously on the stump of a vile-smelling cigar, rolled it around, then removed it. "You see what he's got up his sleeve? He could tell you to go *anywhere* in that boat."

"That's right," Sixkiller agreed quickly. "No way we can cover you if he picks the right place—and he'll do that, all right!"

Dani shook her head, her chin lifted stubbornly. "Look, we've gone over this a dozen times. There's some risk, but not as much as we thought. There'll only be two of them, and Ben will be right there, armed to the teeth."

"So will their man," Savage nodded. "He might be faster."

"No, he won't take that chance," Dani argued. She was pale, both Sixkiller and Savage noticed, but there was no wavering in her now. "They've got to meet us *somewhere*— and with this little jewel, you'll know exactly where we are."

She held up the watch that lay on the table before her. It was a large watch for a woman, but not extremely so—especially for a sports watch. She looked at it, remembering how Hidalgo had explained it to her: *It'll keep good time, Miss Ross,* he'd said, *but it'll do more than that. It'll give off a signal that can be picked up two miles away. You wear this, and no matter where you are, we'll have it plotted. We can send men ahead in cars, boats, or choppers, so that you'll be ringed at all times with enough firepower to wipe out a fair-sized city!*

Dani studied the watch, then nodded with a confidence she didn't feel. "And all I have to do is touch this button to call in the cavalry?" she asked.

"That's it," Hidalgo nodded. "It gives off a different signal, and when we hear it, we close in." He frowned, stuck the cigar back in his mouth, and shook his head. "I still don't like it, though. It ought to work, but if Cain's come up with some sort of place we can't cover, you and Savage could get creamed. Or Cain could get away."

"He wouldn't get away with much," Sixkiller observed. "Only the first two layers of that heroin is the real stuff. The rest is nothing but powdered sugar."

"And what if they test a bag of that instead of the real dope?" Savage demanded.

"Well, you'll have a real problem on your hands—which is one reason I'm still not sure about this thing."

The argument went on for half an hour, but finally Hidalgo gave up his last-minute attempts to call off the operation. "All right, we'll get the stuff loaded. We've got a twenty-two foot cruiser we caught last week, packed with Acapulco Gold. You know how to pilot a boat, Savage?" He took Savage's nod, then got to his feet. "All right, here it is—I'm betting the drop will take place in the Gulf. Which means we'll need choppers as well as coast guard. But it also means we'll have trouble staying close. Can't use the choppers to follow—Cain would spot them in a minute. What we'll do is have a man in a commercial fishing rig follow you. He can stay just in range of your electronic alarm and keep the ring posted, so they stay out of sight. Then, when you signal, he gives us the green—and we close in."

He waved the three out and was picking up his phone and barking orders as they left. For the next two hours they worked frantically, checking equipment and going over and over every possible problem they could think of.

Finally, Sixkiller said, "Ben, I'm going with Dani."

"No good," Savage shook his head. "Everybody knows you, Luke."

Anger and frustration washed across Sixkiller's face, but he knew Savage was right. He turned to Dani, saying, "Let's call it off—delay it for a day. We're not ready."

"We'll never be ready, Luke," Dani answered. "There's no way we can know what Cain's going to come up with." She put her hand on his arm, knowing the strain he was under. Sixkiller, she knew, would not blink if he were forced to charge into the face of certain death. But he was afraid for her—and she was touched.

"We'll be all right," she said gently.

But Sixkiller could not be comforted so easily. "It's not right," he said, gritting his teeth. "You haven't been trained for this kind of thing!"

"But Ben has," Dani nodded. "He'll be right there with me all the time."

For some reason this didn't placate Sixkiller. He gave Savage an odd look, then finally shrugged and left the office, saying, "I've gotta go down to the dock. I'm going to be in the lead chopper, and I want to see what it looks like from the air."

"Touchy, isn't he?" Savage grinned.

"He's worried about us."

"About you, Boss."

Dani shook her head. "No, Ben. About both of us. Luke thinks the world of you."

Savage looked at her, the grin fading. "I think he's right, you know. This is too risky for you."

Dani said, "You'll take care of me, Ben. You always have."

She patted his arm fondly and turned so quickly she didn't see the startled expression on the Savage's face. "Come on, let's do it," she said, and walked out of the office.

"See anything?" Dani asked nervously. She had stared out for the past hour over the water that stretched out in front of the *Lucinda*, and the brilliance of the late afternoon sun burned her eyes.

"Not yet." Savage was wearing dark glasses, his hand held lightly on the wheel. "Tell me again what he said." He knew well enough what Cain's message had been, but he wanted to get Dani talking. He could see she was growing tense, and they still had a long way to go.

"He said to go under the Mississippi River Bridge, and when we got into Lake Borgne, to cut through the Bay Boudreau. He said to hug the shoreline, and that he'd come out in a boat and hail us."

"Pretty smart," Savage nodded. "All this shore is broken up into hundreds of small islands, and it's filled with small bays. Any one of them could be the spot." He looked overhead, saw nothing, then looked back over his shoulder. A frown creased his brow, and he murmured, "This is pretty shallow. Not sure if that fishing boat can get through."

Dani looked back, too, then said, "He can't get closer, Ben. Cain will be looking for that."

"Yeah, sure."

For the next two hours they stood there, not knowing if Cain would appear from the shore or from the open Gulf. It was possible, too, that he had a seaplane there waiting to take on the heroin. The engine throbbed steadily as Savage threaded the cruiser along the ragged shoreline, past Mozambique Point, then cut back sharply into Black Bay. "That's where the Terre aux Boeufs River feeds into the Gulf," he said. "Really rough country. I don't think—"

"Look!" Dani broke in, lifting her hand to point toward the shore. "There's a boat coming out of that bay!"

Instantly Savage throttled back, his eyes fixed on the approaching craft. "One of those flat-bottomed swamp buggies," he said. Reaching down, he picked up the sawed-off shotgun that leaned against the side of the cabin. He had a Colt Python under his arm and a hideaway Beretta .25 in his sock, but he'd spent most of the night working on the shotgun. It was a Browning twelve-gauge pump he'd used for hunting. He'd sawed through the barrel with a hacksaw three inches in front of the pump, then filed the muzzle smooth with emery paper. He'd removed the sportsman's plug from the magazine so that it now held five shells instead of three, and he'd loaded it with deer slugs and double-ought buckshot.

Giving Dani a sudden glance he said, "If either one of those guys blinks, I'm going to take him off at the neck."

Dani swallowed, but didn't argue. Turning back to face the approaching craft, she said, "It's Cain. He's got one man with him."

Savage shut the engine down; the props made a bubbling noise. He picked up the shotgun and moved to stand beside Dani.

The flat-bottomed craft slowed down, and when it came closer, Cain lifted his arm and waved. He was wearing jeans and a white T-shirt. The wind had blown his hair, and he was smiling.

"Everything's okay," he yelled out. "Come on in." He waved toward the shore, and the tall man at the wheel turned the craft around and moved steadily shoreward.

"I could signal now," Dani said.

"No, he's got to be caught with a smoking gun," Savage

answered. "We'll load the boat and take the dough—*then* you blow the whistle."

"All right, Ben."

They followed Cain's boat closely, and saw it enter into what looked like a swamp or bayou. "I'm guessing that's the estuary of the Terre aux Boeufs River," Savage said. "Take a look at the map and see what it looks like."

Dani grabbed the map, studied it carefully, then nodded. "The river goes northwest through a bayou. You can get to Petite Lake, it looks like."

Savage looked around as the shore of the Gulf gave way to the narrower boundary of the small river. It averaged only thirty feet wide, though it grew much wider from time to time. It was more like a series of bayous than a river, though between the broad sections, the stream often narrowed so that the cypress trees almost touched, giving the river a cathedral appearance.

"I don't like this," Savage muttered. "No way that fishing boat can follow us in here."

"Hidalgo will know that," Dani nodded. "He'll close in so he can pick up the signals from the watch."

"He'd better!" Savage looked out at the wilderness they were entering. "He'd have trouble getting the rescue team into this place."

Dani's mouth was dry, and she stood beside Savage, holding tightly to the rail. It was now past five, and the sun was almost hidden by the tall trees. A ghostly atmosphere always pervaded the bayou country, and she usually liked it, but the sight of the boat ahead and the two men turned it sinister in her eyes.

They followed Cain until finally the lead craft slowed to a snail's pace. Cain came to stand in the stern, cupped his hands, and shouted, "Going to leave the main channel,

Margo! It'll be a little tight for your boat, but you can make it. Just gun on through!"

He was right, for the narrow opening that Cain's boat disappeared through was not much wider than the *Lucinda*. It was shallow, too, and only by opening the engines to a high-pitched roar, did Savage bull the boat through.

When they were clear, they found themselves in a channel about ten feet wide that led through the trees. Cain motioned them on, and they followed slowly.

Finally Savage said, "There it is—watch yourself!"

A slight fog, thick and white in the afternoon light, lay in the tops of the cypresses. The trees themselves were wet and black, and green lichen grew on the waterline where the swollen bases of the trunks rose from the black water. Off to one side, Dani and Savage saw a rough shack on pilings. "Trapper's shack," Dani said.

As they watched, the pilot of the other boat cut the engine and glided to shore, the nose making a mushy noise as it nudged into the mud.

"Right here—beside our boat!" Cain called out, and watched as Savage put the cruiser in next to the flat-bottomed craft. Cain motioned to his companion, and as Savage cut the engine, said, "Let's do this nice and easy, right?"

The man beside Cain was Louie Zapello. He pulled a .45 from his pocket and stood there regarding Savage carefully. Savage lifted the shotgun and moved away from Dani in a slow careful movement.

"Okay if we come and look at the goods, Margo?" Cain asked. He was smiling, but Dani could see tension on his face.

"I'll come and look at the money," Dani said. "You can send your man to check the stuff."

It took some careful juggling, for both Savage and Zapello were like cocked pistols. Zapello moved onto the cruiser, while Dani stepped down into Cain's boat. A two-foot rail circled the rear of the craft, and she had to climb down a short steel ladder. Cain helped her down, smiled, and said, "Here— you can do some banking while Louie's checking the H."

Dani looked at the suitcases—two of them, cheap affairs. Cain picked one up and set it on the table. "Go ahead," he invited, and Dani opened it. It was packed with new bills, and she picked up one bundle. "All in hundreds, just like we agreed," Cain nodded. "Go on, count it. I want this all on the up and up."

Dani began counting the bundles, and when she was almost finished, Zapello called out, "Stuff is good, Mr. Cain!"

"All right," Cain answered. He turned to Dani, asking, "How about if they shift the stuff to this boat while you finish the count?"

"All right," Dani nodded. She was trembling, but determined not to show fear. "Flash, get the stuff into this boat!"

"Sure, Flash," Cain nodded. "You come down and let Louie hand you the stuff. "

Savage stepped out of the cruiser onto the rail of the other craft. When he grabbed the top rail of the short ladder, he kept his eyes fixed on Zapello. But Dani saw that Cain, who had seated himself on a bench built onto the frame, was reaching down.

Something warned her, but she was too slow. She saw Cain's hand move, and at that same moment heard a gasp of agony torn from Savage. Whirling, she saw him leaning back, the shotgun in his right hand—and his left frozen to the steel ladder. His eyes were rolled back, and she saw that the hair on his neck was rising and his body was jerking in grotesque contortions.

"You're killing him!" Dani screamed, and would have

leaped to grab him—but Zapello moved quickly to hold her back.

Cain watched the body of the helpless Savage, a smile coming to his lips. "That's the idea," he remarked.

"Don't! Let him go!" Dani pleaded.

Cain watched Savage for a moment, then shrugged. Reaching down, he threw a switch, and the humming noise ceased. At that instant, Savage fell to the deck, his legs kicking and his lips pulled back.

"Get his gun, Louie," Cain said, and watched as Zapello came down the ladder, collected the shotgun and the Colt, and tossed them both into the water.

Dani ran to Savage, knelt, and held his head against her breast. "Ben!" she cried. "Ben, can you hear me?"

"Thought his name was Flash," Cain remarked mildly. He came over and pulled Dani upright. "He's not dead. Just got a taste of what the guys who get in the chair at Angola feel." He looked at Zapello and nodded toward Savage who was trembling but beginning to try to sit up. "Have lover boy there load the stuff, Louie, then take care of him. I'm taking Margo on a little trip through the tunnel of love."

"I won't go!" Dani protested, but Cain struck her in the face with a lightning blow.

"You're going, babe, but you won't be coming back." A wolfish glitter had come to the eyes of the criminal, his lips twisted into a cruel grin. "Remember the alligators we saw on Miss Annie's swamp tour? Well, they're going to have a nice dessert tonight."

"Better not leave nothing on her, Tommy," Zapello spoke, his voice low and unconcerned. "Don't want the cops finding nothing to identify her."

Cain frowned, then reached out and lifted Dani's wrist. Before she could move, he had removed her watch and tossed it onto the floor of the boat. He yanked off the necklace she wore, then said, "That should do it. Now, get out!"

Dani stumbled as he hauled her to the prow of the boat and then half-dragged her out. She fell to her knees, the black mud clinging to her like glue, but he yanked her upright. As he pulled her across the gumbo mud, she looked back frantically to see Savage getting to his feet, his eyes on her. But when he tried to follow, Zapello struck him in the back of the neck with the heavy gun, driving him face down to the deck.

"No time for long good-bys, doll," Cain said, a soft laugh bubbling in his throat. "I'll kiss you good-by for him."

Cain pulled her across to where a small boat was tied, saying, "Get in. I'm going to give you my own swamp tour."

Dani was thrown into the boat, which she recognized vaguely as a pirogue. She fell face forward, and by the time she rolled over, Cain had stepped into the small craft and picked up a paddle. He shoved off from shore, sending the boat into the water, and as it skimmed over the black, oily water, Dani knew that she was a dead woman.

If she had had any hope of pleading for mercy, the sight of Cain's evil face, half shaded by the tall trees, would have let her know there was no use. Cain was standing up, paddling the pirogue easily, and he was smiling—as if he had been given a very special present.

23

The Quality of Mercy

As the small boat wove an intricate pattern between the swollen knees of the giant cypress trees, Dani was trying to think, but her mind seemed to be frozen. Once before she had felt like this—when she was skidding on an icy road into the path of a blue pickup truck. She had tugged at the wheel, stomped on the brakes, but her car had gone on sliding as if the controls were not attached. Her mind had gone blank— and it was like that now as Cain moved deeper and deeper into the swamp.

What she felt was not so much terror as regret. Regret that she would not be around to help her mother. That she would not be there to stand with Allison, who needed her, and with Rob who was struggling in a terrible web of guilt.

She thought suddenly of Ben, and remorse tore at her. *I got him into this!* she thought, and at that moment, she felt a keen grief for the hazel-eyed man who had stood beside her so often—a grief much sharper than she felt for herself.

Cain was slowing down now, and she knew it would not be long before he would turn his attention to her. In the half-light, she studied his face—handsome, with regular features and a deceptive pair of blue eyes that seemed almost mild.

Now, as she regarded him, she waited for the hatred to rise as it had done before, and was faintly surprised to note that she felt very little. She thought of her father, and the aching emptiness that had been her companion since his death was still there. But now that her life was measured out by a few strokes of the paddle in Cain's strong hands, she found it was difficult to recover the hate that had burned in her heart.

Why am I feeling like this? she wondered. *He's still the man who killed my father. But the bitterness that I had for him—it's not the same.*

She had no time to wonder more, for Cain suddenly put the paddle down and squatted down in the bow of the pirogue.

"End of the line, Margo," he remarked. He watched her face closely; his eyes narrowed. Dani knew that he was watching her for a purpose—to see the terror that he was sure would come.

"You don't have to do this, Tommy," she said in an even voice. "You've got the money and the drugs. What harm can we do to you?"

"I don't like to leave people like you around," he remarked. "You'd be staying awake thinking of ways to get even with old Tommy. Too bad—you're quite a gal, Margo."

When Dani didn't speak, he seemed troubled. "End of the line. Aren't you scared?"

Dani shook her head. "No. I'm not afraid."

And it was true, to her great surprise. She'd always wondered how the martyrs could face their deaths so calmly. And she'd always felt that she was made out of different stuff. But now that her time was come—except for a mild regret over the things she'd never do—there was peace in her breast.

Cain scowled, not liking what he saw. He'd looked forward to hearing her beg and cry for mercy, and her courage made him angry for some reason. Perhaps he had doubts whether he was man enough to take such a thing so calmly. But he didn't give up. Reaching over into the water, he dipped his hand down and came up with a fistful of black goo—half sand and half mud.

"Know what this is?" he asked, his eyes bright. When she didn't answer, he nodded and grinned. "It's quicksand, babe. Heard about it a lot, but never saw it—not till last year." He squeezed the ooze between his fingers and watched it fall back into the water. "A Cajun trapper brought me back here, hunting deer. We were in a boat like this one, and I got a shot at a big buck. We followed him here, but the hunter stopped the boat. 'Sand, he's got him,' he said. Well, I looked, and there was the buck—not bad shot, but he was caught in this stuff." The memory brought a slight shudder to his shoulders. "He was being sucked down, and there wasn't anything he could do. The water's only about six or seven inches deep, so he struggled until all that was left was his head—and then he got pulled down, just like something had hold of him."

Dani looked at the water, noting that the bottom was clearly visible. "That's what you'll do to me, then?" she asked.

Cain frowned at her. "I was going to shoot you," he said, "but I've decided not to." He picked up the paddle and drove the boat about ten feet further, next to a cypress. "Get on those knees," he said.

Dani looked at the large Cajun knees—projections that lifted upward around some of the larger trees. She looked at

Cain, who grinned. "I'm giving you a break, doll," he said. "I'm going to give you a chance to live."

Dani didn't believe him for one moment. And at just that instant, the sound of a single gunshot echoed through the bayou.

Cain smiled, his eyes glazed with pleasure. "That'll be Louie putting your boyfriend down," he whispered. Then he shook himself and said quickly, "Crawl on those knees. Maybe you can wade out. But if you don't, the big gators will come to visit you pretty soon. The place is thick with them."

He seemed nervous now; he reached down and picked up the shotgun. "Go on—get out." He stood up and waved the shotgun toward Dani.

There was, she saw, no hope at all—except, maybe—

He was watching her carefully, but he held the shotgun loosely. His finger was not on the trigger.

One chance—just one!

She grabbed the side of the pirogue with both hands and collected her feet under her. She could feel his eyes watching her, but she gripped the edge of the small boat as hard as she could—and with all her strength she threw herself backward.

"Hey—!"

A pirogue is the most unstable craft in the water, and as Dani jerked at it, Cain was thrown off balance. He tried to sit down, but as the shotgun clattered into the bottom of the boat, the pirogue skittered sideways, and Cain fell over the side with a tremendous splash.

Dani was almost thrown from the boat, but she managed to sprawl flat, striking her head on the hard edge, so that sparks flashed before her eyes. But even as she felt the blood that ran warmly down her forehead, she scrambled into a kneeling position and looked wildly for the shotgun. There it was—only a few feet away! She scrabbled along, throwing herself at it, caught the barrel in her right hand, then reversed it and sat down abruptly, staring around wildly.

Then she saw Tommy Cain.

He had fallen flat, and even as he hit the water, he knew that the shotgun had fallen into the pirogue. Forgetting everything, he came to his feet, teetered, and tried to take a step—then looked down with horror, for he was sunk into the black quicksand up to his knees!

Dani never forgot the look of blank terror that washed across the face of Tommy Cain. She heard his hoarse cry of rage and panic and watched as he reached down and grasped his leg, straining to pull it free. But as he did, he forced his other leg deeper into the ooze.

Dani sat there watching, taken aback by the unexpected reversal of fortune. And even as she watched, trying to decide what to do, she saw that Cain was up to his thighs in the water. He screamed and fought, his face blank with blind panic—and the more he struggled, the more he sank.

Then he stopped, and sanity came back to him. He looked across the short span of water at Dani, and his eyes focused on her.

"Help me!" he begged. "I don't want to die!"

Dani knew that she could not let him get his hands on her; he would take her with him. And if he got the shotgun, he would, she knew, kill her instantly.

He saw her waver, and even as he spoke, he settled down another two or three inches. The water was up to his belt now, slowly, imperceptibly, he was being sucked down into the oozing sand. "Don't let me die, Margo!" he pleaded.

Dani said, "My name's not Margo. It's Ross. I'm Dan Ross's daughter."

She had never seen such an expression on a man's face—never. There had been some hope there, but her statement drove his head back as if she had struck him in the face. He opened his mouth in a soundless howl, and his eyes went dull, as if a curtain had washed over them.

At that moment, his eyes caught a movement to his left, and he turned, twisting his body to the side. He screamed, and when Dani turned to look, she saw a V-shaped wave. At the apex appeared a scaly snout and a pair of walnut-shaped eyes—a giant alligator.

Dani could not breathe for a moment. Then, as Cain began to thrash in the water, screaming in the highest pitched sounds she'd ever heard, she lifted the shotgun, aimed, and pulled the trigger.

The bayou suddenly echoed with the thunder of the explosions. She pulled the trigger steadily, pausing after each shot to bring the short muzzle back to bear on the monster. Finally there was a click—and she could do no more.

There was a terrible roiling in the water, the gator rolling over and over, thrashing its mighty tail. The water that showered the trees was red with blood, and finally the thrashing died away.

Dani dropped the shotgun, then turned to see that Cain was up to his armpits in the black, oily water. He had gone white, and his mouth was twisted and pulled down in a mad expression.

Another five minutes and he'll be dead—and your father will be avenged!

The thought came to her, rising from deep within.

Let him die!

Dani could almost hear a voice, whispering in her ear. *Let him die! He killed your father. He had Ben killed! He tried to kill you!*

Cain was staring at her, his eyes glazed and his chin almost touching the water.

Don't let yourself hate—let love come out of you!

Now it was the voice of Dom Lanza she seemed to hear—
and then she had a sudden vision of her father's face as she
had seen it a thousand times—calm and loving, but also it
seemed to her, reproachful.

Suddenly Dani picked up the paddle and desperately drove
the pirogue forward. It glided over to Cain, and she cried out,
"Grab the edge of the boat, Cain, and stop fighting!"

Cain did as she said, hope coming into his eyes. But though
he grasped the boat, he still felt the terrible power of the quicksand.

"No use!" he gasped. "I'm going down!"

"No, you're not!" Dani said. "Quicksand will let you go,
but you have to relax! Stop fighting. That's what's pulling you
down!"

It was something she had read, years ago, in an old Tarzan
comic book. She had no idea if it were true, but she let no
doubt show in her face. "Just relax, Tommy. Don't try to get
away. See, you're not going down anymore!"

Cain blinked his eyes, and whispered, "I—I don't think
I am."

"Just hang on—it'll be all right!"

All right? Dani knew it was never going to be all right. No
help would come, for there was no one to help. Ben Savage
was dead, and her watch was on the floor of the swamp boat,
useless. Zapello had to have heard the shotgun fire, and when
Cain didn't return, he'd get in the other pirogue and come to
see what had happened to his boss. And even if he didn't,
there were sure to be other gators. . . .

Time passed, and there was nothing to do. Cain said once,
"Look—I'm coming out of it! If I stretch out, it takes the pressure off—I can feel the sand letting go!"

"Good," Dani replied listlessly—and at that moment she

heard the sound of a boat approaching. Cain heard it too, and at once yelled, "Over here, Louie! Over here!"

Dani sat back in the boat with her back to the sound of the approaching boat; Cain could not see from his position, but he kept up a constant crying to Zapello.

Finally the sound of a paddle breaking the water was right behind her, but Dani could not bear to turn. She dropped her head, closed her eyes, and waited.

"Hello, Boss—you need a little help?"

"Ben!"

Dani jerked her head up, twisted in the boat, and there he was—Savage kneeling in the small boat with a smile on his dark face.

He pulled up beside her, and she reached out and took his hand, then pulled him close, holding him with all her might and crying, "Ben! Oh, Ben!" over and over again.

Savage kept them from capsizing by sheer good balance, holding her fast with one arm. Finally, she lifted her face, pulled his head down, and kissed him full on the lips. She clung to him, holding him tightly, and his arm drew her closer.

Finally, she drew back, her eyes wet and lips soft and vulnerable. "Ben—I thought you were dead!"

Savage held her closely, saying only, "Louie got careless." Then he added, "Boss, I didn't know you cared this much."

Dani suddenly felt her face flush. She pulled away and settled in her own boat, so full of mingled joy and pain she couldn't speak.

"Well, you got ol' Tommy where you want him, I see." Savage gave her a curious look. "Want to leave him for the gators?"

Danielle Ross, daughter of Dan Ross, suddenly stared at Cain, who had grown quiet.

"No, Ben. I don't want to do that."

Savage saw the look on her face, and a pleased expression came to his face.

"That's my old Dani, he whispered. "Welcome home, Boss!"

Dani smiled and looked with pleasure around the table, letting her glance linger on each face. Her mother, Ellen. Allison. Rob. All laughing and happy.

And Luke Sixkiller across from her, with Ben Savage next to him—both looking handsome enough for any party, but especially this one. It had been Ellen's idea, having a victory celebration on the day Tommy Cain was indicted.

At first Dani had been uncertain, thinking it might bring back harsh memories for them. But she had been wrong. At the very beginning of the supper, Ellen had said, "We're not celebrating what's happened to Tommy Cain tonight."

Sixkiller spoke up, "He's not going to bother you. Looks like we'll get him for Judge Horstman's murder. The D.A. thinks he can put Cain away for at least the rest of his life. Even if that doesn't happen, he'll draw twenty years in the federal pen on drug charges."

Ellen looked around at her children and smiled. "I told you that's not what we're here for. We're celebrating our family— that we've survived. That Dan Ross is here—as long as we are here." Her eyes came to rest on Dani, and she added softly, "And I know one thing—Dan would be very proud of all three of you tonight. In fact, I think somehow he *is* proud of you!"

Rob still had dark circles under his eyes, but there was a faint glow of hope in his eyes. Dani had talked long to him, and prayed along with him, and he was on his way to forgiving himself.

You're going to make it, Rob, Dani thought, feeling her love for him spill over. She glanced at Allison, who sat as close to

Ben as she could get, and said, "When are you going to show us that new thing you claim Ben taught you on the trampoline?"

"Right now!" Allison jumped up at once, her eyes bright. "Rob, you set up the trampoline while I change!"

The pair of them left, and Ellen said quietly to Sixkiller and Savage, "I'm glad you two are around. They need you."

"They'll be all right," Sixkiller said. He was careful not to look at Dani—she was so beautiful that he'd stared at her all during the meal. The four of them got up and went to the yard, where Allison appeared and gave them a spirited performance.

"You'll be in the circus yet," Savage nodded. "Maybe I'll get in shape, and you and I will take to the traps—the Flying Grobinskis!" he teased.

The evening lasted long, ending in the den, where they stayed talking until nearly eleven. Finally, after Allison and Rob had gone to bed, Ellen said, "I'll do the dishes, Dani. You talk with Ben and Luke."

"No chance, Mom," Dani said, and led the way to the kitchen, saying over her shoulder, "You two can talk to each other."

When they were alone, Sixkiller got up and began to walk around the den. He stared out of the window, and then wheeled to say, "Ben, I wish you'd go home."

Savage blinked at the abrupt statement, but a stubborn line came to his firm lips. "Not just yet, Lieutenant. But you could go—if it's past your bedtime."

Savage's jibes usually didn't bother Sixkiller, but he flushed slightly. "It's pretty late," he urged pointedly, then added, "I want to talk to Dani alone."

Savage nodded. "So do I."

"Well, you can talk to her tomorrow, can't you?" Sixkiller was getting angry, his big frame growing tense.

Savage settled down in the chair. "I guess tonight will do me."

Sixkiller glared at him, and then came to stand over him. "Come on, Savage, quit fooling around. I really need to talk to Dani—alone."

Savage felt somewhat at a disadvantage with Sixkiller's bulk looming over him. He got up with an easy movement, shrugged, and said, "Don't try to lean on me, Luke. You can do that with the dudes on the street, but I'm not impressed."

"You may be if you smart off again!" Sixkiller clamped his lips shut, then tried to speak more reasonably. "Look I—I want to talk to Dani about—well, about our future."

Savage stared at him. An impish light came to his dark eyes, and he shrugged his trim shoulders. "You'll have to get in line, Sixkiller. *I'm* going to ask her to marry me—just as soon as you go home!"

Then Sixkiller made his mistake. He was a man accustomed to being obeyed, and in many cases he had to back up his commands with muscle. So he reached out, grabbed Savage by the shoulder, and whirled him toward the door, saying, "I'm through arguing, Ben—now get out!"

With most men that would have ended it. But even as Sixkiller steered Savage to the door, the smaller man gave a sudden twist. Without hesitation he sledged the rock-hard edge of his hand in a driving blow that caught Sixkiller on the neck.

The big policeman was driven backward, his back slamming into the wall. A Monet print in a gold frame crashed to the floor beside him. Sixkiller stared blankly at Savage, who said, "Don't put your hands on me, Luke—"

But before he finished, Sixkiller sprang up and threw himself at Savage. He missed with a thundering right hand that would have ended the fight, but did catch the smaller man with a short left that opened up a cut over Savage's eyebrow.

Savage let fly a lightning-like kick that caught Sixkiller in the thigh, but did no more than slow the big man. The two of them bounced around the room—Sixkiller, at two hundred pounds of bone and muscle, was capable of ending the fight with one blow; and Savage, much smaller, but faster than a striking snake, slashing and kicking and always just out of reach of the larger man.

Sixkiller finally got a grip on Savage's arm and threw him through the French doors. But as he ran to finish the job, Savage lifted a small cricket table and brought it down on his head. As Sixkiller fell, he grabbed Savage's ankle, and the two of them rolled across the carpet in a wild melee.

"Ben! Luke! What are you *doing*?"

The two men froze, both of them twisting their necks to look up at Dani and Ellen. A movement caught their eyes, and they saw Rob and Allison rush into the room, only to stop dead still as they stared first at the wreckage, then at the bloodied faces of Sixkiller and Savage.

Sixkiller let go of Savage's throat and staggered to his feet. Savage lowered his fist and did the same.

They stood there, clothing torn, knuckles scraped, with blood on their faces.

Dani's eyes were wide with shock as she gasped, "What—are—you—fighting—about?"

Both men looked at the floor, unable to meet her eyes. It was Sixkiller who finally lifted his head. He gingerly touched a tender spot on his forehead and licked his lips.

"Well—we were discussing—that is, we were—"

Savage looked up and gave Sixkiller a contemptuous glance. He looked Dani in the face and said bluntly, "I was trying to make him go home—so I could propose to you."

"That's a lie!" Sixkiller exclaimed. "He's the one who wouldn't leave!"

Ellen Ross began to laugh. She had a fine laugh, full and rich, and now she let it ring out. It was infectious, and Rob and Allison lost their worried looks and began grinning.

But Dani was red with anger. Her eyes flashed. "Mother— it's not funny!"

But Ellen could not stop laughing, and finally she said, "Come on, Rob and Allison, you're too young to see how the course of true love never runs smooth."

Dani stared after the three of them, and when they were gone, she shook her head. "Well, aren't you a pretty sight."

"Well, Dani, I just—"

"Oh, shut up, Luke!" Dani snapped. "Come on, both of you."

They followed her to the kitchen, where she sat them on high stools and, pulling out clean cloths and a first-aid kit, began cleaning them up. "I hope it hurts a lot!" she snapped, dabbing antiseptic in the cut on Savage's forehead. She dabbed harder, and finally got the two of them patched up.

"Now—get out of here!" she growled.

Sixkiller looked at her, then at Savage. "Well, I never had any experience proposing. So I didn't do it right, huh?"

Suddenly Dani could not control the smile that began deep inside. Her lips trembled and then curled upward, and finally she began to laugh. She had a good laugh, like her mother, and the two men stood there watching her.

Finally, she took a deep breath. "Go home before I call the police," she said, and there was suddenly a gentleness in her smile. She reached up, drew Sixkiller's head down, and kissed him on the cheek, then did the same for Savage.

"Get out," she smiled, but then she shook her head and added, "Come back tomorrow and clean up your mess."

She wheeled and left the room, going upstairs. She found her mother sitting on her bed, as she had known she would be.

"Well, which one are you marrying?" Ellen asked, getting up to stand beside her.

For some reason, the sound of her mother's voice made Dani feel like a little girl again. She turned and grabbed at Ellen, clinging to her, and there was a catch in her voice as she said, "Oh, Mother! Why don't they just go away and leave me alone?"

Ellen held her daughter, a smile making her lips broad and maternal. "They'll never do that," she said quietly.

The two stood there a long time. Downstairs, the two men were leaving, not speaking at all until they were outside.

Finally, Ben said, "Sorry about that, Luke."

"My fault."

They got into their cars and drove away. The engines disturbed the crickets, who stopped their monotonous symphony for a few moments—then, as the sound of the automobiles faded, began again.